For Sheila, Sarah and Nicholas

# PART ONE

# Chapter One

# Hi-ho, Hi-ho

My interview had been at the main social-services building in Hammersmith so I hadn't actually seen Clifton Avenue before my first day there. In my mind I had it down as the big Edwardian villa on the corner of two suburban roads. I had driven past it a hundred times. It looked light and airy with bright curtains hung in the windows and the garden was lovely. I rang the doorbell and a girl of about twenty-two opened the door. She looked smart and clean and had kind, enquiring eyes.

'Hello?'

'Hello! I'm Rachel Bidewell.' We shook hands warmly. 'I hope you're expecting me. I was told to ask for Rob.'

The girl looked puzzled and screwed her eyes up with concentration. 'I'm sorry, are you here to talk about Lily? I don't think they're due for another hour.'

We looked at each other blankly.

'No. I'm the new Residential Care Assistant. I was told just to come along today to get my bearings.' I began poking around in my bag for the letter confirming the post.

'You're not looking for Clifton Avenue Residential Home, are you?'

'Yes. Isn't this –?'

My lovely new colleague laughed. 'No, no. This is Clifton Park – we're a retirement home. You're wanting Clifton Avenue, it's about fifty yards up and on the right.'

'Good heavens. I always thought that this was . . . I'm so sorry. Up on the right, you say. Sorry.'

And so the door closed and I did an about-turn. It had begun to drizzle. There *was* a building on the right and it undoubtedly was Clifton Avenue Residential Care Home. It had obviously been purpose-built in the 1970s and now looked tired and scruffy. There was what must have once been a trendy glass wall down one side. But once the residents had moved in, it had presumably meant that they had no privacy and so a vast net curtain had been fitted which rather ruined the effect. Now the curtain was grey and coming off its tracks in places. It was all rucked up in one corner, where someone had shoved a rather nasty sort of tea trolley against the window with jigsaws and board games heaped upon it. The window was dull with years of dirt and muck from the traffic on the road. The garden was unkempt. The whole place looked unloved and sad and as the drizzle turned to proper rain, I had the urge to turn and run.

I fished around in my bag and brought out my letter again. 'Residential Care Assistant working with vulnerable adults . . . Must have the ability to liaise confidently and knowledgably with a broad range of outside agencies . . . Must develop caring, professional, sustaining relationships with a challenging, diverse client group.' Surely they weren't looking for me? Surely the only man for this job was Nelson Mandela.

The door opened and there was Denise, the manager and my new boss. She had been immaculately turned out on the day of my interview and I had assumed that she had dressed up for it. But, no, today she was equally smart. She had a little suit on and high, shiny court shoes. Her hair and make-up were perfect, with a big red slash at her mouth as if she had only applied her lipstick a second before opening the door.

'Rachel! Welcome, welcome. Come in out of the wet. Horrible, isn't it?'

'Vile,' I said, grinning and shaking her hand. It was bony and greasy from newly applied handcream.

'Now, I know you've just come for a little look about today. It's very quiet because all the residents are at the day centre or work. This is as good as it gets! I'm going to leave you with Rob, my deputy. He'll go through all the paperwork and tell you exactly how the whole place works, but first of all let me just say how happy we are to have you join us.'

'Thank you,' I said gratefully and followed her down a

narrow corridor illuminated with harsh strip lighting. Her tight skirt rustled as the lining rubbed against her tights. The brown, institutional carpet was tufty and acrylic and she seemed to skate across it in her shiny, smooth shoes. The air was hot and dry. I could feel the static electricity passing up through the soles of my feet and I was worried that my hair would start standing on end as if I'd been rubbing it vigorously with a balloon.

Denise knocked on a door and we went into what looked like the general office. There were two computers, two desks and a number of large pinboards covered with out-of-date leaflets and notices about Health and Safety and union directives. On the back of the door was a massive laminated calendar marked: !!!ROTA!!!

'Hi there, you must be Rachel, I'm Rob,' said a man sitting at a desk. He was very Scottish and friendly. We went to shake hands and a bolt of lightning shot between us. 'Occupational hazard,' he said. 'It's the carpets. If you touch the door handle in the laundry room your fillings buzz.'

When I was about eleven, my family had been friendly with a family called the McCormacks and we had holidayed together in Devon for some years. There came a time when their eldest son hit puberty, and from that day on he was ruthlessly referred to by my father, and then by us all, as Bum-fluff Boy.

Looking at Rob now, I immediately recalled Bum-fluff McCormack. A patchy line of wispy stubble hovered sadly above his top lip. To add to the general sadness of his appearance, as he stood up to offer me tea and to switch on the kettle in the corner of the room, I noticed that his trousers just brushed against the tops of his ankles – and not in a youthful, boy-band way. All in all, the combination had the effect of making Rob look like one of the residents and for a moment I was wrong-footed.

'The one thing I will ask you to look at today is the rota,' said Denise. 'It's all worked out for the next month. Please, please take note of the weekends that I have put you down for. Now, a lot of the staff want to chop and change their weekends but that really does throw a spanner in the works, so, if you could make a note and then stick to the rota, it would be very much appreciated.' She shot Rob a look that indicated that at some point he had asked for a weekend off and chaos had ensued. He grinned at me over her shoulder and slightly raised an eyebrow but I was too nervous to grin back. I obediently got out my diary and began scribbling the dates down.

Denise sashayed out cheerfully and Rob began to run through the routine of the job and what would be expected of me. I'd had a Saturday job in a similar place when I was a teenager and during the long holidays from university, so had a pretty good idea of what the job entailed. It all seemed straightforward, but the more Rob talked, the more my conviction grew that this was going to be a bad move. That I wasn't ready. I took the last swig of cold tea from the dregs of my mug, and found I had a mouthful of limescale that crunched against my teeth as I struggled to swallow it down.

As Rob talked on about the average day at Clifton Avenue, a man with Down's syndrome shot into the room like Eddie the Eagle. 'Rob! Rob! Some bastard has got my coat. Some bloody bastard has taken my coat.' He was short, with a Humpty Dumpty girth and thick glasses.

'Alright, Malcolm, calm down. What coat? Where from?' asked Rob gently.

'*My* coat! Some thieving bastard has nicked it.'

'Which coat were you wearing when you arrived today?' Malcolm shook his head, confused.

'Was it your green one? The puffy one? Is that the one? Come on, let's go and have a look around. You might have left it somewhere else.' Rob wearily made to leave the office.

'Do you want me to look with you? I'm Rachel and I'm coming to work here.' My voice sounded strained and too eager to please.

'It's not there!'

'Let's just have one last look around, shall we?' Rob gave me a grateful nod and I followed Malcolm, who stomped out of the office to a line of coat hooks in a corridor. The only item there was a huge pair of lady's pants draped across two hooks.

'You see! Not there!' said Malcolm.

'No, but I've been looking for these everywhere.'

I grabbed the voluminous knickers and held them up to my hips. Malcolm gave me a withering look and said irritably, 'They're Theresa's,' and stalked back towards the office. 'It's not *there*. Mrs Wheeler will be looking for me and my mum's going to wonder where I've got to. I'm going to tell her, Rob. I'm going to tell her that a thieving bastard from this hostel has taken it.'

'Did your mum drop you off this morning or did Mrs Wheeler bring you?' asked Rob.

'My mum.'

'If you came in the car and didn't have to wait for the minibus, maybe you just came in your sweater. Did you forget to put a coat on?'

Pause. Then a huge rueful grin spread across Malcolm's face. 'Forget my head if it wasn't screwed on, eh Rob? Forget my head. I came with my mum! I didn't *bring* a coat!'

'What are you like?' laughed Rob, cuffing the man on the arm. 'Now, official introductions: Malcolm, this is Rachel, she's going to be working here with us. Malcolm comes to us on a Wednesday and when his mum needs a bit of a rest.'

Malcolm was still laughing to himself and shaking his head in disbelief. 'Hello, sweetheart, you've gotta watch me – hasn't she, Rob?'

'She has indeed.'

'I'm trouble, I am. You've got to watch out for me, Rachel.' Malcolm's bright blue eyes twinkled as he put his chubby hand out to be shaken. 'Forget my head if it wasn't screwed on.'

Then a kindly looking middle-aged lady arrived at the door – Mrs Wheeler, I presumed. 'Hello! Is Malcolm hiding in there with you? Let's get going, gorgeous, or your mum'll think we've eloped again. I've got your coat. You left it on the bus this morning.'

Malcolm winced, smacked his hand across his forehead and looked sheepishly at Rob. 'Mrs Wheeler's got my coat.'

'So I see!' said Rob, laughing.

'Coming, my darling,' Malcolm chirruped theatrically and did a funny little Fred Astaire skip across the office. 'See you, Rachel. Bye, Rob. Mrs *Wheeler's* got my coat.'

Rob let out a deep sigh, turned to me and said, 'Welcome to the wonderful world of Clifton Avenue.'

It was dark by the time I left, and the light on the bus was so harsh that instead of looking out of the window, I found myself staring at my own bedraggled reflection. I tried to make sense of my first few hours of work in more than ten years. I think it was fair to say that it hadn't been an overwhelming success. 'Early days. Early days,' I said to myself, a puny mantra that struggled to keep at bay the fear, resentment and sheer panic that threatened to scupper the whole thing.

I had planned the remainder of the evening based on

the bus trip home taking roughly half an hour. I had not taken into account the fact that it was now rush hour and the bus was stationary. Would it be quicker to walk? We were miles from home and surely the traffic couldn't be like this all the way up Kilburn High Road? Could it? The anxiety in the pit of my stomach spread through my body and into my fingertips. Everyone else on the bus looked resigned and bored and I looked from one to another hoping I might catch an eye and see reflected in it the same panic I was feeling, or perhaps someone would lean over and gently say that this bit was always a nightmare but once we got past these traffic lights it was a breeze. I had exactly twelve minutes to get home. Dom had insisted that as it was my first day in my new job, he would leave work early and pick up the children from school. As a result I had given Marlene, the au pair, the evening off. Dom had said he had to be away by 6.30 and I so wanted to be calm and in control and home on time.

I found my mobile which had a little dribble of life left in it, perhaps enough juice for one call. I decided to save it and pray. And then – Jesus! – I remembered: I had forgotten to buy Alec a disposable camera for the Year 6 Outward Bound week – five days in Swanage with the school, referred to by those in the know as 6OB. It was his first time away from home. The entire year – but Alec in particular – were beside themselves with excitement and anticipation. The camera was the one thing he hadn't got from the checklist and it had to be handed in tomorrow as it was classed as a valuable and so the teachers would take responsibility for it. They weren't allowed to take phones and Alec had never had a camera. Dom never let him within an inch of the family one, and so he'd got genuinely excited at the prospect of having his own for the week. It was yet another of the 6OB rites of passage that the children all got so heady about. I leapt off the bus and into a newsagent.

The man behind the counter resembled Colonel Gaddafi and seemed to be irritated to have been disturbed by a customer.

'Do you sell disposable cameras?' I asked, feeling as if my life depended on his answer. Not only did I have to buy the damn thing but if I couldn't get one here I had no idea where to go and whether I would ever get home.

'No. No camera,' he said, looking as if I had just asked him for a packet of poo.

'Do you have any idea where I could find one nearby?'

A long, bored pause. 'Is possible, Dixons?'

'No. I don't want a camera. Just a disposable one. You know, the ones you just throw away when you've finished with them?'

'Garage,' he said, lazily flicking his thumb in the direction of the Shell garage about half a mile away and returning to his paper.

Bloody, bloody, bloody hell. I was going to have to ring Dom. It was now 6.22, I was due home and was miles away without a camera.

I dialled his number and he said 'Hello?' in a pompous way that suggested he had no idea who was on the end of the phone, which always irritated me, because obviously my name came up whenever I rang.

'It's me.'

'We're just on our way. Where are you?'

'Shit. Look I've got to get Alec a –' And with that the phone gave out and it was a close-run thing to say who was judging me the more incompetent, lousy parent, Dom or me.

I ran. Proper running: knees up, arms pumping. The Shell garage looked bright and welcoming in the dark, and bloody miles away. When I got there I had to make a choice between two queues of bored, grey motorists and opted for the slightly shorter one but the one that included people with shopping. I stood on tiptoes, straining towards the front of the queue like a greyhound at the starting line, as if that would somehow make it move faster. When it got to a horsey woman's turn, she suddenly realized that her carton of milk was a bit wet and she was worried that it might have a leak, so she left us all waiting in the queue and went to get another one.

'Oh dear!' she called out from the milk section, 'I wanted semi-skimmed and that must have been the last one.'

'No problem, love,' said the helpful lady behind the counter. 'We'll have some more out back. Raj? *Raaaj*? Can you bring through some semi-skimmed.'

Raj, unseen from out back: 'Semi?'

'Yes, love. Semi.'

'Milk?'

'Yes, love. Semi-skimmed.'

Dear God. I thought I was going to explode.

I was frantically scanning the back of the wall to see if there was anything that even vaguely looked like a disposable camera amongst the Anadin Extra and Marlboro Lights. Finally, when I got to the front of the queue I asked, 'Do you sell disposable cameras?' like an addict enquiring after heroin.

'Do you know . . .' said the lady, slowly and thoughtfully, 'we used to . . . I think we might still have a few. Have you looked over near the maps there?'

I ran and began darting wildly down the aisles. 'Where? Here?'

'No, just to your left, love. Can you see any?'

'No, here?' Spinning stupidly with my hands outstretched. 'Here?'

She ducked under the counter and came to help. It was now my turn to feel the eyes of the rest of the queue burn into me with a mixture of exasperation and loathing.

'There we are. We've stopped doing them so it's your lucky night, isn't it?'

There were two rather sad disposable cameras left on a shelf.

'Oh thank you. Thank you so much. You have saved my life.'

They were obviously left over from some sort of Disney promotion because they were pink and plastic with a princess on the side. But hell, I was beyond caring. 'Thank you. Thank you so much.' And I followed the lady back to the counter and forked out £7.99 for my prize.

I ran into the street and thankfully a black cab was coming towards me. I threw myself into the back and allowed myself to breathe normally. I didn't care about the cost I just wanted to get home. Please God, don't let Dom be there before me. Please God, don't let him be there.

As my taxi drew into the dark street, I saw Dom's car outside the house. I scrambled to pay the cab and find my keys and try to pull myself together. My hands were shaking as I put my key into the lock and went in. I put my head round the door of the sitting room and there were the kids, watching TV and looking bored.

'Hi guys.' Three little heads looked up and smiled.

'Hi, Mum.'

'How was it?' asked Alec.

'Early days,' I said, trying to look enthusiastic.

I pushed on to the kitchen and there stood Dom, padding back and forth in his socks and clutching a mug of tea as if he'd never left. As if the last six months had never happened.

'I'm so sorry, Dom. Teething problems. I've got to get my timings sorted –'

'It's fine. Not a problem. I will have to rush now though. I thought you'd make an effort to get away in good time –'

'I did, I did. But I had to get Alec a dis–'

'Well, you're here now. I'm afraid I haven't fed them yet. I don't know what you were planning to give them. Do you want a hand? I can stay for five minutes.'

There was next to nothing in the house – the Tesco delivery wasn't due until the next morning – and it was going to have to be scrapings from the back of the freezer. I was anxious for Dom to leave before this became evident. But no, having the moral high ground for the first time in months was a rare treat for him and he was making the most of it.

He looked in the fridge, then a cupboard, then returned to the fridge and squatted down on his haunches to survey its darker regions as if miraculously since last he'd looked a roast chicken or possibly a steak and kidney pie had appeared. We'd had to have a horrible row to stop him letting himself into the house willy-nilly when he first left and now here I was, standing contrite in the corner while he rummaged in my kitchen cupboards and peered into my bread bin. The old Dom would have been bloody furious but now he was being patient and kind and that was far worse.

'Look, you get off,' I said apologetically. 'I can get them something, I was just going to do a snack anyway.'

'They're really hungry, Rach. They're going to need more than a snack. You should have said and we could have fed them.'

Oh *we* could, could we, I thought.

'I know you don't want to hear this,' he went on, 'but we can help. I know things are really tough for you at the moment and I wish they weren't. But you don't have to do everything on your own. Besides, it isn't fair on the kids not to call on us if you need help.'

*Fair*? I wanted to hiss in a demented whisper that had become familiar of late. *Fair*? It's not *fair* that they have a father living halfway across London with God knows who. It's not *fair* that I'm having to take some stupid job just to make ends meet . . .

Instead, I took a huge breath in and said, 'Look, this is a one-off. I'll have Marlene now anyway, once we get into a routine. I'm really sorry but you can get off now.' It was concealed rage and shame that made my voice crack and my chin wobble. 'It was my first day –'

Dom opted for world-weary. 'OK, OK. Look, I've got to go. Deborah's sitting in the car because Alec was worried you'd be upset if she came in.'

'Yes, well, he was right.'

And that was the most mortifying part of the whole day, to know that while I was clambering out of the cab, dropping my purse, running to the house like a demented donkey, Deborah had been sitting in her warm car, probably listening to the radio and watching me. And now Dom was going to get into that car and tell her what a useless, hopeless idiot I was who couldn't get home on time and didn't even have food in my fridge. Deborah would probably feel an intense jolt of love for him because he was so wise and so great with his kids.

I knew what the children needed. I knew that chaos and a hysterical mother were not healthy. I knew that and all I could do was try harder and harder and hope that in some distant, far-off time I would be OK and so would they.

## Chapter Two

# No, I Can't Stand the Heat, But I Am Prevented from Leaving the Kitchen

I was out cold at about 3 o'clock the following morning when Jessie crawled into my bed. I made no move to repel her because I didn't want to fully wake up, so instead I folded her warm little body into mine and nuzzled the back of her head. It was only then that I realized that she had a very soggy bottom. I leapt up and ejected her from the bed.

'Have you done a wee?' I said.

'No,' she whimpered, 'but my bed's all wet and I can't get back to sleep.'

'Come on, we'll get you into a clean nightie.' I tried to sound matter-of-fact but my voice was croaky and I was still sufficiently sleepy to have trouble focusing. I got up and switched the light on and it felt as if someone was hammering nails into my eyes.

'I haven't done a wee. I'm five! I don't do wees any more. Not in my bed!' In Jess's case it wasn't that anxiety had set in and she was now a bed-wetter. She had never stopped being a bed-wetter in the first place. She slept so deeply and happily, we'd never really ever got her out of nappies. This week had been a no-nappy trial but apparently not a very successful one.

I held my hand out wearily and Jess scuttled along behind me and took it. I managed to find the landing light and then – still not fully awake – made my way drunkenly along the narrow landing, heavy-footed, like something out of the 'Thriller' video. We went through to her bedroom and it became apparent that the position she had been in when the leak had sprung was such that she had managed to wee over not just her duvet, undersheet and mattress but also her pillow and Upsy Daisy. I trudged to the airing cupboard and got out fresh bed linen. Jess was wide awake and followed me around, chatting happily.

Since Dom's departure we had become a house of bed-wetters. In fact, I was the only one who managed to hang on until morning on a regular basis. Luke would shout from his bed, 'MUM! MUUUM! I'VE WET THE BED!' And I would go to him and he'd pass me his sodden PJs and pass out again as soon as his sheets were changed. You always know where you are with Luke, he is open and honest and can be unbelievably sweet and, of course, unbelievably horrid, but you know where you are. He will sit on the end of my bed and say, 'Mum, I'm worried. Really worried. I'm supposed to say this poem in assembly and I don't think I can do it . . .' And you can advise him and help him and guide him and feel like you are ticking the good-parenting boxes. He'd wet the bed, I'd sort it and he'd go back to sleep without giving it a second thought.

On the other hand, Alec would say nothing. I would come across him stuffing his sheets into the washing machine, hoping that he could get them on the quick wash, in the dryer and back on the bed before I noticed. Not because he was sneaky or ashamed or scared to tell me, but because he wouldn't want to upset me. I knew that, as he is eleven and Luke only eight, the age gap to some degree explains this, but then again they are so very different. I always feel glad that I had more than one child because sometimes I think it's only when you have a second child that you truly know your first. If I hadn't had Luke I might have thought that all six-year-olds took twenty minutes to eat one Cadbury's Chocolate Finger or that all nine-year-olds insist that Jeremy Clarkson must be revered as a god. I might not have appreciated how direct and bonkers and uncomplicated and joyful Luke is, or how deeply kind, thoughtful, quirky – and frail – Alec is.

I was awake now. Since Dom's departure, if anything woke me in the night, that was it, there was no getting back to sleep. I went downstairs to the kitchen and made myself a cup of tea and out of desperation read the business and then travel section from the Sunday papers. There was a double-page spread about the best and cheapest family holidays to be had in the British Isles. There was a paragraph about a campsite in Cornwall that we had stayed in the previous year and a photo of its lovely swimming pool bathed in sunshine with kids bombing and splashing and hurling themselves in jubilantly. Was it really only last year? I thought of our own holiday snaps, of us all looking relaxed and happy. And all the time, presumably Dom had been nipping off and calling Deborah and telling her how he missed her and how much he wanted to be with her and that it wasn't long now until they could be together . . .

I put my head in my hands and tried to stave off the familiar wave of panic and loneliness. I reminded myself of my dad's stance on the whole thing; that self-pity is always a wasted emotion and never attractive. And I made the promise to myself again, that tomorrow I would be something more like my old self.

Recently, things had been on a bit of a slide when it came to getting to school on time. Usually, we left the house a good ten minutes later than we should and in a state of frenzy, stuffing school bags with swimming kit, gym kit, homework and forms saying 'Yes, I *do* wish to take part in the Annual Walkathon' that actually took place the day before, and legging it down the road, hair standing on end, me shouting 'MOVE IT!' with all the irritability and menace of a senior officer having a bad day at Guantanamo Bay. I would race through the park doing a strange half gallop, half power-walk, with groaning children in my wake, and we would get to school with seconds to go, me bursting into the playground like Roger Bannister having just completed the four-minute mile, gasping for air and retching like a cat.

It doesn't seem to matter what time we get up. Sometimes, I make a real effort and get everyone up fifteen minutes early. I check my watch, all is well, it is a new dawn. I do not shout. I am calm. In fact I barely speak above a whisper. We have perhaps twenty minutes to complete breakfast, gather our things and brush our teeth. So, FOR THE LOVE OF GOD, will someone explain to me what happens between 7.45 and 8 o'clock that means that however in control I am, however ahead of myself I think I may be, something always happens and I will be found screaming at 8.05: 'What do you mean you put your library book in the laundry basket? And anyway, IT ISN'T THERE NOW!'

After the chaos of the night before with Dom, and knowing that I had only had a couple of hours' sleep, I wanted to start the day efficiently and calmly. It was Thursday and Thursdays mean an early start. Luke has Running Club before school and so we drop him off and then Alec, Jess and I go round to the café next to the school for hot chocolate until school starts. But now we were getting later and later and everything was going to be ruined.

Luke is an early riser and had been awake at 6.30. As

usual it remained a mystery to me that, although first up, he was the last one to be ready. Despite a lot of faffing about, Jess and Alec were ready to leave at 7.50 – not too bad – and then Luke suddenly disappeared off upstairs saying that he'd just be a minute. What can he possibly have been doing with the eighty minutes from when he got up to now? I thought. It's not as if one day I would be tidying under his bed and find a replica of the Taj Mahal made out of toenail clippings, or that he was teaching himself Mandarin.

'Luke!' I yelled up the stairs. '*Luuuuuke*! Come! On!' Eventually, he came gallumping back down the stairs two at a time and announced that he couldn't find his trainers. We all frantically searched until he finally concluded that he must have left them at judo. 'Well you can't do Running Club then, can you?' I said.

Luke shrugged and said, 'I'll just run in my school shoes.' And once again he had managed to flick that switch that mothers on the school run have somewhere in their chests, the one that unhinges them as mums and makes them want to kill their own offspring.

'No, Luke, you can't! Of course you can't wear your school shoes for running in.'

'I don't see why not.'

'Oh don't you. Well perhaps you would like me to explain it to you.' I leant forward so that my face was inches from his and, trying to stay calm, continued in a murderous whisper – like Gollum. 'Those school shoes are expensive, they have to last you the year and I can assure you that if you use them as trainers whenever it takes your fancy because you were too lazy to bring your real ones home from judo, they will fall apart.'

He looked defiant, turned and ran upstairs. 'Where are you going now?' I shouted after him. He came bombing back, his face red and angry.

'I'll wear my old ones.'

'Great, the old ones. The old ones you said didn't fit and hurt your feet and that you couldn't possibly wear for another minute and so I *had* to go and buy new ones that day for a small fortune.'

Luke ran off again and returned with the old trainers. He sat on the floor and began squeezing them on but as ever couldn't be bothered to undo the laces and so opted for wearing them like slippers, his heel squashing the backs down.

'How many times do I have to tell you not to wear them like that, Luke? You can't run in them like that!' I shoved him back on the stairs and began to put his feet properly into his too-small trainers but not in a loving way, more like throttling two puppies.

Finally we were ready to leave and as I lurched down the hallway I picked up Jess's scooter that was blocking the way. As I did so I clonked myself on the ankle. If you have never experienced this I can tell you that whacking your ankle with a child's metal scooter results in a pain second only to childbirth and on a par with getting the skin from between two fingers caught in one of the harness clips on a buggy – or standing on the battleship from a game of Monopoly in bare feet.

If I was Jess, at this point I would have sunk to the ground and started wailing. I would have looked for blood and insisted on a plaster whether blood had been found or not. But I am a grown-up, so I leant against the wall, rubbed my ankle ferociously and breathed deeply. At five you can wail because someone will come to make it better. At thirty-eight you could scream all you like but you'd feel foolish afterwards and you'd just be running even later.

Finally we left the house. We would have to take the car to stand a chance of making it in time. Everyone piled in, Luke and I still in foul moods, and as I thrust the car backwards, there was a terrible wrenching sound as the wing mirror hit a post, smashed and fell off onto the pavement in a thousand pieces.

Now I would have to get a new wing mirror and it would cost a fortune. No doubt I would have to tell Dom to check if we could get it on insurance and he would shake his head and tell Deborah what a mad, useless thing I'd done now. I felt so tired and sick of always being late and rushing and nagging, of telling myself never to take anything out on the children only to find myself about to do just that all over again. 'Well done,' I shouted. 'Well done. I blame all of you for that! For making us late. For mucking about. We were supposed to leave the house twenty minutes ago. Was it *me* who held you all up? I got up on time. I got breakfast ready. Was it me who made us late? Was it? Now, Jess, get your seatbelt done up.'

'Like *we* were driving,' said Luke sulkily.

'What did you say?' I murmured. 'What did you just say?'

Luke looked panicked, knowing he'd been unwise to speak. Alec punched him in the arm and Jess started to cry.

'I want Dad!' she wailed. 'I just want my dad!' This was a constant refrain from Jess, one that I had become almost immune to and had learned to cope with, but not this morning.

I felt the sickening internal slide from routine school-run frustration to rage and I lost it. 'Yes, well so do I. So do I! But you know what, Jessie?' I couldn't stop myself. 'He isn't bloody here, is he? And he's not going to be here any time soon because he's off God knows where with the lovely Deborah, who you all seem to think is so wonderful, and you're stuck with me. So bloody do as you are bloody told and do your seatbelt up *now*! DO YOU UNDERSTAND?'

Everyone sat in silence, listening to my ragged breathing and the sound of Jess's little fingers trying to do up her seatbelt.

About ten minutes later we drew up outside school, despite everything, still in time for Running Club. I switched the engine off and everyone remained silent. I didn't know where to begin to say how ashamed I was.

'Sorry, Mum,' said a tearful Luke and did a sort of belly-flop from the backseat and slithered into the front and onto my lap, lodging himself awkwardly between me and the steering wheel. Alec stretched his arm from the seat behind and squeezed my shoulder and then Jess did the same.

'No, I'm sorry,' I said. 'I just get a bit upset sometimes now Dad has gone, and I go a bit –'

'Mental,' said Luke.

I laughed sadly. 'Yes, darling, mental.'

To my horror out of the corner of my eye I saw Miss Sharp and the Running Club emerge from the school side entrance about 300 yards away.

'Oh no, I missed them,' said Luke, resigned.

But no! I would make up for last night, for this morning. I would do the right thing. I went into hyper-efficient we-can-do-this mode and we drove squealing round the complicated one-way system to the entrance of the park in the hope of meeting the runners on the way through. We abandoned the car and looked around anxiously. We were too late. We scanned the horizon like uneasy meer-kats until we spotted the group about 500 yards ahead. 'Come on!' I cried. 'We can easily catch them.' And I set off at quite a lick, determined to reach them, the children following behind, legs and arms motoring.

I was forgetting, of course, that they are a *running* club and as the best pace we could possibly manage – me in wedges – was the pace that they were already at, no matter how fast we ran and no matter how exhausted we became, we never actually got any closer to them.

'Miss Sharp!' I squeaked. 'Miss Sharp! Please wait!' We ran on until Jess crumpled to the ground with a crippling stitch. I was so far ahead I didn't even notice and it took Luke to go into a heroic sprint and shout from fifty yards away, 'We have a man down! We have a man down!' I ran to her and yanked her up into my arms and continued the pursuit of the Running Club.

At that moment, a little weedy chap at the back of the group noticed us and called to Miss Sharp, and with one last push we drew level. Miss Sharp was now irritably jogging on the spot and so I nodded at her – unable to form words – and gestured at Luke to join her. Once he was in her care, Alec collapsed and lay face down on the ground gasping for breath like a fish on a line. I dumped Jess and bent over double, clutching my waist and trying not to throw up. The really tragic thing was that Luke was also a spent force and so Miss Sharp deemed him unfit for purpose and sent him back to us. So we all sat together in a row on a bench in silence, trying to get our breath back. It was too late for hot chocolate but too early to go to school. So we just sat there, throats dry and hearts pounding, and agreed that Miss Sharp is a cow.

For the next few days I kept my temper, tried my upmost to be patient and hoped we were entering a new phase in which, with the help of Marlene and the new job, I would be more reasonable and less tired and not take any of my frustrations out on the children. My first day at Clifton Avenue had not been hugely inspiring but I was trying not to judge the whole place on the experience of one afternoon and was determined to summon up a bit of enthusiasm for my next shift. Until then I would concentrate on getting the house cleaner than ever before.

I let myself in after the school drop-off, desperate for a cup of tea. I would have five minutes with yesterday's free evening paper and that would fortify me for a good wrestle with our decrepit Hoover. It was freezing, but I was determined not to put the heating on in the day when the kids were at school, and so left my coat on. I switched on our battered kettle and put a piece of toast in our ancient toaster which allowed only Alec and me to use it. Others tried to make toast but it just spat back black charcoal squares or squidgy, uncooked lumps. For me it made proper toast because we had been together for many years and it was under the impression that I loved it – although in reality I just knew that you had to push the lever down with the force of a hundred men. Anyway, I couldn't justify getting a new one when it was still functioning – just.

I covered a piece of wholemeal toast with butter and then Marmite, mesmerized as they melted together and started to steam. The anticipation of a quiet sit-down with toast, tea and a paper was lifting my spirits, when I heard the sound of heavy feet on the stairs. It was Marlene.

She had been with us a fortnight and was doing a part-time course at a local language school. The deal was that she would pick the children up on the two weekday evenings that I was working and give them tea, in return for bed and board and a small wage. However, it was becoming clear that she had an on/off boyfriend that she stayed with in New Cross and that the relationship would be on whenever I needed her and off when I didn't. I had hoped that even when she was not on duty, she would be a spare pair of hands around the house, a fun, positive influence who would stay home to let the plumber in and generally help out, but unless she was working she was never there. She was the best friend of my friend Mel's au pair, who had said she was hard-working, from a good family and 'loved the little children'. I was beginning to have my doubts but kept telling myself it was early days and things were bound to be uncomfortable at first.

Even when she was in the house, Marlene stayed in her room unless it was absolutely necessary to come out and we had begun communicating via notes on the kitchen table. Mine read something like: 'Marlene, HELLO! I forgot to mention that my husband has an old television he said you can have for your room. He's going to drop it round later. Hope all is well with you, Rachel xx', and hers: 'THERE IS NO EGGS.'

Marlene walked into the kitchen and her face registered

pain at seeing me there but she tried to look pleased – we were still making a fist of being civil to one another and I hoped things would soon feel less strained between us. Her shoulders were hunched and her arms tightly folded across her chest. She was wearing pyjamas, a dressing gown, big fluffy bed socks and a massive scarf that was pulled up over her mouth. I felt a twinge of guilt about the heating. I think she was weighing up turning tail and returning to her bedroom, but the desire for breakfast won.

'Hello,' I said. 'How are you?'

'Not so good,' she said bravely. 'My monthly pains are bad.'

'Oh dear. Can I get you a hot-water bottle?'

'No thank you. I have one but I need to get some bread for toast.'

With that my second piece of toast popped up loudly. 'Oh have this one,' I said, and I started to butter it for her. 'Would you like Marmite?'

'What is Marmite?'

'You've never had Marmite? You are in for a treat, Marlene. A very British invention, Marmite.'

She stepped forward, picked up the jar and sniffed it. She looked dubious but didn't want to appear rude. 'OK I will try it.' She took the knife and spread it thickly onto the toast.

'Actually, it's one of those things people either love or hate. It's probably not a good idea to put so much on if you haven't –'

She took a massive bite, paused and then turned to me making a face like someone who was about to sick up a toad.

She ran to the bin and made a big thing of spitting her mouthful out and then standing over it and gagging. Finally, she turned to me and said, 'This thing is disgusting. I cannot eat it.'

I was surprised to see how genuinely angry she was. I made the mistake of trying to make light of the situation and laughed. 'Well, it is quite an acquired taste. I'm sorry, I thought you might –'

But she was furious. She swept out of the kitchen, clunked up the stairs back to her bedroom and slammed her door shut.

I decided not to throw the kettle at the back of her head. I could not afford live-out care and an au pair was the perfect solution. However, after that little display of pique, the thought that I handed over my children for two evenings a week to this sour little cat was awful. I would have to find an alternative and, once I was settled at work and things were on a bit more of an even keel, I would.

In the meantime I should make an effort to be nice. I began to feel guilty. She was only nineteen, away from home, in a foreign country and perhaps she just needed a bit of TLC. Of course, I knew people for whom the whole au-pair thing had been a storming success: the girls had been made godmothers to their children and they'd gone on family holidays to the Czech Republic to stay with the girl's relatives. Had I got a dud or was it just that I wasn't trying very hard? Maybe the Bidewell family was not such a great gig. She was in Luke's old room – he and Alec now had to share – with bits of Transformer stickers on the headboard that I'd failed to remove with a kitchen knife, a thin duvet and a noisy, inefficient radiator. Her boss was distracted and showed very little interest in her and the children were quite a handful.

I padded up the stairs and knocked on her door clutching a packet of painkillers and a glass of water. She had placed a large 'KEEP OUT' notice on it and so we did. She had said that I did not need to clean it and that it would be her responsibility. Fine by me. But when she came to the door, I was quite curious to see what if anything she had done with the room. I peered around her head, but she had opened the door about an inch and was determined not to let me see in.

'I've bought you some Nurofen. They're really good for period pains.'

'Thank you but I have painkillers from home.'

'Oh, OK. Well I hope you feel better soon.'

'Thank you,' she said, shutting the door so fast she nearly had my nose off. What was she keeping in there? A forest of marijuana plants? A fully grown tiger?

As I went back downstairs I heard her begin yet another of her interminable phone calls to one of her friends. When she was on the phone she was an entirely different girl, one that we hadn't yet seen a glimpse of. She laughed and chattered and shrieked and sighed and I wondered why she kept her real self so hidden away. Did she really mistrust and dislike us that much?

The following day, Marlene was picking the children up from school and I was to be on duty from 4 p.m. to 10 p.m. for my first full shift at Clifton Avenue. All the residents seemed to have made it back from their various jobs and day centres, and Rob with the prisoner-of-war-trousers advised that I just take a wander and introduce myself to people. He admitted that what he should be doing was giving me everyone's care plans and sending me off to read them all. But he said that it was much more useful to get a feel for everyone before you were swayed by the assessments and judgements of others. Fair point.

First there was Nettie, a lady who reminded me of an elderly bushbaby with tiny crooked hands and large, darting brown eyes (and quite a bit of facial hair). 'Hello, sweetheart,' she said. And as if straight from central casting, she had a southern Irish lilt to her voice. 'Aren't you lovely? You're lovely you are.' If she had any false teeth I got the feeling that they had long since been lost in the bottom of a handbag, but she didn't seem to mind. As she smiled, a huge expanse of shiny, wet gum was revealed and her lips somehow didn't seem to fit her mouth any more. They slipped and slithered about as she chuckled and got out her glasses to give me the once over. She smelt of lavender and Rich Tea biscuits.

'I bet you you've got a boyfriend, haven't you dear?' Then giving a wicked little laugh she said, 'Of course you have. A lovely, young thing like you? I bet you've got hundreds.' She talked to me as if I was sixteen and for that moment I felt it. She leant over, took my hand and squeezed it very tenderly. I was incredibly moved by this simple gesture and squeezed back. She looked into my eyes and assumed a very serious face. 'Because *you* are lovely, I can tell. Just lovely. Better than the other cunts in here.' And then sweeping her arm in a grand theatrical gesture she said loudly, 'They're all a bunch of cunts in here.'

I moved on quickly to check out the kitchen just as chef Pete – looking not much older than Alec – was craning his head out of the window to suck the life out of the last bit of cigarette. I said hello, but without appearing to have heard me, he popped his head back in and expertly shot the butt into the bin at least ten feet away across the kitchen. Then he carefully folded up his copy of the *Daily Mirror* and placed it in his back pocket. Just as I was beginning to feel awkward, he raised his head and gave me a very broad smile. 'You must be Rachel.'

At that moment one of the residents, Theresa, a big, ungainly girl who had the gait of a startled ostrich, spotted Pete.

'Peeete!' she boomed across the sitting room. 'It's Peeete!' Lots of faces craned round to confirm the sighting and yes, indeed, hallelujah, it was Peeete. Four or five residents jumped to their feet and made their way across to the kitchen hatch.

'Hello, mate!' said Malcolm and leant forward to smack Pete on the back in a warm, brotherly show of obvious affection. Theresa was by now in the kitchen and was saying, 'Hello, you rascal. Where've you been then?'

Presently, a small crowd had gathered at the hatch and without exception, everyone was just delighted to witness the return of Pete. He kissed various ladies and high-fived a few of the men and said that it felt great to be back.

When the fuss had died down and everyone had reluctantly returned to their seats giving Pete the thumbs-up, he winked at me and said, 'Yesterday was my day off.'

We had a lively tea with me being introduced to everyone, while trying to stop the people with weight problems overloading their plates with chips, and ensuring that anyone who looked too skinny did. Being new, I held back, but was encouraged to see Pete and particularly Rob, handle the whole meal with warmth, good humour and efficiency. When the last dish had been cleared away, Rob asked me to come and see him in the office.

'How's it going?' he said.

'Fine. Absolutely fine.'

'Who've you spoken to?'

'Nettie and –'

Rob winced. 'Our Nettie doesn't have a very high opinion of this place.'

'Less the place, more the staff.'

Rob laughed. 'All she wants to do is to go back to living with her sister in Morden. She hasn't lived there for ten years but her sister and brother-in-law take her out for the afternoon about once a year and to keep her quiet, make all sorts of promises about when she can go home. It's not fair because they have absolutely no intention of having her back. They don't even have her for Christmas. The next thing she'll try and get you to do is write a letter to them on her behalf.'

'What should I do if she asks?'

'Just tell her to have a word with me. I'm her key worker – so she hates me more than the rest of the staff put together.'

'Poor you.'

'Poor her. Speaking of which, as you're part-time and will mostly be in at weekends – no time for paperwork – we're going to start off by having you be a key worker to just one resident. Is that OK?'

'Yes.'

Being a key worker for a resident meant that you were their 'special' member of staff. You were expected to forge a good relationship with them, make sure that they were looking after themselves properly, that their toothbrush wasn't too worn-out or hairy, that they had clean socks and pants. Most importantly you would work on their care plan to establish what progress they should make over the next few months, what level of care they needed, and it was up to you to liaise with other care professionals and family to institute this.

'Now,' Rob continued, 'everyone's really settled at the moment, so I'm thinking I might give you a new guy who's due to join us in the next couple of days. Philip Johnston, he's called. He's about thirty-nine, we think.'

'Think?'

'Yes, he's lived with his mum all his life and until she died on Tuesday, the authorities had no idea that he even existed.'

I looked appalled.

'It's not like he was kept in a cupboard or anything like that, it's just that he's never been to school and there are no medical records for him. He's a big man – his mum fed him on white bread, two or three loaves a day with butter and not much else.'

'You're kidding.'

'No, he's been admitted as an emergency to another residential place out of borough, and they've had to ship in special supplies of sliced white to calm him down. I met him there earlier. He's got poor communication skills but then again he's completely traumatized – he sat with his mother's body for two days until he finally fessed up to the milkman what had happened, poor sod. There are health issues that are going to have to be addressed – I think his mum had been ill for quite some time and I don't think he left the house – but also I think it's going to be our job to introduce him to the world in general. He's never been to

39

the cinema or the beach or probably even a supermarket. Just spent thirty-odd years in that house with his mum, watching daytime telly and eating Mother's Pride. A neighbour brought in essentials and kept an eye on them. Oh and Philip's got a really nasty bump on his forehead, nobody knows where it's come from but we'll need to keep an eye on it.'

'Do you think I'm up to it?' I asked.

'Who knows? It's Day One – you might not last the week. Few return after the first shift! The downside is that I might be forcing you to bite off more than you can chew but the upside is, if you do a good job, you'll earn Denise's good opinion and without that you may as well pack up and go home now. I'm sticking my neck out for you here. Are you up for a challenge?'

He brought the file containing Philip Johnston's notes down on the table with an almighty thump. I jumped and we both laughed. I was beginning to like Rob and was grateful to him for having a bit of faith in me. Philip Johnston. I felt a very small surge of excitement. The feeling was short-lived; a bright little fizzle in my stomach that lasted just a nano-second. But it was a start.

'Yes, I am. I definitely am.'

'Good, and I'll be your supervisor and oversee any training that you do on the job – so any problems, come to me.'

The following day passed in a fuzz of housework and the making of four cottage pies – one for that day and three for the freezer. All part of the new regime now that I was working. Henceforth, my fridge would forever be full of home-cooked meals and my laundry basket empty.

Eventually, it was time to pick up the kids. As I crossed the playground to get Jess, my shoulders drooped at the sight of Alessandra. Alessandra is the most beautiful mother at our school. Along with fine bones and straight, thick blonde hair the colour of Shredded Wheat, she wears chic, understated jewellery and her clothes are well-cut and very expensive.

I'm as fond of her as I can be of someone with whom I have nothing in common and whose legs end roughly where my armpits begin. She's not a friend but then she's more than an acquaintance. Dom and I have been to supper at her house and big, good-natured family Sunday lunches. Her husband Mark is probably a total git to live with but he makes me laugh and is really good company. He's very rude to her and teases her incessantly and she doesn't seem to notice or if she does she doesn't mind. She is Italian and her son is in Luke's class. He is called Lorenzo which she pronounces 'Lorennnnzo'. I am ashamed to say that it gives me huge pleasure at going-home time when all the children and the teachers chorus: 'See ya, Loz,' and she winces.

All week, Luke had been saying, 'I'm going to see Lorenzo on Sunday,' and I hadn't taken much notice. I was due to be at work and Dom was having the children so there was no way he could go anyway. But as he tumbled out of the classroom, his arm around Lorenzo, he was saying, 'And have you got a Wii? What games have you got?'

'Hi there,' I said and both little boys looked up, clasped together as if they were taking part in a three-legged race.

'On Sunday, can I take my *Guinness Book of Records* to Loz's house?'

'No, sweetheart. I told you, you're going to Dad's on Sunday.' I was aware that Alessandra was now standing next to me. One glance at her made me uncomfortable. She took a deep breath and said awkwardly, 'Actually, they *are* coming to us on Sunday.' She tried to sound chatty and matter-of-fact. 'Mark used to work with Deborah's father many years ago and they have stayed in touch. So you can imagine when they made the connection, Mark said that they should all come to our house on Sunday for lunch and . . .' She petered out. I could feel my mouth had set in a strange grimace and I was turning red.

'I see. Of course. Of course.' I grabbed Luke and steered him towards the gate. Jess trotted along behind us.

'Mummy, are we going to Loz's house?' she kept asking.

We galloped along the road, dodging children, mothers, scooters and buggies, and made it to the car.

'Mummy! Are we going to Loz's house?'

I sat down, shut the car door and put my head in my hands. I squeezed the tips of my fingers hard against my closed eyes, trying to pull myself together just as there was a little click and Alec let himself into the seat beside me.

He squirmed along and put his arm around me. 'Mum? What is it? What's happened?'

'Nothing darling, I'm being so stupid,' I said, determined not to let great black tears of yesterday's mascara start running down my cheeks. Is this what a breakdown was? When you couldn't last five minutes without either blubbing all over your children or screaming at them like an irate chimpanzee?

'Are we going to Loz's house?' Jess said irritably from the back seat. 'My seatbelt's all twisty. When are we going to their house? Mummy? Are we going to Loz's house with Dad? MUMMY!'

'Yes, Jess, alright! You're going to Loz's house.' I turned round and leant over the top of the seat trying to fix her seatbelt.

'Are we?' said Alec.

Trying to sound cheery I said, 'Apparently, you're all going over to Alessandra's house on Sunday with Dad and Deborah and it just gave me such a shock that's all. It's the sort of thing we used to all do together.'

'I won't go. I won't go to Lorenzo's house. Do you want me to come home on Sunday? I'll come back and we can do something together.'

This made me get a grip. I swept my hands across my face and gave Alec's knee a squeeze.

'No, honestly, I'm being ridiculous.'

At that moment someone hammered on the window. It was my friend Grace. Beautiful, calm, wonderful Grace. I was so flustered that although I pushed every button at my disposal, I managed to put down both the back windows but not the one she was at. So she just shouted through the glass, 'Tea?' and I gratefully pointed the car in the direction of her house and sanctuary.

Mel was in full swing. Grace had set off an emergency flare and here we were in her beautiful kitchen, my two dearest friends once again trying to work their magic. Mel is much more in-your-face than Grace. She has curly, auburn hair, to Grace's wispy blonde, and once she has an opinion, she will not stop until she has convinced you – and sometimes herself – that she's right.

'Do you like Alessandra?' she was saying. 'No, not much. Do you want to spend Sunday with her and her awful children in her awful house? No. Let Dom and Deborah go and have a stilted conversation over the lunch table and wade through architectural plans for their house in Tuscany or whatever. You put your feet up and relax and think yourself lucky.'

'Or come over here for lunch,' said Grace. 'I've got the Carters coming but we'd love to see you. Come here.'

Grace made me permanently welcome but I couldn't face sharing Sunday lunch with other whole, perfect families; I might end the meal lying in the foetal position under the dining table and that wouldn't be much fun for anyone, now would it?

The weekends that the children were with Dom were interminable. He would collect them from school on Friday evening – meeting me at the gates to collect their little weekend bags – and then return them on Sunday evening. Their school uniforms would be washed and ironed and their homework done to perfection.

I would put a very positive spin on it for people who didn't know better and when they asked me about my plans for the weekend I would say: 'I've got the house to myself. I've got a really good book and bubbles for my bath and a box of wine.' And people would imagine me painting my nails and watching entire DVD box sets at 3 o'clock in the afternoon or having long lunches with single girlfriends and shopping for clothes.

The reality was less seductive. I couldn't face seeing anyone and yet I couldn't face the silent house on my own. I would go and see films that I couldn't go to with the children in an effort to enjoy some grown-up time for once. I'd take a snack I'd bought from home in a Tupperware box to save money. Now we were experiencing the lean years, it no longer felt appropriate to spend £10 on a box of popcorn the size of a washing machine. A family bag of Maltesers was too big for one and it simply wasn't possible to buy a normal-sized packet any more. I was aware that I looked a bit sad as I furtively drew out a cheese sandwich halfway through the film, and I did draw the line at a Thermos flask. And of course, because they were grown-up films looking at adult themes, they would be about love – fresh, new, hopeful love or sad, old, decaying love – and betrayal and death and fear, and I would emerge blinking onto a dark high street, depressed and dreading putting my key into the lock, knowing that the house was empty and cold and that it was still only half-past six. I cannot tell you how desperately depressing it is to watch *The X Factor* on your own.

'It's not that I want to go to Alessandra's – of course I don't really. I suppose I just feel that Dom shouldn't be allowed to do normal things with normal people, like going round to Sunday lunch with a family from school. With Deborah!'

Mel looked exasperated. 'God, surely lunch with Alessandra is punishment enough. Forget it. Let it go. You have so much to worry about now –'

'Thanks!'

'Well you do! You've started a new job. You've got zero money. Just let this one go. They say choose your battles; well choose your meltdowns too. This is not a meltdown situation. You have melted down in error. Hasn't she?' Mel looked at Grace for confirmation.

Grace said: 'The thought of them all sitting down cosily together as if it's the most normal thing in the world does make me want to scream.'

'Vomit!' interjected Mel. 'But if you want to think of

Dom doing penance, just think of the *good* people he's missing out on. Us for a start. Anybody with half a brain has taken your side.'

This wasn't entirely true. In the initial aftermath I was very aware of people sticking by me. But after so many months I was sure that many of Dom's old friends now felt that it was safe to go for a drink with him or take him to a football match. I'd seen it so often; I'd sat at supper where the topic of conversation had been a couple that had recently split up and the same old platitudes had been rolled out. I'd probably even rolled a few out myself: 'There are always two sides to everything.' 'No one knows what goes on behind closed doors.' 'He's probably been wanting to leave for years but stayed for the sake of the children.' 'I'm not going to take sides. I'm here for both of them.' Or more specific: 'Apparently she let the children sleep with them every night and he ended up in an Ikea mini-bed. What did she expect?' Eventually, someone might say, 'Well, let's face it, she could do with losing a few pounds and she makes no effort with her appearance. She was asking for trouble.' At this point I would go quiet, feeling the hairs on my legs sprouting through my tights and my Spanx digging painfully into my waistline.

Every day I looked at my marriage, pulled it apart, held it up to the light to see where it had been found fatally wanting. I cringed at the thought of all the times Dom had come home knackered after a long day only to find me screaming at the children or moaning at him because he'd forgotten to pick up some milk or drop off the dry-cleaning. I remembered all the times he'd slid into bed and put loving, hopeful fingers out to stroke my back or the inside of my thigh, only to be met with a handful of tracksuit and an irritable wiggle away from him. Yes, I was sure that I was to blame in a thousand ways, so to have Grace or Mel tell me that Dom had done a terrible thing and that they would never ever forgive him, made me feel as if I wasn't going completely mad. Their common sense kept me going and stopped me being engulfed by regret and self-recrimination.

Alec came in. 'Josh says you *can* take your iPod to 6OB.'

Josh looked guiltily at his feet.

'Josh is a lying little toad, aren't you, Josh?' said Mel.

'Well everyone took them last year.'

'Yes, and got them confiscated en masse. Ignore him, Alec.'

Josh was Mel's son, a year older than Alec, good-looking, cool and at secondary school. Alec worshipped him. I worshipped him too because he was kind to Alec and hung out with him whenever we visited. The 6OB trip was set for Sunday evening. It was the high point of Year 6 and Alec had been looking forward to it for so long that I didn't see how it could possibly live up to his expectations. There would be midnight walks, abseiling, teams building rafts to get across the river, canoeing, and then there was a last-night disco. Alec so deserved this week of just letting off steam, of being eleven and mad and carefree. He felt responsible for everyone and there was nothing I could do to stop him. For months now, I'd looked at his tired, drawn little face, so full of concern and angst, and just kept thinking, Thank God he's got 6OB to look forward to.

The next morning, I was scuttling out of school when RebeccaClassRep found me. She had actually volunteered to be the PTA class rep for the past three years running and so while everyone liked her and admired her and was extremely grateful to her, we all knew that underneath she must be as mad as a snake. Mel had christened her after a new parents' drinks party where she had introduced herself with 'Hello! I'm RebeccaClassRep!' while shaking the hands of maybe sixty strangers for all she was worth.

'How are you, lovely?' She was wearing the look of concern that mothers at the school gates wore when addressing me these days. 'How's it all going?'

'Fine . . . really well. How about *you*?'

'Oh God, you know, busy – think my head's about to spin off . . . but . . . are you coping?'

'Yes, yes,' and wanting to deter her from any more sympathy I said, 'I've actually just started a new job. I'm on my way there now.' I smiled brightly and dared her to continue to look so desperate on my behalf.

'Good for you! Well done you!' She squeezed my forearm and left her hand there. 'What are you doing?'

'I'm working at a residential home for adults with learning disabilities . . .'

Her face dropped, in fact it plummeted. What had she thought I was going to say? That I'd just been made Secretary General to the United Nations? She was momentarily lost for words. In her mind's eye, I could tell she was picturing me emptying bedpans and strapping people into straitjackets while they hurled abuse at me and possibly their poo.

Once it had got out that Dom had left me, I'd achieved minor celebrity status at the school gates. I knew that, in the main, people wanted to help and be supportive but up until then, I had been a relatively private person. The thought of everyone – people like RebeccaClassRep – knowing about my private life and talking about me in sad, hushed whispers was unbearable. It's funny how one individual can say something and leave you touched and grateful and another can say exactly the same thing and leave you either mortified, depressed or wanting to stab them. If I had a Walnut Whip for every time someone had said 'Just let me know if there's anything we can do' or 'You know where we are' I would be the size of a barn. When Grace and Mel offered help I would feel grateful and blessed. When RebeccaClassRep asked if I needed anything I wanted to stick my fingers in my ears and start whistling.

'I do so admire you, Rachel. I don't think I could do it, I really don't,' Rebecca was saying, and all the while her crab-like hand gripped my forearm and squeezed and I wanted to shake it off and stamp on it until it was dead.

'Well, just hope you never have to,' I said with a horrid, bitter little laugh, hoping inwardly that she would go home that morning to find Toby, her small, hearty husband, in bed with a cheerleading team.

At last she seemed ready to move on: 'Look, I wondered if I could ask you a favour?' she said.

'Ask away.'

'Could you possibly take Felix to Thomas's go-karting thing on Saturday because I've got a clash with Tash's ballet.'

I felt my throat tighten as I mentally reviewed the children's arrangements for the weekend. It was complicated because the Clifton Avenue rota had thrown things out of kilter; they were with me on Saturday and with Dom on Sunday – going to bloody Alessandra's – and then Alec was leaving for 6OB on Sunday evening. Thomas's go-karting rang no bells.

'I'm afraid I don't know anything about it,' I said and her face froze.

'Really? Thomas Summers is doing a birthday thing at the go-karting place. I'm sure you were on the email list. I thought I checked. Just about the whole class is going.'

I let myself have a momentary panic on Alec's behalf and then gave myself a small slap. Alec was always forgetting to pass invitations on to me. And Thomas Summers wouldn't not invite Alec to his party. Thomas had been to

Alec's trip to the cinema and burger afterwards on his birthday and they were great friends.

'Look don't worry,' I said. 'I'll go home and double-check and if Alec is going I can easily squeeze Felix in. If you don't hear from me, just assume that it's fine for me to take him.'

# Chapter Three

# Drowning and Waving

I don't think I've ever seen a picture of such complete misery. He was a big man and looked about forty-five although he was thought to be younger. He was sitting in a little scrappy armchair clutching a couple of plastic bags filled with colouring books and felt-tip pens. He was rocking gently, back and forth, and every so often would sweep his huge hand across his face and then shake his head as though in disbelief or as if he was trying to shake off whatever thought had just entered his befuddled mind – a gesture of utter confusion and fear.

'Hello, Philip,' I said. 'I've so been looking forward to meeting you.' And he turned to me and despite his bewilderment, gave me the most beautiful, watery smile.

He had a huge lumpy bruise on his forehead.

'What have you been doing?' I said. 'You look like you've head-butted a fridge.' But he said nothing and just looked at his feet.

As I went over to shake his hand, he stood up and a

whiff came off him akin to an elderly wildebeest. Obviously, the first thing that was needed was a bath.

I left him sitting in the day room and told him I'd be back in a minute. I went to the nearest bathroom and ran the biggest, hottest bath, fit for a Roman emperor. Borrowing Theresa's bubble bath I tipped half a gallon of pink goo in and then went to fetch Philip. He meekly followed me down the corridor and back into the bathroom. Once there, the rocking became more urgent and he began feverishly kneading his hands together, so big and white and soft that he looked like a magician on the point of producing two doves. He looked at me and then at the water and then back at me, obviously now in a state of free-fall panic, and simply said, 'No, dear. No.' And then he turned and went back into the corridor, but once he got there he realized that he hadn't any idea where to go, and so he just stopped like a wind-up toy that had run out of oomph.

I went to his side and took his hand. 'You need a bath. We can't go and get you unpacked and sorted until you're nice and clean. Ruth has bought you some new clothes. I'll help you. I'll stay with you but we have to get you bathed.'

'No, dear.' And he shook his head repeatedly, not in defiance but as if a fly were buzzing in his head and he couldn't stop it.

'Philip, you have to have a bath. I don't think you've had a wash for quite a while and so we have to get you clean. Ruth will be back later and she's going to want to see you all shipshape and smelling lovely. Come on, let's get you into the bath.'

'No, dear.'

And so we stood there, looking at each other in a polite stalemate. It wasn't as if I could grapple this man with the proportions of a grizzly bear into a headlock, strip him naked and heave him writhing into the bath. I didn't want to upset him any more than he had obviously been upset by everything that had happened, but there was no option, he had to have a bath. He had reached the putrid stage, and if I couldn't manage to get him clean then what good was I as a staff member? Plus his social worker, Ruth, was due to visit and she would expect to see some progress.

At that moment, to my immense relief, Rob bustled into the corridor. He took one look at me weakly clutching a flannel and a bar of hairy soap and assessed the situation.

'Come on, Big Man. It's a bath or we throw you onto the streets. And besides, you have the lovely Rachel to help you. God, I bet there's armies of men who'd pay good money to be in your position.' He took Philip's other hand and we both led him back into the bathroom – me grinning stupidly, out of practice at being complimented. Was it Rob's natural authority or a man-to-man thing? I didn't care, I was just so relieved.

'Thank you!' I said. 'I thought I was going to have to hose him down in the car park.'

'Good luck!' said Rob with a good-natured smirk and left.

Philip and I got down to work. Very gently I began to take off his smelly, stiff jacket and his smelly, stiff shirt and his smelly, stiff trousers. As I did so, he started to tremble and although he said nothing I saw a huge tear dribble down his nose. I was breathing entirely through my mouth, which hung open stupidly, so as to avoid catching any whoosh of fetid air that might escape from his arm-pits, feet or nether regions, and I was making a sound like the young Darth Vader. A small lurch of his shoulders gave way to a little hiccup of a sob. I put my arm around him. When I spoke I sounded as if I had a very heavy cold but I still could not risk a full intake of air through my nose as there was every possibility that I would keel over and hit my head on the sink on the way down.

'Oh Philip. Please don't. You're going to feel so good once you've had a bath and it won't take five minutes until you're dressed again and you know what? I'm going to have you looking like James Bond by the time I've finished with you.' And once again, there it was, the lovely, fearful, brave smile.

He was huge. Or rather his torso was. He must have been six-foot-three but he had little legs, like wobbly bird's legs which, as he stepped gingerly into the bath clutching my hand, looked as if they would snap at any moment. At the end of these stork-limbs were the most hideous toenails I had ever beheld. It was as if someone had crafted a cheese and onion crisp onto the end of each toe and I couldn't take my eyes off them. I felt a bit overwhelmed. I didn't know where to start. I began to wonder what quirk of fate, what complex or serendipitous moments in my history and Philip's history had brought us to this point, where I was the one who was trying to negotiate past these pork scratchings and clean in between his hairy, foul toes.

For some reason that song from *The Sound of Music* came into my head, when the Captain and Maria are finally united and they cannot believe their luck. He is convinced that he must have done something 'goood' in his past to be worthy of such good fortune. So what the bloody hell had I done to deserve this? Leaning up to my elbows in now lukewarm, progressively scummy water, no husband and Philip Johnston's toenails? Cruelty on a major scale, surely, or perhaps just a touch of genocide in a former life?

I felt overcome by fatigue mingled with a bit of nausea and had to stand up. I went over to the window and looked out, although the glass was frosted and all I could see were grey shapes outside. I folded my arms, breathed in deeply and put my head against the window to steady myself. I thought of Dom and of the unmade beds at home and the breakfast dishes and all the things I had to do and had a feeling of floating.

Then a voice from behind me said, 'Sean Connery,' and Philip was looking at me with a face full of concern and apology. And I wanted to put my arms around him.

'My favourite too,' I said, lathered up the flannel and set about his back.

I always remember my father telling me a story about the time he was in hospital when he was a teenager, and a kindly, lady nurse had been instructed to give him a bath. He had been mortified as she briskly went about the task as though this awkward boy was a car or perhaps a labrador. Just as it got to the point when he could take it no longer and the inevitable was about to happen, the nurse said, 'I'll let you do your own toffee apple.' And my father had nearly died of gratitude. Well, Philip's tummy was so large that I was actually having problems locating his inner thigh let alone a toffee apple. I gestured for him to stand up, but still no sign of it, as his stomach hung in a thick band of soggy limp skin almost to his knees.

'I'll let you wet your own whistle,' I said weakly, but he obviously had never washed himself in his life, and so just looked down at me apologetically. There was no alternative, I lifted up the wodge of skin with one hand and with the other vaguely wafted the flannel where you might expect genitalia to be and hoped for the best. All the while wondering if the balance of his huge tummy was so out that it had in some way been ingested. Eventually I decided that I was not being paid enough to go on a definitive toffee-apple hunt and so left it at that.

I chit-chatted and asked lots of inane questions, but they were all brushed off with a shy smile and after a good twenty minutes of scrubbing I was no further on in getting him to open up. Finally, sodden and freezing, I was done. It was at this point that I reached into his bag to find the towel that he had brought from home and realized that it was as rancid as his feet had been an hour ago. The thing I remembered most regarding bathing the residents was that you should never leave anybody unsupervised, even for a minute, and that someone could drown in an inch of water – so I was a bit stuck.

'What I'm going to do, Philip, is that I'm going to drain the bath and leave you here while I go and get a big, clean towel. Is that OK?'

He just looked at me as if I'd said that I was going to abandon him on the fast lane of the motorway with nothing but a canoe. So when the last dregs of the bath had gurgled away I ran as fast as I could to the laundry room – a good mile and a half away it seemed – hoping to find a spare. I grabbed the first towel I saw and galloped back to the bathroom. Philip had gone. Shit. Shit. Shit. Shit.

I hadn't passed him on the way so he must have gone towards the office. I belted down the corridor, into the office – no sign. Finally, I heard one of the big fire doors clunk and followed the noise at high speed. There was Philip in the sitting room where I had first met him, standing stark, bollock naked and rocking from side to side.

'I thought you'd done a runner,' I said breathlessly, wrapped the towel around him and tried to usher him into the corridor, but he wouldn't move. 'Are you looking for your things? Your colouring books? Your pens?' He nodded, on the point of tears. 'They're all safe. I've got them for you. You mustn't worry. Let's go and get dressed and take everything up to your new room.'

He nodded and as he headed for the door the towel came adrift.

'Philip! What are you doing?' Denise was in the corridor and Philip had given her a fright. He froze in the doorway in a panic. He was too big for me to squeeze past so all Denise saw was a pair of hands snake either side of his tummy attempting to reapply the towel.

'I'm so sorry,' I said, finally squeezing into the corridor. 'It's me. Philip decided to go walkabout after his bath but it's all OK now.'

Denise didn't look impressed and I winced inwardly. It was such early days and it was so important for her to see me as a safe pair of hands, looking after Philip in the way he deserved.

'That's my towel!' she said and we both surveyed it with surprised expressions.

'Oh . . . I'm so sorry. I didn't realize. I just grabbed the first one . . .' I said apologetically as we gazed at Philip, now swaying gently, resplendent in a towel decorated with pink bulrushes and a turquoise swan.

By the time I'd sorted Philip out I was late leaving and so didn't manage to get home to check emails before I was due to pick Alec up from school. So I thought, Hell, I'll just give Thomas's mum a ring and sort out the go-karting arrangements. Thomas was a lovely boy who we knew quite well, well enough to know not to serve macaroni cheese if he visited and that the landing light had to be left on if there was a sleepover.

'Hi, Kath. It's Rachel Bidewell here. Look, I bumped into Rebecca this morning and she asked me for a lift for Felix on Saturday morning and I realized that Alec hadn't told me about Thomas's party. She said she'd seen my name on the email list so I hope you don't mind me ringing.'

There was a pause. 'Oh God, Rachel. I'm so sorry. I feel absolutely awful but you see the thing is it's one of those things that we just can't take everyone to. There was a real pressure with numbers and . . . it was so hard for Thomas to come up with the final twelve. God, I feel awful.'

I wanted to shout, Twelve? You're taking *twelve* boys and Alec hasn't made the cut? Thomas would be in Alec's top four! And don't you know what a tough time he's having? Didn't it occur to you to try and steer Thomas towards inviting Alec when going through this terrible heart-searching process of coming up with the final *twelve*?

But for Alec's sake I was determined to sound unmoved and instead said cheerily: 'Oh don't be silly. I've been there. Honestly, it's absolutely fine. It was just that Rebecca said I was on the list. Don't give it another thought. I'm sorry I put you on the spot.'

'Look, I haven't heard back from everyone yet. If

anyone can't make it Alec will be the next on the list I'm sure.'

Leave it, forget it.

'Fine, whatever. Have a wonderful party, Kath, and give our love to Thomas.'

I wanted to hammer nails into Kath's eyes. And yet the poor woman was obviously mortified, I couldn't have made her feel any worse than she already did. My main worry was why – why was Alec not on the list? What was going on? Was it just that he and Thomas weren't getting on all that well, or was it more worrying than that? Sometimes I was aware at home that Alec was withdrawn or very quiet – no prizes for guessing why – but I'd hoped that he was the same Alec at school. Not the most popular boy in the class, a bit shy, a bit quirky, but appreciated by those boys who knew a good thing when they saw it.

I waited in the car for him to catch my eye as he rounded the corner outside school and then climb into the seat next to me. I wasn't sure how to play it. Should I just gently come out with 'I hear you're not going to Thomas's party on Saturday?' or should I say nothing. Alec wasn't stupid. He must have known that Thomas was having a party, the others must have all been talking about it surely. He'd chosen not to mention it. Should I just respect that? Did he in fact not give a shit and it was just me stressing about it? My kids did have this amazing ability to surprise me by taking something in their stride which I thought would totally floor them and then having a meltdown over something I had deemed small and inconsequential. I decided to leave it and see if it came up naturally.

He slid into the car and reached across to give me a quick kiss. 'Good day?' I said.

'Alright.'

Luke and Jess had clubs and were being dropped home later, so we prepared to drive off. But then there was a bang on the window. It was RebeccaClassRep. Please, please Rebecca, not now. I put the window down as she hopped from one foot to the other in the middle of the road.

'Did you speak to Kath. Is it OK for Saturday?'

Alec stared at his feet.

'No, I'm so sorry,' I said very quickly. 'I was going to ring you. Alec's not going on Saturday.'

'Did you ring Kath? I'm sure he was on the list.'

'Yes, look, apparently he wasn't.'

Alec continued to stare intently at this feet.

'Oh God how awful. I'm so sorry,' and then craning her head into the car, 'I'm sorry Alec. I just assumed . . . They must be really tight on numbers . . .'

We drove off. If a Fiat Multipla could limp we would have.

'What's happened? Is Thomas having a party and I'm not going?' Damn. Damn. Damn.

'Well, yes, but I think that he was only able to take a few boys from the class. I don't think it's anything you've done.'

'Who *is* going?'

'I honestly don't know, darling.'

'How many?'

'I'm not sure.'

'Well obviously it's Alexander and I bet Max, Raf, Ross and Harry and Will P and Will B. I bet it's just me and Isaac and Dean who aren't.'

'It's just one of those things. You didn't take everyone on your birthday treat, did you?'

'Yes, but I took *Thomas*. Of course I took Thomas!'

'But you didn't take Will B and you felt really bad and you didn't invite Dean until the last minute.'

'But you only let me bring six people and Will B and I aren't even in the same class. I only took Dean because you said I had to.'

'Well, look we'll just say rubbish to them and do something really cool on Saturday. You name it. What do you want to do instead?'

'Nothing. We'll only be able to do something really lame because Jess and Luke will have to come too, and anyway you said that we had to get a cagoule for 6OB on Saturday.'

'I'll see if Dad can have the others and you and I can go and get the cagoule and then do something together . . .'

He nodded. A brave little nod and we drove home in silence.

I was on the phone to Dom. 'I know, I know we talked it all through but things have changed. I want to spend the morning with Alec. If you could just have the others. The thing with Thomas has upset him I think and I said that we could do something together while they were all off go-karting. It would just be until twelve-ish. I could drop them off and pick them up. I'm sorry to ask it's just –'

'Let me talk to Deborah. We were planning on a shopping trip for the house on Saturday morning –' flinch – 'but maybe we can go in the afternoon. Hang on a minute.'

Dom put down the phone and I could hear him talking to Deborah in a muffled tone. He was gone for ages. I was convinced he was going to come back and say that it was not possible because *Deborah* had other plans for them and I was in full attack mode when he returned to the phone.

'I've spoken to Deborah and she's really happy to help out but look, I think that the best thing is if *we* take Alec. He can come along with us and –'

'Dragging him around John Lewis on a Saturday morning is hardly going to cheer him up.'

'If you'll let me finish. We thought we could take him for a big breakfast and make a fuss of him and then as we were shopping for stuff for the kids' rooms anyway, he could come along and we'll devote the morning to getting stuff for him. I want to get him a lamp and a desk so that he can get on with his homework when he's here. We'll do Ikea and then he can get a duvet cover and all that kind of thing. And then as I've got them Sunday he can just stay over Saturday night and I'll meet you at the school Sunday evening for the big 6OB send-off.'

'Oh right. It's just that then I won't see him before he goes and I –'

'You did agree to me having them Sunday because your work rota means I'll potentially miss a weekend.'

'Yes, I know, it's just –'

'It makes perfect sense. You said yourself he needs a bit of time away from the others – some VIP treatment. We'll take him for a Chinese in the evening and he'll be in heaven.'

'Well, he needs to take it easy because it's a big week for him next week.'

'Fine. We'll have him in bed by ten. Honestly, I think it makes sense.'

'You'll need to get him a cagoule. He hasn't got a cagoule –'

'No problem.'

Right. That was that then. As Dom said, it made perfect sense. The fact that I wanted to lock Alec in his room and never let him go to his father's let alone to Swanage for an entire week was of course irrelevant.

I went upstairs, banged on Alec's door and put my head round it.

'I've just spoken to Dad and he says he wants to take you out on Saturday morning. I was actually asking him to have the others so that we could do something but he wants to take you to Ikea to get stuff for your room. And he wants you to stay over . . .'

'Just me?'

66

'Yes, just you. He's going to take you for a Chinese in the evening and you can get your new room straight.'

'Brilliant. He's going to get me my own desk and lamp –'

'I know, Dad said. Are you happy with the arrangement? It's just that I had hoped we could spend the morning together before you go off to 6OB.'

A great cloud of unease had spread over his face. I had pushed Alec's guilt button again.

'Oh well look. Don't worry, Mum, I can tell Dad –'

'Don't be silly. Of course you should go and spend some time with Dad. I'll just miss you that's all.'

'You can get the wing mirror fixed on the car.'

'I can get the wing mirror fixed on the car. Exactly. It will be the perfect opportunity and once more we will travel like normal people and you won't have to hang out the window every time I need to go into the left-hand lane.'

'Are you sure?'

'Absolutely. And Dad's going to get you a cagoule.'

'Oh no. You get it for me. Dad'll make me get one suitable for forty degrees below zero, up Mount Everest.'

'With a built-in tent and GPS. I'll get you one from Millets.' I stood behind him and kissed his smelly, little head. 'I'm so sorry about the Thomas thing. I hope there's oil on the track and they all spin off and die horrible, bloody deaths.'

'It's OK, Mum, honestly. I'm fine. Thomas sent me an

email and I think his mum is going to email you this evening and invite me for a sleepover when we're back from Swanage.'

It was my second shift looking after Philip. He was standing in front of me in his vest, pants and socks, newly bathed and spring-fresh next to the sink in his bedroom.

I wiped his face with a damp flannel so that his hair was out of his eyes

'Smile,' I said.

He smiled. To my relief, his teeth were beautiful. His former hygiene hierarchy had obviously had teeth at the very top and toenails way, way down at the very, very bottom.

'Lovely! Now, I want you to show me how you keep those teeth so fabulous. Here . . . is a brand-new toothbrush I bought on the way in.' I held it up for him to see and then put it back down again. 'And this –' I picked up the toothpaste – 'is your toothpaste. Now show me what you can do.'

It was like throwing a ball at a man with no arms and shouting, 'Catch!' Philip did not move.

'Just show me how you would normally brush your teeth if I wasn't here.'

He looked awkward and full of regret, but again, did not move. So I took his hands and helped him to lift the toothbrush and the toothpaste. Then I helped him to squeeze the toothpaste out onto the bristles of the toothbrush. When I say 'helped him', his hands and arms were a dead weight and I was a reluctant mario-nette with a massive puppet.

I turned him towards me and held onto his wrists. 'Can you just give your teeth a brush now? Can you do that for me?'

His face said, I'm trying – I really am. But I have abso-lutely no idea what it is that you are asking of me.

I made the motions of brushing my own teeth. 'Can you show me?' I said again. 'Like this?' But he just drew his lips back and hesitantly bared his teeth.

We stood looking at each other face to face, Philip now wearing the expression of a Rottweiler uncomfortable with the order to attack. 'I'm guessing your mum used to do this for you. Did she?'

Silence.

'Did your mum brush your teeth for you?'

After a pause he said, 'Pearly whites,' looking at me ear-nestly. 'Pearly whites. Come on, handsome!' His voice trailed off and his hands dropped to his sides, letting the toothpaste and toothbrush fall to the ground. His gaze drifted off and he turned his head towards the window.

We stood in silence for a moment and listened to some-one in the building whistling merrily while Philip's grief seemed to engulf the room.

Eventually I said, 'Well, your mum did a very good job. She could have been a dentist.' And bending down to pick up the toothbrush, I said, 'Let's see what we can do.'

I pulled his armchair over and made him sit down facing the mirror. I put a towel around his shoulders and rested my hands on them.

'Right, Your Excellency,' I said, 'will it be teeth and a shave today or just the full body massage?' It had dawned on me that if his mum had brushed his teeth for him, then it was unlikely that shaving was his forte.

It way *my* Saturday morning. Until 10 o'clock, I had all three children to myself. I was in the kitchen. It was 8.45 and because Mary, Dom's wonderful mother, had been in and done a bit of my ironing the day before, Radio 2 was blasting through the kitchen. A great wave of easy-listening, Saturday morning heaven. We'd had a bit of Squeeze, a bit of Wham! and even some Neil Diamond. I was making bacon sandwiches and as I fried the bacon, Jess had wrapped her arms around my waist from behind and was making me sway to the music. Her feet kept leaving the ground and she was laughing like Peppa Pig, her head buried in the small of my back. Marlene was at her boyfriend's, Luke was sprawled in front of the television next door and Alec was stirring somewhere upstairs.

'No! I don't have to wear a uniform. I'm not a nurse.' I was talking to a very confused Jess about work.

'Well what are you?'

'I'm a helper. I help the grown-ups who can't do things very easily for themselves. I had to brush a man's teeth last night and give him a shave.'

'Really!' Jess's eyes were huge. 'Is he nice?'

'Yes. Very. His name's Philip. I'll take you to meet him one day.' I thought of Philip's face as I had shaved him and smiled. He had relaxed and been so keen to help, craning his neck this way and that, every now and again making small Chewbacca noises.

Jess and I laid the table and I put on a saucepan of hot chocolate for the kids. The glorious smell of the bacon brought the boys in and Elvis came onto the radio. Jess began dancing as if it was the overture from *Swan Lake*, twirling and leaping and then pulling up her nightie to reveal a bare bottom and tummy. Luke gave her a good-natured whack on her behind and then began dancing around with her, now like something out of *Strictly Come Dancing*.

'I love this song.' Alec tried to get past them and idly leant down to check the mail on the computer screen.

'There's nothing,' I said. 'Nobody loves us except Amazon. And Amelia Knight's mother who wants to know if anyone has got Amelia's school skirt. You haven't have you, Luke?'

'Yes . . . and her school bra,' he said in his lady's voice, fitting his hands over his chest like two coconuts. Alec shook his head with good-natured exasperation while still checking the computer. I made a lurch to pull Jess's nightie down but she leapt away shrieking and so I chased her around the kitchen, half-chasing, half-waltzing, with Luke trying to stand on my feet so that I could drag him round with me.

I sang along to the King: "'. . . *in the ghett-oh*!'"

Alec's face contorted with a pained expression as he tried to concentrate on the music with the rest of us all cavorting around him. "'*Da de da de da de da da . . . And something or other, and he something or other . . .*'" and Alec sang: "'. . . *in the gecko . . .*'"

"'Gecko'?!' I said, laughing out loud. 'It's not "gecko"! It's "ghetto". Did you just say "gecko"?'

Luke and Jess joined in. 'Gecko?!' they screeched, although they had no idea what the real words were either. 'Gecko?!'

'It's not a skink! It's not a lizard!' said Luke in a sing-song voice, laughing his head off along with Jess and me.

Alec shot over to the radio and swept his hand viciously across the tabletop so that it crashed onto the floor. The room went quiet.

'Shut up. Shut up you bloody, bloody tossers. Why can't you just all shut up for one single minute? I thought it was "gecko". Big, bloody deal.' He was roaring at us and crying and I don't know who was the more stunned, him or us. Alec never minded being teased. He always took it with such gentle grace and he never swore. But now he kicked the radio with his bare foot and sent it skimming across the wooden floor.

'You all think I'm such a joke. I'm not a bloody joke. You're all a bloody joke. I wish you'd all just die.'

And then all the rage left him as quickly as it had

appeared. As if coming to from a bad dream, he looked around him, horrified and panicked.

I was paralyzed. I had no idea whether to shout back, tell him to apologize and get out, or to drop to my knees and hug him.

'It's OK, Alec. We were only teasing you. We didn't mean to upset you. We just thought it was funny.'

'You think everything's funny, Mum. You laugh at everything.'

And then the pan of hot chocolate boiled over on the hob, making a fizzing sound and putting out the gas.

On Sunday morning I drove Jess and Luke over to Dom's. It was a Victorian semi almost identical to ours. Dom worked as the operations director for a big, charitable housing trust – a noble and worthy occupation that he loved, but not well paid. He had met Deborah there when she worked as his assistant. She had left once their relationship became common knowledge, to work for a very swanky architects' practice. She was now on a good wage, but even so, I knew that Deborah's parents must have been paying the bulk of the mortgage on their new house – there was no way Dom could, when meeting ours was always a struggle.

We'd got into the routine of me telephoning Dom's house when I was two minutes away. I would let the phone ring twice and then by the time we arrived, Dom would already be standing at the door and I could just let the kids out and drive off with little more than a nod in their father's direction. It was one of those things that I did automatically, but if I let myself stop and think about it, it made me want to weep. What a sad little dance. Still, at least it meant that Deborah could lurk in the house and wait until the coast was clear to come and greet the children. I think if I'd had to witness them running into her arms I may have driven headlong into the garage door.

It was Alec waiting for us and he made a big play of being very helpful and getting Jess out of the car. He looked a bit sheepish but I was reassured to see him looking rested and relaxed.

'Did you get what you wanted yesterday?' I asked casually as I got the kids' coats out of the back.

'Just about,' he replied, knowing that listing his brand-new purchases would have been painful for us both.

'And you're OK?'

'Yes. I'm fine, Mum . . . really.'

I put my arms around him and rested my chin on his head for a moment, then let him go.

I went home and tried to get on with some bits of admin but I felt restless and listless all at the same time. By lunchtime, I was exhausted from re-running the events of Saturday breakfast in my head over and over again. Also, I'd had enough of imagining Dom and Deborah quaffing Mark and Alessandra's Chianti. When I could not bear to look at the four walls for a minute longer, I grabbed my coat and fled. I went to Clifton Avenue, crept in the back door, sneaked past the office and found Philip, who was dozing in front of *EastEnders*.

'Fancy a walk?' I said. Philip looked a bit bemused but stood up slowly to get his coat. I didn't want to see any of the care staff and so just told Pete the Chef we'd be gone for an hour.

I felt that walking would do Philip good. It's not as if sending him to a gym was an option at this stage but he had to start getting some exercise and losing some weight. Also, it was a gentle way for him to start experiencing the world outside and would be good for his soul.

A weak autumnal sun was trying to warm us up and I felt my head clearing as we wandered along, Philip with his arm in mine and me chatting inanely. Laurel and Hardy, alive and well and ambling through the park. Alec had seemed OK that morning and he'd obviously had a good day with Dom. As I walked I allowed myself to think that his outburst on Saturday was understandable and nothing to panic over.

Without warning, Philip suddenly became agitated. He stopped dead, donkey-like, in his tracks and began rocking from side to side and shaking his head feverishly as if in a trance.

'What's the matter?' I asked.

But he couldn't speak. He just gazed at me with an expression so panic-stricken that it looked as if his face was melting, and then he began the head-shaking again.

'Philip? What's wrong?' And then more sternly because

he was beginning to really worry me. 'Philip, what is it? Look at me. What is wrong?' I held him by the shoulders to try and get him to focus on me and to calm down, but he was staring at a nearby tree as if it were writhing with snakes. I looked over to try and understand what on earth was going on, just as a little dog trotted out from behind it. It had not seemed possible that Philip could become any more agitated than he already was, but I was mistaken. He began frantically to bounce up and down while making the high-pitched wailing sound of a hysterical turkey, like some vast warrior from the Masai Mara. People began to stare at us, either laughing or freaking out themselves. One little boy fell off his bicycle.

'Stop it, please, Philip. Stop it. It's not going to hurt you.' The dog was a tiny thing – virtually a guinea pig on stilts – but as it veered towards us Philip screamed a great big girl's scream and tried to leap into my arms like he was Scooby-Doo and I was Shaggy. I was struck in the chest with the force of twenty sandbags, bringing me thudding down backwards onto my bottom. Embarrassed and winded I scrabbled to get up but once on my knees, Philip threw himself over me in a kind of crouch, bending me over backwards and whimpering in my ear, as the dog's owner grabbed it and ran for his life.

I decided that the best thing to do was remain in that position until we had both regained our composure. I tried very hard not to think of the ten or so remaining spectators who were gaping, open-mouthed at our strange tableau, not one of them asking if they could help or if we were alright. Eventually, I struggled to get one arm free, and with all my weight on the other arm, I began to give Philip's great head a stroke. He rested it on my shoulder murmuring, 'You're alright, my darling,' and I realized that what he had actually been doing in pinning me down was protecting me from what he saw as a terrible threat. My hero – like Batman having eaten all the Mother's Pride in Gotham City.

'So, Philip,' I said, scooching out from under him and onto my bottom as he gazed past me, focused on some point in the near distance, 'you don't like dogs.'

He dropped his head and shook it.

'How are we going to cheer each other up with lovely walks in the park if you don't like dogs?'

He continued to shake his head but as I began to laugh so did he and eventually we just sat there next to each other in the dirt, waiting to summon the strength to head for home.


'Go away, you beastly boy.'

It was the 6OB send-off. I had Alec clamped to me and I was clamped to him. When I was a little girl and didn't want to go to school, my mother had two means of getting me back on track. One was to lift me up by the elastic at the top of my woolly tights and swing me round – I have experienced such joy since, but rarely. Or she would grab my hand, make me straighten my arm and do a pumping motion. 'I'm pumping you up with love for the day,' she would say gravely and I would stand feeling as if I genuinely was being filled with the strength to get me through to home-time.

Right now, particularly after his outburst in the kitchen on Saturday, I wanted to pump Alec up with whatever it took to last him an entire five days – in Swanage. Other boys loitered furtively, their mothers knowing that hugs and kisses were out of the question. I felt so lucky that Alec had still to cotton on to the fact that allowing your mother to squeeze the living daylights out of you in public was not the done thing. I think the longest I had been away from him was the three nights when Dom and I went on a disastrous mini-break to Prague, and Dom got an abscess on his tooth and we'd spent the weekend in grey dentists' waiting rooms or trying to find antibiotics on a Sunday when all the chemists' were shut. Now Alec was to be gone until Friday – five nights.

'Take care. Don't do anything daft and just enjoy it.' I tried to take him slightly away from the throng and whispered to him. 'You so deserve to have the best time, Alec. You really do. You've been so amazing these last few months and –'

'He's got to get on the bus, Mum. Quickly! They're going to go!' Luke was about to faint with the anxiety of it all.

'Alright, alright.'

Alec swung his bag over his shoulder and tried to

swagger away with it but the thing was clearly too heavy for him and so instead he had to do five or so little steps and then stop, put the bag down, take a breather, heave it back up again and do five more. At that moment, Dom, who had been hanging back, came and took the bag from him. He ruffled Alec's hair and went over to the side of the coach to deposit the bag. I watched him efficiently throw Alec's stuff in and then assume the role of Chief-Bag-Thrower-Inner as other dads came over with their children's cases and handed them to him.

'I could always kidnap the coach and run her down at high speed.' It was Mel, here to say goodbye to her daughter Issie who was in Alec's class. 'I cannot believe he's brought her here.' For one second I looked at her blankly and then followed her gaze over to Dom's car and saw Alec hugging a tall, slight young woman with long, straight, beige hair, wearing jeans and a red, all-weather jacket. It was Deborah. Then I watched as she held Alec by the shoulders and spoke to him earnestly. I imagined her saying, 'You so deserve to have the best time, Alec. You really do. You've been amazing these last few months and your father and I are so proud of how you've looked after your poor, mad mother, but now you deserve some time for yourself.'

Then Alec got onto the coach. It pulled away and we waved and we waved and we waved. Jess and Luke raced along behind the coach. And he was gone. As Dom was getting into his car, he looked over the top of it and raised his hand at me, like a Red Indian saying 'How!' and then drove off. Deborah had resolutely looked at the windscreen as they left and I stood staring at the place where their car had been sitting for some time.

We drove back to Mel's for a late tea and she wittered away, full of outrage and bile. She hadn't seen Deborah before and she was unimpressed. 'To think that that mouse is the best he can do. I'd expected huge tits at the very least. All this time waiting to catch a glimpse of her and she looks like Peter Crouch.'

'She does not look like Peter Crouch. She looks like Jodi Foster.'

'Yes, and she's a lesbian!'

On the occasions that I had seen Deborah since the split, I was always surprised by how young she looked. I knew she was only twenty-nine but still, every time I saw her in the flesh it was a shock. And she looked so normal. She didn't look like a husband-stealer, a marriage-wrecker. She looked like a rather nice, fit, outdoorsy sort of young woman who probably exercised every day and had done the London Marathon more than once for a very good cause. She wasn't a beauty but she looked . . . nice. Did she care what I looked like? Was she remotely curious when she saw me or was I just Dom's ex? Worse still, was she sitting in the car now and thinking, No wonder he left *that*?

Since Dom had left me, I had been heartbroken of course, but by far the most immobilizing emotion had been rage. I couldn't sleep for rage. I couldn't eat for it.

And if I wasn't feeling rage, I was feeling grief, a sense of terrible loss akin to when my mother died – but the person who I was grieving for would suddenly be on the end of the phone wanting to know whether the car insurance was up to date or when Alec's piano exam was. And then the rage would return again – like someone in the room with me howling. At first it was focused on Deborah, the evil, wicked Deborah: Lady Macbeth, Lucrezia Borgia, Cruella de Vil. Terrible, biblical rage would choke me and I began to worry that I would develop a limp and forget to change my clothes or wash my hair or feed the children; that ultimately I would be found wandering down Kilburn High Road with a can of Thunderbird, shouting obscenities and spitting at passers-by while trying to punch a policeman.

Seeing Deborah, slight, unremarkable Deborah, hugging my son and twiddling nervously with the zip of her jacket, I once again had to face the fact that she was probably just young and thoughtless and idealistic. And that it was Dom – *my* Dom, my husband whom I had loved since I was nineteen, the father of my three children – who was the unbelievable shit.

I decided the one thing that would stop me fretting about Alec too much was to make some progress with Philip. A few days later we were up in his room and today saw the start of Operation Daily Hygiene Routine. I thought we would begin slowly with tooth-brushing, work up to shaving, and ultimately showering somewhere around the next millennium.

I had bought him a new wash bag – a stripy, jolly affair – and a bright red flannel. I had also brought in my own wash bag. I realized that by comparison it was a sorry sight. The plastic lining had ripped so that you could see a layer of thin, mustard-yellow sponge inside. Hence *sponge* bag I thought distractedly with the same sense of moderate wonder I had experienced recently on a school trip with Jess, when someone explained that a cupboard had once been a board that you kept your cups on. Or maybe it was just the bag that you kept your sponge in. I was stalling.

Philip was once again in his vest, pants and socks but it was a bit chilly in his room so I found his old dressing gown hanging on the back of the door and put it on him. As I fished around for both ends of the towelling belt and tied them up over his stomach, I was pleased to see that he had already lost a bit of weight.

'Goodness me!' I said. 'Well done, mate. We could barely get this done up a few days ago and look at you now.' He ate well at Clifton Avenue but just cutting out the white, sliced bread was obviously having a dramatic effect. I was delighted. I tapped his tummy. 'Come on, Twinkle-toes, let's get started.'

I put aside the unused dental floss, free moisturizer samples and gently oozing, out-of-date Calpol sachets that had taken up permanent residence in my wash bag, and started my demonstration. I carefully spread the toothpaste on my brush and talking all the time through froth and dribble did a step-by-step breakdown of what the process involved. Philip seemed focused and alert.

Then I guided his hands as we repeated the actions slowly and carefully together. At one point I had to get him to sit down as his height meant I had to stand on tiptoe, which was exhausting and faintly ridiculous. So now I was on my knees, holding his hand as we made bold strokes up and down across his top teeth and then bottom. All the time I talked to him and explained what we were doing and why. I was confident that things were going well.

The final and crucial stage was to get him to do the whole thing on his own. I told him to stand up and face the mirror and I laid the toothbrush and toothpaste out in front of him. 'Right,' I said encouragingly, 'let's see what you're made of, Mr Johnston. Now you do it.' Like a nervous hostess revealing a surprise-party buffet table, I stepped back from the sink and gestured to Philip to dig in.

He didn't move.

'Come on,' I said. 'Give it a go.'

Nothing. So I squeezed the toothpaste onto his brush to make things easier and waited for a miracle. I gestured towards the sink again. Ta-da! Still nothing.

So we started the whole process all over again. Only this time, I popped out to borrow another resident's toothpaste to see if the one I had got was too minty for Philip. To my annoyance, when I got back I saw Philip disappearing down the corridor and before I could stop him, he shot into one of the lavatories and shut the door very firmly behind him. He now had his mind on other things and experience told me he would be a while.

Great, I said to myself. 'Thank you, Rachel. This afternoon has been most informative. What would I do without you?' 'Don't mention it, Philip. Just doing my job . . .'

Later as I was speaking to Denise about a problem with one of the dryers, I noticed that her eyes kept travelling down to my chest. As I followed her gaze, I saw dried toothpaste splattered down my T-shirt like bird poo. Self-consciously I pulled my cardigan around me to hide it but I had already sensed her wince with disapproval.

I had spent the rest of the afternoon at Clifton Avenue, lurching from cup of tea to cup of tea. I was not really sure what was expected of me and wished Rob was around so that I could ask his advice on Philip's oral hygiene and generally have someone on my wavelength to talk to. It was a relief when the residents all came home and we could get stuck into teatime.

A huge debate was going on about whether or not their recent Halloween party at the hostel had been attended by Theresa's sister. Theresa was one of my favourite residents; warm and funny and incapable of speaking in anything but a bellow.

'You,' Theresa was saying to another resident, Stewart, waving her knife in his direction, 'are well out of order. Linda came *and* she brought the boys because Matthew was wearing fangs.'

'No,' said Stewart definitively, taking a large mouthful of fish pie. Theresa was Sophie's best friend and Sophie was Stewart's girlfriend, so there was a lot of niggling between the two rival parties.

'Hear that, Rachel? He says "No" like he knows more about whether my own sister was at the party than me! He takes the biscuit, he really does. You, Stewart, take the bleeding biscuit.'

Philip was at the table and so I tried to encourage him to join in. 'Well, Philip and I will be newcomers next year. Is it wild this party?'

'Spoooky!' said Sophie, happy that the conversation had shifted.

'Will we have to dress up?'

'Ooh yes! Spoooky!'

'Do you like Halloween?' I said looking at Philip, but he just smiled and vaguely shook his head. He had started to talk more but just in stock phrases that his mother had obviously used again and again. 'I'm watching you!' he'd say good-humouredly and, 'Here comes trouble!' but not much more.

'When's your birthday, Big Fella?' said Theresa. 'We'll

need to do a big party then won't we Rachel?' and I could have kissed her for trying to involve him, but again he shook his head, lowered his eyes and just smiled.

'Very good point, Theresa,' I said. 'We'll have to check that one out.'

'You're only allowed a party if Denise says it's OK,' said Stewart smugly, 'or if your family take you out and pay for it.' Stewart's main problem was that he was a severe epileptic whose fits were only just controlled. As a result, the drugs he was on really took it out of him and he was constantly dozy and his speech and movements painfully slow. For all that, he still managed to be pretty annoying when he wanted to, and liked to remind everyone what the rules were at all times, especially new, inexperienced members of staff.

'I'm sure we'll sort something out,' I said.

'Ooh yes!' said Sophie. 'I hope it's tomorrow!'

Although the staff at Clifton Avenue watched Sophie's diet very carefully, she went home every weekend, and her mother had fed her until she was the size of a squat moose. Apparently, her parents had been advised by a nutritionist who specialized in Down's, but her mother was of the opinion that poor little handicapped Sophie had such a miserable quality of life that a few sweets, a chip buttie and a litre-bottle of Fanta were her only source of joy. The fact that Sophie had a better social life than me, with Mencap bowling on Tuesday evenings, salsa, Zumba and various treats at the day centre each week –

*and* a boyfriend! – just didn't seem to compute with her mum. What also didn't compute was that a potentially rich and rewarding existence was being increasingly threatened by her obesity.

Her mum was quite elderly and had given birth to Sophie, the last of five children, in her mid-forties. Consequently, Sophie was the baby, and her mother loved her to pieces and dressed her in pretty dresses and lots of pink. The effect was not good. Clifton Avenue would dress her in comfy, adult clothes in an effort to give her a bit of dignity, but her mum would mysteriously lose these items of clothing at the weekend and return her to the hostel in bobby socks. And we would have to check her bag for chocolates and sweets, which we always found, shoved into secret pockets in her coat or in her rolled-up socks.

Denise spoke disparagingly about Sophie's family, but there was no mistaking the love that they had for their daughter. Misguided they might have been, but at least they thought they were doing their best for her and she was loved and secure. In fact she was the envy of half the other residents whose families had given up on them years before.

I was on duty with Lucy, a single mother in Doc Martens, hanging off brittle little legs in black, opaque tights patterned with purple squiggles. Her hair and make-up were equally uncompromising, with lots of black eyeliner and tufts. The overall effect was part Siouxsie Soux, part irritable poodle. She had no time for me.

'Here she is! Here's Lucy!' chirruped Sophie. 'Ooh Lucy, you're as posh as a dog today.' A compliment from Sophie always entailed an adjective linked with something from the animal kingdom, but the link between the two was not always immediately apparent. 'As pretty as a pony!'

'Thank you, Soph. Rachel, we try and have tea done by six and it's ten-past now.'

'Sorry, yes of course.' I started madly clearing the plates.

'Let the residents do that. We're not their skivvies.'

'No, it's just if we're getting late I . . .' But she'd moved on. I felt a bit lost. I let out a deep sigh and, as I caught Philip's gaze, I rolled my eyes in the hope of getting a little support, but he was looking at his hands again.

The doorbell went and gave me something useful to do. Philip's social worker, Ruth, was on the doorstep. She was carrying a cardboard box and said that there were four more in the car. I was shocked to hear that Philip's mother's funeral had been that day. So shocked that I didn't even question Ruth about it – it didn't seem to occur to her that Philip might have wanted to attend. She told me matter-of-factly that his mother's house was going on the market. The neighbour had helped clear up and put a few things by that Philip might like to have.

I took the boxes up to Philip's room. They looked incredibly forlorn in the middle of this empty, dull space. I went to get Philip, thinking that we could spend an hour unpacking and making the room more cosy, and perhaps I could get him to talk to me. He obediently followed me but showed no sign of recognition at any of the things in the boxes. I'd hoped that there might be a photo of him when he was younger, or perhaps of him with his mum, but there was just one of a girl of about twenty-five in a mac at the seaside. The day looked wet and cold but she was smiling a toothy grin and doing a little sort of wave, squinting into the camera.

'Is this your mum?' I asked. But Philip just looked blankly at me and stood, his hands clasped in front of him, gently rocking on his heels.

'Oh my goodness, look at him!' I pulled out a knitted toy that perhaps had once been a jolly bunny. I showed it to Philip but he just stared at me. I continued to pull stuff lamely out of the boxes and to arrange the contents around the room, all the time chattering away, but there was no response. Eventually, I went downstairs to make myself a cup of tea and to check Lucy didn't need me, leaving Philip finding his pyjamas.

I offered to make Lucy a cup and tried to build some bridges.

'Is it OK to use these mugs?' I asked by way of an ice-breaker.

'Yep.'

'Oh great.' I surveyed ten or so faded, unappealing mugs that looked as if they would render tea into sludge the minute they came into contact with it. I went for the least unappetizing.

'Is this one OK?'

'I said you could use any of them.'

'Oh right . . . How long have you been here?'

'Two years. I'm being sponsored by the borough to do a social work degree next year.'

'Oh great.' Why couldn't I think of a single thing to say? 'Rob said you had a daughter. How do you cope with childcare and everything?'

'My mum. I'll start the drugs run. You should make sure that Philip's OK. He's not really up to getting himself ready for bed you know?'

'Yes, I know. I was just giving him a couple of minutes to acclimatize to his room with his old things in it.' I was trying not to sound prickly. 'I know he needs help at bedtime.' I began to hurry out of the kitchen, feeling that I'd been chastised again. I knew Philip needed help, I didn't need reminding. I turned and in an effort to gain just a morsel of respect from Lucy, said: 'I gather from Ruth that it was the mother's funeral today. I wish someone had told me, I could have gone with him.'

'Oh he didn't go,' said Lucy. 'Denise didn't think it was a good idea and the social worker had something else on.' She looked triumphant.

When I got back upstairs, Philip was still fully clothed and standing in the middle of the room, only now he was clutching an ornate, mint-green plate. On it was written:

PHILIP: from the Greek *Philippos*,
meaning 'lover of horses'.
Strong and Purposeful. A leader.
An idealistic nature with a desire to help others.
Abbreviation: Phil
Namesakes: His Royal Highness the Duke of
Edinburgh, Prince Philip

'I bet your mum gave you that? Did she?'

He nodded. I tried to take it from him but he clung onto it tight. Although his face registered absolutely nothing, as I touched his big, soft hand, I realized that it was shaking. I gave it a miniscule stroke with my knuckle.

'Would you like to go back to the flat? You and me, and we'll see if there's anything else you want to keep? Any photos? . . . A bread bin?'

He smiled, that lovely watery smile, and shook his head.

'Come on,' I said, 'let's get you ready for bed.' He handed the plate to me but made no move to get ready so I continued to stroke his great hand. I marvelled at the grief and loss that this man must have been feeling, and yet he had no way to express it or to share it with me or anyone. I felt lost and useless in Clifton Avenue but compared to Philip, I was having a holiday. How he must have longed to turn the clock magically back to where he was just a short time ago: safe and secure, living with his mum with everything feeling like it was for ever.

'*Here* you are, Rachel!' The door burst open and Denise swept in. 'Lucy's downstairs doing the drugs on her own! I've only popped in to drop off the rota. You're needed down there. There are twenty-two other residents in this place, I know you're his key worker but Philip is not the only one.'

'Yes, of course. We were just unpacking some of his things.'

She looked exasperated but not unkind. 'Well, now really isn't the time. This is the sort of thing that should be done when the others are at the day centre. You should keep him home for the day if you want to concentrate on interior design.' She was trying to be patient but was clearly frustrated by me.

'Sorry. I didn't know. I'll come straight down once Philip's in his pyjamas.'

'Right, I'll see you down there. Please hurry.'

She left the room and I took in a large breath of air to stop myself flinging Philip's precious plate at the wall.

He gave my hand a little stroke. 'Here comes trouble,' he said.

I entered the office and Lucy and Denise sprung apart like guilty lovers. Obviously they had been discussing me.

Denise's head did a tiny nod and Lucy tactfully left the room.

'Rachel,' said Denise formally, 'we've got to get you out of mummy-mode. When you're working a shift the priority is that the evening should run smoothly. Don't do too much for the residents. We are here to facilitate them to live as independent lives as possible, not to treat them like our children.' She softened. 'I know it's tempting to help out more than you should but in the long run it's actually the very worst thing you can do.'

'Yes, of course, I know, I just –'

'You haven't the time to indulge all the residents' individual needs. No peace for the wicked, Rachel – we have to get through tea, get the drugs run done and get everyone settled and into bed. Above all, we have to support the colleagues that we are sharing a shift with.'

'I know. I'm sorry. I appreciate Philip took up a lot of my time this evening.'

'I'm worried that perhaps Philip is too much for you to take on at his stage. Lucy tells me you feel you should have taken him to the funeral. I really didn't think it was appropriate. Can you imagine how distressing it would have been for him?' She bit her lip. 'I don't know . . . do you think you're up to being Philip's key worker?'

I tried to sound confident and sure of myself. 'I think that with the right help and supervision I am. I would hate to have to let him down now.'

'Let him down?' This struck her as funny and she said

gently, 'That one doesn't know what day of the week it is.'

'It's early days, I think we're both just finding our feet . . .' I said weakly.

'Well, I'll have to talk to Rob but it's possible that we may have to re-evaluate this arrangement. OK?'

I hadn't realized it but Philip was the only thing keeping me going at Clifton Avenue, keeping me going full-stop. Making me feel that despite everything else, amidst the meltdowns, bed-wetting, sulky au pair and absent husband, I could prove to myself that I wasn't completely useless. I couldn't bear to think of someone else looking after him and him having to go right back to the beginning with someone new. I couldn't say any of this to Denise as she looked at me with her little tight lips pursed and her head on one side like a disappointed cockatoo. I wished the kind Rob was there to fight my corner, I knew that he was the one person with faith in my ability to help Philip.

'Well, keep me posted,' I said weakly.

'Oh I certainly will *keep you posted*,' Denise said, laughing a wheezy little laugh.

My God, was that the phone ringing? Where was it? Not in its holder next to the bed. I sat up and looked around. A phone was ringing. It was 2.32 a.m. The phone stopped.

Then my mobile started. Down in the kitchen, probably in my handbag, but I could just hear it. I got out of bed quickly, suddenly feeling a pang of real concern. By the time I got to the kitchen my mobile had stopped but immediately the house phone started ringing again. It had been left on the stairs.

'Hello?'

'Rachel?' It was Dom. 'Why haven't you answered your phone? It's me. Look I've just had a phone call from Mr Peters in Swanage. Apparently Alec has disappeared.'

A bolt of adrenalin hit me in my stomach, bowel and chest. 'What? What do you mean disappeared?'

'There seems to have been a bit of an upset at supper-time and Alec hasn't been seen since.' Dom's voice was tight and he sounded as if he was doing everything in his power not to panic. 'They checked his bed about two hours ago but he wasn't there. They've searched the grounds and they think he may have run off.'

'Run off? Where? Oh Jesus, Dom. Jesus. How long has he been missing? It's half-past two in the morning.'

'I'm not sure. Long enough for them to be worried. Look, I'm going to drive down there now and I'll call you as soon as I know anything.'

I tried to think clearly. There was no way I could sit and wait for information. 'I'll come too,' I said.

I ran to Marlene's door and banged on it. There was no answer. She must have been at her boyfriend's. I would have to drop the others at Mel's and Dom could pick me up from there.

I woke up the little ones and pulled a sweater on over my pyjamas. My hands were shaking so much I could barely get the keys into the car ignition and my legs trembled as I tried to drive and appear normal. I wanted Luke and Jess to think that this was all actually a jolly good adventure – a bonus sleepover at Mel's – and I was still telling myself that, by the time I reached her house, Alec would probably have turned up.

Mel said: 'He's fine. I know he is. You'll look back on this and laugh.' Whatever the outcome, I knew I would never, ever look back on this and laugh.

Dom and I drove to Swanage with the sat-nav lady, icily calm, saying 'Turn right at the next junction. Take the first exit,' as our thoughts raced. We couldn't comfort each other. We couldn't reassure each other. We just sat in silence – terrible nightmare scenarios running through our heads.

Dom's mobile rang. I answered it. Please, please let it all be OK.

'Hello?'

'Hello, is that Mrs Bidewell?'

'Yes, yes it is.'

'It's Sergeant Travis here, one of the officers looking for Alec.'

'Yes? Has he turned up?'

'No, not yet but we're doing all we can. Look, there seems to be a bit of confusion here as to what exactly he would be wearing. Can you clarify what jacket he might have on? Obviously, we need to put out a description of him and the teachers aren't sure.'

My mind was blank. Then I pictured him walking up the steps of the coach, shyly turning to wave at us, trying to stop a huge, broad grin from splitting his face in half. 'He's got a navy fleece jacket that has a zip up the front . . . and a hood. And a cagoule. A dark-green cagoule, with a camouflage pattern on it . . . from Millets.'

'Right, well, that's very helpful. Are you on your way, Mrs Bidewell?'

'Yes, we should be with you in an hour.'

Dom was saying, 'Ask them where it is. Ask them where it is.'

'Can you tell me the postcode for the centre? We've no idea where it is other than Swanage. I've got the details somewhere but I left the house without –'

'Yes, of course. One moment . . .'

I tried to put the numbers into the machine but I had no idea how. I pushed a red button and the whole thing switched itself off. Dom was trying to keep his eyes on the road while getting it started again, all the time cursing under his breath. He jabbed at the machine and it flickered on and then straight off again and he leaned in closer to look at what was going on. As his eyes darted back to the road again, he swung the steering wheel violently and the whole car lurched away from the central reservation that was millimetres away. One small van braked hard to avoid us and we swerved again and shot onto the hard shoulder. Then we ground to a halt in a vibrating, gut-wrenching skid.

The phone had been thrown to the floor. I picked it up and heard Sergeant Travis still trying to communicate the postcode to us. I passed the phone to Dom and put my head in my hands. If anything has happened to Alec, I thought, I will die.

We arrived and parked outside what looked like a huge, sprawling school. It was empty and dark and we didn't know where we were supposed to go so Dom swung and jerked the car round recklessly. Eventually, we drew up at the back of the main building to find what seemed like a film-set from a low-budget disaster movie. Sergeant Travis came out to meet us and introduced us to two other policemen who were obviously in charge. Extra lighting had been rigged up and its glare was harsh and dizzying. As the men had their backs to the light I couldn't actually see their faces and the noise of the generator made it very hard to hear what they were saying. It was drizzling and bitterly cold and I felt foolish for not having dressed in more suitable clothes. Dom ran back to the car and returned with two rugged-looking fleeces and a waterproof picnic blanket. I put on Deborah's fleece and wrapped the blanket around me but I may as well have covered myself in tissue paper, it was so cold. Over all the shouting and activity you could hear the sea and great waves crashing on a beach near by. We were introduced to all sorts of people and I envied everyone their sense of urgency and purpose. I wanted one of them to give me something to do, anything, but we were treated like chief mourners at a funeral.

'Try not to worry,' a policewoman kept saying to me and I wanted to laugh and head for the beach and run up and down screaming Alec's name. I vaguely recognized some of his teachers and couldn't understand why they were hanging around looking uncomfortable when they could have been out searching, but then I realized that the police were so efficient and busy that you would feel like you were getting in the way if you tried to help. Dom's face was grey and his mouth strangely taut; I knew that he felt as useless and desperate as I did and I wanted to put my arm around him or squeeze his hand, but I couldn't.

Someone official arrived and tried to be reassuring. The beach was being searched, the dunes, the road, the railway station, the bus terminus, the cliffs. There seemed to be police everywhere. I was torn between feeling hugely grateful that they were obviously taking it very seriously and appalled at how grave they seemed to think the situation was. I'd half been hoping to arrive to find one policeman on a bicycle saying that this sort of thing happened all the time and that Alec would be back for his breakfast. Everyone seemed to agree that once the morning came the search would get easier. Helicopters and boats would join in, partly because they were more effective by day but also because by then Alec would have been missing for a longer time and the search would automatically be wrenched up a gear.

All we could do was squint into the darkness beyond our little hub of activity and shiver. Someone brought me a cup of tea and I burned my mouth on the first sip. Now I stood in front of the centre, clutching the cup and blowing on the tea with strange, thick, trembling lips that I didn't trust to work properly. Mr Peters, one of Alec's teachers, was talking, saying that there had been a bit of a fuss after tea but that everyone had gone to their rooms quite happily and that he'd checked them all at 9.15. Alec hadn't been in bed but he'd assumed he was in the bathroom. He'd checked with his roommates and they had confirmed this. It was now 5 a.m. At the very least, Alec had been missing for eight hours. And it was so cold. Mr Peters gave the impression of someone desperately concerned for this lost boy in his charge, but also desperately trying to cover his back.

Dom was coping by asking lots of questions about timings, and security and whatever the incident was that had taken place after supper, and who had been involved, and what the weather forecast was for the coming day.

I felt as if a great stone had been dropped onto my chest, stopping me speaking or even breathing properly. I was grateful that by this stage nobody tried to make light of it, nobody tried to say it was all going to be alright, they just got on with whatever they were doing and let a WPC get me tea. Where are you, Alec? Whatever has happened it's OK. Just be OK. We can sort it out. But where the bloody hell are you?

The police seemed very anxious to determine how he had bolted. Had he planned it? Packed his bag? Got food from the kitchen? If so, they hoped he'd turn up trying to thumb a lift, although with this scenario there was more chance of abduction.

Just the word made me want to scream. We were asked to inspect the things he'd left in his room and it seemed to be just about everything. His bag was there, dirty socks and pants and the *Top Gear* magazine I'd bought him as his big, holiday-reading treat. Everything was strewn around his bed. No, this little boy had not been planning to leave – in fact this little boy was wearing his pyjamas. The hooded fleece was hanging on the back of the chair where his cagoule was sitting, folded up in its small pocket, unused.

In an article about something like this in a crappy women's magazine, you always read, 'It all felt so unreal. It was like some hideous nightmare; one I couldn't wake up from.' And it was. That was exactly what it was like. The same piece would say, 'You never think anything like that is ever going to happen to you, do you?' And I would always think, Well, as a matter of fact, yes, I do. I always think that something awful is going to happen. That one of my children will be snatched or blown up or drowned. Dom said that I worried too much, that I shouldn't be so neurotic, but now I was being proved right. Eleven years of worrying, justified in one night.

I'd lost all sense of time. I kept looking at my watch.

One minute it would feel as if three hours had slipped away without me even noticing and that the situation had gone from bad to worse in a horrid, grey, slick of time that was floating past imperceptibly; the next it would feel as if time was going backwards. It couldn't still only be ten-past six, could it? It was five-past six an hour ago.

As the day came, it was a relief to be allowed to join the search. We were to re-tread the steps of the police in case they'd missed anything in the dark or Alec had looped back. I went onto the beach with about eight staff from the centre who had come in specially: catering staff, admin staff. I was incredibly touched that they were all there and kept thanking them as if they were helping me clear up after a children's birthday party. 'This is so good of you. Thank you so much. I am so very grateful . . .'

But still no sign of Alec. Alec was still missing. The whole thing felt surreal but at the same time it was all so familiar, like we were involved in our very own episode of the *The Bill*. When a boy's shoe was found on the shore-line and brought to me, it was like a terrible TV cliché. No. It was too small. It had silver planets on it. More suitable for Jess.

The beach was grey and cold and drizzly. After a couple of hours we were told to take a break and help ourselves to something to eat. We were taken back to the centre and into the brightly lit canteen. All the food had been sitting in stainless-steel containers under a heated light for hours. It was nearly midday. The rubbery scrambled egg caught in my throat and made me gag.

Suddenly, the heavy, glass fire-doors swung open. A young policeman burst in. 'He's been found. He's been found. The boy's been found.'

We'd run, following the young policeman and we were weeping and laughing and tripping over. He was fine. Just tired and cold. He was safe. Someone put us into the back of a police car and we drove for what seemed like miles. At last, Dom and I were able to grip each other's hands and squeeze like mad. We arrived at a little lane and stopped and I caught a glimpse of Alec in the back of an ambulance. We bolted out of the car and I ran to hug him; to clutch him to me, to squeeze him as hard and as tight as I possibly could, but his body in my arms was limp and unnaturally yielding and it was like trying to hug liquid.

We went with him to hospital with cheery paramedics and efficient breezy nurses. We filled in forms and answered questions but all the time Alec just sat, a blanket draped over his little frame, looking incredibly sad. He was checked over and they said he had hypothermia and so we stayed in the hospital all afternoon while he slept. We rang everyone to say that he was safe and I stood and looked at my feet as Dom rang Deborah and cried with exhaustion and joy. We passed a strange few hours eating tasteless sandwiches and drinking instant coffee just waiting for Alec to wake up and for us to get some sort of an explanation as to what had gone on.

'What happened?'

Finally, it felt like the right time to ask. We were all sitting in an empty classroom back at the centre; Dom and I perched on child-size chairs, me still in boots, Deborah's fleece and pyjama bottoms. It was about 8 o'clock in the evening and we'd been allowed to leave the hospital and were now back at the centre to pick Alec's stuff up. I'd wanted just to hold him the entire day. Carry him around in my arms, let him wrap his legs around my waist and bury his head in my neck like he had done when he was little. But he was closed-off and unapproachable and wretched, and when I held his hand, it was lifeless and unresponsive in mine.

Alec had been found about twelve miles from the centre by a man walking his dog. He'd run off at around 7.15 p.m. and eventually headed for what he thought was the main road, but having run all night he had finally collapsed with exhaustion. He had been deathly pale when I first saw him, but now that he had slept and eaten and eaten again, he was looking more like his old self, though still tearful and frightened by how out of control everything had become. He had spent the day hidden behind a wall of exhaustion and shame and at no point had it seemed appropriate to ask for an explanation. Until now.

'It was at tea,' he said, looking up at me and then quickly

away as he forced himself to remember. 'I wanted to take a picture of the dining room so you could see what it looked like and I went to get my camera. And Mum, it's pink. It's bright pink with Disney princesses on it. The others all started to tease me and call me gay and everything but it wasn't too bad. Then after tea we all went back to the dorm and while I was putting it in my bag, Will B snatched the camera from me and he started throwing it about to all the others: Thomas, Hassan – they all joined in and I tried to get it back but they just kept throwing it around to each other and saying, "Yuk! Don't touch Bidewell's gay camera." And I tried to get it back but then they all sat on me. They got me on the floor, Mum, and there wasn't anything I could do. They were sitting on my arms and my chest and I was on the floor and I was crying and I was saying, "Get off me! Get off me!" But they just laughed and then Ollie took the camera to the bathroom and I could see through the door they were trying to flush it down the toilet. And everyone thought it was so hysterical. Even Thomas and Will C, and I just went mad.'

He put his head in his hands at the memory.

'I went totally mad . . . and I was really, really crying. I tried to get up and I was hitting and kicking everybody and Ross was pulling on my trousers to stop me getting away and they were coming down! Everyone saw my bottom and my willy and Ross was pulling my pyjamas down even more and someone else held onto my arms so I couldn't pull them back up. And everyone thought that was even more hysterical and I was going, "Give me my camera! Give me my camera!" And then Will C just threw it at me. It had been in the toilet and it was all wet and disgusting and covered in germs. I pulled up my trousers and I just ran out. They thought I was going to get Mr Peters so they were all shouting, "Gay, gay. Get the teacher, gay boy." I thought I'd just go somewhere to get away from them so I ran to the beach and I just kept running and running and then I got lost and . . .'

He'd run out of steam.

I said gently, 'Why didn't you try to telephone anybody? Call 999 from a phone box?'

'I thought everyone was asleep. I didn't know they'd ring you and Dad and I didn't know what time it was till the man found me. I was going to find someone and ring you, Mum, when I thought you'd be back from dropping the others off at school. And anyway, I just couldn't. I couldn't go back with all them laughing at me. I knew they'd tell everyone about me crying and my pants coming down. I knew that the girls would know.'

'But you *must* have known everyone was worrying. You must have known that people would be looking for you.' Dom had got down onto his haunches and had put his hands on Alec's knees.

'I didn't think. I just thought everybody would just be asleep. Can we just go now? I don't want to stay here.'

'Of course. Of course,' I said and got down onto my

knees too and the three of us had a sort of group hug, with Dom and I crouching uncomfortably and Alec leaning unnaturally forward. But we all hung on for dear life.

Dom started to gather all our stuff together and then a little posse arrived: Thomas, Will B, Will C, Ross, Hassan. They shuffled and looked at their feet under the stern eye of Mr Peters. Some of them had been crying. They said they were really sorry and Thomas gave Alec his own disposable camera and Alec looked so grateful and forgiving that it nearly broke my heart.

We drove home along the motorway, with Alec sleeping in the back. Dom and I were so shocked by everything that had happened, it was all so huge and we were both so exhausted, that we opted to say nothing at all.

# Chapter Four

# Racing Piglets

Alec slept for twelve hours. When he woke he was still shaky and quiet. I didn't want to let him out of my sight. I had to plan for the weekend. The kids were due to spend it with Dom but it seemed impossible in the light of what had happened in Swanage. So I called work and spoke to Rob, who predictably tied himself in knots trying to rejig the rota. I was touched when he came up with a fabulous plan which involved him working forty-eight hours straight, but ultimately Denise vetoed it. Dom said I was mad because he was having the children anyway and now was the time to try and keep things as normal as possible. When I asked Alec he said he was 'cool' with going to his Dad's.

Dom had already been in touch with the school and arranged for us to meet Alec's head of year, Mr Withers. I arranged for Dom's mother, Mary, to sit with Alec. She was going to make him pancakes. I wouldn't have left him with Marlene even if she had offered – which she hadn't.

Dom and I sat outside Mr Withers' office, Dom telling me in a hushed whisper how he wanted us to handle the meeting. Handle it? Surely we were just there to try to get to the bottom of what had happened with Alec. Shouldn't we just engage in an open and frank discussion? Then a voice from within said, 'Come' and we shuffled in.

Mr Withers' office smelt unsurprisingly of polish and school dinners, but some kindly soul had thought to put in a movement-sensor air freshener so that when we entered, a great squirt of spray emitted from it with the aroma of sickly, synthetic roses and lavatory cleaner.

'Welcome, welcome, Mr and Mrs Bidewell.' Mr Withers greeted us with all the charisma of a stoat. He shook our hands awkwardly and we all took a seat.

I suppose nothing that was said was unexpected. Mr Withers felt that Alec's behaviour was a direct result of everything that had gone on with Dom and me. That he had been withdrawn for some time, was not the cheerful boy he had once been and did we think counselling would be a good idea. I clung onto the fact that his work remained consistently good and in some subjects had even improved. Mr Withers said that in many cases when children were 'experiencing turmoil at home' they would seek to control one thing in their otherwise chaotic world, and that this was often schoolwork, so it was not uncommon for the child's marks to get better.

Mr Withers was a nervous stringy man, who clicked his biro on and off throughout the interview. At one point he was clicking it so fast that I was conscious that I was gabbling to keep up with the rhythm. 'Alec's very aware that his well-being is vital to us and so I think he does have a tendency to try and protect us from what he's feeling,' I said.

Click-clack, click-clack, click-clack went Mr Withers' pen.

'In the past I think he was very open about his relationships at school – if things were going well, if there'd been a fall-out – and I just wonder whether he's been keeping things to himself and that it all got too much and exploded in Swanage.'

'Do you think, Mrs Bidewell . . .'

Click-clack, click-clack, click-clack. Stop.

'. . . that it was a cry . . . for help?' He didn't look like a man who had much of a rapport with eleven-year-olds or indeed one who could distinguish a cry for help from a whoop of mild concern. One could only assume that he had gone into teaching because he didn't have the imagination to think of anything else.

The three of us were forced to sit in such low, comfy, put-the-parents-at-their-ease chairs that our knees were up around our ears. As a result, the bottom of Mr Withers' suit trousers and the top of his brown work socks were some inches apart and the resulting expanse of spidery, fleshy leg was mesmerizing. Try as I might, I couldn't stop my eyes wandering to it and at one point, obviously feeling a little uncomfortable under my scrutiny, he made an effort to cross his long legs. But, as he was so low down, he was forced to throw a wild, balletic kick high into the air not far from Dom's nose and so halfway through he thought better of it.

Despite all my misgivings about him, I had no choice but to take all he had to say on board. Phrases such as 'the family home in crisis', 'the father no longer resident', 'the emotional needs of the child being over-looked' hit me like a baseball bat in the gut but I gritted my teeth and nodded my head. Of course he was right, what other explanation was there? We should look into the counselling option and we should get to the bottom of what had really made Alec bolt.

Dom on the other hand, merely said, 'Well if it was so obvious that my son was unhappy, why had nobody been in touch?' We'd both been in and spoken to Alec's form teacher when we split and she had vowed to keep a close eye on Alec and to let us know immediately if she was worried about anything. Dom then took Mr Withers to task about the school's bullying policy, about whether they were reviewing it when it came to school trips and staff-to-pupil ratios. He wanted to know what action was being taken with regard to the ringleaders of the trouble.

'I can assure you that all the necessary action will be taken, Mr Bidewell. But we do not want to get into a situation where things are made doubly hard for Alec when he returns to school.'

'Agreed, but that is no excuse for you to do nothing.'

Eventually, after forty minutes of polite recriminations

and Dom trying to make out it was *all* the school's fault and Mr Withers trying to make out that it was *all* ours, we left. I didn't feel positive. I didn't feel reassured. I wanted to know what it was that I could do to make things better for Alec and that was all that mattered.

As we walked away, Dom said that he bet the school was punching the air that we had separated because then they had something to blame it on. He said that if they couldn't blame it on Alec's home circumstances then presumably questions would have been asked about the nasty little shits who persecuted him and how Mr Peters had mislaid a pupil for seventeen hours.

I pointed out that if we had still been together we probably wouldn't have been there in the first place as Alec probably wouldn't have bolted. I wanted him to see that Mr Withers might have had a point but he rounded on me:

'Don't use this as just another opportunity to play the guilt card, Rachel, please! Do you honestly think I need you to point out that this might all be down to me?'

I was too tired and too sick to speak.

'I know that you're going to think that I have gone completely mad, but what about going to Bramley Farm?' I said to Alec about an hour later. There was no question of him going to school, I wasn't working and the day lay before us.

'Bramley Farm? Mum, I'm not six!'

'I know, but we could go and see Paddy and we could

have lunch and a walk. When are we ever going to get the chance to go again, just you and me? It'll be quiet as well because it's the week and if we leave now we could be there in half an hour.'

'Bramley Farm? Are you serious?'

'Why not? Come on. I even think the sun's trying to shine. Go on.'

'Alright, alright. This is so mad but if that's what you really want.'

Alec pretended to get his coat on in a state of world-weary resignation at the day ahead, but secretly I knew that this was exactly what he wanted to do.

In the pre-school years, Alec and I, and then Luke, Alec and I – Luke in the pushchair, Alec balancing on the buggy board – had spent hours at Bramley Farm, a great big sprawling place just off the A3 that had chickens and goats and guinea pigs and unfeasibly large rabbits and llamas and trampolines and rock-climbing walls and a rather camp Santa at Christmas. We had so many happy memories there and when he was about four, Alec had adopted a Shire-horse foal named Paddy as a birthday present from my mother. We'd been to Paddy's stable to inspect a little plaque where along with about 8,000 other children's names were the words: 'ALEC BIDEWELL has adopted PADDY. Happy Birthday, love from Grandma and Grandad, 12.05.2006', and he had nearly burst with pride. Elsewhere, plaques from my parents for Luke and a meerkat called Spike, and Jess and a guinea pig called Lucifer had gone up, but Paddy had been something a bit special.

As we sped along the A3 at eighty, the chance of sunshine seemed to have increased somewhat and for the first time in days I felt light-headed and easy. Alec had flicked over from *Woman's Hour* and Capital was blasting out something by the Black Eyed Peas. We'd had to stop to get petrol and I had been weak and emerged from the shop with Fanta and cheesy Wotsits. We sat swigging and munching, Alec in the front seat next to me, both of us singing and getting our hands and clothes covered in bright orange, lumpy, Wotsit dust.

I had been right in thinking that Bramley Farm would be quiet and we parked right next to the entrance.

'What first?' I said.

'Farmyard Corner.'

We bought a white paper bag full of strange, mustard-coloured pellets and we took them round to Farmyard Corner. Here, we fed the pellets to small sheep with shaggy coats and an incredibly persistent goat that, if you took your eyes off him for a second, tried to eat your handbag. YOU MUST NOW WASH YOUR HANDS said a notice on the exit and so we obediently did this only to find that the paper towels had run out and the hand dryer wasn't working. So we jumped about flicking our fingers in each other's faces until they were dry.

Then Alec wanted to go for a bounce on the trampolines. I was feeling all girlish and brave and was yanking my shoes and socks off in preparation to join in, until thoughts of three children and a dodgy pelvic floor made me beat a hasty retreat. Then lunch. To my surprise, Alec spurned the little cardboard picnic boxes that he had always loved, with a free toy and a choice of sandwich, crisps, fruit, flapjack and drink. Instead, he went for a huge plate of spaghetti bolognese that he ate with such relish that it was a pleasure to watch.

We talked about the Porsche Boxster versus the Carrera, Chelsea versus Man U and everything and anything that I never talked to him about normally because I was too irritable and didn't have the time to listen. We ignored the existence of school or Dom or Deborah or even Luke and Jess. Part of me felt that I should be steering the conversation towards more important stuff, but he was so happy and relaxed, it just seemed criminal to do so.

Luke and Jess were being picked up by Dom and we had until 4 o'clock. A plan was formulated: we had completely forgotten the tradition of the Bramley Farm Piglet Races and were determined to catch one. Then we would go on the Woodland Trail and finally to the shire horses to look for Paddy. Alec wanted to save the best till last.

The piglet race was at 2.15. You placed a bet on one of seven or so piglets and then if you won you got a packet of sweets – all for 50p. We took our position at a wooden fence at the bottom of the hill. Inside the large enclosure was a course that the piglets would race around with the spectators cheering them on. All the school children on day trips and toddlers with their mothers started to come to the fence as well until there was quite a crowd.

A large blackboard informed us of the names of the competitors:

1. RED – JAMES RUNT
2. BLUE – MICHAEL SCHURASHER
3. GREEN – DAMON SWILL
4. PINK – NELSON PORKAY
5. BLACK – LEWIS HAMILTON
6. ORANGE – BACON BUTTON
7. YELLOW – LESTER PIGGIT

We ignored the fact that some of the names of the piglets hadn't changed in ten years but the piglets obviously had, and went to place our bets. Alec went for Lewis Hamilton and I went for Lester Piggit. The course was a big one. The piglets had to race down the hill towards us for about 100 metres and then belt back up the hill and down again to the finish.

The PA fizzled into life and a pale young man of about eighteen tried to inject a bit of tension and excitement into the proceedings, but he was no Bruce Forsyth.

'My name is Martin, I'm one of the Animal Maintenance Assistants here at Bramley Farm, and I would like to welcome you all, ladies and gentlemen, boys and girls, to the Bramley Farm Grand Prix. Now please be ready to cheer your piglet on and make as much noise as you can. I shall fire the starting pistol and Ian –' a hairy youth in the far corner of the field gave a wave and a weak smile – 'will begin the race by opening the gate and letting the piglets fly. Are you ready, everyone?'

Small, self-conscious 'Yes!'

'I said, ARE YOU READY, EVERYONE?'

Slightly larger but just as self-conscious 'Yesss!' Alec and I seemed to be the only ones getting into the spirit of things and cheered '*Yeeesss*! Bring it on!'

'I feel the need, the need for speeed!' yelled Alec.

'Five, four, three, two, one . . .' Bang! The gun went off and the piglets came belting down the hill as if the big bad wolf was on their curly tails. Pigs aren't built for speed but they shot past us like pink bullets, their miniscule trotters pounding the earth, their heads bobbing up and down with all the concentration and heroic effort of Shergar. Where were they going? They had no idea. Why were they going there? They hadn't a clue. They just kept on thundering down the course towards us, bemused but determined. As they neared us they went into the turn, some of them skidding and losing their footing and some of them going so fast it actually looked as if they might leave the ground and fly to the finish line.

Now it was time to watch their little bottoms disappearing up the hill.

'Come on, Mum!' Alec grabbed my hand and dragged me towards the finishing line. The leaders were once again charging towards us and for one second I felt an affinity with them. That was me! I was a racing piglet! Where was I going? No idea. Why was I going there? Hadn't a clue. I just kept charging along feeling as if a butcher with a massive cleaver was bearing down on me. Get up, feed the kids, go to work, get the shopping, pick the kids up, make tea, put the bath on, don't think about the past, keep up with the mums from school, keep the plates spinning. Why? I don't know. What for? I've no idea. The sight of those plucky little pigs, racing for all they were worth, when the chances were their days were numbered and all their efforts hopeless, struck me as terribly moving but also hysterical and I started to laugh. The sort of laughter that's not altogether in your control and goes on and on until it starts to unnerve you a little. That was me – Rachel the racing piglet!

I don't know if Alec knew why I was laughing or whether it was just a welcome release, but he started laughing as well and when Lester Piggit came in last we laughed and cheered all the more.

Feeling a bit weak but happy, we made our way to Paddy's stable. To be completely honest we didn't know which one he was but when we asked a man with a broom he pointed to such a magnificent, enormous beast that Alec and I just gasped. When he was little Alec used to feed him Polo mints and I'd bought some in the garage earlier. He fed a couple to Paddy, who nuzzled Alec as if he recognized an old friend. Alec looked completely delighted and his eyes sparkled and a grin so wide and beautiful spread across his face that it threatened to reach his ears.

'He knows me, Mum. I really think he remembers me. Hello, old buddy. Hello, you beauty.'

It was getting dark now, the temperature had dropped and Alec and Paddy's frozen breath mingled in the bright, electric light. Eventually, Alec tore himself away and we went to look for his name plaque but it had gone. 'Gutted!' he said, but nevertheless had to accept that as the whole adoption kit had cost my mother a tenner – certificate, free visit to Bramley Farm, animal-shaped sweets and a T-shirt – it would have been a miracle if his name could have hung there for all time.

As we drove back, Alec dropped off and I kept glancing at his lovely face. Did Dom wish he'd never married me like he claimed? Did he really think it was all a huge mistake? I couldn't believe he thought that. We had made three miraculous children and whatever had happened or was going to happen in the future, I knew he could never regret that.

# Chapter Five

# Don't Happy, Be Worry

When Dom had the children, the worst moment of the weekend was waking up in a quiet house. I used to be desperate for just five minutes more sleep when Dom had been there and the house had been noisy and the children would squirm into bed with us and pester us and cuddle us and sing tunelessly along to the radio, which they had slapped on at full volume.

The irony was that now I always seemed to wake up at 5.30 in the morning with such a bolt of adrenalin that I couldn't get back to sleep. I would imagine what they were doing. Would the children get into bed with Dom and Deborah? Were they all in a sleepy, warm heap, chatting and laughing? Or was Jess already in their bed, having crept down in the night in need of some comfort? It was unbearable to imagine her hot, smooth little body snuggled up to Deborah. Or her sitting on the end of the bed going through Deborah's make-up asking what everything was and whether she could just try on a little. Deborah probably said 'Yes! Go ahead, angel!' and Jess would be allowed a smear of pink lipstick and a dab of blue sparkly eyeshadow and be thinking, This is brilliant! Mum never lets me do this. And when she asked Deborah if she could help her get dressed and choose her clothes for the day, did Deborah say 'Of course, my love'? Did she go out to Waitrose in a floral, summer dress in January with purple kitten heels and a pink frilly bra underneath because it made Jess so happy and proud? Especially as she was used to me ignoring her pleas and throwing on jeans and a black polo-neck.

I got out of bed at about seven and wandered down to the kitchen feeling sluggish and miserable. I had so much to do, so I should just get on with it. I had anticipated this Saturday morning to be a cleaning frenzy – bathroom, kitchen, the lot – but now that it was here I felt tired. Everything that had happened in Swanage had played over and over on a loop in my head in the middle of the night.

It was part of the weekend ritual for the absent parent to ring the children on Saturday morning – usually at about 10 o'clock. It seemed like such a long time to wait so I made some breakfast and a pot of real coffee and read last Sunday's paper. Every time I looked at the clock it seemed to have stopped. Finally, at around 9.15 I rang. Alec picked the phone up and I spoke to him and Luke. Jess was nowhere to be found as she off with Deborah, so Alec promised he would get her to ring me later. I tried not to think where they were but the familiar tussle in my head started again; of course it was best for everyone if the kids had a good relationship with Deborah, but whenever I was confronted with evidence of this it made my insides squirm.

The thought of going into Clifton Avenue didn't help. I was working with Scott, an agency worker who was happy to do the bare minimum and it was to be my first sleepover duty. I was due to start at 2 p.m. and to finish the following day at 10 a.m. I would take some residents for a walk, I thought. But then was it too cold? Would I be deemed irresponsible and reckless? Perhaps I would help Nettie give her bedroom a long-overdue clear-out. It was dusty and neglected and needed a bit of sprucing up. But was that allowed? Would I be stepping on someone's toes and would it be mentioned at the next staff meeting? I found myself again wishing that Rob was going to be on duty, as he was the only one that seemed actually to like the residents and care whether I was OK. The shifts passed more easily when he was around, because we could have a laugh and he was happy to let me get on with things.

Later, I got off the bus and walked up the road. It was November and it was bloody freezing; there was no way I would get any of the residents out for some fresh air today.

I let myself in and slipped past Yellow Kitchen. The hostel was split up into three sections – Red, Blue and

Yellow – and each had its own little kitchen, sitting room, bathroom and bedrooms. There was a communal sitting room and central area for eating, but during the day most residents stayed in their own section. Red was for the residents who coped fairly well on their own, Blue for those who needed a bit more support, and Yellow for those that needed full-on supervision.

In Blue Kitchen, Margaret was pacing up and down with a cold cup of coffee on the table and shouting, involved in an endless, tragic conversation with people who had long-since died or abandoned her. She was about fifty or so and always wore the same outfit of brown polyester trousers, cream shirt and beige V-neck sweater. She had about four of each item and just rotated them day-in, day-out. When she was in her teens she'd had a child that had been given up for adoption and all these years on, she still carried around all the hurt and the anger from that time and would shout and rail at her parents and the authorities that had made her give up the child. She smoked incessantly and so spent a lot of time in the garden, pacing and smoking and shouting, whatever the weather. When in the sitting room or at tea, she always sat in stony, tense silence, but whenever she was on her own she would begin her bitter monologue.

I could hear her as I entered the building. 'Yeah! You do that! You useless pile of shit. See if I care. It's got nothing to do with you. Nothing at all. Yeah? Mind your own bloody business and fuck off!'

I put my head round the door. 'Hi, Margaret.'

She went quiet and just nodded curtly at me. As I went back into the corridor I heard her grumbling to herself. 'New bloody staff. Mind her own bloody business.' So that buoyed me up no end for the shift ahead.

Once in the office, I said hello to Scott: six foot, skinny, ineffectual. I'd only worked with him on one occasion but it was enough to know that the reason he worked for a supply agency and had never been offered a full-time job was because of his skinny ineffectualness. Nevertheless he seemed to work at Clifton Avenue a great deal and indeed had done so on and off for about three years. Saturday was laundry day, so I said that I would get on and check up on how Yellow were getting along.

Denise was sitting at the computer and she turned and smiled. 'Hello, my darling,' she said. 'Put the kettle on.'

'Sure. I thought I might make this evening a bingo night. There's a whole set in the cupboard,' I said tentatively. 'I've bought some chocolate as prizes, just a couple of Kit Kats, and I thought we could have it in the dining room, before *The X Factor*.'

'Sounds lovely,' said Denise, looking back at the computer.

'Well, you'll need to have something other than chocolate for the diabetics,' said Scott dryly, 'and make sure you've got receipts for the Kit Kats otherwise you'll never see the money.'

So, not a whole-hearted roar of approval, but then he hadn't refused point-blank to join in.

It was beginning to get me down that, for most of the staff a culture of cynicism seemed to have taken hold at Clifton Avenue, which meant that you stayed in the office and if you did anything more than the absolute minimum, you were somehow a fool. If Rob was on duty they might be shamed into doing something but otherwise they just stayed put.

On the other hand there was Lucy, who worked incredibly hard but was completely joyless. She entered the room to do the hand-over. She had been on duty over night and all morning. She sat on the desk and swung her DMs.

'Carlos, George, Martin and Sophie are all out for the weekend. Although Sophie's due back tonight because her mum's got something on tomorrow.'

Without looking up, Denise made a sniffy sound from her computer that told us what she thought of Sophie's mother.

Lucy continued: 'We've got Malcolm this weekend in Blue 4 and his brother's going to come and take him out for lunch tomorrow. Nettie's chest infection is on the mend but she's had to go on antibiotics. They're in the drugs cupboard and they are in a syrup form because you know what happened the last time she was given tablets.'

I didn't, but guessed they'd been found down the back of the sofa or fed to the goldfish.

'Margaret's about to run out of cigarettes so I've said that one of us will take her to the garage this afternoon to get some more.'

I was standing closest to the door, so when Malcolm came careering down the corridor, I was the first to see him.

'Rachel! Come quick! Blue Kitchen. We need you.'

Denise's head sprung round, her lips pursed and she glared at me. Mindful of our exchange about getting me out of mummy-mode, I said: 'Excuse me, Malcolm, but we are in the middle of hand-over with Lucy. You can see we're busy, so please can you give us five minutes and then I can talk to you properly and see what it is that you need.'

He nodded apologetically and stood against the wall outside the office with his head bowed obediently. Denise smiled encouragingly and gave me a 'You see it isn't so hard now is it?' look and went back to the computer. Lucy resumed her hand-over.

'The radiator in Derek's room still isn't working – his sister's on the warpath about it –' Another sniff from Denise in the corner – 'so I've put him in Red 2. Pete's left sandwiches for tonight – they've all had a good lunch – and Angela from the agency is cooking tomorrow. She normally comes in about ten. I think that's it. Oh and Scott, can you just run Rachel through the procedure for a sleep-in duty because you've not done it before have you?'

'No. Thanks, Lucy, that would be a big help.' I was touched by her thoughtfulness.

'It's not rocket science, just common sense,' she said in such a way as to ensure that I didn't mistake her doing her job for her being kind. She jumped off the desk and reached behind the door for her coat.

'Right Malcolm, you can come in now,' I said as Malcolm shuffled in and took centre-stage, 'but please in future remember not to interrupt us during hand-over.' I knew Denise was listening and that she approved. 'Now, what was it that you wanted to talk to me about?'

'Margaret's dropped the kettle and her hand's all burnt.'

'Oh my God!' shrieked Denise and all five of us ran to Blue Kitchen. Margaret looked ashen and very frightened but she said nothing. Thankfully, she was standing running her hand under the cold tap under Stewart's instruction, but it was a bad burn and she would have to go to hospital.

I felt horribly responsible and at one point I saw Denise catch Lucy's eye and do a little shake of her head as if it was all my fault, but if Denise hadn't been there I would have run round to Blue Kitchen like a shot.

A debate followed about who would take Margaret to A&E, and Denise said that she would do it. I was surprised, but thought, Good on you. She sat Margaret down in the office and got an icepack for the burn, all the time reassuring her that everything was going to be OK. She called for a taxi and gently put Margaret's coat around her shoulders, but just as she was leaving, I saw her go over to the filing cabinet and take out an overtime form.

'All the nines, ninety-nine!'

'Oh you beauty!' yelped Malcolm. 'Only two more to go!'

'Six and two, sixty-two. At the gate, forty-eight.' Bingo-calling had never really been my thing. 'On the line, twenty-nine.'

'Thank you, God!' thundered Theresa and crossed her fingers and looked to the heavens theatrically.

The bingo set that I had such high hopes for had seen better days. Half the numbers were missing and so many of the players were doggedly playing on unaware that there was no chance of them winning. I have to confess that I had given the doomed cards to residents from Yellow who couldn't identify the numbers in the first place. Scott was sitting with them and trying to help but I could tell that he was bored and slightly embarrassed by the whole thing. Philip was sitting next to me, but preferred just to watch rather than join in. His card sat in front of him untouched.

'Big fat knee, twenty-three!'

Scott gave me a sideways glance, aware that my style was becoming more and more unorthodox.

'Hope I get to heaven, forty-seven . . . I like wine, fifty-nine . . . Rachel is great, seventy-eight.'

'Biiiiii-ngo!' Theresa leapt to her feet and punched the

air. 'Yes!' She shimmied into the centre of the room and did a little victory dance. 'Oh yeah! Oh yeah! Oh yeah! I'm Queen of the Bingo!'

'You don't say "Bingo", you say "Full House", don't you Rachel?' said a very disgruntled Stewart.

'Oh, I don't know, but I think Theresa has won fair and square. Well done, Theresa!' Everyone – except Stewart – gave her a clap and I went to present the Kit Kat.

'You have to check her card. It's not official until you've checked her card.'

'Quite right, Stewart, thank goodness you're here to help me. What would I do without you? Theresa, your card please.' I put out my hand soberly and Theresa presented me with her winning card.

On not terribly close inspection, it became apparent that Theresa had just been slamming the numbered discs on to non-corresponding numbers, willy-nilly. She was either totally innumerate or a big fat cheat. I didn't know her well enough to be sure and decided to give her the benefit of the doubt. Besides, bingo had not been a rip-roaring success and the thought of starting another round made me feel suicidal.

'All seems in order here,' I said. 'Congratulations, Miss Theresa Fisher.'

Just as I was about to hand her the Kit Kat, Stewart yelled: 'Stop!' He had come up behind me and was looking at the card over my shoulder. He was furious. 'Stop! Stop! This is a bad business. The numbers are all wrong.'

'Get stuffed, Stewart. Mind your own beeswax,' said Theresa, grabbing the Kit Kat out of my hand and making off with it. Stewart was in hot pursuit. He rugby-tackled her to the ground and tried to prize the Kit Kat out of her hands. Before I could stop them, they were wrestling on the ground.

'Stop them! Stewart, *nooo*!' Sophie was wailing like Scarlett O'Hara and I waded in.

'That's enough! That's enough!' I said and grabbed the Kit Kat. Scott looked on like a great useless pudding and I suddenly felt a bit out of my depth. Philip was shaking his head in a panicky way and rocking forwards and backwards. Theresa now had her hands around Stewart's neck and was squeezing very hard. 'I'll kill 'im. I swear I'll bloody kill 'im,' she was saying in a murderous whisper with her jaws clenched.

What was the procedure? Should I throw a bucket of water over them?

Eventually, I managed to pull them apart, having been whacked on the chin by Stewart's elbow, and the three of us sat on the floor panting. What now? Should I send them both to bed or alert the authorities? It was already dawning on me that I would have to admit in the duty log that my bingo session had deteriorated into a brawl and risk Denise's disapproval again.

'You should be ashamed of yourselves,' I said when I got my breath back. 'Fighting? *Fighting*?!'

'Sounds like my kind of party.' Everyone looked around

and, to my eternal gratitude and joy, Rob was standing in the doorway. The tension immediately dissipated and the residents ran to welcome him. He looked at me with an amused, quizzical expression, and began to distribute cans of beer to those that wanted it from a huge bag.

'What are you doing here?' I said.

'It's the birthday boy!' chirruped Sophie, hanging her arms around his neck and giving him a big kiss.

'Did nobody mention it? Well that's nice. It is indeed my birthday and I promised some of the gang that I'd pop in. This is my wee warm-up before the festivities really take off.' He waggled his eyebrows to suggest that his plans for later that night were ambitious. 'I've even brought a cake.' From out of the bag he produced a Tesco's cake in the shape of the Tardis. 'It's a sad day when a man has to buy his own birthday cake, but what a cake!' He pushed a button on a plastic thing imbedded in the icing and the whole cake started to make the shuddering, rasping noise of the Tardis materializing. Everyone cheered.

'Fantastic!' I said laughing, 'but for God's sake, take that bit off before someone swallows it.'

Stewart poked me in the shoulder and in his slow, monotone said, 'Denise will not be happy if she hears you've been giving cake to the diabetics.'

'Stewart,' I said, 'I'm not about to start handing out –'

'Bugger Denise!' shouted Theresa and Rob caught my eye and laughed.

I took the cake into the kitchen and stuck on three very

old, very pink candles. I was thinking that when I'd rung after Swanage and asked for this weekend off, Rob had volunteered to cover for me and so must have been prepared to work on his birthday to help me out. I already knew that he was someone who'd put himself out for you, for anyone, but this was a revelation.

I lit the candles from the huge industrial gas ring, which nearly took my eyebrows off as it whooshed into flame, then making sure that someone had switched the lights out, returned ceremoniously and we all sang 'Happy Birthday'. It's fair to say that Clifton Avenue singing en masse sounded like a group of donkeys being stoned but we got through it. Even Philip was smiling broadly. Rob blew the candles out and everyone clapped and whooped.

'Make a wish, make a wish!' implored Theresa, now standing with her arm draped around Stewart's shoulder, all hostilities forgotten. Rob screwed his eyes tight shut.

'What did you wish for?' asked Sophie.

'Ah, now that'd be telling,' was all Rob would answer, but then he leant over to me and whispered in my ear, 'I wished for Denise to die a slow and horrible death.'

I was shocked. I looked at him for some kind of explanation but he had already moved away and was swinging his arm around Sophie as if he'd never said a word.

'Presents, your majesty,' said Malcolm, going into a low bow and presenting Rob with a gift. It was socks; grey, acrylic and uninspiring, bought and wrapped by Malcolm's mum. But Rob opened them slowly and carefully and then held them aloft, showing them to the crowd, like Charlie Bucket with the golden ticket.

'Thank you, mate. Thank you so much.' He gave Malcolm a big smacker on his forehead and Malcolm looked like the man who had just got to hand over the World Cup.

One of the residents had bought Rob a can of beer of the same variety that he had been handing out so liberally just minutes earlier, but he didn't seem to notice and looked thrilled. Theresa had wrapped up a bar of Galaxy for him and someone else a massive bar of Dairy Milk.

'You'd better watch yourself, Rob,' said Malcolm, stroking his ample tummy, 'you're going to get one of these.'

Rob stuck his own tummy out until he looked pregnant and stroked it too. 'I'm working on it, mate. I'm working on it.'

Finally, Sophie galloped into the room with her large present. She gave it to Rob coquettishly, grinning and laughing. She just could not wait for him to open it up.

Rob slid the paper off and revealed something grey wrapped in cellophane. 'Well, I hope this is what I think it is,' he said, looking at Sophie. 'Don't tell me I've lucked out again!'

Sophie nodded an excited, nervous little nod, and Rob opened the package and slowly drew out a pair of nylon trousers from British Home Stores, quite possibly even shorter than the pair he already owned.

'I am going to have a word with your mother, Sophie

Manning. You spoil me, you really do.' He held the new pair up to his hips and did a little wiggle. 'Oh my God! They are amazing. Even better than last year's. What do you think?'

Sophie stood back and looked at the overall effect. 'I like them,' she said. 'I like them a lot . . . You're as handsome as a hedgehog.'

Rob left, and as everyone was winding down, I turned off all the lights downstairs, locked up and finally went to find Philip to get him ready for bed.

During his ablutions it was customary for me to chatter inanely about the kids, the television programme I'd watched the night before, what I was having for tea, anything and everything, in the hope of getting a response. I had no idea if he was interested or whether one day, as I was telling him the tale of, say, the Boots ham sandwich and its lack of ham compared to the one I got from a petrol station he would suddenly scream at the top of his voice, 'Enough woman! Enough of your incessant dirge! I will not tolerate it for another single second!' In a way, I wished he would, at least it would mean he had developed the confidence to stand up for himself. And it would be less hurtful than Dom saying it, which in effect he had.

Philip seemed relaxed and as if he'd enjoyed the evening, so I decided that it was a good time to introduce him to one of Jess's treasures that I had stolen from home. It was a pink and sparkly toothbrush with little silver stars along its side, a stocking filler from last year that was deemed so precious it had never been used. It was designed for a five-year-old girl so looked preposterous as I put it into Philip's great hand and spread toothpaste onto its small head.

'Now,' I said, 'if you brush your teeth by yourself, this toothbrush has a surprise for you. Try it.'

I helped him to put the toothbrush under the running tap and then brought his hand up to his mouth.

'Go on,' I urged and began to make an up-and-down motion with the brush. As I did so I pushed a small button on its base and it began to sing its little tune: '*Daisy, Daisy, give me your answer, do . . .*' The notes started to dance out and into the room. '*I'm half crazy . . .*' Philip grinned. '*Da da da dee da dooo. . . .*' went the tinny little melody. It was a song Philip seemed to recognize and he began to nod his head just a little and sing the odd random note. He looked at me and made another delighted face and scrunched up his nose.

I switched the tune off. Philip looked shocked.

'It only plays when you brush,' I said. 'You have to be brushing to hear the tune.' I held his hand, pressed the button and started brushing again. The song began. This time I let it play for longer.

'It plays for one whole minute so you know when you've had a really thorough go at getting your teeth clean,' I said and switched it off again. I let go of his hand. 'Now you try.'

'Pearly whites,' he said cheerfully. 'Pearly whites.' But

he made no motion to bring the brush up to his mouth.

'You have to do it, Philip,' I said firmly. 'You have to brush your teeth yourself for it to work, for the toothbrush to play its tune.'

He jerked his head back three or four times and then was still again. He looked at the floor and said to himself distractedly, 'Pearly whites ... Handsome.' Then he looked up and slowly, his eyes on mine, brought the toothbrush up to his mouth. I made the tune start to play and very weakly and ineffectively, he started to brush at the space in front of his teeth. I turned the tune off.

'Come on,' I said. 'You can do this! It will stop playing if you don't brush properly.' And he made his lips into a shape as if he was about to say 'ch' and put the toothbrush into the little space he'd made and onto his teeth. Then he began to make the brushing motion again, his face grave with concentration. I switched the toothbrush back on. As the tune started up, so he began to brush more vigorously.

'That's it!' I laughed. 'That's it!' And as Philip warmed to the task he started laughing and brushing his back teeth and his front teeth and the cheery little tune urged him on. White foam was building up around his mouth. I started clapping. 'Perfect!' I said. 'That's the way. Keep going!' My face was looking up at him and as he laughed delightedly so great gobs of toothpaste hit me between the eyes.

I sang along, "*It won't be a stylish marriage, I can't afford a carriage . . .*'" I grabbed Philip's free hand and we did a little turn around the bedroom. "'*But you'll look sweet, upon the seat, of a –*'" And the tune stopped abruptly.

'That's it!' I said. 'You've done your minute. All by yourself! You genius, Philip. You bloody genius!' I couldn't have been more proud of him. 'Shall we go again?' I asked. He nodded and started brushing for the second of the eight times he would complete the process that evening.

I got home the following day after popping in to see my mother-in-law, Mary, for a catch-up. I had a quick tidy round before Dom was due to drop the kids off at 6 p.m. I put *Pick of the Week* on the radio and made some sand-wiches and chopped up some raw carrot so that they would have something to eat before bed, knowing full well that I would be eating left-over raw carrot all evening. Humming 'Daisy, Daisy', I started to sort out the uni-forms and gym kits for the week ahead. I was putting Jess's library book into her school bag – *Rabbits and How to Care for Them* – when I heard Luke crash onto the door mat and start to shout through the letterbox.

'It's us! We're back! Open up in there!'

I opened the door and he flung himself at me, wrap-ping his arms around me and squeezing very hard. Dom came up the path carrying a very weary-looking Jess and handed her to me like a little chimpanzee. He knew he wasn't going to be invited in and put their bags on the doorstep. I looked behind him and then towards the car for Alec, but he wasn't there.

I looked at Dom and said 'Where's Alec?'

'He's not here, Rachel. We've talked about it and decided that it's best for everyone if he stays with me.'

# PART TWO

# Chapter Six

# Screaming with the Volume Down

'You cannot let this situation continue, Rachel. It's not right!' It was a month later and Dom's mother, Mary, had asked me to go round. She had held her tongue for long enough and felt the time had come to speak out. She'd prepared a speech but things weren't going to plan.

'I can't stop him,' I said, shaking my head with frustration.

'Of course you can! You can drag him through the courts if need be. He can't just take Alec away because the fancy takes him. There are laws to protect the child in this sort of situation but you just seem happy to lie down and let Dom walk all over you.'

'Listen, Mary, if I went to court, the judge would ask what it was that Alec wanted and he would say that he wants to live with his dad. Dom isn't a child molester, he has a perfectly nice home and a respectable girlfriend and Alec loves him.'

'What? You're saying that a judge would take the word of an adulterer over that of the boy's mother?'

'Yes! That's exactly what they'd do because Alec is a big boy now. If it was Jess or Luke it might be different, but it's Alec and he's eleven years old. And what's more *I* have to respect what Alec wants. He doesn't want to upset me, he's sorry to have done what he's done but all the same, he is absolutely sure that he wants to be with his dad.'

'And you think that poor child knows his own mind?'

'Yes!'

In all the time I had known Mary, we had never rowed; a few huffy silences over Sunday-roast preparation maybe, but we had always agreed on the big things. She had even stood by me when Dom had left and they hadn't spoken a word since.

She went on: 'You keep saying "he's eleven years old, eleven years old", as if he's thirty-five. He's *only* eleven. He's still a little boy and he doesn't know what he wants and it's up to you to do what's right for him and that is to keep him living at home with you.'

'I'm not sure that's how the court would see it! The one thing I am determined not to do is to get Alec mixed up in some terrible, bitter, drawn-out custody battle.'

'But you could go to that lawyer for advice, just to see what your options are.'

'It doesn't work like that, Mary. For a start I couldn't afford it. Do you fancy coughing up?' Mary seemed convinced that a judge would take one look at the situation and insist Alec be returned home.

'So you're just going to roll over yet again and let Dom and Deborah do as they please.'

'I haven't any choice. Please, Mary! Please understand that I just have to accept that this is what Alec wants. What happened in Dorset was a huge wake-up call – it was not the behaviour of a happy, secure child. I have to accept that –'

'Nonsense.' Mary threw her hands up in the air with furious exasperation.

'How can it be nonsense? Listen! The school have suggested counselling but Dom won't hear of it. Alec has started wetting the bed. Whatever it is he wants or he needs to make him happy, I'm not giving it to him.'

'The only thing that child wants is for his parents to get back together and you can't give him that – and neither can Dom. Not now.'

'Brilliant!' I slapped the kitchen table with my hand. 'Thank you. That's the one thing we're all agreed on. Dom's not coming back.'

'So in a couple of years' time you'll let Luke go to Dom and Deborah's and then Jess and be left with nothing?'

'No! Of course not. That isn't going to happen.' I took a deep breath and tried to explain it all over again. 'I've thought it through, I really have. It's not as if he isn't going to come home every other weekend. I'll see him at school. Alec has always been the most organized and sensible of the lot of us.' I tried to keep my voice steady. 'He wants the stillness of life with Dom without the little ones. He wants routine. He wants a bit of peace and quiet, civilized meals, his own computer and a room of his own to do his homework in, and you know what? I don't blame him. He's had enough of us all – of me.'

Mary was too angry to be moved by my hopelessness. 'Rubbish, I've never seen a boy more bonded with his mother. He adores you, he always has. To think that Dom has persuaded him that . . .' She was getting weepy now.

I went over and put my arm around her; in an instant the fight had gone out of both of us. She was big and soft and easy to squeeze, the sort of middle-aged lady who keeps a tissue permanently up her sleeve in case of emergencies and as she tried to access it now with shaky fingers it fell onto the floor. I went down onto my knees to retrieve it and for some reason stayed down there. I suddenly felt too drained to stand. I sat on my bottom with my knees drawn up and my head back against a kitchen cupboard.

I'd had the same conversation with my dad, Mel and Grace, but with Mary it was so much worse. All I had wanted from her – the only other woman as shattered by Alec deciding to live with Dom as I was – was for her to listen and understand.

'Look,' I said, staring at the lino, 'I probably haven't been the best of mothers since Dom left. I shout, I'm permanently tired and generally a bloody misery. I'm not there half the time now because of work and Marlene is no fun to be around. When I am home I sit down to help Alec with his homework or just hear about his day and then Jess needs me to do something or Luke decides to bump his head. I try to make him his favourite meal but then the other two decide they won't touch it so it's pizza again. We lurch from one crisis to the next and now with this job . . . I can't blame him. I really can't blame him.' Then I stretched back up on weary legs and gave her the tissue. 'Perhaps he just needs a break.'

'That is such nonsense,' she said, blowing her nose. 'And as for that girl, thinking that she can do a better job with an eleven-year-old boy than his own mother. Who does she think she is?'

There was nothing that Mary could say about Deborah that wasn't already festering in my chest so I just nodded and went to the loo.

Mary lived in a small flat five minutes from us and it was as neat as a pin. It was everything my house wasn't and I loved it. Sitting on the side of the bath now, steeling myself to go back into the kitchen, I remembered the hours Dom and I had spent helping do it up. The bathroom tiles had little white flowers on a soft, lavender-blue background. The matching curtains were as clean and perfect as if they'd been hung that morning. The bath was lavender-blue and the loo paper was lavender-blue. On the sink was some lovely lavender hand cream and I helped myself to a squirt. When my children visited, as at home, they would always forget to flush the loo and I would rush round as we left to check they had not left a stagnating yellow wee or worse in the bowl. In my house this was always annoying, but in this little bathroom it felt like an abomination. I walked back to the kitchen.

When I'd had the children, Mary had been fantastic. Particularly so with Jess because my mum was already ill and hadn't been able to come and stay. Mary must have made herself ill wanting to wash the muslin squares before they went stiff with sicked-up milk, or to empty the dirty nappy-bin before it got up and made its way to the dust-bins of its own accord. But she kept her own counsel and was nothing but supportive and loving and there.

She worked as a receptionist at our local GP surgery and – a traitor to her race – was helpful, accommodating and sympathetic when people rang up needing last-minute appointments or repeat prescriptions or test results. The practice was her domain and her social life revolved around the district nurses who worked out of it, other administrative staff and some colleagues who had retired. They cooked suppers for each other, went to the theatre and to the cinema; a gaggle of middle-aged ladies she referred to as 'the girls', although not one of them was a day under fifty – Phyllis, Carol, Jean, Barbara, Maureen, Joyce, Natalie and Sue – and they made each other laugh and laugh. She'd been widowed in her early forties but now with her job, the church, her social life and her grandchildren, she led a very full and contented existence and I couldn't bear for it all to be undone by my family misery and me.

'I need to buck up,' I said, coming back into the kitchen, 'and then maybe Alec will come home. It's like a boyfriend; if you wail and scream and slash his tyres he'll keep running. But if you carry on and look strong and confident and as if you're coping, then he's much more likely to have a change of heart.'

'Has that been your strategy with Dom?' Mary asked innocently.

'God no! I wish.' I looked down at my terrible trainers and ill-fitting jeans and stretching my arms out to the side I said, 'It's a bit late for that.'

Mary allowed herself to laugh. Maybe I hadn't done enough to fight for Dom. Maybe I had let him drift away. Was I doing the same with Alec?

That evening Alec rang as usual before he went to bed.

'Hello, Mum?'

'Hello, darling. How was your day?'

'Good. Didn't do much school-wise. How was Grandma?'

'Lovely. She sends her love and says she'll pop over when you're home.'

'Are you OK? You sound a bit sad. Are you?'

'No! I'm fine.'

'Sure?'

'Yes, honestly. I was sad. You know I was. But I'm fine now, honestly.'

'Do you want me to come home?'

'Yes, of course I do . . . But Alec, I do understand why you need to get away. You want to be at Dad's now and that's OK.'

'I'm sorry, Mum.'

'I know. But don't worry about me, just worry about yourself for once. The most important thing for me is that you are happy and if being at Dad's makes you happy then that is where you should be.'

'That's what Deborah said you'd say.'

'Right . . . well, she was right. It's just really, really important that you know that you can come home whenever you want to. Whenever. You do know that, don't you?'

'Yes. Do you want me to ring you tomorrow?'

'Only if you want to, sweetheart.'

'Well, I think I will. Night, night.'

'Night, night. I'll see you at the weekend anyway. I miss you.'

'I miss you.'

I wanted to put work on hold for a while and to crawl into a hole. With Alec gone I felt the same way I had after my mother died; I just didn't know what to do with myself. On the one hand I thought I should stay upbeat and jolly for Jess and Luke but on the other, I would worry that they didn't think I was missing Alec and that I didn't care. Trying to find the right balance was hard. The incident at Clifton Avenue with Margaret burning herself had made me feel more than ever that I was on probation and not in control. My one triumph was Philip, whose ability to brush his own teeth – ineptly – had made life worth living. With daily little nudges and shoves, I hoped he was beginning to find a bit of peace and warm to his new life and I just hoped that Denise could see it.

One afternoon I was filling out a form to allow him to apply for some money from his mother's estate to get some nice things for his room and some new clothes. Philip would be worth quite a lot of money once his mother's flat had been sold. The flat was grotty and unloved but in a good location just off Queen's Park. The form had taken me hours. I had written an accompanying letter to Philip's solicitor and copied in his social worker.

Denise came in, looked over my shoulder and carefully read the contents of the letter. 'Good work,' she said. 'Well done.' Then she let out a hoot of highly amused derision. 'Where on earth did you find that headed paper? I thought it had all been chucked. Honestly, Rachel, you do make things difficult for yourself.' She hooted again.

'What's wrong with it?' I sat back and scanned the paper through puzzled eyes. I was baffled.

'Look!' she said.

I studied it again and then turned to look up at her and shrugged.

A plum-coloured nail pointed to the line under the address. 'There!' she said.

I still couldn't see anything wrong.

'That's our old phone number and there's no email. We haven't used this paper for ages. Where on earth did you find it?'

'Under here,' I said, shuffling back and opening the cupboard under the desk to reveal about forty sheets of the stuff. Denise grabbed it and stuck it into the recycling bin. Then she went over to another cupboard and pointed to a wedge of the up-to-date paper.

'Honestly, it's just here.'

'Sorry. I didn't realize . . .'

Denise squeezed my shoulder kindly as if to say that I mustn't beat myself up about it. I wanted to say, 'But nobody has ever told me what paper to use. I'm not an idiot, just not bloody psychic.'

'Come on, we're going to be late,' she said. 'Shall I make us both a cup of tea to give us the strength to get through the staff meeting?' I nodded gratefully as she swished out of the room smiling and waving my dirty mug at me.

A minute later Rob came in. 'Have they started?' he asked anxiously.

'Not yet. We're having tea to fortify us first.'

'Oh good. I thought I was late. I'll go and get myself a

coffee.' As he hung his coat on the back of a chair he asked, 'I haven't seen you for a while. How's it going?'

'Oh, OK,' I replied with a sigh.

'And Philip?'

'Getting there. I think we've cracked tooth-brushing.'

'Well done! That's great news!'

He seemed genuinely pleased and I told him all about Jess's toothbrush.

'Inspired,' he said admiringly when I'd finished and I grinned, like a child being given a house-point by its favourite teacher.

'Except now I have to give his shaving some thought. Any ideas?' I asked.

'Brazilian – every time,' he said and I let out a short bark of laughter. As he signed in, leaning across me, I noticed that Rob looked different. Better. Much better. He said casually, 'You know he doesn't have to have a wet shave. Perhaps an electric razor might suit him, at least to begin with.'

'That's a brilliant idea. Thank you!' Once again, I was grateful for Rob's help but I was also excited for Philip; if a singing toothbrush had unlocked something for him, an electric razor might have him joining MENSA. 'And talking of shaving,' I said, screwing my eyes up and surveying Rob's face, 'you look different.'

Rob's hand immediately went to his smooth upper lip and stroked it. 'End of the month,' he said, 'thank Christ.'

'Oh! Were you growing a tash for charity?'

'Yes!' He looked appalled. 'Dear God, don't tell me you thought that I was growing that thing out of choice. You didn't . . . did you?'

I was laughing guiltily. 'Well, I didn't know, did I?'

'I looked like a teenager! I cannot believe you thought it was a deliberate style choice.'

We were both really laughing now and it felt good.

'What look did you think I was going for? Tom Selleck? Hercule Poirot?'

'I'm sorry! I didn't know!'

'Shame on you. The whole thing was a bit of a disaster. I thought I'd be able to grow something half decent but if I'm honest, I've had girlfriends with more facial hair than that.'

'Did you raise much money?'

'Well, I don't think I saved any lives but between me and a few mates I think we'll keep a testicular cancer nurse in paper clips for a year, so not a complete waste of time.'

Reluctantly and still chuckling we made our way towards the meeting room.

'So, everyone is happy for the staff first-aid kit to be kept in the green cupboard in the office from now on. I'll put a note on it making it absolutely clear that residents are not allowed to interfere with it.'

There was a murmuring of half-hearted yesses from around the table and Denise went on. 'Now I think that's everything.' She looked over her agenda for one last time.

Thank the Lord, I thought – I was beginning to get twitchy about picking the kids up in time. It was always the same with the Wednesday staff meeting: it just went on and on. Faff, faff, faff, and we never seemed to be any further on when we'd finished.

I looked around at the team, twelve people in all, some of whom looked like contestants from a 1970s edition of *University Challenge*, plus drippy Scott, two agency workers smelling of fags who I'd never even seen before and snarling Lucy. When I'd worked for social services when I was younger, the staff had been vibrant and warm and good communicators; this lot looked bored and fed up, as if they'd wandered into social work by mistake on their way to a Dr Who convention. Rob had told me that keeping permanent staff was proving very difficult and that was why there were so many agency workers. This was bad for the place – it meant high turnover and a lack of commitment and consistency.

'Just one final point.' Denise turned to me. 'Rachel, I've given it some thought and I really don't feel that it is appropriate for you to continue to be Philip's key worker. I think that you need to concentrate on finding your feet here before you take on such a demanding role.' And without waiting to hear my response she turned to the rest of the table. 'I don't know who is best placed to work with Philip at the moment; does anyone have a particular yearning to take him on . . .'

I could feel myself going scarlet with rage and embarrassment. We were in the meeting room – an airless, dark place lit only by overly bright strips of light that made us all look like we were terminally ill – and twelve pairs of eyes were looking anywhere they could but at me. I was getting somewhere with Philip, I knew I was.

Trying to sound relaxed, I took a deep breath: 'Can I just say something, Denise?'

She nodded irritably.

'I'm really shocked. It's early days for Philip but I think that we're getting somewhere. Slowly, *really* slowly, but he's started brushing his teeth on his own for the first time in his life. Just today he told me that my socks were "fancy".'

Denise stared at me blankly so I heaved my foot up to show her some awful socks patterned with pink reindeers which Jess had bought me for Christmas and I was wearing hidden under jeans. She gave a little shake of her head, not understanding me.

'I think that's progress,' I said. 'He's beginning to notice things around him and to contribute little opinions about things and to find his voice. I really do think that given time he can do so much more . . . and having started the process with him I really do want to carry on.'

She made a face like a clown with her mouth turned down at the corners. 'Sorry, Rachel. But you must understand that from where I'm standing, I see little or no progress from Philip and a member of staff who is – to be honest – out of her depth.'

I didn't know what to say next. She hadn't seen me with him. I couldn't remember a single time when she had been in the same room as Philip and me apart from that very first day with the towel. She never ventured out of her office. Had somebody said something? I looked around the room feeling panicky and paranoid but still no one caught my eye.

Then, to my relief, Rob spoke up. 'As Rachel's supervisor, I wonder if we could talk about this after the meeting.' His face looked grim and determined.

Denise gave a little shrug. 'I'm sorry Rob, but this is our staff meeting and I think it's something that we should sort out as a team.'

'I think that if you wish to discuss Rachel's performance and her suitability as Philip's key worker, then that is something that should be discussed privately, either with her directly or, as her supervisor, with me.' He was speaking very slowly and deliberately.

Denise pretended to look shocked and formed her mouth into a little 'o'. 'Well that's as maybe, Rob. But I don't have the time, I'm too busy to have private meetings with staff members when this is a perfectly good forum to air these issues.' She turned to me. 'I'm not having a go at you, Rachel, I just think we've given you too much responsibility too soon.'

'Yes, I know, I just wish –'

Denise turned back to Rob, smiling. 'You see? She's a big girl, she can take it. Can't you, Rachel?'

Rob pushed on. 'I know,' he said, 'but I'm thinking about Philip and I've seen them together. I've witnessed the way Rachel works with him and they're really getting somewhere. The poor man's been through enough, he's still grieving for his mother and I think it would be cruel to take Rachel away. I really do.'

They were at stalemate.

'Can I just say something?' Lucy had spoken. I shot her a look of pure loathing.

'I think that Rachel is doing a good job. I've been really impressed the last week or so and I think there's a marked difference between Philip on the shifts when Rachel's here and when she isn't. I'd like to get her take on how we can best manage Philip when she's not around so that we can all start to build up his confidence.'

Denise looked completely wrong-footed. 'Fine, fine. Well, I don't want a *riot*, so OK Rob, if you want to talk about this later we can.'

Rob smiled. 'Thank you, Denise.'

Denise glanced at her watch. 'It's ten to three and I'm due at head office, so if there's nothing else anyone wants to raise we should pack up now. Rob, you're on duty tonight, aren't you?'

'Indeed I am.'

'We can talk later.'

*

*Due at head office.* I knew that Denise would slip home. She had a house on site, it went with the job, and so she had made 'working from home' an art form; doing sod-all from home more like, I thought resentfully. I could picture her now slipping off her shiny shoes and wiggling her toes as she dunked a biscuit stolen from Clifton Avenue supplies into a hot cup of tea and clicking the remote control on a hunt for Noel Edmonds.

As I put my coat on, Rob came to find me. 'I'll do what I can,' he said. 'I'm pretty sure I can talk her round. But that was a bolt from the blue, wasn't it? I thought I was gonna hit her!'

'Next time give me warning and I'll hold her down.'

'Honestly, sometimes I think she's got a screw loose. You and Philip were my success story . . .'

'Why do you think she wants me away from him? I don't think she's ever even seen us together.'

'God knows, I think it might be partly my fault because I kind of rail-roaded her into letting you have him in the first place. I mean in a way she's got a point, he probably should have gone to one of the more experienced members of staff but, having met him, I thought you'd click. It was just a hunch. Also, she has a funny way of operating, Denise. She's probably just jealous as hell. You're younger than her, attractive, the residents all like you and you're bright.'

He spoke very matter-of-factly, not in the least bit flirtatious, as if me being attractive and bright was just an undisputed fact that everybody knew. I felt absurdly flattered and my cheeks flushed. I found myself hoping that this was his personal view and that he wasn't just describing the attributes of an esteemed colleague.

'Haven't you noticed,' he went on, 'that she normally likes to surround herself with dullards that she can bully?'

'Like you, you mean.'

He laughed. 'Obviously she couldn't turn *me* down. Anyway, she's not stupid. She knows that to get away with being such a lazy bastard she needs a competent deputy. It breaks my heart – this place has so much potential and I feel that Denise just wants to squeeze all the joy out of it. The minute something goes right and I feel it's all gonna change, she always comes in and buggers things up.'

'Well, thank God you're here and thank you for sticking up for me.'

'No problem, but I haven't saved the situation yet. Anyway, it's Lucy you need to thank. She really stuck her neck out for you.'

'Yes, I couldn't believe it. What came over her?'

Rob looked pained. 'Don't be too hard on Lucy. Don't be fooled by how she comes across. She doesn't give a toss about the staff, but have you ever seen her doing Margaret's hair? She couldn't be more careful or take more time if it was her own mother. And that miserable old stick just loves her for it.'

I felt my cheeks flush red again. 'I'll go and find her

now,' I said, slapping on my coat and racing out of the door to catch Lucy before she got on the bus.

She was fifty yards ahead of me, stomping down the road like an angry little crow. 'Lucy!' I called out and she looked round irritably, saw me but did not stop to wait. 'Lucy, wait!' With a shambling run I caught up with her. 'I just wanted to say thank you for standing up for me.'

She stopped dead and turned to me. 'Philip should have gone to his mum's funeral. You should have gone with him. I told Denise that day that he should and I was so embarrassed when you walked in and asked me why you hadn't been told about it. What sort of a place do we run, that doesn't even make it a priority for a son to go to his own mother's funeral? And now this? It's a bloody joke.'

Her bus was coming so she ran off. We went our separate ways. Once on my bus, I started to entertain all sorts of bizarre fantasies about kidnapping Philip. The other residents were becoming fond of me I hoped, but they had all been living in institutions for a while; they were used to staff members coming and going. Philip was the only one that I felt really needed me. Although God knows why I thought that. It's not as if he would fling his arms around me when I arrived on shift or express any affection. If Denise is going to ruin things, I thought, I'll smuggle Philip out and he can come and live with us all in Queens Park. Or better still we could all run away and go and live on a Scottish island à la Enid Blyton; away from

Denise, public transport, school, homework, Deborah and Dom ... Except that now we'd have to leave Alec behind as well.

When the kids and I got home, Marlene was doing some washing up expertly with one hand, while holding her phone with the other. She was gabbling away and didn't draw breath as we came in, just nodded. Oh Alec, what the bloody hell are you doing and why aren't you here?

I wearily dropped my bag on the floor and went over to the kettle. As I filled it, I waved it at Marlene and she nodded gratefully. I opened the fridge to see what we could eat. There was nothing edible except for a few bits of indescribable grey meat that belonged to Marlene, like a lot of lolling tongues hanging out expectantly as I opened the fridge door. She would make pilgrimages to a Czech shop halfway across town and come back with all sorts of over-sized sausages and off-cuts and would then just nibble a bit off the end and leave them in the fridge for me to dispose of when they started to belch independently. I felt a stab of irritation.

'Marlene?'

She looked up from her phone call and I felt spitefully happy to have interrupted her flow.

'Can I ask you to have a clear-out of the fridge? I'm not sure what's fresh and what needs throwing out. It's a real mess.'

'OK, no problem,' she shrugged and carried on with her conversation.

Then Jess wandered through. She was wearing a school cardigan that obviously belonged to someone else, someone large. I curled the collar back but there was no name inside it. Presumably some heffalump of a child was lumbering around with Jess's cardigan on. As Jess began to tell me about her day, I wound up the sleeves so that, when she gesticulated, her hands were liberated and I ceased to be hit in the face by random swipes of bobbled polyester.

Jess's teacher was pregnant and it was lovely for all the five-year-olds to watch her tummy expand. She let them touch her bump and press their ears up to it and shout instructions down her belly button. She had been for a scan and had been told she was having a boy. For Jess, this was terrible news. She chattered on while I made myself some toast. As I sat down at the kitchen table, I noticed that Marlene was off the phone and hovering.

When Jess drew breath, I asked if everything was OK.

'I would like to have a little word with you please, Rachel.'

'Sure,' I said and sent Jess back into the sitting room.

'My college work is now different. I have changed my course.'

'Oh. Are you enjoying it?' I asked tentatively, not sure where the conversation was going.

'Yes, but now the schedule has changed and I must do

a tutorial on Thursday afternoon at five. Is this good with you?'

I was non-plussed. Surely she knew that in no way would it be good with me. 'Well no,' I said uncomfortably. 'As you know, my hours at work differ from week to week. I may need you on some Thursdays. Not every week but –'

'Can you ask of your boss that she does not make you work on Thursday at five?'

'No, Marlene, I'm afraid I can't. That's not how it works.'

'But I have changed my course.'

'I know, but you shouldn't have changed your course until you had spoken to me. I thought your English course lasted a year and it was mornings only.'

'Yes, but I have changed my course,' she said loudly as if I was feeble-minded.

I sighed, completely at a loss to know how to explain things. Finally, very slowly and clearly, I said, 'I need you here to pick up the children on the days I am working. That is why you are here. That is what I pay you for and why you have a room in my house. That is what we agreed when you moved in.' God knows it wasn't for her company that we had her living amongst us.

At that moment the door flew open and Jess came hurtling in, eyes blazing. 'Luke bit me!' she shrieked.

'No I didn't,' came a lazy drawl from next door, 'I just *pretended* to bite her. It was a fake one.'

'Oh for heaven's sake, you two,' I said exasperated, and Marlene took this as her cue to leave. I followed her out of the kitchen. 'I'm sorry not to be able to help, but it just won't work. I can give you a copy of my rota and then you can see what Thursdays I'm working for the next month at least.'

'It's OK, no problem,' she said coldly and left.

A few days later, as I dropped Luke and Jess at school, I caught sight of Alec getting out of what must have been Deborah's car. He looked happy and relaxed and gave Deborah a jaunty wave as she shot off in a little unpretentious, sporty number. Neither of them saw me.

I went back to the house. The front door was double-locked, which meant that Marlene was out at college. Hurrah. She had left a note on the kitchen table: 'IRON BROKEN'. I resisted the temptation to scrawl 'SO?' across the bottom.

After toast, tea and a read of the *Week* – which wasn't actually from this week, last week or even the week before but nevertheless made me feel like I was vaguely catching up on things – I had to get on with some housework.

First, I bound a kink in the iron's flex where the wires were showing through with about fifty foot of gaffer tape. Eventually I was satisfied it would last a few more months, if not years – as long as you ironed at the correct angle.

Alec was coming home for the weekend and I wanted his room to be beautiful. I made Luke's bed and then changed the sheets on Alec's, putting on a plain, navy blue duvet cover rather than the usual cheery stripes or animals. I hoovered throughout and then dusted all Alec's knick-knacks; the dreadful bits of pottery he'd made at school that any other self-respecting mother would have thrown away on sight, a photo of both boys with my mother and father and Mary at Jess's christening, some fossils, a model of a lion cub from the Cotswold Safari Park, a hippo from Newquay Zoo. Finally, the 'Excellence in Sports' trophy he had been given after a football course which I was momentarily proud of until I realized that every child on the course had received one and that all you had to do to get one was turn up.

I got on my hands and knees to clean under the bed and retrieved a couple of stray Match Attax football cards which were obviously breeding somewhere in my house, because no matter how often I cleared them away another hundred would be strewn across the floor by morning. The room was looking good and smelled of Mr Sheen. I had bought Alec another *Top Gear* magazine and I placed this on his bed. I knew Luke wouldn't mind because he'd come with me to the newsagent to buy it and was as excited as I was when Alec came home. Two weeks felt like such a long time these days. I tried to divide the room into two halves allowing Luke's half to remain the same but to give Alec's half a more mature look. I made sure all the soft toys were on Luke's bed and sorted the bookshelf on Alec's side so that it only contained his books. I went downstairs and found a mini bottle of water, which I put on the *Top Gear* magazine, and then I laid them both on one of the best towels, the towels that the children weren't allowed near because they were huge and luxurious and expensive. Finally I went into the garden, picked a couple of big Michaelmas daisies and put them into a tooth mug by his bed. I stepped back and surveyed the room with satisfaction.

Then it struck me: I had laid the room out as if a guest were coming to stay. This is what I would have done for a *guest*. Alec was now a visitor in this house. He didn't want to live here any more and so the tidiness was artificial and strange; the mini water bottle and towel made the room look as if I was trying to run a B&B. This was Alec's room: it should be untidy and he should be grumbling at Luke to keep his stuff over his side and never pulling his duvet straight in the morning no matter how many times I asked him. There should be pants and socks spilling out of the laundry basket and Alec's Lamby should be under his pillow. Lamby had been his special toy which from the age of about six months he couldn't sleep without – Luke had had Feelie and Jess still had her thumb. Lamby had once been white and fluffy but now he was grey and bald and looked like an out-of-date chicken breast with eyes. He smelt like one too. We'd once left Lamby in a service station on the M4 and Dom had travelled eighty miles back down the motorway to get it. Inevitably, he'd fallen out of favour as Alec got older but I suddenly realized that Lamby wasn't here and so Alec must have taken him to Dom's and put him under the pillow in the house that he now considered his home. Lamby belonged here!

It felt as if the reality of Alec being gone hadn't hit me until this moment. I'd been too busy defending his decision to everyone else, giving the impression to Jess and Luke that everything was fine. I stood in the doorway motionless, hearing the penny drop in my head with a great clunk. Although my throat felt constricted and tight, I was beyond crying; my eyes felt dry and prickly and tired. To cry would have been self-indulgent and a waste of time and anyway I couldn't.

I made my way to the bathroom on autopilot, put on *Woman's Hour* and started to rub off the knobs and smears of dried toothpaste in the sink with a towel that was going into the wash anyway. When I went to get the Cif from the cupboard under the sink I realized it wasn't there. I went down to the kitchen to look under the sink there, but no. There was a little basin in Marlene's room and I wondered if it was in there. I hesitated at the door, knocked just in case, and when there was no reply I walked in.

It was like walking into one of the room displays in John Lewis, one that was also showing off all the latest additions to the small electrical appliances department. It was warm and clean and bright. In one corner was a plug-in storage heater and it was doing a great job. Along her shelves were all sorts of very expensive beauty potions and lotions and in another corner on a little table she had a mini kitchen set up. There was a kettle, a mini fridge that hummed happily, some mugs, some teaspoons with chunky, purple handles, a breadbin and a toaster. She must have bought it all very recently because the stainless steel was shining as if it had never been out of its box. On the floor there was a huge white adaptor, presumably so that she could have everything going at once: hairdryer, radio, fridge, DVD player, toaster, kettle, heater and presumably a Jacuzzi once she could find the space. She'd put down a cheerful rug to cover the carpet, horribly stained after an incident with a fountain pen my father had foolishly given Luke for his birthday. She'd even put up one of those squares that go around a light switch, so where there had once been a rather nasty grey patch from little sweaty fingers reaching up to switch the light on, there was now a square of shiny, purple, spotty plastic. She had a beautiful cream and mauve duvet cover with a matching pillowcase. God, it looked inviting, and I was so tired. I felt as if I hadn't slept a wink since Alec had left and, fully aware that it was crossing the line between owner of house looking for Cif and freak, I sat on the bed and then very slowly put my head on one of Marlene's brand-new, bottomless pillows. I didn't let my feet and legs follow onto the bed as then I knew I would be lost. So I just lay at a rather strange angle, breathing deeply and allowing my eyes to close just for a second.

*

'Mrs Bidewell. Rachel!' I opened my eyes. Looming over me looking aghast was Marlene. I leapt into the air like a rabbit that had just been shot in the bottom by an air rifle.

'Oh, Marlene! I'm so sorry.' As I spoke I realized that one side of my chin was distinctly moist, and both Marlene and I looked at a patch of dribble on the pillow roughly the size of a teabag. She said nothing, but looked at me with eyes as big as milk-bottle tops, appalled.

'Please forgive me,' I said. 'I was looking for the Cif and you've made this room so lovely and I just couldn't help myself . . . and I must have . . .' I was an ageing, panicking, slightly overweight Goldilocks. '*Have* you got the Cif?' I asked weakly.

'No,' she replied curtly and, mortified beyond imagining, I left the room and got ready to escape to work.

'Philip! There's someone here to see you!' I said, and Philip, without showing any sign of emotion, stood up and meekly followed me into the corridor.

'It's a lady called Pearl,' I said. 'Mrs Deakin, your old neighbour. She's just arrived out of the blue. Do you want to see her?'

He looked at me and shook his head, but Philip shaking his head didn't necessarily mean that he didn't want to see her or in fact that he did. He just shook his head a lot.

'Shall we go through and say hello?' Still nothing. So I decided to press on.

When we came into the meeting room, Philip reacted

in a way I hadn't seen before. He became agitated and could not sit down, but he was excited; there was no mistaking that he was pleased to see the little old woman who sat at the table. She looked about a thousand, and although she had taken her waxy old raincoat off and put it on a chair next to her, she still seemed to be wearing many, many layers; her little head wobbled atop a mound of home-knitting in the sort of colours you never see any more except in the United Kingdom's few remaining wool shops – peppermint green, salmon pink and even a flash of primrose. She looked as if she'd spent a lifetime knitting clothes for new babies and made up her own multicoloured wardrobe from the leftovers. The few strands of white hair that she still had clung limply to her livery, yellow skull. Her eyes were pink and watery and I got the impression she couldn't see a great deal. Pete the cook had provided her with tea and biscuits and as she reached for a digestive I saw that her fingernails looked as if she'd been digging the Channel Tunnel by hand.

'Here's trouble!' danced Philip, 'Here's trouble!' and he began hopping about and rocking vigorously to and fro like a happy little budgerigar in a cage delighted with a newly acquired mirror and swing. He was smiling and smiling and he kept putting the palm of his hand on top of Pearl's head as if she were his pet. She laughed and put her hand on top of his, as if playing One Potato, Two Potato. It was a strange, mixed-up attempt at an embrace but it obviously expressed what they both wanted it to.

'Hello, my friend,' she laughed. 'Hello, my old darling.' A tiny voice, strained with age. A little cockney sparrow but with someone standing on its windpipe.

'She's trouble, Pearl!' Philip said, jumping in the air and wagging his finger at her like a camp headmaster. 'She's trouble, that one.' Then he snorted and pranced over to the window where he stood and looked out grinning, still at last.

'Well, someone's pleased to see you!' I said. 'I'm Rachel, Philip's key worker.' I put my hand out and she shook it with a tiny, warm claw.

'How lovely,' she said. 'And do you look after all the poor children here?'

'Residents, yes. I work here and I have special responsibility to keep this one happy, don't I, Philip?' I didn't add 'for as long as they'll let me'. Philip bounced from one foot to another and shook his hands as if he'd lost a towel and was trying to get them dry.

She tutted. 'Shame. Phil's mum used to say to me, "The Lord wanted to punish me and he gave me a retarded child."' Shaking her head she said kindly: 'It's such a shame.'

'You'd be surprised. Philip's settling in really well here. He's making lots of progress and lots of friends.'

'Aaargh, bless you.'

'So you used to live next door to Philip?'

'Yes, dear, for thirty-odd years. I was there the day they moved in. Hey, you!' She turned awkwardly towards Philip and shouted, 'Wasn't I? Eh, Phil?'

Philip put his hand back on the top of her head and let it rest there.

'My son says I can't cope no more on my own so I'm going into an 'ome. Van's coming to pick me up tomorrow at eleven. I says "I've got to say goodbye to my Phil first."' She looked at him and said loudly, 'Eh, Phil? Can't go without saying goodbye to my friend Phil!'

'No, Pearl. Say goodbye to Phil.' Philip laughed high and loud and shook his head.

'Where are you going to?' I asked. 'Is it nearby? Can we come and see you?'

'No, darling, it's not I'm afraid. My son's got it all sorted. It's up near 'im.'

'Where does he live?'

'Bedford, dear. You can't come and see me all that way, can you?'

'We could try.'

'No dear, Phil couldn't come all that way, could you, Phil?'

'She's trouble!' He laughed again and she joined in.

There was a silence and then Philip suddenly said in a high-pitched voice, 'Sooty! Puss, puss, puss. Sooty!'

'Oh my Sooty's gone, Phil.' Pearl looked sad and shook her head slowly. 'He was old. Too old. I said to my son, "I'll hang on 'ere as long as Sooty can," but once he was gone, it seemed like the right time to move on.'

Philip's hand moved round so that his palm was now

pointing down onto Pearl's cheek and then he dropped it onto her shoulder.

'It's bloody quiet round our block now. Not much to stay for really. Now my Phil's gone and his mum. New pair moved in.' She sniffed dismissively. 'Stuck up. I miss our singsongs, Phil! I bet you do. You do, don't you?'

Philip now looked pensive and shook his head.

Pearl began to sing 'Some Enchanted Evening'. Her voice had changed and now she warbled with the enunciation of an early BBC radio announcer. 'Come on, Phil . . .'

'"*Daisy! Daisy!*"' sang Philip and stopped abruptly, smiling.

'That's what him and 'is mum used to do. They liked a good singsong.' She started on a medley: 'I Dreamed a Dream' from *Les Mis* and then Gloria Gaynor's 'I Will Survive'.

Philip gave a big yacking laugh and the room fell silent. He broke it with: 'Sooty! Here, puss. Sooty, Sooty, Sooty.'

'No,' said Pearl, looking at him and raising her voice as if talking to a foreigner. 'He's gone, Phil. My Sooty's gone. He is *dead*!' She looked at me sadly. 'He doesn't know what I'm saying does 'e? Do you, Phil?' she shouted again.

He laughed. 'She's trouble. Pearl's trouble.' Then he went back to the window.

'Oh I think he takes in a lot more than we think. Can I ask you a question?'

'Course you can, fire away.'

'Did Philip ever go to school? Did . . . what was his mum's name, I can't remember.'

'Muriel. Or Mo I called 'er.'

'Muriel, of course. Did she ever send Philip to school?'

'No, dear. She couldn't, could she? He's retarded. He couldn't have managed it. He can't cross roads, you see. He can't go down the shops. She couldn't leave him for a second. He couldn't go to school, dear.'

'But there are schools for retarded children and day centres for people like Philip. Places like this. Didn't he ever come to anywhere like this?'

'No! He 'ad his mum. He didn't need looking after by no strangers.'

'I see. Was his dad ever on the scene?'

She shook her head and sucked her breath in. 'No, darlin'. His dad didn't stay around long enough even to see 'im born. She was on her own from day one. She wasn't a young thing. In her thirties and I think she thought this was her only chance. Her mum and dad didn't wanna know. So she says "I'm going to have this baby" and she did!' Pearl paused and her brow furrowed. 'I think if they'd been able to tell at birth that he wasn't right, they'd have put 'im away, wouldn't they? But they couldn't so it was just the two of 'em. She got very big those last few years so it was hard for her to get out. I'd go up the shops for 'em and get 'em this and that. If she needed to go up the Post Office or whatever, I'd keep an eye on 'im but never for more than an 'alf hour. I think it's what killed her in the end. I was staying with my son when it happened. I'll never forgive meself. Massive heart attack. Pouff!' She clicked her fingers and that, it seemed, was that for poor Mo.

Pearl rooted about in her bag for a hankie. 'Never forgive meself. Never. They say he was in such a state.' Her face was so ancient that it was hard to read and I was surprised when she wiped her eyes and her shoulders gave a little shake. 'A terrible, terrible state.' I touched her arm and gave it a squeeze. 'Oh take no notice of me, love. I'm a silly old cow. Honestly I am.' And she gave my hand a pat.

There was so much I wanted to ask her, not just from a personal point of view but also things that would inform much of Philip's care in the future. But she was tired and suddenly struggling. Making ready to go, she pulled out a Tesco bag from under her coat and produced a box of Cadbury's Heroes for Philip.

'There you go, Phil. Don't eat 'em all at once.' He hopped to her and took the box. Unkindly, I felt a pang as I thought of how many calories he would consume. Then she pulled out another box. 'And these are for all the other children,' she said. 'Poor souls.'

'Thank you, Pearl,' I said. 'Please let us know where you'll be. Philip's really making so much progress. I'm sure we could come and visit you or write even.'

'No, darlin', he can't write! Anyway, it's too far!' She slowly got up to leave and Philip put his forehead on the back of her shoulders. She turned round and took him in her little arms. He went very stiff. She gave him six or seven slippery little kisses on his cheek and looked at me. 'You look after this one,' she said raising her voice again. 'He's my Phil. He's my friend, aren't you, Phil? Eh? He's very special.'

She shuffled out into the corridor after much palaver with the half pack of digestives that I insisted she took, her walking stick and the Tesco bag, which she folded and put in the front pocket of her handbag. Then Philip and I watched her leave and walk down the road towards the bus stop. At one point she turned and waved her stick with a flourish.

'Well,' I said, turning to Philip. 'Wasn't that a lovely surprise? What a great lady.'

'Here, puss, puss, puss,' he said. 'Here, Sooty.'

'I'm sure I can find out where she is. We can send a card at least. And you're a bloody dark horse you are, Mr Johnston.' I poked him in the chest. 'You can sing!'

He laughed and put his hand on top of my head.

'*Muuum*!' It was later that day and Luke was bellowing down the hall like a walrus.

'Coming.'

'*Muuuuuum*!'

'I'M COMING!'

'MUUUUUUM!'

'Yes, alright, Luke, I'm coming. I was on the loo! What is it?'

To my horror Luke thrust the phone at me. 'It's some-one called Rob?'

I made an appalled face at Luke like someone out of a silent movie, but he just handed me the phone and shrugged. 'Hello?' I said.

'Hi,' Rob said hurriedly. 'Look, I've finally got Denise to tell me what she's going to do regarding Philip.' He sounded grave and professional.

'Oh yes?' I said warily.

'I can't get her to back off. At the end of the day it is her decision. I think that if it hadn't been for the incident with Margaret burning her hand that time when you were on duty –'

'But, she was there too. I only –'

'It's OK. I know, I know. She's just using it as a justifica-tion. My worry is that this will set you back. Whatever you do, don't let this affect how you're doing here. It would be a shame if Denise dented your confidence and you lost your way.'

I wasn't really listening. I just couldn't imagine how I was going to tell Philip and how I had let this happen.

Rob went on, 'The problem with this place is that we have an unmotivated, bored staff team – it all comes from the top – and if you left I think that would just about finish me off.' He paused. 'I'm trying so hard to keep this professional, but you know I really do think that this is a mistake with Philip. It's so wrong and I'm so sorry.'

'I'm not worried about me, it's just Philip,' I said.

Something about the kindness in Rob's voice made me want to sob. 'I've promised him so much. We were going to decorate his room together, I wanted to take him to the pictures for the first time. And his feet! Who's going to take him to get his feet done now?'

'Well it will be Scott. Scott's going to take over from you.'

Scott! Monosyllabic, ineffectual, inept Scott? This was madness. I might not have been brilliant at the job, I might have been inexperienced, but I was better than Scott.

'The appointment's on Monday – he just won't go with Scott, I know he won't,' I said.

'Well, isn't that your ultimate revenge? Scott is now responsible for those monstrosities.'

I felt unable to explain that I had actually been looking forward to taking Philip to get his feet sorted. I had pictured us on the bus, perhaps having our lunch in the hospital canteen and above all, me being the one to look after him. He had an appointment with an uber-chiropodist – presumably one that had power tools – and he was very nervous and fretful about the whole thing. I liked the fact that when I'd taken his hand and given it a good squeeze and said, 'Don't you worry, mate, I won't leave your side,' he'd looked at me with such gratitude.

I stayed silent. I couldn't trust myself to speak. Rob said, 'Look, if the appointment is on Monday, we should probably cancel it. Don't worry. I'll get on and do that, the number will be on his file. I'm so sorry, Rachel, I feel like I've let you down.'

'Don't be silly. It's not your fault. I'll see you soon.'

I put the phone down and sat on the sofa. Luke looked up from the TV and on realizing that something was wrong, shuffled along on his bottom and plonked himself on my lap, eyes fixed back on the screen. The phone rang. I picked it up – it was Rob again.

'Look, I know how freaked out Philip is about this appointment. Perhaps you should go ahead as planned and take him on Monday. We'll need to do a gradual handover with Scott anyway and I think it would just be cruel to send Philip with a virtual stranger.'

'Won't Denise go mental?'

'I'll deal with Denise. I really do think it's the right thing for you to take him yourself. It's the right decision for his well-being and for his peace of mind and whatever Denise thinks we shouldn't lose sight of that.'

'Thanks, Rob.' I felt relieved and again grateful for his kindness.

'Leave it with me,' he said.

'God, my room looks amazing. Thank you, Mum.'

It was Friday evening and Jess, Luke and I had taken Alec up to his room. He hurled a big overnight bag onto the bed.

'My goodness, what have you got in there? You've got everything you need here.' I tried hard not to sound peevish but what was so desperately important that he needed to bring it the three miles from Dom's house?

'I don't even know what's in there, Deborah packed it for me ...' He looked momentarily bereft and couldn't think what to say next, worried that the 'D' word might have upset me.

'Well aren't you the lucky one. Eleven years old and *two* women waiting on you hand and foot!'

He looked relieved and I tried to sustain the queasy smile on my tight lips. I noticed him delve into the bag and put Lamby under his pillow.

'No prizes for guessing what's for tea.'

'*Macaroni, macaroni, macaroni cheeese,*' sang Jess – one of her own compositions.

'Great!' said Alec with real pleasure and I wondered if he'd been living off capers and pudding wine since he left.

'Good, well come down when you're ready. I'll leave you to Jeremy Clarkson,' I said, backing out of the room.

And once again, it felt as if Alec were the nephew of an old school friend come to London; a nice boy but everyone giving each other a wide berth because of the inevitable awkwardness.

As I came downstairs the phone went. It was Mel. We were all going over there for lunch on Sunday.

'How's it going?' she said.

'Oh I don't know.' I took the phone into the sitting room and shut the door. 'When Alec's here we're walking on eggshells a bit – which is ridiculous.'

'Why's it ridiculous? It's bound to be awkward; he's feeling guilty that he's gone to Dom's and you're trying to look as if it's OK when it obviously isn't.'

'Yes, I s'pose so. It seems mad to think that until recently, this was Alec's home and now . . . well, we're all just feeling the strain a bit. Luke's being so nice to Alec it's heartbreaking. And even more freaky, I've washed my hair and put on a skirt.'

Mel laughed. 'Dear God! Steady now, girl. Friday was the hardest bit last time wasn't it? Just get through this evening and then things will feel more normal in the morning.'

'That's the thing! I keep wanting things to feel like normal and then I remind myself that *normal* was what he needed to get away from.'

'Well then you're doing exactly the right thing; trying to find what the new normal is going to be. It's bound to feel a bit strange.'

'Yes, I know. Look, I'd better go. I have a macaroni cheese that looks like something from *MasterChef* to serve up.'

'Go girl. I just wanted to warn you that Josh isn't going to be here on Sunday. I'm so sorry. He's got some bloody paint-balling party somewhere in Surrey to go to.'

'Oh.' Although it was always a bit sad for my bruised and battered little crew to be around such a happy, chaotic family, especially as in the past Dom would have been with us, we were always relaxed at Mel's house and it was

180

always good fun. I had actually asked her if we could come because of Alec's devotion to Josh, thinking that a day with him always puffed Alec up a bit. Josh was a year older and he was effortlessly cool and kind and a laugh. Also, as Dom was now not allowed over the threshold of Mel's house, it was also somewhere that was just ours.

Mel went on: 'He's going to set up the Scalextric in his bedroom anyway and he'll leave Alec in charge. I'm really sorry but I just hadn't realized this bloody thing was in the diary.'

'Not to worry. It can't be helped.'

'We'll make a huge fuss of Alec – I'm going to do a roast and then a massive crumble. Everybody likes crumble, don't they?'

As we said goodbye I wandered back into the kitchen, reflecting that no, alas, not everybody does like a crumble, not in the Bidewell family anyway. Already I could picture the scene: Alec would eat the bottom but not the top; Luke would eat the top but not the bottom; Jess would refuse to eat either the top or the bottom and as a plate was put in front of her, her eyes would fill up and she would look as if we'd put a bowl of medieval pig's innards in front of her. I would eat two or three massive helpings with custard to compensate and would go home feeling bloated and fat. Hey ho.

The macaroni cheese was indeed a triumph. The cheese bubbled and the topping had gone nicely brown. I put some peas in a dish and they steamed contentedly with a knob of golden butter slithering across them. As it was a special occasion I had put bits of bacon into the macaroni and breadcrumbs on the top. I had laid the table nicely and had even ironed some napkins that hadn't been used since the last time we had people for supper before Dom left. I'd put them into the wash earlier that day as they still bore the scars of a fish pie I had made 'with real fish!' as Luke had excitedly told the guests when they arrived. He was used to Findus boil-in-a-bag – 'plastic fish' as Dom used to call it – being plunged under a mound of lumpy mash and couldn't believe I'd actually used something that once sported gills.

I drew the curtains and surveyed the kitchen, which looked warm and inviting bathed in an electric, orange light. I yelled up the stairs that tea was ready. Then again . . . and then again. Finally, three pairs of feet came thundering down the stairs. Perhaps it was all going to be OK.

Alec was telling us some long convoluted story about a games lesson where they'd all had to pick up litter off the school field before they were allowed to play football. I'd put orange squash in a jug and was trying to follow him while pouring it out. I was delighted that in front of him was a huge plate of food and that he was enjoying it so much he couldn't decide between talking and eating and so kept waving his fork around when faced with the inconvenience of swallowing.

Suddenly Jess screeched, 'Not the pink one! Not the pink one!' as I tried to fill up her cup.

'But you like the pink one. It's the one with the butterfly –'

'Not the pink, Mummy.' And she shot up from the table and began rooting around through the cupboard looking for a more suitable receptacle for her squash.

His flow interrupted, Alec rolled his eyes.

'Jess, come back to the table; you don't just leave the table when you feel like it. You know that,' I said.

'I want the blue one with the spots. It tastes funny in the pink one.'

'Oh don't talk such nonsense, now get back to the table and stop being so silly.'

She ignored me and continued to rifle through other perfectly serviceable cups.

'Jess, will you please come back here.'

'Jess, stop being such a baby!' Luke said. He was as keen for the meal to go well as I was. He loved having his big brother home again and I'm sure somewhere in his small head he was thinking if this goes well Alec might decide to stay. 'Have mine! You can have mine,' he said and grabbed the pink cup and substituted his green one.

To my relief, Jess came back to the table and clambered up onto her chair but then immediately squawked, 'I don't want the green one. I never have the green one!'

'Well you've got it now and I've got the pink one.' Luke took a big swig. 'You can't have it back, it's got my germs now,' he said, hoping that would be the end of the matter.

'I don't want this one. Give me the pink one. You can't have pink. Give it back!' Jess lunged across the table at Luke and as she did so she caught Alec's cup. She knocked it flying and a wave of orange squash hit not only the table but Alec's meal. Bits of macaroni and bacon lifted up off the bottom of the plate in a sea of watery juice and the cheese sauce immediately went lumpy and fragmented and thin.

'Jess!' I grabbed Alec's plate and tried to drain off the excess liquid into the sink. Then I threw the pink cup violently into the sink making a great clatter. I was so furious with her for ruining everything. 'Jess, that serves you right for being so silly. Just for once I thought we could have a nice meal all together. Honestly, you naughty girl – you've ruined Alec's tea. Five years old and behaving like a spoiled baby. There's nothing wrong with the green cup or the pink one.' I knew that the one thing I mustn't do on Alec's weekends was lose it and here we were, not even 6 o'clock on Friday evening, and I was ranting.

'It's OK, Mum. It's fine. I'm sure it'll be OK,' said Alec, surveying his gelatinous meal.

'No, Alec, you're not eating this, Jess is. You can have Jess's.'

'It was an accident,' wailed Jess as I swapped the plates around, 'I didn't mean to.'

'It was not an accident.'

'It was!'

'No, a true accident happens completely by mistake, this was the result of some very silly, selfish behaviour.'

Jess burst into tears looking at the soggy, congealed pasta in front of her and her perfect plate in front of Alec.

'It's OK, Mum, I'll have it. It's fine,' said Alec. Jess's sobs were rising to a wail.

'No, you won't. Why should you have your meal ruined?'

Huge tears were running down Jess's bright red, screwed-up little face. 'I'm sorry. It *was* an accident, Mummy. It was just an accident. I'll have the green cup. I like the green cup!'

'OK. OK,' I sighed heavily, 'I'll have it,' and the dance of the macaroni cheese continued as I swapped my plate for Jess's. We all sat in silence with the children staring anxiously at me as I tried to swallow slimy, cold macaroni cheese that tasted of cheap orange squash.

That night when the house was quiet, I took a sleepy Jess for a wee and then went into Alec and Luke's room. Luke was prostrate, as if he'd just jumped off a skyscraper. I tidied him up and slotted all his limbs back under his duvet. Alec was huddled cosily inside his duvet already and all I had to do was rescue Lamby from falling down between the bed and the wall. I put him in the little nook between Alec's fists and his chest and he grunted gratefully in his sleep. He was tall for his age but skinny and slight, far too grown-up for Lamby now but far too young to have left home.

I crept over to the other side of the room and began to unpack his bag for him. I didn't recognize the bag itself and inside I found that he had new pants and new socks, very grown-up trainers and a polo shirt. He had a shiny, black, sporty sponge bag with a brand-new toothbrush and toothpaste, a comb, a flannel and some dental floss. Were combing and flossing a part of Alec's new existence? It made me want to laugh out loud. A tablet of soap was still wrapped in cellophane in a black soap box. Presumably Deborah had packed this bag. Did she honestly imagine that we didn't have toiletries for him here? That we didn't use soap but perhaps our own spit to get ourselves clean? As I fished about a bit more I found another copy of the *Top Gear* magazine that I had put on Alec's bed and a towel. She'd packed him a towel.

I tried to picture her getting this bag ready. Was this the work of an arrogant little cow, who thought how ghastly it was for poor Alec to have to come and stay in such a dump, so she'd packed him a case which said, 'This is the world you belong to now, where you floss and your soap box matches your sponge bag, because you are better than the world you have left behind and my standards are higher than your mother's'? Or was she a young woman trying desperately hard to please this child and her new partner? Was there something touching about how much effort she had put in, how she didn't want to leave anything to chance or Alec in need of anything? Had she popped out in her lunch hour and stood in Boots wondering whether to buy the executive black sponge bag and matching soap box or the one in the shape of a Power Ranger?

The rest of the weekend passed without incident but I never really relaxed or managed to turn in a performance of my old, pre-Deborah self. On Monday morning after drop-off, as I headed back to my car, I was apprehended by RebeccaClassRep. She was standing at the school gate and to my relief chatting animatedly to someone else, so I slithered past, trying not to break into a trot as I made it onto the pavement.

'Hang on, Rachel!' she chirped and then screwing up her face and talking in an exaggerated whisper she said, 'I just wanted a quick word.'

I nodded, grinning. 'Sure. What can I do for you?'

'Do you know, I don't think I've seen you since all that awful business in Swanage.'

No coincidence there, Rebecca; I've been avoiding you.

'I was just appalled. I kept thinking of Alec out all night. Well it was just awful. We all were just appalled.' By 'all' I assumed she meant all 300 other mothers with whom she'd no doubt had PTA coffee since the unfortunate disappearance of Alec Bidewell. However, she did look genuinely sorry and I felt myself warm to her. 'How is he now?'

'Well he seems to be OK. Obviously it was a terrible shock but I think he's settled down again.' I just couldn't bring myself to tell her about Alec living with Dom. It wasn't any of her business and she would tell the world. Also, I knew that if I did, she would tell me how brave I was and then try to hug me. I couldn't face it. No, it wasn't necessary for her to know everything.

'Well, I think what you've done is very brave.'

Oh, hell's teeth. 'What?'

'Letting him move in with his father. It must be utterly heartbreaking for you but I'm sure you're doing the right thing.'

'Are you? Well that makes one of us.' I gave a bitter little laugh and regretted it.

'Oh no, I'm sure you are. Now I know you've been in to see Mrs Graves.'

I had indeed been to see Alec's form teacher and explained the situation to her. She was a lovely girl of about twenty-six and had managed not to look embarrassed or judgemental or even, thank God, sorry for me.

'And I know this is the most awful bore and must be the least of your worries, but that was why I needed to catch you; I wondered where you wanted Year 6 and PTA emails to be sent now that Alec isn't living at home.'

'Still to me. Of course still to me.'

'OK, but are you happy for me to send a copy to your husband as well?'

'No, it's not necessary, I can pass on anything that is relevant.'

'Oh, well, that makes things a bit awkward because I did actually bump into your husband's new partner yesterday. We had a chat as she's very keen to get to grips with how all the PTA stuff works. Is it Deborah? And she did ask that all communications be sent to your husband's email address in future.'

Oh she did, did she? 'Fine, Rebecca. Well as of tomorrow, send them to both of us – it's not like it's a waste of paper, is it?' I tried to sound jaunty. Why did she have to make everything so complicated? Why couldn't she just send the damn emails to Dom and me without having to talk about it at all? Did she enjoy this sort of meaningless organizational stuff?'

'I hope you don't mind me fussing about it but I thought it best to clarify the whole thing with you.'

'Well, I'm glad you did. Thank you.' I turned to leave – surely she was done.

'I really hope you don't think I'm making a mountain out of a molehill, but then I thought, well, I've known Rachel long enough and she'll tell me to bugger off if she wants to!'

*Bugger off.*

'Take last night's email.'

*Bugger off.*

'I sent it to you but then worried it should have gone to your husband instead. Did you get it?'

'Probably, I haven't looked yet today.'

'Oh, well, apparently someone in Alec's class has got nits – again! – and I have to inform the parents. I know I don't need to remind you that Alec will need a treatment tonight otherwise the whole class will be facing another infestation – God help us – and it just makes sense to get the lines of communication sorted. You don't mind, do you?'

*Bugger off!* 'No, of course not. I'll pass the information on. Look I've got to get back. Thank you again.'

'Bye bye. And Rachel?'

Let me go, woman. Please just let me go.

She hugged me and stepping back looked me in the eye gravely. 'Children do surprise you, you know. Sometimes I don't think we give them enough credit but they are incredibly resilient.'

It's funny, like Catholics are always devout, Jews are practising, bullets are speeding and cancer patients riddled, so the children of a divorce are always resilient. They don't 'bounce back'; they don't show 'fortitude' or 'resolve'. No, they are 'resilient'. They actually have no choice, because they are children and no matter how badly or shoddily you treat them, you are the grown-up and you are in charge. I don't think all children are resilient; they're just not in control and so have to get on with life regardless of how damaged they feel. I didn't think running away and spending the night in sub-zero temperatures in pyjamas was a sign of resilience. I thought it was a sign of despair and that's why I had to tolerate Alec staying with Dom for the time being, in case I was the problem and it was the solution.

# Chapter Seven

# I'm Sorry, I Know It's Only a Bit of Milk, But Just for a Moment I Was Overwhelmed

'Hello, my lovely. Is it Philip? Philip Johnston, sweetheart?'

The time had come for Philip's feet to meet their match. He stared blankly at the pretty, young girl with blue hospital trousers, a blue tunic, white clogs and a broad Birmingham accent.

'Yes,' I said. 'This is Philip and he's a bit nervous.'

'There's nothing to worry about, silly! I'm Leslie-Ann and I'm going to take good care of you.'

We had travelled all the way to the hospital on the bus, with Philip gripping my hand till the blood had left it completely. It had been hard enough getting him on the bus in the first place, taking a lot of soothing and cajoling and eventually one monster shove. Now they'd kept us waiting for forty-five minutes and I could tell that Philip had wound himself into a state. He had brought a catalogue which I had gone through with him a few days earlier when we were ordering the new furniture for his room. At first we had looked at it together in the waiting room, with me pointing out the stuff that we had ordered, but now he sat obsessively flicking through it through it back and forth without looking at any of the content. He was rocking and shaking his head and making unnerving little snorts. The other two or three people in the waiting room were sneaking furtive glances at us as if to make sure Philip was not a silverback gorilla, heavily disguised in beige slacks, slip-ons and an anorak. All we needed now was for someone to walk in with a Pekingese.

'There's nothing to be nervous about, lovely! Nothing at all,' Leslie-Ann continued. 'We're going to have lots of fun. It'll just feel like a little tickle, that's all.'

The word perky had been invented for this girl and, as she led us busily through to her consulting room, the words 'lamb' and 'slaughter' sprang to mind.

'Now, my darling, I just need you to pop your coat and your socks and shoes off and sit on the chair here and then we'll get started.'

Philip looked at me with pleading eyes as I took his coat and hung it on the back of the door. He was rooted to the spot.

'Come on, now. Sit yourself down,' I said, trying to sound sympathetic but also distinctly no-nonsense.

He sat on the chair, all the while staring at me and shaking his head. His socks remained resolutely on.

Perky sat down on a funny little seat and wriggled herself around on her bottom until she had maximum access to every millimetre of Philip's right foot. That'll wipe the smile off your face, I thought.

'Now, sweetheart, I'm not going to do anything that will hurt you or cause you any discomfort whatsoever. If at any point you *do* feel that I'm hurting you, all you have to do is tap me on the shoulder or say, "Leslie-Ann, please could you stop?" and I will. OK?'

Philip stared at her as if she was about to take out a small hand-saw and hack both feet right off.

Undeterred, Leslie-Ann switched her eyes to me. 'Shall we get started?' she whispered kindly.

I nodded. 'You're OK, aren't you, Philip? You're happy for Leslie-Ann to get going, aren't you? Remember, just tap her on the shoulder if you're not happy.'

He said nothing but continued to stare like a cat in the path of a juggernaut. She looked over at me again and I nodded for her to start.

She leant forward and began very gently to peel the sock off Philip's right foot. During the final stages she paused, a little tell-tale pause, as if she suddenly had an inkling of what was in store. *Courage, mon brave*, I thought. *Courage*.

She carried on gingerly. On revealing Philip's toenails, long and curled, yellow as Cheddar and hard as concrete, her shoulders gave a little droop, but she seemed to steel herself and without saying a word, turned to a tray of elaborate instruments and surveyed them to see which one was up to the task. Alas, there was no chainsaw.

'I just need to pop next door and have a quick word with a colleague,' she said to Philip, and she turned to me and said in a hushed, serious tone, 'Do you know what length of appointment you booked for today?'

'No,' I said, 'we were just told to come here at ten.'

'Right,' she said. 'Would you just excuse me for one minute?' She shot out of the door as if she were on springs and returned a few minutes later.

'OK!' She was her old self again. Perhaps her colleague had told her to pull herself together because Philip was a chiropodist's once-in-a-lifetime dream, her Everest. 'My associate is going to look after my next two appointments, so we really should be able to make some progress today. However, I think you are going to have to make a few return trips until we can truly say we're on top of the problem. OK?'

'Of course,' I said. 'Absolutely.'

'Right! Philip, my lovely, let's get started! I'll just give my hands a warm up.' As she sat down again she began rubbing her hands together with relish. 'OK!' she said again as she turned to her tray of instruments and took hold of a strange-looking one with a hook on the end. 'Now we'll need to give these a really good soak I think, but first I just want to –'

Philip had seemed resigned and relatively calm, but as Leslie-Ann put his foot in her lap and lowered her face to within inches of it, so he suddenly panicked. As a spasm of fear overtook him, his foot jerked forward with all the force of a demolition ball, and he smashed it into her face so that she was thrown backwards, sprawling halfway across the room. She instantly brought her hands up to her nose and shouted a muffled, 'Oh my God! Oh my God!'

I don't know who was the most appalled, Philip, Leslie-Ann or me. I shot across the room and got down onto my knees. 'Oh my goodness!' I said. 'Leslie-Ann, are you alright?'

Her hands still covering her nose and mouth, she struggled to say, 'Fine, my lovely. I'm fine. I just might need a bit of assistance.' And as she spoke, great bubbles of blood started to leak between her fingers.

I ran to the door but couldn't leave the room as Philip, now standing, was swaying and shaking his head and moaning. He looked imploringly at me and then glanced around frantically as if looking for an escape route. Any minute now I feared he would leap through the window in the style of Starsky and Hutch and end up in the hospital car park three floors below.

'Hello!' I shouted urgently down the corridor and stepped out of the room. 'Hello? We need some help in here. Hello?' A man in the same blue robes and white clogs stuck his head curiously out of the next-door room.

'What is it?' he said.

'It's Leslie-Ann. There's been an accident. I can't leave the room because I'm in charge of Philip Johnston and he's very distressed and I can't leave him.'

The man stalked past me into the room. 'Good God! What on earth has been going on?' He threw himself on the floor next to Leslie-Ann. She now had a huge wad of blood-soaked NHS tissue stuck to her face.

'It's alright, Graham. Honestly I'm fine, I just can't seem to stop the bleeding.'

Graham pulled her up and led her out of the room, leaving a trail of blood spots that hit the floor with a splat.

'I'm so sorry,' I kept saying. 'He was just very frightened. I think he panicked. He wouldn't hurt anybody for the world.' I shouted after them, 'Do you want us to wait?'

'No!' barked Graham, leaving Philip and I looking at each other, neither of us quite sure what had just happened or what to do next. Eventually, I put his shoes and socks back on, grabbed his arm and frog-marched him back through the chiropody department. Quite a crowd of people was waiting now and having just seen the bleeding Leslie-Ann being led away, they looked at us with cold fear in their eyes.

'I don't know what I'm going to say to Denise. I'm going to have to tell her because the hospital will probably write to her. What were you thinking of? That poor girl . . .'

We were sitting in the hospital canteen. I was eating a ham sandwich that tasted of cardboard with a hint of fish and drinking a cup of cold tea the colour of a ginger nut.

Philip was calmer now and sat looking unmoved, with his hands in his lap and a sandwich made of stiff, shiny cheese on a hospital-green plate in front of him.

'They won't let you come back now, will they? Your feet'll never be fixed and they must be so sore. Apart from anything else it's just such a wasted opportunity! Honestly, Philip, what I'm supposed to be teaching you is how to live away from Clifton Avenue, so that maybe in the future you can have your own life and do things independently. That's never going to happen if you go about breaking the noses of people who are trying to help you, is it?'

I didn't know if he was taking any of this in – he was gazing at the till machines – but I was on a roll.

'Can you imagine what Denise is going to say?' I couldn't explain that this was our last outing together and that I'd hoped we'd have been in and out in no time and now would be walking along arm in arm and deciding whether to go to the zoo or the aquarium. And I couldn't explain that a small stupid part of me had hoped that maybe if the trip had been an unqualified success Denise might have rethought her decision. He'd never once given me cause so much as to raise my voice to him, but today, and I think with good reason, I was furious with him. However, no matter how much I banged on, his expression just registered boredom and distraction.

'She wouldn't have hurt you. What did you think she was going to do? She's an expert. She was bending over backwards to be kind and gentle. If she'd been horrid to you I could have understood – well, it still would have been a terrible thing to do but at least I . . .' I could only see Philip's face in profile as it was turned away from me towards the till, but when I stopped to draw breath, I realized that his eyes were red and I saw a tear leak out and run down his left cheek.

I ran round to the other side of the table. 'Oh don't, Philip. Please. I know you didn't mean to. I know it was a mistake. Who cares what bloody Denise says? We'll ring the chiropody department now and check that Leslie-Ann is OK. I'm sure she is.' I scrabbled to find my mobile. 'Come on, cheer up, we'll get your feet sorted even if I have to rip off those toenails with my own teeth.'

Very awkwardly, he lowered his head a foot and a half and put it on my chest. I put my hand in his hair and gave his great big head a stroke, still clutching my mobile.

'What are we going to do with you?' I said gently. We seemed to have attracted the attention of most of the other diners, who were having a good stare. I gave the top of his head a kiss.

I eventually got through to the chiropody department and a very sharp woman said that Leslie-Ann had been sent home but that it didn't look like any long-term damage had been done. This and the tea raised my spirits significantly.

It was still only 11.30. If this really was going to be the last time Philip and I would be able to do something officially together, then I thought that we ought to make the most of it. My shift finished at 3 o'clock, nobody at Clifton Avenue knew when we were due back and Rob had given the distinct impression that if I wanted to take Philip to Disney World and back he'd cover for me.

'Come on,' I said, 'I'm going to take you to the pictures.' Sod the bus, I thought, and flagged down a black cab. 'Whiteleys, please,' I told the driver and we set off; for some reason I was suddenly feeling very happy – as if we were bunking off double maths. After such a disastrous morning it seemed imperative that we turn things around.

We got to the cinema and one of the films looked like it would fit the bill. It was an animated kids' thing about space and so I thought it would be fairly innocuous. We bought our tickets but still had ninety minutes to wait until it started, so we went into Marks & Spencer and then Gap. Thanks to the improved diet at Clifton Avenue, Philip's clothes were now beginning to hang off him. In both shops we had nice assistants who took us to the XXXL sections, but Philip did not engage. In the end I bought him two pairs of navy blue cords – trying them on seemed a step too far – but Philip was agitated and even as we stood in the queue I was reassuring him that he didn't have to wear them if he didn't want to. Next to the tills was a display of belts. I grabbed a brown leather one; I thought Philip probably needed a belt more than new trousers for the time being. As I stood holding it, his hand rested on mine and to my surprise he was holding a rather jaunty blue belt.

'Do you want this one?' I asked. 'Do you want the blue one instead?'

He pretended not to hear me and continued to gaze at the ceiling.

'You sly dog – tell me you want the blue one and I'll buy it,' I said. He didn't look at me, so I pulled his chin down to face me and looked into his eyes. 'Say "Rachel, I would like the blue belt please." And if you can do that we'll buy it. We'll buy six! It's your money not mine that will be paying for it so the colour is your choice, but you must tell me that you want it.'

He looked pained and waited a minute before saying, 'Here, puss!' very loudly and rather camply. We got a couple of looks from startled shoppers.

It was our turn to pay. A miserable cow behind us in the queue looked irritable and huffed a bit, so I stepped away from the tills, dragged Philip with me and waited. 'Say "Rachel, I would like the blue belt."'

Philip shook his head, rocked to and fro and then looked at his feet. He became totally still and we waited in silence.

'Come on,' I pleaded with him, 'I know you can.'

Eventually, still looking resolutely at the floor, he said

quickly, 'Keep 'em up, Phil. Keep 'em up . . . get the blue one, mate.'

'The blue one! An excellent choice,' I said, wacking him on the arm delightedly. 'Let's get the bloody blue one.' And with that we joined the queue again behind the cow and Philip laughed and made a noise like a whale searching for its young.

We still had a while to wait, so I took Philip into Starbucks. After the turn of events at the hospital, I was aware that in taking him to the pictures I was running the risk that he might freak out and start taking bites out of the usherettes, but there was also the chance that he might just love it, and the risk was well worth taking. Buoyed up by the blue-belt success, I couldn't wait.

I stood up to get us some tea when my phone went. It was Miss Emma from the school office.

'Hello, Mrs Bidewell?'

'Yes, hello, is everything OK?'

'Well, I'm just ringing because I've got Alec here in the office, and I'm afraid he's not feeling too bright.'

'Oh right. Could I have a quick word with him?'

'Yes, of course. Alec, it's your mum.'

I waited and then a little, weak voice came on the line trying to sound chipper. 'Hello, Mum.'

'Hi, darling, what's wrong?'

'I just really feel like I'm going to throw up.'

'Have you been feeling sick all morning?'

'Yes, I was nearly sick after breakfast.'

'Why did you come to school?'

'Dad's really busy at work and Deborah's gone to Bishop's Stortford so I came in. I honestly did feel OK.'

'Well, don't worry. I'm working but I'll come and get you.'

'I didn't know whether to call Dad or you. Do you think I should call Dad?'

I was thrown. What was the etiquette here? When the child of separated parents is ill, who does he call first? Alec didn't live with me any more but I was his mum and surely when you're sick you need your mum.

'What do you want to do?' I asked.

'I want you to come and get me.' Thank you. Thank you, God.

'Then I will ... And I'll call Dad, so don't worry.' I would have to go and get Alec and take Philip with me. Not ideal. But fine. Then I'd take Philip back to Clifton Avenue and concentrate on Alec.

I rang Dom.

'Hello? Dominic Bidewell.' He said.

'Dom, it's me.' You *know* that, my name's on your phone. 'Look the school just rang and Alec isn't well. I'm going over to pick him up but he's worried that you don't know.'

'OK, Rach. Don't worry. Either Deborah or I will go and get him.'

'There's no need. The school rang me and –'

'They should have known to call me now. Just tell him

to sit tight and Deborah or I will come and get him. He was perfectly fit to go to school this morning –'

'Well, obviously not. Anyway, Deborah's in Bishop's Stortford, isn't she? I've told him I'm on my way now. I'm only in Bayswater. I'll call you later and let you know how he is.'

'It's probably only a sick bug, Rachel, I'll get him. I'm leaving now.'

'No, I'm on my way.' I switched my phone off, grabbed my bag and then Philip and ran. I was nearest. I'd get there first.

I felt elated. Alec was two boys now: mature, urbane Alec with Dom and Deborah, who was allowed to stay up until 10 p.m., and *my* Alec, the same as he'd always been, less mature, making fewer demands on himself and just a boy. Now that he was sick, he was my Alec again. Anyway, I knew exactly what Dom would do with Alec and that would be to take him back to work and make him sit in the office until Dom was ready to go home.

Philip and I burst out into Queensway and a cab was just hurtling past. 'Taxi!' I yelled so loudly that half the street turned round to see who had such a great pair of lungs. 'St Joseph's School in Blythe Road?' The cabbie nodded. We gently drove off and continued at a moderate pace until we joined the back of a long line of waiting traffic. I leant forward and knocked on the partition. 'We're in a hurry. My son's ill.' The cabbie nodded and rose to the challenge. He swung the cab round at gut-wrenching speed and we shot off in the opposite direction and then took every back way and short cut he knew.

We arrived at the school ten minutes later. 'Wait here,' I said to the driver. I had hoped to leave Philip in the car but both men looked decidedly uncomfortable so I yanked Philip out and onto the road. I galloped up the school steps, with Philip lumbering behind in a state of high confusion. As I rang the bell, I saw Dom's car crawl past; he was looking for a parking space.

'Rachel Bidewell,' I panted into the speaker by the door, squinting up and grinning into the camera.

The door sprang open automatically and we ran down the entire length of an echoing school corridor with Philip still holding my hand. Then we ran out of the fire doors and across the Lower School playground, turned right at the boys' lavatories, left at the library, along the Reception corridor past the gym, and right again into the school office. There was Alec, looking waxy and pale on a chair next to Miss Emma, the school secretary.

'Hello!' I said breathlessly. 'How's the patient?'

Alec's face lit up and with that look I knew I'd done the right thing. Relief spread from his chin to his ears and the ends of his hair. I'd keep that look, file it away and the next time I doubted myself or my ability to do the right thing by him, I'd dust if off and remember that I was still his mother and that I knew best.

'This is Philip,' I said, remembering that at any minute

Dom was going to burst in and ruin everything. 'Come on, Alec, I've got a cab waiting outside.'

Alec and Miss Emma looked a bit alarmed at my hectic, breathless state and at the weird stranger whose hand I was holding. However, they seemed to appreciate that there was a sense of urgency and Alec grabbed his bag and we ran.

We raced back across the playground and burst through the fire doors. I looked back and saw Dom coming squinting into the playground by the upper-school door, and asking the caretaker the way to the office. He thought he could be mother and father to Alec but he didn't even know his way around the school. This was classified information for mothers only, who knew their way blindfolded from the myriad times they had collected a sickly child, or picked up tickets to the carol concert, or dropped off a form for a school trip or rummaged around in the lost-property bin. Ha!

As the cab pulled away I got Alec and Philip comfy on the back seat and hovered on one of the pull-down ones. Looking out of the back window I saw Dom emerge out of the main doors still looking lost and livid. I felt triumphant, euphoric . . . until I looked again at Alec.

I reached for his hand and said, 'Are you feeling awful?' He nodded. 'We'll get you home. We just have to drop Philip and that should only take ten minutes.'

Marlene's phone was switched off so I gave Mel a quick ring and she said that she'd pick Luke and Jess up for me. Then with typical thoughtfulness and generosity she casually offered to give them tea so that I could concentrate on looking after Alec, and said she'd drop them back later.

Philip was looking at Alec with a broad grin on his face. He seemed absolutely delighted to meet him. I had never introduced the children to any of the residents but I was completely confident that Alec would be cool.

'I've told Alec all about you, Philip, so he knows you're trouble.'

Philip chuckled delightedly and then he leant conspiratorially over to Alec and whispered, 'Pictures.'

'Oh no,' I said. 'We can't go now because –'

But I was interrupted. Alec had gone green and said, 'Sorry, I think we're going to have to stop.'

We did and Alec slithered out of the cab and threw up violently into a drain at the side of the road. As he leant over, his whole skinny body continued to wretch until finally there was nothing more to bring up. I rubbed his back and gave him an ancient tissue from my pocket. We found a wall to sit on and for a minute he went limp and let me prop him up with my right arm around his shoulders. With the taxi fare now in the region of a thousand pounds, I hoped that we could drop Philip off really quickly and get Alec home to bed. However, after a few minutes, he blew his nose and straightened up.

'Better out than in,' he said with a grin and all the

colour seemed to have come back into his cheeks. 'That did the trick. Where to now?'

I looked up from where I was using the same poor tissue to remove a couple of splashes of sick from my shoes. I made him do a little walk up and down the street, taking deep breaths before getting back into the car. He was suddenly very chatty and animated and seemed OK.

As we got back into the taxi, the long-suffering driver asked me where we were headed. I turned to Alec: 'You don't fancy going to see a film, do you?'

We arrived with about three minutes to spare. We shuffled into our seats in the gloom. We had the pick of the place as there were only three other people who wanted to see *The Space Adventurers* at 13.55 on a Thursday afternoon in Bayswater. Surprisingly enough, they were pensioners.

Philip sat in between Alec and me. I kept leaning round Philip's tummy to whisper, 'Are you *sure* you're alright?' to Alec and he would just nod and say, 'I'm absolutely fine! Honest.'

We sat through a couple of adverts and then it was finally time for the film to begin. 'It's starting,' I whispered and Philip clapped his hands delightedly and made a whinnying noise like an ecstatic colt in a field. The other three cinema-goers looked around a bit startled and Alec sniggered.

I was sure that the tickets had said Screen 2 but when the black censor's card came up it was for Steven Spielberg's

*The Color Purple.* We had wandered into the Thursday Film Club. Alec leant over and gave me a puzzled look and I gestured for him to get up and make his way out. He did, but Philip didn't.

'Come on,' I whispered urgently. 'This isn't the film we wanted to see. This is the wrong one.'

In a good-natured but resolute way he shook his head and smiled.

'I don't think you'll enjoy this one,' I said as the music started swirling and the opening credits began with little black girls running through cotton fields. I tried to heave him up but he wouldn't budge. Alec was chortling again.

'Come on.' I said to Alec. 'Give me a hand.' But we couldn't get Philip to move. Alec gave me an 'Oh well' shrug and so we gave up and sat back down to watch nearly three hours of black suppression, lesbianism, sexual abuse and depravity in the 1930s American Deep South.

I'd forgotten how good it was. I started to sniffle a little about twenty minutes in and never looked back. Towards the end, when Celie is reunited with her children all the way from Africa, the three of us were so transfixed that the cinema could have burnt down around us and we wouldn't have noticed. At one point Philip reached out for my hand and for Alec's and the three of us watched the reunion in a joined-up row.

When the lights came up we were exhausted. How much Philip had understood was irrelevant, he had loved it, and knowing this gave me a surge of the sort of uncomplicated pleasure I hadn't known for ages.

We got back to Clifton Avenue at about 5 o'clock. It was teatime and Alec seemed genuinely interested and excited to be there and so I said we'd stay and help with tea. Plus Rob was working and I was really looking forward to seeing him. Over the last few occasions that we'd worked together – his birthday bingo night, his defence of me at the staff meeting – something had shifted in my attitude towards him and at work I didn't feel secure or myself if he wasn't there. More worryingly, I was beginning to look for signs of how he felt about me.

I thought I ought to give Dom a call and tell him that I'd keep Alec for the night. When I switched my phone on I realized that he had been trying to get me and I felt guilty. As I dialled the number I went into the laundry room and shut the door. The first thing Dom said was, 'Where have you been?'

I took a deep breath and said, 'Look, Alec is a hundred per cent better. I took him to the pictures with one of the residents from work.'

'You're kidding,' he said.

'Give me some credit, Dom, he's absolutely fine. We've actually had a lovely afternoon and now he's helping me give the residents some tea.'

'Well I've got something on but Deborah will come and pick him up. Clifton Avenue, isn't it? What number?'

'There's no need. He's really, really happy. I'll just take him home with me and drop him at school tomorrow.'

'It's not necessary. Deborah can come and get him and –'

'Listen, Dom, you've won. You've got him. I haven't made a fuss, I've respected your wishes and his. But just for today he wants to be with me and I can't tell you how great that feels. Let him just do this night with me.'

'No, it isn't fair on him.'

'Look, leave Alec with me for the night and you can see him tomorrow. Please, Dom, he's not been well and it's what he wants.'

The phone went dead.

The door opened and Rob walked in. To my surprise, my heart did a little gambol. 'Everything OK?' he said gently.

I nodded. 'My son's here.'

'Which one?'

'Alec, the biggest one. I'm just going to hang around and help with tea and then we'll be out of your hair.'

'No hurry,' he said. 'Stay as long as you can.'

'Thanks,' I said and looked at my feet awkwardly.

'How did it go with Twinkletoes?' Rob asked.

I told him all about my morning at the hospital and as the full horror of it came back to me I thought he might be appalled. But instead he threw his head back and laughed and laughed and I felt a hundred times better.

Rob returned to the office and I went to find Alec, who

had joined Theresa and was tucking into a huge bowl of spaghetti bolognese.

'Is that wise?' I said. 'I don't want you bringing it all up again in five minutes.'

'Leave him alone, Mum. He's having a chinwag with his Auntie Theresa, aren't you, sweed'eart?' she boomed and Alec nodded happily.

'He's as handsome as a fox, isn't he, Rachel?' said Sophie. 'You'd better watch that one.'

'Are you mentally handicapped?' Stewart asked Alec.

Alec looked nonplussed and then said simply, 'No, I don't think so.'

'Me either,' said Theresa.

'You bloody are!' snorted Stewart and the two of them were off again. Alec rolled his eyes at me as if he'd sat at this table a thousand times. He was very relaxed in this lovely, crazy company and I was so proud of him.

I left him to it and walked through to the office. Lucy was just coming out. 'I've just met your boy,' she said.

I looked puzzled. 'Alec's eating tea in the dining room,' I said, just as the door to the office opened and Denise's stout, sullen son, scuttled out.

'I've finished on the computer,' he mumbled in the voice of a young Mr Toad. 'I've switched it off.' Then he waddled off down the corridor and you could hear his thighs rubbing together in his school trousers.

When he was out the door, I turned to Lucy. 'That's

not my son!' I said in a shocked whisper. 'That's Denise's boy, isn't it?'

'Thank goodness for that, Rob said your son was in and I thought –' she said, starting to laugh.

Rob joined us. 'That little shite's been on the computer for hours,' he said. 'Denise obviously thinks that his school project takes priority over any work we might have to do. Apparently, his printer's broken. And not so much as a please or thank you – he never opened his miserable wee mouth. I offered him a biscuit and he looked at me like I was a paedophile!'

Lucy had got the giggles. I realized that I'd never seen her really laugh. She brought her hand up to cover her mouth but couldn't disguise the fact that she was laughing.

I took them through to introduce them to Alec, who was now tucking into some treacle pudding. I was delighted to see him talking to Philip. Both of them had their heads bowed and were looking at something on the table between them. Philip was nodding as if taking in everything Alec was telling him in minute detail about Match Attax cards and the vagaries of collecting them. Alec passed his prize card to Philip for inspection and Philip held out a photograph of Ronaldo surrounded by gold lettering for me to see and exclaimed excitedly, 'Fancy pants!' This made Alec crack up. He'd grown out of Match Attax ages ago and my guess was that Dom hadn't realized this and was buying them for him again to aid the transition.

The doorbell went and Theresa shot up to answer it.

'That's more like it,' said Rob as he shook Alec firmly by the hand, staring into his eyes intently. 'It's a pleasure to meet you, Alec, a real pleasure.'

'SOMEBODY TO SEE YOU!' roared Theresa. We all looked over to the doorway and standing there, looking awkward and unhappy, was Deborah.

I felt myself go scarlet. Alec's face dropped and he looked at me nervously.

'Your dad said you needed a lift,' said Deborah weakly.

I wanted to say, No he doesn't, he's fine, he's staying with me, just for tonight, just for this evening.

'What do you want to do, darling?' I said. 'Whatever is fine by me.'

'I'd better go,' he said, unable to meet my eye. He'd gone limp and looked ill again.

'That's absolutely fine. Come on, we'll get your stuff.'

'I'll wait in the car,' said Deborah and we both pretended she hadn't spoken.

Once in the office I handed Alec his school bag and gave him a hug.

'Sorry, Mum, it's just that Dad will be expecting me and I don't want to cause any trouble. I just feel . . .'

He ran out of steam and I hugged him again and nearly broke all his ribs. 'Don't worry, darling. We've had a good afternoon, haven't we? And I'm really glad that you've met Philip and all the people I work with. You go off now and I'll see you next weekend.'

'OK. Don't come out.'

'No, I'll stay here.' I waved him off down the corridor.

I picked up my bag stiffly and put on my coat. I needed to be back in time for Jess and Luke. I thought I might give their baths a miss tonight.

I walked back into the main dining area just as Rob was coming in from the opposite side.

'Did he get off alright?' he asked.

'Yes, fine.'

'Listen, I'm off after tea. Could you use a drink?'

I felt my chest constrict with disappointment; I had to get back for Jess and Luke but I wanted more than anything to go to a pub with Rob. I smiled sadly. 'Yes, I could use a drink, a very big, very alcoholic drink, but I've got to get back for –'

'Yes, of course,' he said quickly. 'Of course.'

'Another time . . .'

'Yes, another time.'

As he watched me walk out he said, 'You know we've got to plan the handover to Scott and how we're going to handle telling Philip.'

I stopped and drooped in the doorway. 'Yes, I know.'

'We're on together on Saturday. Shall we do it then?'

I nodded. 'I'll see you then.'

The next day Dom rang as I was in the kitchen trying to resuscitate the Hoover. Minutes earlier it had started making a strange smell, gasped a little and then, like a heroine from a gothic novel, died in my arms.

My electrical appliances were ganging up on me, I was sure of it.

'You know I came to the school yesterday to get Alec,' he said sourly, 'but you'd already left.'

'Oh, sorry. Did you?'

'I thought you realized I was going to get him.'

'No, sorry, I must have got the wrong end of the stick.'

In my head I could hear Luke saying: 'Liar, liar pants on fire, bogies up the telephone wire.'

'How was he this morning?' I asked.

'Fine, I think he must have eaten something.'

Something you or Deborah cooked for him, I thought.

'Look, it just highlights the fact that we really have never sat down and talked through the ground rules of this arrangement. It's still early days, so no one's to blame.'

'Not me,' I snapped stupidly.

'No, not you,' he said irritably, 'not anyone. I feel it would make sense for us all to sit down together and talk through how it's all going to work. Deborah hasn't ever had to look after an eleven-year-old before and I think, understandably, it's all a bit of a mystery to her. Yesterday proved that we need to communicate more efficiently.' He was trying very hard to stay calm but I didn't see why I had to.

'Well, she should have thought of that before she decided she could take him on. Perhaps you both should have asked for my opinion in the first place or for my help, instead of just not giving him a lift home one night.'

'Well that's what we're doing now, Rach.' Dom was endeavouring to keep his temper and I knew deep down that he genuinely wanted to do the right thing.

Then something clicked. 'When you say "all", are you saying that you want you, me and Deborah to sit in a room together and discuss this?'

'Yes, I don't see why –'

'You are joking?'

'I'm thinking what's best for Alec. I think we should put our personal feelings to one side and –'

'No, Dom. Absolutely not. You want me to sit down with you both – with Deborah – and give her instructions on how to care for my son? If she can't cope then just tell her to send him back to where he belongs.'

God! How dare he? Once again he was going to make out that I was the one who didn't have the kids' best interests at heart when he was the one who had walked out on them. When Dom took the moral high ground I felt as if I would kill him, violently, terribly. But as the life-blood ebbed away from him and I stood over him, blunt instrument in hand, I knew his last words would be: 'Now how do you think this is going to be beneficial to the children?'

'If she can't handle it,' I went on, shouting now with the receiver jammed into my neck and pacing around the kitchen as I emptied the rubbish bin, 'it's because she's never had children of her own and if she doesn't know what time football club ends it's because she hasn't stood on the touchline bored out of her skull for the last six years. Or if she doesn't know how the long-division homework should be taught it's because she wasn't at Mr Ashton's "Maths Can Be Fun!" evening in the school hall. If she doesn't know what to say to his friends or what books he should be reading or whether his soap box needs to match his sponge bag, well then perhaps she should have concentrated on having her own family instead of stealing somebody else's husband and son!'

'Have you finished?' asked Dom. 'I think I should tell you that we are in the car. We have rung you to have a civilized conversation about how best to help Alec and we are on the speakerphone . . . Deborah is here with me.'

There was a terrible silence. I screwed my eyes up and hit my forehead with my fist repeatedly, gritting my teeth. 'I'm sorry,' I said, all the vitriol draining out of me. I kicked the Hoover. Then a voice said: 'Rachel, I know that this must be really hard for you, I do understand –'

'Please, Deborah,' I said, 'please. You don't understand. You don't understand anything. Let me give this some thought and, Dom, I'll ring you back.'

I put the phone down and kicked the Hoover again.

I kept forgetting to tell them about the nits.


On Saturday I made sure that I was at work in good time. I felt ill and nervous and sad, dreading what we were going to say to Philip. The children were with Dom and so I had had my usual fretful Friday night and woke up at dawn. I was relieved to be doing the sleepover duty and so wouldn't have to try and fall asleep in an empty house again.

Clifton Avenue was quiet for a Saturday afternoon and to my surprise, Denise was in the office when I walked in.

'Hello Rachel!' she said good-naturedly. 'Fit and raring to go?'

'Absolutely,' I said, dropping my heavy overnight bag like a stone on the carpet. 'But I definitely need tea before I do anything else. Can I get you one?'

'Ooh, yes please,' she said, leaning back on her chair and stretching like a playful cat. 'That would be a life-saver.'

I wandered through to the kitchen and saw Rob and Scott. We all said hello and Scott talked me through what had happened on the previous shift.

'And what are we going to do about Philip?' I said eventually.

'Scott is off at five,' said Rob efficiently, 'so I think it makes sense for the three of us to sit down with him in the next hour or so.'

I felt sick.

'I think he's in his room probably having a snooze, so best we leave him for half an hour.'

I nodded.

'How do you think we should play it?' asked Scott breezily.

Rob looked at me to decide.

'I think I should take the lead,' I said, 'and just be honest, say that as I'm a new member of staff, Denise thinks that it would be better for Scott to be Philip's key worker and stress the positives; that I'll still be around whenever he wants to talk to me, that Scott's a great guy and . . . Oh sod it, I don't know what I'll say but I think I should be the one to say it.'

The others nodded. 'How much do you think he'll take in?' asked Scott.

'I've no idea,' I said, sighing heavily. 'Sometimes I think he has a handle on things and then sometimes I just seem to lose him. We'll have to see . . . and we'll have to tread very carefully.'

Rob said, 'Look, there's too many residents in for me to cover on my own but I think Denise is still in. Maybe if I could persuade her to hang around, you could both take Philip up to the café or something. And Rachel, you could talk through all the things that might make the Big Man anxious; the furniture order, buying new clothes, his feet . . .'

'OK by me,' Scott said and I felt grateful on Philip's behalf.

'I'll ask her.' Rob looked relieved. 'It's a shame there's just too many in for me to cover alone otherwise I would.'

'I know you would,' I said.


It was only 4 o'clock but already it was dark and murky outside. Since I was there for the night, I went around turning all the lights on and saying hello to any of the residents who were around. Finally I remembered I was supposed to be taking Denise a cup of tea and so made it and went to the office. Rob had just got there before me.

'It's fine, Rob, it's already done,' Denise was saying. I felt a jolt of apprehension. Rob's expression was bleak and his jaw tight. 'He's absolutely fine about it. I went to his room just now and I've told Scott to go and have a chat with him. I'm not sure he even knows who his key worker is.' When Rob's expression didn't change she looked a little guilty but covered it up with exasperation and threw her arms in the air. 'Oh, Rachel, there you are. I've told Philip about the changes I've put in place and he's fine with it. Scott's off at five and I really did want to get it sorted today. Too much fuss has been made about this whole thing as it is.'

I stared at her and just couldn't think what to say.

She went on, 'I think now it's done you'll feel a real sense of relief and when the time comes we can really take some time to assign you to someone who is better suited to your level of experience.'

'And he was OK?' I said weakly. 'Are you sure? I think I'd better go and have a word.'

'Please don't,' she said gently but firmly. 'Scott might be up there now and they need time to get to know each other without you poking your nose in. Would you mind starting the drugs run?'

I went over to the drugs cupboard and unlocked it mechanically. Rob said nothing but busied himself with picking up my bag and offering to take it to the sleepover room. As he left I looked at his profile and saw an expression I had never seen him wear before: it was rage. Denise sat at the desk and started to rustle a few papers.

As I sorted the various medicines, my mind raced and my hands shook a little as I dispensed the pills into little paper cups.

Then I became aware of a thudding sound coming from somewhere in the hostel. I stood still and shook my head trying to decipher where exactly it was coming from. It went on, persistent and unnerving. Thud. Thud.

Denise looked up. 'What's that noise?' she asked and I shook my head.

'I don't know. Where's it coming from?' I went out into the corridor and realized that it was coming from upstairs just as Rob came through the fire doors.

'It's coming from Yellow Landing,' he said, puzzled but also concerned. We began to walk and then run towards the staircase. By the time we reached it, the thuds were so loud that we ran up the steps three at a time. Just before we reached the top Scott came through the fire doors.

'It's Philip,' he said. 'I can't stop him. I'm going to tell Denise.'

'Oh Jesus.' I grabbed the banister and yanked myself up the remaining steps as fast as I could and then ran onto Yellow Landing. The thudding was now very loud. Philip's door was open and he was standing in the doorway hitting his head again and again, brutally, violently, against the frame.

'Don't, Philip. Stop it,' I pleaded and, running to him, I grabbed his arm and tried to pull him away. 'Philip, stop it! Stop it now!' But he just carried on as a livid bruise spread across his forehead and he began to bleed.

'Philip, it's me, it's Rachel. You're hurting yourself. It's going to be OK but you must stop it. Please, Philip.' I was panicking now but he was unmoved, unseeing. I put my hand up to his face to try and claw it away from the door but he was so strong it made no difference.

'Come on, mate,' said Rob and he went to grab an arm and tear him away from the door. But Philip pushed Rob over and sent him spiralling back, falling and hitting his head on the bedhead. Still he carried on. I would never have believed him capable of such self-destructive fury.

All the time I was saying, 'Philip, stop it. Please stop it. You're hurting yourself. You've hurt Rob. You must stop it.' But it was as if he was deaf.

Denise came running along the corridor. Her voice sounded frightened and hysterical. 'He needs sedating – I've called an ambulance. This is exactly the reason why it was totally inappropriate for you to be given responsibility for Philip in the first place. I saw this coming!'

Rob sprang to his feet. 'This is your doing, Denise. Your doing!'

'Not now, ' I said. 'Not now. This isn't helping!' I was still pulling on Philip's arm and now blood was beginning to splatter over my face and shirt. I had an idea that if I could just get a duvet over Philip's great grizzly head, I could stop him hurting himself. Thud went his forehead again. The others looked at me as if I was insane as I grabbed his bedding and threw it over him.

I managed to grab both his hands and he just stood still. We all watched him frozen, too frightened to say anything in case it set him off again.

'Would you like to come and sit down with me?' I said, pulling the duvet down from Philip's face. 'Perhaps Rob can get us both a cup of tea.' He didn't move.

I tried to lead him over to the bed but he didn't budge and when Scott stepped forward to try and help me move him, he went to start again, so we all froze and I stood gripping Philip's hands for what seemed like an age.

Other residents were coming out now and looking on in horror. Rob told them to go back to their rooms and stay there. They did so meekly, only too pleased to avert their gaze.

To all our relief we heard a siren. 'Thank God,' said Scott and ran down to the street to direct the ambulance to us.

Within seconds two ambulance men flew up the stairs and began asking questions.

'What's his name?'

'Philip. Philip Johnston.'

'Alright, Philip. Come on now, mate, we need to get you to calm down. Has he consumed any alcohol?'

'No, definitely not.'

'Any drugs that you're aware of?'

'No. None.'

Almost immediately they administered a sedative. Philip's whole body went limp. The ambulance men tried to hold him steady but he sank to his knees in slow motion and began to cry. Finally, he toppled onto the carpet and lay there like a great felled beast.

I got down on my knees next to him and began to stroke his big head. His eyes were rolling, huge and frightened, and I felt myself begin to cry too, out of pity for this dear, sweet man. I tried to comfort him until the paramedics moved me out of the way so that they could see to his wound.

The ambulance men had paperwork to be filled in and forms to sign. They said that Philip would be groggy when he woke up but that that shouldn't be for a while. We were to give him painkillers for his wound and to see that it stayed clean. They recommended that we take him to A&E to get his head checked out, but when I explained he was frightened of hospitals, they were understanding and gave me a leaflet on head injuries and what to look out for. They said to keep checking him through the night

When they left, Rob, Scott and I went round the residents to calm them down and reassure them that Philip was fine. When we got back to the office, Denise was there. She picked up her handbag and made to leave but she stopped in the doorway and turned to us all.

'I'll call in tomorrow morning and see how he is. We'll have to do some serious thinking about this on Monday.' She was very shaken and her mouth twitched – was it remorse? 'Rob,' she said quietly, 'I hold you responsible for this. It was negligent to have let Rachel take charge of Philip's care. I don't blame you, Rachel, you weren't to know. But as I say, we will have to do some very serious talking on Monday. We will also have to work out what we will say to his social worker.' She suddenly seemed to find the resolve to leave and said almost casually through a sigh, 'You should just be grateful, Rob, that he's no family to speak of. Otherwise you'd have to justify your actions to them.'

Rob looked incredulously from me to Denise. 'What?'

'Please, don't raise your voice to me,' she said calmly.

'No, Denise! You – you! – need to think about justifying your actions here, not me.'

'We'll talk about this on Monday.' She spoke slowly and deliberately.

'You know full well what's happened here tonight is a direct result of what you did. Of you having no thought or sensitivity in the way you handled things. Of your total . . .' Rob was unable to express himself. He was paralysed with frustration. Finally he went on: 'You just charged in because you wanted to get away and you wanted to show us that you were boss. You've no understanding of how Philip works. You've no understanding of how this whole thing could have been handled with empathy, with love –'

Denise snorted.

'Yes, love! You've no bloody love for any of the people here and you can't go on treating them – and us – like this. You can't even see what you've done tonight, can you? You have no idea. I don't know if you're trying to pass the buck or whether you genuinely believe that I'm to blame – I don't know what's worse.'

'Rob, I'm going to leave before you say anything more that you're going to regret. I will see you on Monday and we will talk this through rationally and –'

'My only regret is that I haven't said any of this earlier. God knows what we've done to Philip this evening. And I wouldn't blame Rachel for a minute if she walked out tonight and never came back. We finally get a great member of staff who is brilliant for this place, who genuinely enriches the lives of the people living here – which by the way, Denise, is what our job is – and all you see is a threat and all you can do is undermine her and humiliate her and it makes me realize that as long as you are here, this place is doomed and I can't fight you any more. I'm out of here.'

Rob pushed past Denise and stalked off down the corridor.

Denise was ashen. 'I think that everyone needs to calm down,' she said, trying to collect herself and then she picked up her handbag, put it on the desk and pretended to search for something in it as she regained her composure.

She found a tissue and did a little sniff into it. Finally she left, but then in the corridor she must have bumped into Malcolm and I heard him say innocently, 'What's all the shouting about?'

I stepped into the corridor to see if he was OK. In trying to get past him, Denise had managed to get her handbag buckle caught in one of Malcolm's sagging belt loops and the two of them were doing a frantic little pas de deux as Denise desperately tried to free herself and leave.

Not realizing I was in the doorway, she turned on him, whispering nastily so that no one would hear. 'Get out of my way, Malcolm! Mind your own business and get back to your bed.' Her neck had gone red and blotchy. 'And look at the state of you. Do your flies up will you and look at your sweater, you're filthy.' Having got her handbag free she gave Malcolm a nasty shove to get him out of the way. 'Oh get out of my sight, man, I can't bear to look at you. You make me sick!'

Malcolm looked as if he'd been slapped. He opened his mouth to speak but Denise hadn't finished.

'And don't tell me you'll go and tell your mum, because if you do I'll tell her a few things about you you wouldn't want her to know. I know all about you, Malcolm Brewer. Mucky magazines in your locker. I've seen them.'

I walked forward and put my arm around the horrified Malcolm. Denise saw me for the first time and for a moment looked stunned but then widened her eyes as if to say 'What?' and walked out.

'It's alright, mate,' I said. 'Let's get you back to bed.' It was true he had one rather old copy of *Nuts* in his locker. He'd bought it because it contained pictures of one of the girls from *Coronation Street* in a bra.

I sat with Malcolm for a few minutes in his room to see that he was OK and he started showing me photographs of a holiday in Margate the residents had been on years ago. There was one of him and Denise – he was grinning with his thumbs up to the camera and she had her head thrown back and was laughing. I knew from her expression that the laughter wasn't kind.

'That Denise,' said Malcolm. 'We go back a long way. She'd do anything for me, she would. She's a wonderful girl.' His voice was quiet and his smile unsure.

For the first time I began to wonder how Denise had got the job in the first place. Presumably she was highly qualified and extremely reliable when it came to keeping on budget. Scott had inferred that she was sleeping with someone high up in the council but that hardly seemed likely. Surely you wouldn't gift a house, a car and the responsibility for all these vulnerable residents in return for the odd bony shag with Denise. Or perhaps you would. Maybe it was the house she'd wanted. She was divorced with the one stout, sulky son, but he never came into the office apart from that one time or interacted in any way with the residents or with us. Perhaps a roof over both their heads had been the attraction of the job.

I would have forgiven her anything if she had been good with the residents, but I could see now that she treated them all like annoying children. How on earth had she ever decided that social work was her vocation? Another mystery. When my mother was in hospital the chemotherapy had made all her hair fall out and a woman came round with a catalogue, the NHS wig specialist. She was bored and unhelpful. She gave no advice about what models might suit my mother and made no effort to cheer her up at all. She said that the wigs would itch and that many people opted not to wear them at all, and you got the impression that she was urging my mother to do the same so that she wouldn't have to bother with her. My mother was appalled, and as she never had been the sort of person to throw a Gypsy Rose headscarf around her head, in the end we went to a wig-maker that we found in the Yellow Pages, one who specialized in theatrical wigs but made them for cancer patients as a sideline for next to nothing because she was kind. After my mother died, Luke had stolen the wig, thinking that it had huge comedy potential, but thankfully I think it always reminded him of his beloved Granny, and so to this day it was lurking at the back of his pants drawer.

I remember thinking that, for the right person, being the expert who advises sick people about their wigs would have been such a lovely job, one where you could have done so much good. Someone who'd been positive and reassuring, and who'd told my mother that all was not lost would have meant the world to her, given her a bit of hope. She needed to be told that how she looked was still important, and that a bit of vanity, after all she'd been through, should be relished. And if she had, we would have all gone home – my mother, me *and* the wig specialist – with a warm glow. But no, this woman had chosen to see her job as depressing and boring and too much like hard work. I felt the same way about Denise: if she had enjoyed being around the residents and derived satisfaction from caring for them and giving them the best quality of life that she possibly could, then she'd have loved her job and her life and she'd have been a better person. Instead, I think she saw herself as a terrible martyr, caring for all these ghastly people and fending off their ghastly families, and she was bitter and miserable as a result. She managed to be positively captivating around anyone from head office and was thought of as a saint by all her associates there. Unfortunately, she didn't think the residents worthy of such charms. Why hadn't she taken a job which would have suited her more? A dentist, perhaps, or a traffic warden or taxidermist?

I really wanted to find Rob but he had disappeared. I searched all around the building not knowing which was the more painful, seeing him distraught or the thought of him leaving. Scott was in the kitchen fixing himself a sandwich and said he would stay and see if Rob turned up and if not would finish his shift for him – out of character for Scott, but even he had been moved by the day's events. We did the final rounds together and eventually he left.

I went into Philip's bedroom. He was sleeping soundly. I tried to wake him briefly as I had been advised and to my relief he lifted his head up, stared at me vacantly and immediately went back to sleep.

I didn't want to leave him. I didn't want him to wake up and feel the pain from his head. The painkillers would wear off in the night and what would he do? Would he wake up and remember what had happened? I decided to stay with him. I went to the staff bedroom and heaved my mattress off the bed and down the corridor. Once I'd put it next to Philip's bed I went back for my bedding, my nightwear and my toothbrush. I made up the bed as quietly as I could and began to get changed when I heard the clunk of the fire door in the corridor. I looked round and it was Rob. He stood in the doorway, unsure whether to come into the small dark room.

'What are you doing?' he whispered.

'I'm going to sleep in here. I don't want him to wake up and not –'

'I'm sorry,' he interrupted. 'I messed up.'

We stood looking at each other, me feeling exposed in just a long T-shirt, big socks and no pyjama bottoms. I didn't know what to say.

'I can't stay on here,' he said eventually, still whispering.

'You can. On Monday you can say you're –'

'I can't say sorry because I meant every word.'

I couldn't be half-dressed for this conversation and so as I talked I wrapped Philip's dressing-gown around me. At any other time Rob would have laughed out loud but he seemed not to notice.

'Oh, Jesus, Rob,' I said. 'What'll happen to this place if you go? Anything good in here comes from you. It isn't so terrible. The residents aren't unhappy.' I couldn't bear the thought of him going.

'No,' he said sadly. 'They tick along. We all tick along. We should re-christen this place the Good Ship Status Quo.'

'If it ain't broke . . .' I remarked weakly and immediately regretted it.

Rob looked at me angrily and his brow creased with incomprehension that I should be so stupid. 'But that's not our job! Our job is to push the residents, inspire them, empower them, make them be the best they can possibly be and, God forbid, enjoy life a little. Every shift we should be pushing a boulder up a hill and instead we sleepwalk through the day. All day. Every day.'

'I don't! Lucy doesn't! And you're by far the best person here.'

'But imagine this place with a bit of energy and colour and commitment. Last year Theresa's mum and dad did a bit of fundraising. Just a barbecue for some friends with a few raffle tickets and a couple of quid for a hot dog. Do you know what Denise did with the money?'

I shook my head.

233

'Bought that new headed paper for the office. Absolutely legitimate, head office had refused to update ours but . . . Jesus. What we could have done with a couple of hundred quid. We could have had a day out, got a DVD player that worked, a new bloody bingo set, anything! It should be so different here and I'm ashamed that as the deputy I've let it all slide. This whole thing with poor Philip has been a wake-up call. He may never come back from this.'

'Denise made a mistake,' I said hopelessly. 'We made a mistake in not talking to him earlier.'

'Oh come on, you know as well as I do, this is far more than Denise making a simple mistake. There's a phrase, I think it's Russian: "The fish always rots from the head down." Denise'll stand by and see this place stagnate – along with all the other Philips we have the privilege to care for – and as long as the books balance at the end of the day nobody will say anything and so it goes on.'

'Well she is efficient, this place does run smoothly. I suppose I just didn't realize she was so . . .' I petered out.

Rob stared at me miserably and then without warning stepped forward and took my hand and then dropped it almost immediately. An awkward, joyless gesture. 'I wanted you to understand why I've let things get like this. It really matters to me that you know I didn't mean for this to happen to Philip.'

'I know that. Of course I know that,' I said.

'When I first came here, five years ago, Denise had breast cancer.' Rob's glance fell to his feet. 'She was in the middle of radiotherapy. She was tired and sick and on her own with a little boy. I really admired how she coped. It went on for months and months and she was pretty magnificent if I'm honest. I think I've been making excuses for her ever since.'

'Is she well now?' I asked.

'Completely.' He rubbed his forehead with his thumb and forefinger in an effort to clear his head and stave off exhaustion. 'I thought I understood what made her tick but –'

'You can't blame yourself. She's your boss.'

He put up his hand wearily to silence me. 'I'll see you Monday,' he mumbled and leant forward and kissed me very gently on the cheek. His temple lingered against mine for a second and then he left. I thought for a moment about running after him but I couldn't leave Philip, and besides, what would I say? A middle-aged crush seemed idiotic after all that had gone on that night.

I lay awake and wondered about Denise being so ill. I thought about Alec in his new bed and Jess and Luke. I thought about the first time I'd met Dom – compared it with the slow-burn attraction I was realizing I felt for Rob. I thought about my mother and Deborah and Marlene and my mind raced and raced. Most of all I thought about Philip and how on earth I was going to make sense of all this for him. Eventually, I made a cup of tea and sat staring at him, waking him every hour or so to make sure he was OK.

Philip slept in for most of the next morning. I'd taken tea in to him but he was still very sleepy. The wound on his head looked sore and I gave him some more of the pain-killers but he appeared not to remember what had occurred.

Sunday is a big laundry day for most of the residents and they need a lot of help, so Scott and I passed the morning shift quietly and efficiently but without much reference to the night before. I put my head around Philip's door as I left but he was dozing with his face to the wall.

Once I got home I spent the afternoon worrying about Philip and wishing I'd stayed. I wanted to ring Rob just to see that he was OK and to try and persuade him to stay. When I did finally pluck up the courage and find his home number, there was just an answer machine with a woman's voice on it and although I left a message he didn't ring back. I rang Clifton Avenue and was told by Scott that Philip was watching television and had eaten a good lunch.

Fortunately Marlene was out so I just got the uniforms and stuff ready for the week and caught up on some admin. At about 6 o'clock the doorbell went and it was Dom with Luke and Jess. The kids had spent the afternoon making jewellery for me from a kit – some dangly earrings and a matching bracelet and necklace. They were very pleased and proud of their efforts and urged me to try them on immediately with Dom looking on. To be honest it was hard to drum up too much enthusiasm for purple, green and pink homemade clay beads strung inexpertly together on silver string, but I made all the right noises and put them on.

'Deborah helped us because Alec was on the computer,' admitted Luke. 'They were too fiddly to do all by ourselves and the kit was for ten-plus. There's a card too, have you seen the card?'

Indeed there was a card, obviously made by Jess, with glitter and stickers all over it. I opened it up and saw a message written in what I could only assume was Deborah's handwriting: 'To the Best Mummy in the World, Happy Birthday, with Lots and Lots and Lots of Love.' And then all three children had signed the bottom – Jess and Luke in their usual childish scrawl but Alec with an unfamiliar, overly dramatic adult signature that took me by surprise.

'We couldn't wait. Do you like them? Do you really like them?' asked Jess, hopping up and down on one leg because she was desperate for a wee but couldn't bear to tear herself away from the grand trying-on of the birthday gifts.

'Oh they're lovely!' I said with as much conviction as I could muster. It was my birthday the following Tuesday but I had completely forgotten. I couldn't get the clasp on the necklace to do up and with huge awkwardness, Dom offered to help and scooped my hair away from my neck.

He was in such a hurry to bring this unwelcome burst of intimacy to an end that his fingers became like sausages, the clasp got caught in my hair and the whole business seemed to take an age. Finally, I looked down at my chest and patted the necklace with pride. 'That is really, really lovely. Thank you so much.' I kissed both children on the head and they looked suitably pleased with themselves. 'Now come on, let's get you in the bath.'

I turned to let Dom out and as the kids said their good-byes and raced up the stairs Dom said quietly, 'I think that's such a lovely gesture. It's Deborah's way of telling you that what happened in the car the other night was OK and that no matter what happens, you'll always be their mummy. She's no threat to you, I wish you could see that and we could all have a civilized relationship. It's what she wants more than anything.'

'I don't need any reassurance that I *will always be their mummy*. Of course I will. What makes you think I need reassurance? I am their mummy.'

'Yes,' Dom sighed deeply and said patiently, 'and she is just acknowledging through these presents – which she sat and made with the children all afternoon when she could have being doing any number of other things – that she knows that.'

When Dom had first informed me that he was leaving, I remember he said that the reason he had been so attracted to Deborah was because she reminded him of me when I was younger. He'd even taken my hand and squeezed it as he said it and then was taken aback when I didn't take it as some sort of compliment. I felt the same slightly unhinged rage now, as I did then.

'No matter what your personal feelings are,' he went on, 'you must try and put them aside. It's in the kids' interests for us to all get along. It will be so much better for them in the long run if we do.'

I knew that. Of course I knew that. So I just said sadly, 'How's Alec?'

'Good,' said Dom. 'Really good.' And he left.

When the children were in bed I decided to have an early night. I put my new jewellery away – although I was tempted to pop it in an envelope and send it to Deborah with a note saying, 'You bought the kit. You did the work. YOU wear it, and the next time you want to look really smart, Jess will run to find it as the absolute thing that will make your outfit complete and you'll find yourself meeting the Lord Mayor with a lump of Play-Doh bouncing between your breasts.'

I had a bath. But although I was exhausted, I felt restless. Eventually, I went into the boys' bedroom to have a last check on Luke. He was sleeping peacefully and snoring very gently with his mouth ajar. I looked over to Alec's empty bed and the sight of it was unbearable so I climbed in and slept there.

As soon as I arrived at work on Monday I went to find Philip. He was in one of the day rooms watching *This*

*Morning* while fiddling with his felt-tip pens. He rarely seemed to do any drawing but he seemed to like the colours and having something that belonged to him. I watched him from the doorway, methodically taking the tops off the pens and then replacing them one by one. He looked calm and relaxed.

'Hello,' I said, getting down on my haunches and looking into his face. 'How's that head?' And he just froze. Left his arms out-stretched mid-air with his hands clutching a pen and its top and just froze.

'I'm here, Philip. Look at me. I'm so sorry about what happened on Saturday but I'm still here. I'm not going anywhere.' But he stayed frozen, his eyes focused on a spot on the carpet just next to his feet.

Denise was in the office. She was smiling, friendly and efficient and left me in no doubt that she had won whatever battle had taken place on Saturday night. I had formed a plan to talk to Philip's social worker, Ruth, and see if I could get her to intervene and perhaps support me to continue as his key worker, but Denise was way ahead of me. She asked me to write an account of what had happened and put it in the logbook and then said that she had a meeting with Ruth that afternoon.

'Would it be possible for me to attend?' I asked.

'No, that isn't appropriate. Besides, it's at 4 o'clock and presumably you'll need to be on the school run.'

'No, not today. I thought there might be some fall-out

after Saturday, so I arranged for my au pair to pick the children up.'

'Oh, well, that's extremely thoughtful of you, but honestly it's not necessary.'

'I think it's important that I'm there,' I said defiantly. 'I may not be Philip's key worker any more but I was involved in the build-up to the incident, and so I think my contribution will be vital.'

'"Vital"?' Denise was amused. 'Well if you're here I suppose you may as well come along but I've known Ruth for years and I think she will get the measure of what has happened very quickly. There's no need for a great post-mortem of events.'

'And Rob?'

'Rob made it perfectly clear that he no longer wants to play a role in the running of this institution. Of course I'm sorry but it's his decision.'

'Is he leaving?'

'I've spoken to him this morning and we have agreed that he must work out his full notice. He can't just leave when it suits him. I need to recruit a new deputy and, less a few weeks of leave he's owed, he'll be here for another couple of months . . . I think he'll regret it when he starts to look for another job. There's very little out there and he can't expect a glowing reference.' She seemed to be talking to herself more than to me. 'Good luck to him,' she said lightly.

The doorbell rang and a delivery man was there holding a large cardboard box. I signed for it and carried it awkwardly along the corridor and into the office. It looked like some computer equipment. Thank God, a new printer, I thought as I heaved it into the corner of the office to unpack later. Denise looked up but didn't register any interest in the box.

'I'd kill for some tea,' she said brightly.

'I was just going to make one,' I said coldly and rose from my chair.

'And a slice of toast?' she asked playfully.

'Sure – no problem.' It was a relief to leave the room.

When I came back into the office five or so minutes later Denise had disappeared. I put her tea and toast on the desk and went to hang up my coat. On returning, I noticed that the box containing the computer equipment had gone. It had definitely been addressed to Clifton Avenue Residential Centre. I looked at our sad old printer still in place attached to the office computer. The odd Jammie Dodger was one thing, but surely Denise wouldn't have helped herself to a whole printer. I remembered her stout son, shuffling out of the office having been forced to do his homework in there because his printer was broken on the day Alec had been with me.

I looked through the window at Denise's house and noticed that the lights had come on. Surreptitiously I sat at the computer and looked up our latest order from Atkinson's, our office and IT suppliers – the one approved by social services, through which we got a hefty discount. And sure enough there was an order made by Denise for a new printer on Clifton Avenue's account, a brand-new laptop with a separate invoice for a resident called Emily, plus three or four other orders from the last year that made no sense and bore no relation to anything that we used around the office. I felt my heart begin to beat just a little bit faster and almost jumped out of my seat when Denise came back into the room.

'Is that mine? Thank you!' she said, reaching for her tea. Her eyes quickly flicked to the computer screen just a fraction of a second after I closed the page. 'You'll be pleased to know that Philip can go back to the day centre tomorrow. His head is clearing up nicely and he seems absolutely fine. We're still giving him some anti-inflamatories but he seems as right as rain.'

'Oh great,' I said cheerily. 'Right . . . well . . . I'd better get on. I'll just go and wash out my cup.'

I stood up as casually as I could but my joints suddenly felt stiff and clumsy. Rob was scheduled to work with me that morning but I had no idea if he was around. There was a free bedroom that some of the staff used when they had to get on with paperwork and needed peace and quiet. I marched along the corridor feeling as if I'd just drunk ten double espressos and stopped outside the door. I knocked and walked straight in. Rob was sitting at a computer with his head in his hands and his shoulders drooped. I had a sudden urge to smooth his hair and stroke his poor, tense back. He turned and looked at me as I shut the door behind me and leant against it. He looked tired, anxious and really rough.

'Hi there,' he said. 'I'm composing my resignation and I'm going to file an official complaint – I have to. Not that it will do any good. All Denise's cronies have their feet well and truly under the table at head office – that's how she got the job in the first place –'

'I think Denise has just taken delivery of a printer meant for the office and installed it in her own house. And I think she's bought a laptop for Emily and lord knows what else.'

He looked bemused. 'What? What do you mean?'

I told him about the order forms and how the box had disappeared.

His eyes widened with anger. 'Sneaky bitch,' he said, rubbing his chin. 'Robbing, greedy, sneaky bitch.' He sat forward suddenly. 'Are you sure?'

'Yes – I'm sure. And I'm sure we can prove it. One minute there was the box in the office, the next it was gone and she was in her house. Look up the Atkinson's account, it's all there.'

Rob started typing furiously and again the invoices came up in Denise's name for hundreds of pounds' worth of equipment that had never made its way to the office.

'Can you get some copies of this?' I nodded as Rob went on, 'I've got a key to her house that she gave to me for safety ages ago – I can get in and confirm the printer's there. Then we'll be completely sure of the facts when we confront her.'

The more the enormity of what I thought Denise had done sank in, the more angry and determined I was becoming. 'Good idea.' I said.

'I think it's bloody brilliant.'

We looked at each other in silence – both of us processing what had just been said.

'Are we right to ignore the official route?' I winced at how prim I sounded.

'Probably not, but if we do that, it'll take months – I had a supervisor once who threw a can of baked beans at a resident's head. He was suspended on full pay for six months and then was right back as if nothing had happened. By the time it's been sorted I'll be long gone.' Rob was fired up. 'Ruth's coming at four, isn't she?' he asked. 'Denise'll be tied up with that so I can get in then and get a picture of the printer on my phone. Then we'll take it from there – confront her if necessary or go to head office.'

'Right,' I said. I felt queasy from great squirts of adrenalin forcing their way into my system. What Denise had done was outrageous. 'For now I'll just get on as usual. I've got to write up what happened on Saturday too.'

'OK.' He stared at me intently, his eyes wide. 'It is unbelievably good timing, Rachel – it might just save me my job.' The expression on his face was triumphant.

'I know, I know.' It was hard to resist his enthusiasm. I felt like running round in circles and punching the air.

He turned back to his computer screen, still rubbing the stubble on his chin. I could almost hear his brain whirring. Just as I was out the door he lurched sideways and grabbed my hand, pulling me back in.

'I'm sorry about Saturday – me mauling you and getting so maudlin and self-righteous. I wanted to ring you back yesterday but I just didn't know what I'd say. I think the emotion of the night just overwhelmed me a bit . . . Sorry.'

I felt embarrassed and disappointed. 'Don't be silly,' I said brightly. 'No harm done.'

He was laughing. 'But what do you expect a grown man to do? Leaping about in your undies?'

'I wasn't in my undies and I was hardly leaping about.'

'What, no undies?' he said and I laughed and felt a rich warmth travel up from my chest to my cheeks.

I went back to the office and although I knew Denise was back in her own house, I felt twitchy as I set up our old printer to churn out the invoice. It seemed to take an age for all its bells and whistles to start functioning. Constantly checking over my shoulder for Denise, I went back onto the computer to find the Atkinson's account. I let out a gasp when the pages I had just been looking at with Rob failed to come up on the screen. They had completely disappeared. Denise must have wiped them. I felt a dizzying wave of fear. Was this something she did as a matter of course or had a game of cat-and-mouse begun?

Taking my mobile, I went out into the car park and sat in my car. Having had a good look around to make sure Denise was nowhere to be seen, I rang Atkinson's. A nice girl took my call and I explained that we were having some problems with our computers and needed hard copies of all the invoices from the last twelve months for our records. No problem, she said. She'd get them in the post to me in the next twenty-four hours.

I went back inside and got on with writing my report of the events of Saturday evening and then went to Philip's room to assess the damage to the door frame before we got our handyman in. Seeing Philip's blood still smudged on the splintered wood strengthened my resolve to get Denise and get her good.

I tried to concentrate on the tasks in hand and not to get distracted. Ruth was due and I was delighted with my small victory of getting myself in on the meeting. I wanted to be totally honest with her and to let her draw her own conclusions from what she heard. I hoped she might even recommend that I continue as Philip's key worker. I knew that Denise would be covering up for herself and blaming Rob for everything but hoped that Ruth would see what was going on. She seemed a decent type and must have known Rob through other residents. With me in the room, how much damage could Denise do to his reputation? And now with this thing with the computers, I could suddenly see Denise on very shaky ground.

On my way to the office I knocked on Rob's door and we began to walk together. I was five minutes early for Ruth's meeting and confident that I would be in the room well before it began. As we paused outside the office door, Rob patted his pocket to check he had his phone in order to take pictures of the printer.

'Get Denise to sit with her back to the window, otherwise she'll get a clear view of me breaking and entering,' he whispered.

'Oh God!' My stomach tightened as I heard Denise's voice from the office.

'See you on the other side,' said Rob and I turned the doorknob and walked in.

'Here's Rachel,' Denise trilled as I entered. 'Ruth got here early. Shall we get started?' She had already rearranged the chairs and was sitting opposite a grave-looking Ruth with a prime view of the window and her house.

I was thrown. The phone rang and I grabbed it. 'Hello, Clifton Avenue,' I said distractedly.

'Hello, is that Mrs Bidewell? It's Miss Emma here from the school office. I've got Jess and Luke here. Apparently they say your au pair was supposed to be picking them up today but I'm afraid there's no sign of her.'

I looked at my watch – it was just gone four. Marlene was half an hour late.

'Have you rung her?' I said.

'Yes, but there's no answer.'

Shit. Shit. Shitting shit. 'I'm on my way.' I put the phone down and turned back to the room. 'I'm so sorry. I've got to go. My au pair has disappeared. Ruth, can I ring you tomorrow and just update you on where I am with all of this?'

Ruth shook her head. 'Don't worry, Denise and I should be able to cover everything today. I just want to be reassured that Philip is more stable now and find out what went wrong on Saturday.'

'Of course. I'm so sorry. I can't think what's happened to her. She's never done this before . . .' I grabbed my coat and bag and left. As I came into the corridor I found Rob and just shook my head to let him know the whole thing was off. The last thing I saw was Denise looking apologetically at Ruth and mouthing 'Single mother . . . three children.'

When I arrived at school everywhere was quiet. I parked the car and raced to the school office. I gathered up Jess and Luke, who were unperturbed by their experience, having made paperclip chains with Miss Emma. I apologized again and again and started back for the car. All the time I kept imagining what Denise was saying to Ruth and thinking that if it turned out that Marlene was to blame for me losing Philip I would never forgive her.

As we passed a classroom someone banged on the window and I jumped. It was Alec. I motioned for him to come to the door. We had a mini-hug and I said in a whisper – so as not to disturb the other children in the classroom who were working quietly – 'What club is this? I didn't think you had a club today.'

'I don't!' he said, whispering and rolling his eyes good-naturedly. 'It's the Homework Room. Dad and Deborah are both busy today so they can't get me till six. I'm here till five and then going home with Lorenzo and then they'll collect me from his.' Jess was hanging onto his waist and squeezing for dear life and Luke looked confused and upset.

'Do you want to come home with us?' he said.

'Yes but . . . it's fine. It's all arranged. I'll see you for your birthday, Mum.'

We got in the car and I dialled Marlene's number again. Still no answer, it just went straight to messages. We got home and as we came into the hallway I shouted upstairs to see if she was around, but still nothing.

'I need a cup of tea,' I said with total certainty. I put the kettle on and went to the fridge to get some milk. As I gingerly sniffed at the top of a carton of skimmed milk I noticed that the fridge looked very clean and spacious. Marlene had finally had a cull of the unfortunate meat specimens that she had been collecting. 'Hallelujah,' I said under my breath and then felt a small uneasy jolt in my chest.

Still holding the milk I bounded up the stairs two at a time to Marlene's room. I knocked on the door but there was no answer. I walked straight in and stopped still. It was completely, totally and utterly empty. She had cleared everything out: the rug, the duvet, her pictures, toiletries, the little humming fridge, her mug tree, her mugs. The only things left were the bed, the chest of drawers, the curtains and the purple sticker around the light switch.

I sat on the bed still clutching the milk and then rang her number again. Not surprisingly she didn't pick up and so I left a message. 'Marlene, this is Rachel. There was no need for this. You are a cowardly, foolish girl and I do not deserve to be treated like this by you – and the children certainly don't. I am not an ogre, you could have told me you were unhappy and wanted to leave. You should have said a proper goodbye to the children. Shame on you. Do not expect a reference.'

Luke had come up the stairs and poked his nose around the door. 'Oh Mum! What's she done? Where is she?'

'I don't know, darling. She's done a runner.' Luke's jaw fell open in amazement and as he stared at me astounded, the doorbell rang. 'What now?' I said irritably.

I gallumped back down the stairs to find Mary on the doorstep.

'I didn't know if you'd be in,' she said brightly, slightly breathless from the walk from her car to the front door. 'It's silly but we've had about five boxes of thank-you chocolates given to us at the surgery this week and we just all looked at each other and said, "We can't eat all these!"

and I said, "Well I know a very good home that they can go to."' She was clutching a plastic bag that had once held medical supplies but now was home to a box of Quality Street and two boxes of Celebrations.

'Oh lovely,' I said distractedly. 'Come in. Come in.'

'Are you sure? I was only going to drop these off and –'

'No! Come on.' I stepped backwards and she followed me into the hallway. 'You've just caught us mid-crisis actually.'

She tried to disguise a 'not another one!' expression and I led her upstairs talking over my shoulder. 'Marlene's done a runner. Can you believe it? No warning, no nothing.'

I showed Mary into Marlene's bedroom where Luke was still perched on her bed.

'We don't know where she is, Grandma,' said Luke. 'She's just gone.' Mary looked suitably appalled and Luke looked lost. It was such a shock.

I ran downstairs to put the kettle on again and while it boiled I went back up to ask if Mary would like to stay for supper. I paused outside Marlene's room and looked through the half-open door. Luke was sat sideways in Mary's lap. 'She could have said goodbye!' he was saying in a small, strained voice. His chin was wobbling and he looked bereft.

'I know,' said Mary. 'What a silly, silly girl. Fancy just up and going like that.' And although Luke thought he was getting a bit big for sitting in his grandma's lap, she placed his limp head on her shoulder and rocked him back and forth. As his eyes began to water he drew his head back to look at her, and smiled despite himself. 'I didn't even like her!' he laughed but nevertheless snuffled his head back into her neck and sobbed.

I couldn't move. I sensed that maybe Luke would be able to talk to Mary more freely than to me and so just watched. After a few seconds, he looked up again. 'Do you think she missed Alec so she left?' he asked.

'No, absolutely not,' Mary said shaking her head ferociously. 'I think she left because . . . because she's a very silly girl . . . and because she is utterly thoughtless and . . . because your feet smell.'

He allowed himself a weak smile. 'Not as bad as yours,' he said but then his mouth went into another spasm and wobbled. I could see that his tense little body needed the release and watched Mary rub his back while he had a cry. I knew that somewhere in this small frame was a question he couldn't bring himself to vocalize: 'Dad, Alec and now Marlene. Why, Grandma?'

Eventually, Mary stood him up, gripped his shoulders and looked him in the eye. 'Listen, this has nothing to do with Alec or you. She left because she is stupid and selfish and if she didn't realize that she was the luckiest au pair in the world to be able to look after my wonderful grandson, well then we're better off without her.' She fished about for the tissue up her sleeve and wiped his eyes. 'Now, let's not let Mum see you like this. We don't want her to see you upset do we?'

'But what will we do?' Luke asked anxiously. 'What about after school when Mum's working?'

I suddenly came to. It was as if someone had shaken me. I couldn't let Luke think he couldn't talk to me or that he had to hide his feelings. I was grateful to Mary, but it was up to me to reassure him that this was not his problem.

'That's not for you to worry about,' I said, coming into the room. I sat on the bed next to Mary and pulled him onto my knee. 'I'll sort something out and we will all be fine. We've had far worse things to deal with than this, haven't we?'

He nodded.

'You mustn't worry. OK?'

'OK.'

I squeezed Mary's hand and gave her cheek a kiss.

Jess's reaction was far more straightforward. She bounded up the stairs and looked around the empty room with her hands on her hips. 'Good! She's gone. Luke, you can have your old room back.' Then she turned tail and ran into her bedroom.

We had tea, and when Mary had left and the children were in bed, I rang Mel and told her all about Denise and Philip and Marlene. Her au pair, Anna, was supposedly Marlene's best friend but said she hadn't a clue where Marlene had gone. However, she did say that she'd heard that I had told

Marlene that she wasn't allowed to go to college any more if she wanted to keep working for me.

I was past caring. All I cared about was who on earth was going to look after the children over the next few days when I was working, let alone until they were eighteen.

'Can't Dom help?' asked Mel.

'Maybe,' I said, 'but I really, really don't want to ask. What if Jess and Luke start spending a couple of evenings there a week and suddenly it's all hunky-dory and Dom is suggesting that they move in too? On the other hand, I think the reality of looking after Alec is proving difficult enough. Today Alec was in the Homework Room after school because neither of them could pick him up.'

'Shit . . .' said Mel. 'You know, I remember when I had my first au pair. Do you remember Helena? And she came to me and told me that she had to return home urgently because her mother had to have life-saving surgery back in the Poland. Jesus! I offered to take her to the airport and pay her fare. I told her to make as many phone calls as she wanted home and that we would pay. I was beside myself. I kept thinking what it would be like if I lived in another country and my mother was ill and how terrible it would be. But then three hundred au pairs later and three hundred bizarre reasons for their departures and I've become a lot more cynical. I think if Anna came to me tomorrow and told me that she had bone cancer and only a week to live, I'd ask her to make sure she left her room tidy and to delay her departure until after Sports Day.'

I chuckled.

'Look,' she went on, 'I don't need an au pair. I don't work. I'm just lazy and spoilt and sit on my fat arse all day. So, until you can sort something out permanently I'll ask Anna to come to you. I have a nasty feeling she knew what Marlene was up to so it'll serve her right.'

'Oh, that would be a life-saver.'

'Yes, I am an angel.' She changed the subject. 'What will happen at work? Do you really think that woman is a thief?'

'I'm sure of it and if we can get her thrown out then I can get on with looking after Philip,' I said resolutely.

'Which one's Philip again?' Mel asked, struggling to keep up.

'Oh, the resident I was key worker for . . . with the feet . . . do you remember?' I said limply. I couldn't begin to explain to her all that Philip had come to mean to me. How could I possibly sound like a rational human being if I told her that at that moment it felt as if my happiness was dependent on a six-foot-three giant with no verbal skills and putrified toenails? 'I'll update you when I see you,' I sighed.

'Good, I'll look forward to it. Anyway, you're all coming over tomorrow for tea. We're ordering pizzas, Grace is bringing a cake and I'm providing the fizz.'

'Oh Lord . . .'

'Don't fight me on this. It's your sodding birthday and you *will* celebrate and be merry.'

'OK. OK. You've twisted my arm.'

I sent a text to Dom saying that I'd pick up Alec the next day so that he could come over to Mel's for my birthday and preferably stay the night with me. I didn't hear anything back until I was going to bed at about 11 o'clock and a text arrived: 'Sorry Rachel. Too short notice. Things arranged for Alec tomorrow and too late to reorganize. He understands and looks forward to seeing you on Saturday.'

Great.

# Chapter Eight

# I Do Look Like a Monkey and My Worry Is That I Smell Like One Too

I slept brilliantly for the first time in ages. Thanks to Marlene, I had expected to toss and turn all night and wake up feeling rotten, but instead I leapt out of bed. It was freezing and rainy but for some reason it felt like a good day. Luke and Jess were still asleep so I went down and laid out a birthday breakfast, complete with napkins – Sponge-Bob left over from Luke's party – and started to make bacon sandwiches – unheard of on a school morning. I turned the radio up really, really loud and found that Take That is the perfect musical accompaniment to bacon-frying.

When the kids shuffled in they were ecstatic. They boo-gied around the kitchen, gulping down warm, fatty bacon and slightly old bread with lots of ketchup, and when Luke asked to eat a large jelly snake left over from a party bag that for some reason was loitering in the fruit bowl, I said 'Yes!' and he yanked it in half and gave some to Jess.

I showered, still able to hear another joyous track wafting up from the radio in the kitchen and wobbled naked along the landing humming to myself. It was suddenly clear why I felt so liberated; there was no Marlene. No sour-faced Marlene, huddled behind her door waiting for the bathroom to be free. I didn't need to worry that I'd accidentally used her shampoo or left hairs in the bath or that I'd bump smack into her wearing only my pants. I didn't feel that I should discipline the children more because the children of the Czech Republic are not as dirty/rude/disrespectful/generally disgusting as the ones in the UK. God, it was such a relief to have my house to myself again and to behave normally. I couldn't afford live-out help, but Mel had given me a moment to catch my breath and I was going to make damn sure that whoever I employed now would be someone with whom I could relax. Ding dong! The Wicked Witch is Dead.

I got dressed, and as I made it into the kitchen Jess let out a wail. 'You're not wearing your birthday jewellery! Why aren't you wearing it?' So even though we were now running late I shot back up the stairs and put it on.

It was still raining so we drove to school and as we dashed across the playground with our coats over our heads Luke ran ahead into his classroom. He told everyone it was my birthday so by the time I shuffled in the teacher had got everyone to start singing to me. I went scarlet.

RebeccaClassRep filed out of the class with me. She pulled me into a dry recess and said with her face all crinkled up, 'I hope you're doing something nice.' The subtext being, 'Poor old you. Alone on your birthday. You'll probably be getting shit-faced by yourself watching *Taggart*.'

'Thank you. I am,' I said and floated away across the puddles. Then I surprised myself. I knew that Rob wasn't working so I rang him. I wanted to explain what had happened when I had left work so suddenly but more importantly confirm exactly what we were going to do about the stolen computer equipment. There was no way I was going to let this opportunity to nail Denise slip away. Plus, I just felt good and positive, as if my birthday was the beginning of something and not just a reminder of time passing.

Rob sounded surprised but pleased and we arranged to meet for coffee in a place round the corner from school that afternoon.

It was still raining but I bought some flowers on the way home and then tidied the house from top to bottom. By now I had so much adrenalin racing through my veins I thought I'd better not waste it. I got on the Internet and started trawling through all the personal ads for au pairs and posted a few myself.

The soggy post came and there were cards from my dad, Mary, my cousin, an aunt, two friends from college, my godmother and the local Indian takeaway. My dad had sent me an M&S voucher for £20 and my cousin a book. I had an Alec moment as there was nothing from him, but quickly pushed it aside. Since seeing him in the Homework Room I realized that actually everything wasn't ideal at Dom's house. I had envisioned a new life for Alec of calm efficiency. But no, they were scrabbling about trying to make all the pieces fit together just as much as I was. I must be patient and wait it out. Wait for Dom and Deborah and Denise to trip themselves up and fall flat on their stupid arses. And wait for Philip to trust me again.

I sat at a low table in the corner of the café and watched for Rob to come through the door. The café felt warm and cosy and smelt of everyone's damp clothes and dripping umbrellas.

When Rob did arrive I found myself smiling inanely. There was some kerfuffle with a lady trying to fit a rain hood over a buggy, and as she was coming out he was coming in. He opened the door as wide as he could to let her through and then lifted the buggy down the couple of steps beyond the door as if he didn't notice the rain. He made a face at the baby and smiled at its mother who looked hassled but very grateful. He strode in and I just observed him for a minute. He seemed taller and leaner and was smiling and I was extremely pleased to see him. He was wearing some nice lived-in trousers which reached all the way to the floor. He spotted me and his face broke into another smile. I waved moronically and stood up. As he reached me he squeezed my arm and his lips brushed my cheek.

The first thing I did was to tell him it was my birthday – like a six-year-old.

'Oh you should have said. Right, this calls for a slab of cake the size of a breeze block.'

'Absolutely,' I said grinning.

We ordered cake but were both anxious to talk about Denise. I explained about Marlene and why I'd had to rush off and then said: 'Look, I've thought and thought about the whole Denise and the printer thing and basically I think we both know that she ordered it for herself . . . don't we?'

'Well, it certainly does look like it but I think I've lost my nerve from the other day. Maybe I should just work out my notice, make our suspicions about the printer and the rest of the stuff known and hope the powers-that-be eventually see sense?'

'You're kidding. You said yourself that could take for ever. We have to try and get her out ourselves. Is there nobody at head office you can go to with this and at least get her suspended?'

'Well, there's Martin Sharp, he's decent enough but they're all bound by procedure and at the end of the day it's only a cheap printer.'

'And all the other stuff? The woman's a thief! And besides, we owe it to Philip to do whatever we can. He is absolutely central to all this – not to mention your career.

I think we should do exactly what we planned the other day – get into her house and see if we can match the printer and anything else we find with the invoices.'

'Dear God, you sound like something out of the Famous Five.'

'Alas, that would make me Timmy the Dog. But don't you think what I'm saying makes sense?'

'OK, OK, yes it makes sense. I'm on with you tomorrow aren't I? I'll see you then you crazy woman and we'll get into the house. Did you get copies of the paperwork?'

'Not exactly,' I said and Rob cringed.

'Why not?'

'Well, it looks as if they've all been wiped.'

'Dear God!' Rob rubbed his face in his hands. 'Do you think she knows we're on to her? Jesus, that woman terrifies me, I dread to think what she'd do if –'

'She can't do anything. I've got hard copies being sent to me and once we've got them, and hopefully proof that the printer is in her house, she won't have a leg to stand on.' He looked queasily reassured and we both relaxed.

We carried on having a damn good bitch about Denise. Rob had tried to get the low-down on her meeting with Ruth but she had refused to divulge what had gone on so we assumed Denise's version of events had been swallowed whole. Then Rob made me laugh with stories of when he'd first qualified as a social worker, including the full story behind the thrown baked-bean tin.

As we talked on, Rob kept trying to steer the conversation towards the children and me, but I thought that my life would sound sad and sordid so I kept heaving it back to work. Plus, my new-found attraction to him made normal behaviour nearly impossible. I found it hard to eat my carrot cake, which was determined to stick to my teeth like clay, on account of my saliva glands going on strike. At the same time I lost the ability to lift a cup of tea to my lips, sip and then put it down again. I was grateful when it was three-fifteen and I had to leave to pick up the children.

Just as we got up to go Rob said, 'Can I ask you a question?'

'Of course,' I said, hoping it was something about dinner followed by wanton, wild, abandoned sex.

'Where did you get that necklace?' Bollocks, I'd meant to take it off.

'It's a birthday present – my children made it,' I said, aware that he was about to take the piss.

'Well they're obviously immensely talented,' said Rob. 'You must be extremely proud.'

'This from the man who – just to please our Sophie – wears what at my school were referred to as spaz trousers.'

'Rachel!' Rob looked genuinely shocked. 'Are you sure you're really cut out for a career in social services?'

We got up to leave, sniggering.

At school it was the usual pandemonium at 3.30 on a rainy day. The number of cars quadruples, everyone gets fractious and there's a lot of bad-tempered reversing and horn-blasting and everyone can't wait to get somewhere warm and dry. I picked Luke and Jess up and waved at Grace and Mel in their cars. I hoped that I'd see Alec but there was no sign of him. I waited for a bit and then asked a boy from his class if Alec was around, but he said that he hadn't seen him all afternoon.

He'd ring later, I was sure.

We drove to Mel's with the windscreen wipers on over-drive and the windows steamed up. As our school was a church school with a good reputation, some people trav-elled a long way to attend, having sold their souls and their granny to get in. Mel was one of them and it took us ages to get to her house in the school pick-up rush.

Once there the kids all shot off in different directions and Mel, Grace and I stood in the kitchen with cups of tea. We ordered the pizzas and laid a birthday table.

I was touched that Mel's son Josh was there and not locked in his bedroom with his computer. 'Where's Alec?' he said, having tired of helping Jess and Grace's youngest play restaurants.

I took a deep breath and said as lightly as I could, 'Well since he went to live with Dom, everything gets very complicated with who's supposed to be where and when, and so we thought it was easier just to wait until the week-end to celebrate.'

He looked embarrassed at my directness as if I'd tried to engage him in conversation about the menopause.

Mel cut in. 'As I live and breathe, I do believe it is now five minutes to five and therefore time for a drink. Thank goodness for me.' She opened her vast fridge and took out not only a bottle of cold champagne but also three very fancy, chilled champagne flutes.

She poured out a glass and held it up saying, 'To Marlene, may she rot in hell.' We all clinked glasses and Mel went on: 'I've got Anna picking the kids up tomorrow, doing tea and staying until you get back. Is that right?'

'Yes it is,' I said, taking a huge gulp of cold, fizzy bubbles and kissing her on the cheek fondly. Mel and Grace wandered through to the sitting room and I stayed back to wash the teacups.

I always quite enjoy washing up in other people's houses. Other people's scouring pads and dish cloths always seem so much more enjoyable to use than my own manky ones, plus you always get lots of credit for old-fashioned washing up. Standing with my hands in warm soapy water, hearing my friends laughing in the next room and the kids charging around upstairs, I reflected on what a lovely thing a middle-aged crush was. When I was younger I would have been obsessed with a boy, thinking of nothing else and talking to my friends of only him. I would have mooned and sighed and found it hard to focus on my maths homework. But this crush had crept up on me silently and, rather than dominate my every waking moment, would get completely forgotten in all the chaos of family life only to sneak up on me deliciously when I least expected it. Like now, in my Marigolds, I was suddenly thinking of Rob's hands, of his hair, of his laugh, and it was as if I was an empty house that had stood abandoned for years and somebody had unexpectedly come to live in it again and was walking round switching the lights on. I stopped still for a moment, just to enjoy the sensation. The other lovely thing was that I knew I wouldn't die if Rob never returned my admiration. Initially I'd be gutted of course, but I wanted Alec to come home, I wanted a kind, cheerful au pair and I wanted to be allowed to care for Philip and enjoy my job. Above all I wanted to be my old self again. I knew no man could sort these things out for me but it didn't stop me feeling thrilled that I still had it in me to be attracted to someone and to feel the hope that a new relationship might bring. After Dom, I thought that part of me was dead, but no, it was very much alive.

I came back into the sitting room and Josh was teaching Luke to do some trick which was causing much mirth. Someone had put some music on. I sat on the sofa with Mel and Grace and shouted above the noise. Grace invited me to supper at her house the following week. I could tell from her furtive description of the other guests that she was trying to set me up with someone and for once I felt quite relaxed about it and said I'd see if I could find a babysitter, knowing full well I wouldn't.

Grace got up to open the huge cake-tin she had brought with her, to reveal a cake with 'Happy Birthday Rachel' written on the top and a picture of my face in piped icing.

Baking was her thing and she'd got her kids to help decorate it.

'You're a bit boss-eyed, sorry,' she said apologetically, but it was beautiful. I could have cried.

'Thank you,' I said. 'It's amazing!' And I gave her a hug.

'I'll go and get it ready to serve up after the pizza,' she said, carefully replacing the lid and heading off to the kitchen. After three glasses of fizz she was a little unsteady on her feet. 'Oooh dear,' she said, sounding like Beryl Reid, 'I haven't had any lunch and I think I'm a bit pissed. Mark will have to come and pick us up. I don't think I can drive!'

Mel made a 'bloody hell!' face at me and we both giggled.

As Grace weaved through the door, Jess came whooshing down the stairs, head down and full of five-year-old righteous indignation. 'It's not fair!' she was shrieking. 'It's my turn to –'

And as she smacked into the tottering Grace, so the cake tin flew out of her hands and landed with a very nasty thud on the hall floor.

We all went quiet and Luke turned the music off. Jess had gone very pale. Grace dropped to her knees and picked the tin up. Gingerly she opened it once again and, alas, my beautiful face now resembled Saddam Hussein. That is the bit that was still on the cake and not the bit that was stuck to the roof of the tin having hit it at ninety miles an hour like a bug on a windscreen.

Jess's eyes were the size of chocolate coins. She couldn't

speak because her mouth had gone rigid in preparation for an onslaught of guilty tears.

'Oh, Jess . . .' I said and waited for Grace to be all stiff-upper-lip and say not to worry and that she could definitely resurrect something out of the mess in a jiffy.

'I'm sorry, Grace! I'm so sorry!' Jess whispered and Grace just glared at her.

'I will kill you, Jess Bidewell,' she said. 'I will bloody kill you.' To my relief the champagne had obviously hit an excellent spot and she was laughing. Not only that, but to everyone's disbelief, she slowly scraped some of the icing off the tin lid and proceeded to smear it across Jess's nose. Was this our Grace? Our beautiful, perfect Grace behaving like a ten-year-old? Fortunately, Jess shrieked with pleasure – it could have gone either way. 'I will kill you!' Grace was saying again and laughing. 'Have you any idea how long that took me to make – and that's my second attempt because the first one was rubbish? I WILL KILL YOU.' And with that she got Jess by the throat and started to roll around on the carpet with her while Jess squealed. Grace's skirt rode up to reveal a large expanse of auber-gine, opaque thigh. The kids were cheerfully appalled.

In the midst of all this I heard my mobile ringing. Reluc-tantly I left the chaos and fished the phone out of my coat pocket in the kitchen. Dom's number had come up and I assumed it was Alec, ringing to wish me happy birthday.

I was still laughing when I said, 'Hello! The Birthday Girl speaking!'

'Rachel, it's me,' said Dom. 'Look, have you heard from Alec?'

'No,' I said immediately anxious. 'Why? Isn't he supposed to be with you?'

'Well, yes. Deborah just went to pick him up from the Homework Room – she was running a bit late – but he's not there. She's at the school and no one's seen him all afternoon.'

Oh God, I thought. Not again.

At that moment the doorbell went. 'Pizza!' cried Mel and came running into the hall. As soon as she saw the expression on my face, her smile faded and she stopped. 'What's happened?' she said. 'What is it?'

'It's Alec. He's not at school.'

The doorbell rang again and I moved to open it. There on the doorstep, wet through and freezing cold, was Alec, with a broad grin on his face.

'Hello, Mum,' he said. 'You don't look a day over fifty.'

'It's OK, Dom, he's here, we'll ring you later,' I said and hung up. 'Alec! How did you get here? That was your father on the phone; he's worried sick.'

'I walked. I thought I could get a bus but then I didn't know which one to get and this woman put me on one and I ended up in Archway!'

'Have you walked from Archway? But it's miles and your dad's frantic.'

'I told them I was coming. Anyway, I'm here now.'

*

We all went into overdrive. The kids were just delighted to see him but the mothers were appalled at how cold and wet he was. His fingers were so stiff and blue that he couldn't get his buttons undone to take off his sodden parka. Mel went upstairs and immediately ran a hot bath and put out a big fluffy towel and dry clothes for him.

The pizzas did eventually arrive and while everyone was chowing down, I went to find Alec.

He was sitting on the lavatory lid and drying his skinny legs and feet. He was lobster-pink from the heat of the bath, his hair had gone like a chick's and he looked about seven.

'It's lovely to see you,' I said, 'but I don't think your dad knew you were coming.'

He looked up at me fiercely and said, 'He did know! I told him last night that I wanted to see you on your birth-day. I wasn't going to wait until *Saturday*. I told them, I said I was coming here and I said if they wouldn't take me, I'd get the bus. It's not my fault if they didn't believe me.'

'We could have waited until Sat—'

'Is that what you wanted? Not to see your own son on your birthday?'

'Of course I wanted to see you — more than anything — but with this new arrangement, we're all going to have to make sacrifices.'

'I don't mind doing that — I don't! But Deborah wouldn't drive me here and Dad said he had to work. So I said "Fine! I'll get the bus."'

'You're too young to get the bus on your own. You know that.'

'I'm not! Isaac gets the bus to school every day on his own.'

'Yes but that's a bus he's used to. He knows exactly when to get on and exactly when to get off. You're too young to just set off without telling anyone where you are . . . Aren't you?'

'Yes,' he said miserably.

A silence hovered between us.

'Dad told me Marlene's done a runner?' Alec said to break it.

'Yes. Great bloody birthday present. Thanks Marlene.'

I went over to him, got onto my knees and started drying his feet. With my head down, concentrating on the crevices between his toes, I said, 'I think Dad's going to be very cross and upset . . . and Deborah too.'

'I don't care. A son should be allowed to see his own mother on her birthday, especially when . . . he doesn't even live with her any more.'

I spoke to Dom. He was indeed furious with Alec, but I overruled him and took Alec home with me. He slept with me in my bed. Dom had insisted that everything was absolutely fine but I thought of Alec being shoved into the Homework Room after school, of him climbing onto a bus in the rain and I thought, very calmly: I don't believe you.

The next morning, I looked at Alec's crumpled, dozing face next to me on the pillow.

'Is everything OK at Dad's?' I asked quietly.

He rolled over and sighed very deeply, opening one eye and considering me. 'Do you think he's going to go ballistic tonight?'

'No, I think he'll have calmed down. But you are going to have to apologize. I think he panicked – probably Deborah too – and after what happened in Dorset I don't think you can blame him, do you?'

'No.' He was staring at the ceiling and I rolled over and propped myself up on my elbow so I could get a proper look at him.

'Look, you know you can always, always come home. Your bed is there waiting for you anytime.'

'Yeah. I know that.'

'Do you want to come home?'

He looked so pained that I immediately regretted asking the question. It was as if a physical ache had seized his stomach as he curled up and rolled away from me. I put my hand on his head and rested it there.

Eventually, he turned back and said matter-of-factly, 'The thing is, I've got all my room sorted now and Deborah's organizing something at work so picking me up won't be such a problem. And I'm going to help Dad get the garden straight. I think I do need to stay.'

'Of course. Of course. I totally understand,' I said, adopting the same practical, adult tone as his. 'Come on, we'd better get the others up. You can go and jump on their heads.'

'Right. OK.' He gave a little laugh but was awkward and embarrassed and as he left the room I continued to stare at the door after he'd gone. For the first time I was not sure whether he was saying he needed to stay with Dom because he wanted to or because he felt he ought to.

That day's shift was busy and very frustrating. Denise was at home with a bad cold, plus, as I made a frantic search through the post, there was no sign of the copies of the invoices. I fought with paranoid fantasies that Denise's cold was a front and that she was staying at home in order to smash and dispose of all her stolen computer equipment. Or, that she herself had been through the post and intercepted an envelope with my name on it. To make matters worse, Rob and I were stuck with another agency worker called Vince who was incredibly clingy so we couldn't speak.

I looked at the diary. Ruth had made an appointment for Philip to see a psychologist who specialized in people with learning disabilities, and he had been to see her earlier that day. Plus there was a big note from Denise to Scott to say that Philip's new furniture had arrived. I sought Philip out. He was sitting in one of the day rooms, the tatty furniture catalogue limply clasped in his massive hands. His forehead looked sore but not too swollen. On the floor next to him was a plastic bag containing his felt-tip pens and a pad of paper but he obviously wasn't in the mood for drawing, or anything else by the looks of him.

'Hello, you,' I said quietly.

He looked up, whatever strange thoughts had been rambling around that big head were interrupted. He only moved his head towards me, but not his eyes, and almost immediately he turned away again to look out of the window.

'I hear your new furniture's arrived. Shall we go and have a look?'

Philip meekly rose to his feet and obediently shuffled to the door. He winced when he stood up and my heart lurched – his feet were obviously sore.

We walked in silence to his room. The door frame was fixed and it looked as if nothing had happened. The only clue to the damage was the smell of fresh paint.

'All your new stuff has arrived!' I said, sounding overly chirpy. 'It's going to look great in here. Scott's going to help you get it all sorted.'

His face remained blank and unresponsive. I sat down on the bed but Philip remained standing, swaying gently back and forth on his feet.

'I hear you went to see a lady today who wants to help you.'

He gave a little nod.

'Nobody wants you ever to be as upset again as you

were on Saturday and her job is to help you to deal with your feelings – when you get very sad, or you miss your mum, or you're hurt or . . . angry.'

Philip gave his head a little distracted shake as if startled by a passing wasp and continued to stare at nothing in particular in the corner of the room with his head on one side. He wouldn't look at me. I wanted to run over to Denise's house then and there. Call the police and get her marched off the premises. This was all her fault. 'Slowly, slowly catchy monkey', I heard my mother saying in my ear and I took Philip's hand.

'I'm still here,' I said. 'I haven't gone anywhere. You can always come and find me. I haven't left you. If nobody made that clear to you the other day then I'm so sorry but I am still here.' I gave his hand an almighty squeeze, but it might just as well have been a piece of plasticine.

Lucy had popped in to catch up on some paperwork and was in the office as I came down from seeing Philip.

'What's wrong with you?' she asked. Although she was curt and looked irritable, I knew that was just Lucy. I leant against the wall and sighed. 'You look done in,' she said.

'I just feel like Philip's shut down. We're right back at square one – worse even.'

'Look, it'll take time, it's often two steps forward three steps back in this job, but we'll just have to keep willing him on.'

I shook my head rather hopelessly and she went on.

'Look, I'll keep an eye on him for now. When you're not here I'll make sure he's OK. I might even take him on one of your walks if I can get Denise to let me.'

I stood up straight, I had to get on. 'That would be great. Thank you. Just watch out for any dogs.'

'Oh I think I can handle it' she said casually, and then a thought struck her. 'How do you think he'd cope with going swimming?'

'God knows. I doubt he's ever been.'

'Well, I take Margaret to an assisted-swimmers session at the leisure centre. If you could bring Philip it might be just what he needs. Being in the water is very freeing and he might relax and let you back in.'

'Do you know?' I said. 'It's either the worst idea in the history of residential care or it's the best. I'd have to sneak him out from under Denise's nose – she'd freak.'

'Oh sod her. I pick Margaret up from the day centre. Denise need never know. It would do him so much good and if he takes to it, it could become a regular thing. He needs the exercise and it's going to help with his weight loss. Do it!'

'He'll need trunks. I don't know when I'd have the chance to go into town.'

'If I promise to find him some trunks this afternoon, will you come?'

'Yes, OK,' I said, chewing my lip. 'In for a penny . . .'

'Don't worry! It'll be great.' And with that the front door thumped against the wall in the hall and the residents were back from the day centre. As the internal doors opened, the smell of tea wafted throughout the building. I made a guess at baked potatoes, cabbage and some sort of fish.

'Good evening, ladies and gentlemen!' called Rob who'd gone to greet everyone. 'Tea will be served at approximately 6 o'clock – on the menu this evening we have a terrine of foie gras drizzled with the finest truffle oil, followed by roasted swan and steamed ocelot. Formal wear is mandatory.'

'Shut it, you nutter!' Theresa bellowed good-naturedly.

Everyone filed past the office laughing and said hello to Vince, Lucy and me. Then Rob came in and started preparing the evening medication.

Once the coast was clear, Emily put her head around the door. Apparently, at one time in her life Emily had held down a job as a receptionist and carried on a fairly average life. But something inside had fractured twenty-odd years ago, never, it seemed, to mend itself. And now here she was, living in Clifton Avenue with no family who gave a damn about her and in many ways oblivious to the world around her. She loved pretty things though, they brought her such joy: necklaces, hairclips, rings, china cups and saucers, and bits of clothing. She would collect them and coo over them and often left the house, a strapping lady in her fifties, bejewelled like My Little Pony.

The trouble was that she simply could not stop helping herself to other people's stuff. Once or twice a week we would have to go into her bedroom and find all the bits and pieces that she had pilfered from other rooms and return them to their rightful owners. If we tackled her about them, she would say, 'Are they not mine? No, not mine. Not mine then?' like a little magpie caught in the act. If she spied a piece of jewellery on you that she took a fancy to, she would ask, 'That's not mine, is it? Is it mine?' She didn't seem to care what member of staff was on duty or who she sat next to at lunch or what was for supper. She just cared about beautiful things and making them her own. She scuttled about the hostel locked away in her own private world; a less grim Miss Havisham, constantly searching for a long-lost time that had been beautiful.

She had a problem relaxing. She just couldn't sit still, and so, while others watched TV, you were very aware of her stalking the corridors, marching up and down in an anguished Lady Macbeth fashion. She was tall and substantial with a great crop of grey hair and sometimes, if you went to look for her, you might find her marching towards you at high speed with her hands thrust deep into her pockets. Once she saw you, without appearing to acknowledge your presence, she would do an immediate about-turn like something out of Monty Python and lurch off back the way she had come and you knew that she had gone to return whatever forbidden item it was that was in her pocket.

Today, all was not well with Emily. She looked hot and

bothered, as if she had the most God-awful secret that she had to tell me or else she would die. 'Could I have a word? No? A word?' she said urgently.

'Of course! What's the matter?'

'It's my nipples, dear,' she said emphatically, 'they are screaming. My nipples are screaming.'

Vince pretended not to hear but Rob spluttered from the drugs cupboard and stuck his head out. I let my eyes flick over to his, which was a big mistake, because much as I was trying to remain sympathetic to poor Emily, the look of horror on his face made me want to laugh out loud.

'What do you mean "screaming"?' I said.

She held her hands up as if holding two imaginary beach balls and feverishly wiggled her fingers back and forth while making the face from Munch's *The Scream*. 'Screeeaming,' she said.

'Well, would you like me to have a look?'

Another splutter from the cupboard. Luckily now all I could see of Rob were his shoulders, which were vibrating with mirth as he buried his head behind the drug cupboard doors.

Emily reacted to my offer as if I had gone about her with a cattle prod. 'Noooo!' she wailed and started to sway shakily forwards and backwards, looking at me imploringly and now rubbing her hands agitatedly up and down her thighs.

'Come on, let me take you into Blue Bathroom and you can show me what the problem is . . .'

'Is it very painful? Is it very painful?'

'I'm not going to do anything you don't want me to. We'll just have a little look, shall we?'

'Yes. It's not mine, you see. Is it? Is it mine?'

I took her hand and we retired to Blue Bathroom and, once inside with the door closed, Emily very gingerly lifted up her jersey and there indeed lay the problem. Where a good 38D cup should have been, robustly supporting her ample bosom, there was a thing the size of two teabags strung together that had ridden up to somewhere near her chin. She had obviously been into another resident's bedroom that morning and helped herself to a bit of underwear. And I could see why; it was such a pretty little bra, like something Ken would have bought for Barbie. Alas, on Emily, it looked as if lacy swimming goggles were failing to pin down two semi-deflated party balloons. To make matters worse, she had decided, that morning of all mornings, to wear a harsh woollen sweater with no vest, T-shirt or what she would describe as her 'slip'. The unforgiving, scratchy material had obviously spent the day rubbing back and forth and the result was pure agony. Her poor squashed nipples were protruding out from under the little cups like baked beans.

I went to find Sophie and I asked her to sit with Emily and hold her hand while I rushed off to try and work out the best course of action.

'Is Emily as sad as a pony?' Sophie asked. 'Is she as ill as a seal?'

I probably wouldn't have empathized half so much had the torture of breastfeeding not still been relatively fresh in my mind. In the absence of lanolin cream or a Savoy cabbage leaf, I came back with cotton wool and lipsalve and got Emily to her bedroom. I gave my patient a cool glass of water and laid her down on a bed in the darkened room and over the affected area I draped two cotton-wool squares covered in the lipsalve. I drew the line at applying it directly and was extremely grateful to Rob for the cotton-wool brainwave.

At the end of the shift I felt jumpy and grinned awkwardly as Rob hung around getting his coat.

'Have you got your car here?' Rob asked furtively and when I nodded he followed me out to the car park.

It was bloody freezing and, as I stepped outside and braced myself for the arctic sprint to the car, I shot my hand in my pocket and came upon the offending lipsalve. I made a gesture at Rob as if to say, Do you need a dab of this? and he screamed in mock horror, grabbed it from me and hurled it into the bushes – never to be seen again.

'Thanks!' I said, laughing. 'It'd only been rubbed on a bit of cotton wool.'

'I don't care! The thought of it going anywhere near your mouth . . .' And just him saying the word 'mouth' and especially with reference to *my* mouth, made something tighten in my insides, so when I said, 'Do you need a lift anywhere?' the words burst out in a high-pitched splurt, as if I'd just breathed in helium.

'No, you're alright. I'm being picked up by a mate on the corner. I am in very bad need of a drink after the night I've had, what with Emily and her nipples.' He made no move to invite me along and I tried to ignore the sensation of my crest falling.

'Well I'll see you tomorrow then.' I was thinking of Denise. 'Hopefully the post will have arrived from Atkinson's.'

'OK.' He looked furtively around and said, 'Tomorrow, we're both in till three and Denise is scheduled to be at head office if she's better. I think that just might be our moment.'

'I hope so. I don't think I can take another day worrying about this.'

'Me neither,' agreed Rob and we stood in an uncomfortable silence for a moment.

'See ya then,' I said and for some unknown reason did a sort of mock salute. As I drove down Clifton Avenue cringing, the words 'see', 'ya' and 'then' rolled around my head and by the time I got to the traffic lights, I was convinced that I had said them in the voice of either Orville the Duck or Mr Punch.

As I went to turn right I saw flashing lights and a digger and it was obvious that there were some roadworks or an accident. I decided to go left instead and loop back past Clifton Avenue to take a different road home. As I rounded the corner next to the hostel I saw Rob getting into his own car – an old blue Audi – but it was being driven by a woman, a blonde, and she was leaning forward to kiss him as he got into the car.

'MUM!'

I'd just got in from work and Alec's voice was blasting into my ear from Dom's home phone.

'Hello, darling.'

'Mum! I've got the best news. I feel like crying!'

I remembered that it was the day Mrs McKenzie, the drama teacher, was announcing the parts for the Year 6 show which was going to be *Joseph and the Amazing Technicolor Dreamcoat*. Oh, thank you, thank you, bloody lovely Mrs McKenzie, I thought. I guessed that she had seen Alec struggling at school, knew all about what happened in Dorset, how Alec was living with his father and that she – sensitive, caring, intuitive Mrs McKenzie – had thought, I'm going to boost that boy's self-esteem. I'm not going to go the usual route and use the same old faces. I'm going to give Alec Bidewell his chance to shine. And perhaps she had seen some hitherto unseen spark of dramatic brilliance in my son, which I had always known was there, just waiting to be coaxed out. I braced myself, grinning from ear to ear. I was expecting Joseph at the very least.

'Oh my goodness, it was drama today!' I said excitedly. 'What did she say? What did she say?'

'Oh no, not that. It's much better.'

'Didn't Mrs McKenzie announce the roles for *Joseph* today? She said she would.'

'Yes!'

'And?'

'I'm an Ishmaelite.'

'Oh.'

'But this is nothing to do with the play.'

'Do you have any lines?'

'No. I don't think so. But it's much better than that!'

'Do I have to make the costume? What does an Ishmaelite wear?'

'Mum! Listen to me. Dad and Deborah and me are getting a dog! We've just got back from the breeder. Her name is Fiona Billings and she lives in Hemel Hempstead. We've just got back and we've chosen the most beautiful little golden Labrador puppy. I can't believe it. I'm going to have a dog.'

'Oh . . . That's wonderful,' I said lamely. 'A Labrador. When was all this decided?'

'Well, we were talking about it the other evening because we were watching telly and the adverts came on and Deborah said that she'd always wanted an Andrex puppy.'

'Oh . . . Right.'

'And then without either of us knowing, Dad got in touch with Fiona Billings and we were so lucky because there was just one puppy left in the litter because the lady that was going to have him had to cancel because she gets asthma.'

'Oh dear.' I'd gone onto autopilot.

'So Dad drove us there after school and he wouldn't tell us where we were going and he wouldn't give us any clues and when we got there Deborah and I were just so happy. And we walked in and I just knew immediately which one it was. It was really weird. I just walked in and all the puppies were tumbling around and I just looked at one of them and I said to myself '*That* one is Rufus,' and it *was*. And then we stayed for about an hour and we just played with him and cuddled him and he is the most lovely boy. I can't wait for you to see him.'

'Rufus?'

'Yes, Deborah said that she used to have a teddy bear called that and when she was young she went on holiday once and it got lost and after that she always said that if she got a dog she would call it Rufus. And I really like the name too and he is just *such* a Rufus. The name just fits him perfectly.'

'How lovely.'

'He's nearly eight weeks so we're going to pick him up on Saturday.'

'But that's my Saturday. You're here this Saturday.'

'Oh yes.'

I could feel his disappointment seeping down the phone. 'Sorry. I'd forgotten . . . Well Dad and Deborah can get him . . . I can see him Sunday evening I suppose.'

I was tempted to say spitefully, 'Yes. Yes you can see him on Sunday. Or perhaps you don't want to come home at all now you've got your darling Rufus.' How could I compete with a puppy? Game, Set and Bloody Match, Dom. I steeled myself to do the right thing.

'Look, darling, I'll talk to Daddy and maybe he can pick you up on Saturday and take you to Hemel Hempstead, but I do want to see you.'

Alec was grateful and relieved and he continued to express his wonderful disbelief that he would have his own dog, how he couldn't wait for Jess and Luke to meet him because he would be their dog too, how Dad had said they would all go and kit Rufus out at the pet shop together. Usually Alec trod so carefully, but today his elation had got the better of him – and a good thing too. The joy was coursing through him like bolts of electricity. How could I stop him from going to collect the bloody thing?

We said goodbye and immediately I dialled Dom's number, spoke to him very briefly and said yes, in response to our earlier conversation I did think that it was a very good idea that we meet to discuss the parameters of this new arrangement and no, I did not think that it was appropriate for Deborah to attend.

At 2.35 a.m. in the morning I got up and in an effort to stop my head racing with uneasy dreams about mislaid felt-tip pens, Labradors with long blonde hair and Denise behind bars, I went downstairs and found an ancient episode of *Inspector Morse* to watch.

Since seeing Rob being collected by the blonde, I had given myself a very good talking to. I had been sorely tempted to tell Mel and Grace and even Mary about him and was so relieved that I hadn't. I was furious with myself for letting it all mean too much, become too important. I was a single mother with three children. What had I been thinking? Of course he had a partner and of course she was blonde and attractive. I'd been so shaken when I'd seen her in the car because he hadn't mentioned a partner, not once, and he'd given a good impression of being interested in me. But I realized I'd been very foolish and misinterpreted everything. He obviously wasn't attracted to me but he definitely liked me a lot and saw me as a kindred spirit. That was good enough. I'd had a few days of feeling quite flirty and attractive but today I felt forty, old and frumpy again. But I was cool about it. I was fine.

I went over to the computer to distract myself, and realized that I had some replies to my advert for an au pair. Some of them looked promising: 'I have excellent references and three years' experience. I am outgoing and fun. I embrace challenges head-on and enjoy cleaning.' Some did not: 'Fluent in Englosh. No CRB check please.'

I emailed a few possible girls back and forwarded their CVs to Mary.

When I went back to bed I found Jess there, absolutely comatose but sodden. I wearily went into her bedroom to change her sheets and found under her pillow five or six drawings of a yellow dog. 'I Love You, Rufus' she'd written on one and then covered it in hearts and kisses. She hadn't even met him yet. Another one showed Rufus and his family. Jess had drawn herself, the dog, Alec and Luke and two other bigger people: one was Daddy and the other was Deborah. I don't know what upset me most, looking at this little family minus me, or that Jess felt the need to hide the drawing under her pillow. The refreshing thing about Jess was that she had always been too young to watch what she said or how she behaved but now it appeared that even she was learning about secrets that had to be kept and feelings that mustn't be hurt.

I lay down on my bed, feeling leaden. I closed my eyes knowing that I wouldn't sleep. A great, fetid pond of loss, dwelling somewhere between my stomach and my chest, was in danger of consuming me; my marriage, Alec, Philip, Rob and now my little Jess.

Dom had suggested we meet at a café around the corner from his work. That was fine by me. I think he thought I might rein myself in on neutral turf.

He was idly stirring a by now cold cup of coffee and saying irritably: 'Only you, Rachel, could see a puppy as a threat. You are blowing this up out of all proportion. It's a bloody dog, for Christ's sake.'

Dom was doing something that he'd mastered since our separation – wilfully misunderstanding me. He went on trying to feign confusion. 'What on earth can possibly be the problem with Deborah and me getting a dog? Look out of the window. Every other person owns a dog. It is not a big deal.'

'But you know full well it is.' I was trying not to raise my voice. 'Don't try and make out that this is just me going off the deep end.'

He gave me a look as if to say, Well, isn't it?

'I wouldn't mind but we begged you to get a dog ever since Alec could speak and you always dismissed us out of hand.'

'Well, things change,' Dom muttered with a deep sigh.

'Yes, don't they just,' I retorted and at that moment the waitress skipped up.

'Can I get you anything else? Refill your coffee?'

I said 'No thank you.'

Dom made a big play of collecting our used cups and saucers together for her. 'No. Could we just have the bill please? Would you mind?' he said as if asking her a favour. Had he always been such a ham? When we were married I'd thought that he was a man who oozed kindness and warmth. Today he was being obsequious, and for the first time I realized he had developed a habit of sort of tugging his hair forward where it was receding.

'Two more things: why is it suddenly the norm to dump Alec in the Homework Room after school every night and what made you say you'd pick the dog up on Saturday?

Have you any idea how precious a Saturday with Alec is to me now?'

'Look, the after-school thing is getting sorted – and anyway it was only a couple of days – and Saturday is the day that the breeder asked us to pick the dog up. It's not some campaign to undermine you. If you're not happy for him to come along then that's fine.'

'And stop Alec going to collect his new puppy – a day he'll remember for ever?'

'OK. Well let him *come* then. Honestly, Rachel, why do you have to make everything so complicated?'

'I'm not. I know you can understand where I'm coming from, Dom, so stop looking so baffled. It is still very early days for this arrangement. This is still a period for Alec to settle in. He needs to be level-headed and to take a calm approach to deciding if living with you is right for him. We all do. A puppy throws everything off balance and puts everything artificially in your favour.'

'So this is about you not accepting what has happened with Alec and thinking he'll come home. Face it, Rachel, he isn't, and dog or no dog he wants to live with me.'

'Well, I'm not so sure about that any more and I want him home with me.'

'Yes. Well Jess wants a trampoline for her birthday but that's not going to happen either.'

We sat in silence and for the first time I saw a genuine expression register on Dom's face – regret.

'Look,' he said dejectedly, 'I'm sorry I didn't talk this

through with you. I probably should have done. It was a spur of the moment thing. It's just that what happened in Dorset haunts me – the thought of Alec being that unhappy was such a terrible shock. He puts on a good show for us but I can't help thinking that that basic despair is still somewhere inside him. Then Tuesday's little escapade didn't help. I honestly just thought about a little boy needing a friend and something to cheer him up and to help him get through this transition – something to set the seal on our arrangement. And he is happy, Rach. You should have seen his face when we went to the breeder's.'

I wished I had. That was the sort of moment which I always thought we would share as a family.

'Fiona Billings in Hemel Hempstead,' I said absently.

'Yes,' he allowed himself a small smile. 'Fiona Billings in Hemel Hempstead. He is out of his skull with joy – can it really be such a bad thing?'

'No, I suppose not,' I said wearily. 'I just wish we could have talked about it and I miss him. Plus I get the impression that you and Deborah find it a struggle to have him and if he gets so much as a whiff of that then he will feel awful . . . and he'd be better off with me.'

'Well, we're not. If you remember, I did ask you to meet with me and Deborah to discuss things but you wouldn't. Perhaps if you had sat down with us, you would have been reassured that it is all running very smoothly.'

'Like on Tuesday when he got on a bus to Archway.'

'Obviously there are going to be hiccups but overall,

things could not be better. Can you imagine the adjustment Deborah has had to make? But you know she really does love Alec, Rach, and relishes having him in our home. I know this is hard for you to hear but I know that if you're honest you'd rather it were that way. I'm so grateful to her – it's another of the reasons I want to get the dog, to say thank you.'

'Bully for bloody Deborah,' I said ungraciously as I gathered up my coat and bag.

# Chapter Nine

# Bring It On

Today was the day. I strode into work. I was knackered but had got my head into exactly the right space regarding Denise. I knew that Philip was my priority – not to mention all the other residents of Clifton Avenue who deserved better. As for my relationship with Rob, our connection was Denise and Denise only. I told myself I was lucky to have him as a deeply respected colleague. However, as I walked down the corridor towards the kitchen I heard Rob's deep, generous laugh and my insides did an almighty flip-flop. The chef, Pete, was telling him some tale about getting locked out of a pub and unfortunately I walked in just as he was coming to the denouement. He stopped talking and both men said a hurried 'Hi!' to me, polite but eager for the story to reach its culmination. Feeling awkward, I shuffled out again and went to hang up my coat as the two men roared with laughter in the kitchen.

Thirty seconds later, Rob came round the corner. 'Hi,'

he said again. 'Sorry, Pete's stories of hedonism on the Kilburn High Road take some beating. How are you?'

'Good,' I said brightly. 'Really good.' I bustled past him to the office and he followed. I grabbed the post and sorted through it with clammy hands. To my relief, the envelope from Atkinson's had arrived. I waved it at Rob and said gravely, 'Evidence. This is the invoices.' He nodded and closed the door nervously behind him.

'Today's the day,' he said. We both looked pale and twitchy. 'Denise is at head office so I should get into the house. Once I've been in we'll have to sort out what to do next but let's take things one step at a time. I'll get in there while the residents are at the day centre and it's quiet, get some pictures of the printer and anything else that I recognize as being Clifton Avenue property, even if it's a custard cream, and then we'll take it from there. God, I'm sweating – I'm bloody terrified!'

'Of getting into the house?'

'Yes, that and then how the bloody hell are we going to confront Denise? She's back at about two and then I guess it's . . .' He made the sound of a bomb exploding while mimicking the shape with his fingers. 'You're unbelievably calm,' he said.

'I just keep thinking this is all for Philip and as long as I think that then I'm OK.'

'And me?'

'Of course,' I said dismissively.

Rob picked up his phone. 'I'll see you in ten minutes.

You'll keep an eye out just in case she comes back, won't you?'

'She won't but yes, I'll go and sit in Philip's room where I can see the car park as well.'

'Wish me luck!' he said, looking grave. 'Jesus, has it come to this?'

'Good luck.' I said.

I made my way up to Philip's bedroom. Rob was striding over to the house and as he did so he looked up at the window and gave me a little half-hearted wave. I watched him put the key into the lock of Denise's front door and go in.

With my eyes darting back to the car park, I let myself have a look at the new stuff I'd ordered for Philip. A lot of it was in flat-pack form. Rather you than me, Scott, I thought. There was a desk and a chair, a bedside table, a couple of lamps, some brightly coloured pen pots for his felt-tips, a bookcase and some cushions intended to cheer up Philip's rather dismal bedroom. Why on earth had I ordered two lamps? I thought.

I looked back to Denise's house and the car park. All was quiet. 'Come on, Rob,' I said under my breath. 'Get a move on.'

I picked up the package containing some ready-made curtains. We'd gone for stripes in scarlet and blue and they looked really smart. It was a very heavy package considering that it only contained curtains for a window no bigger than a metre and a half across. I had a little pick at the plastic wrapping. Under Philip's curtains were another pair in a sickly lemon yellow and they were massive. Confused, I hurriedly unwrapped the cushions. There were at least three more than I had ordered, again in a lemon-curd yellow. I scrabbled to find the paperwork and peeled it off the packaging. The order form which Philip and I had completed had been changed. It now had Denise's name as the authorizing signature. Unlike the other residents, Philip had quite a lot of money. As the sole beneficiary in his mother's will he wasn't a millionaire but stood to inherit the proceeds of the sale of his mother's flat in Queen's Park. There was a trust being formed to supervise any expenses and the plan was to get him ultimately to live independently in his own flat under some sort of supervised scheme. Denise would be aware of all of this. Suddenly, her need to replace me with dozy old Scott made perfect sense.

As the penny dropped I heard a noise from outside. I looked into the car park and saw Denise's stout little son dismounting his bike and leaning it up against the side of his house. Shit! What the hell was he doing home at half-past eleven on a Thursday morning? Shit, shit, shit! I bounded down the stairs and outside but he was already putting his key in the lock of the front door. It suddenly brought it home to me that what we were doing was insane. What were we thinking? Jesus, Rob could end up being arrested!

'Hello!' I yelled madly. 'Hello!'

The boy stopped and, looking very wary, turned towards me.

'Hello! It's Stewart, isn't it? Stewart?'

'Stephen,' he said.

'Oh, sorry. Sorry, Stephen. I just saw you and I wanted to ask what . . . what . . . Is everything OK? You're not usually home on a Thursday are you? Are you OK? I know your mum's not in.'

'I've got Mum's cold,' he said, regarding me as if I was some sort of freak. 'So I can't go swimming.'

'Oh dear,' I said. He was clutching a violin case. 'Violin!' I shrieked. 'Violin! I didn't know you played the violin. My son Luke had one lesson and I said that if he ever played it again I would have his arms surgically removed. He made do with a recorder after that. How long have you played for?'

Then there was a loud knocking on the office window. Rob was standing there grinning.

'Well, as long as you're OK I'll leave you to it. Bye!'

'Bye,' said Stephen, scowling, as I sprinted back to the office like a demented gazelle.

I stumbled through the office door, shaking with laughter and relief. 'Oh my God! I thought you were a goner!' I said, gasping.

'So did I. Some lookout you are!'

'I was watching the car park. He must have snuck in from the main road. I'm so sorry! How did you get out?'

'Let myself out the back door and then came round the front.'

'Did you see anything? Did you see the printer or the laptop?'

'Just the printer and then Laughing Boy arrived. But I got a shot of it, there's no mistaking it's the one that was here. It's brand new and I've taken the model number.' As he spoke he started looking for the picture on his phone to show me and I started searching my handbag for the invoices so we could match the model.

'That's definitely the one,' I said when I saw the picture and make.

'We don't need to tell her that I've been into the house, we just need to say that we know what she's up to. That we have the invoices and therefore the evidence that she has been stealing property from this place and that we intend to tell whoever we think is appropriate and –'

'What's going on?'

Standing in the doorway was Denise. I felt the earth sort of shake beneath me and couldn't say a thing. Rob looked as if he'd been shot – his expression made it clear that neither of us was capable of bluffing this one out.

'Stephen's been sent home with this cold so I had to come home,' Denise said calmly. 'It sounds like it's a very good thing that I did.' She grabbed the papers from my hand and then Rob's arm. She looked at the image of the printer still displayed on his phone.

'Have you been into my house, Rob?'

'Denise, we've had our suspicions for some time –'

'If this is about that printer, I can assure you that I have full authorization to have it at home. I do work from home a lot as you know. I think it is completely understandable that I should be provided with the necessary equipment to do so. I suggest you call Adrian Morris at head office and I have no doubt that he will vouch for me.'

Rob looked stunned. Denise went over to the office phone and started to dial the number. 'Go on, Rob, talk to Adrian. I've absolutely nothing to hide. I've also purchased a laptop on behalf of Emily and various pieces of equipment for the residents' use.' She carried on dialling and then held the phone up to Rob, urging him to take it from her. She was trying to appear in control but her hands shook with rage.

'Look, Denise,' Rob stuttered. 'I was concerned that . . .'

I stepped forward and took the receiver out of Denise's hands. In fact I snatched it. Both she and Rob looked baffled.

'Thank you,' I said. 'I'm happy to speak to Adrian Morris. Although I think it makes more sense to speak to Martin Sharp.' Adrian Morris was the Director of Social Services and the man rumoured to have got Denise the job at Clifton Avenue in the first place. Martin Sharp was his deputy, and according to Rob was a decent and conscientious man.

Denise exhaled, sharply and irritably.

The automated voice on the switchboard said, 'Please enter the number of the extension you require or hold to speak to an operator.' I held but wasn't sure how long my legs would continue to support me until mercifully someone said, 'Hello, Social Services.'

'Oh hello.' I breathed in deeply, my voice now calm and even. 'Could you put me through to Martin Sharp, please?'

'Yes, can I tell him who's calling?'

'It's Rachel Bidewell. I'm a residential care assistant at Clifton Avenue.'

'Putting you through.'

There was a click and a voice said, 'Hello? Martin Sharp.'

'Hello, Martin,' I said. 'This is Rachel Bidewell from Clifton Avenue.'

'Hello, Rachel. How can I help you?'

I thought my heart was going to burst out of my chest. I took another deep breath. 'I'm afraid I need your advice. I have discovered some very upsetting information about Denise Mott. I think that we may need to inform the police.'

Ninety minutes later and Martin Sharp was seated at the table in the office at Clifton Avenue. He was a big, kind man in an ill-fitting navy blue suit. Denise was sitting opposite him and was white with shock and indignation. On the table between them were a large pair of lemon-yellow curtains, a table lamp and three cushions.

'You leave me no option but to inform the police,

Denise. I really don't know what else to do,' Martin was saying.

'How you can conclude that I was stealing these items, Martin, is beyond me. Surely you understand that it was merely for convenience that I ordered them via Philip Johnston. My intention has always been to pay for them. And as for the printer and the computer equipment, I work extensively at home and –'

'You know full well that I would not be doing my job properly unless I investigated thoroughly the accusations that Rachel has made. That, in addition to your insistence that she be removed from her position as Philip's key worker – specifically going against the wishes of your deputy and the client himself – does indicate that there is cause for concern. I think it's out of my hands.'

'Well, we'll see what Adrian has to say, shall we? I've put in a call to him,' spat Denise.

'I spoke to him before I left. He agreed, as I'm sure you will, that as you've been friends with Adrian for many years and he is our director, it would be inappropriate for him to oversee the investigation. Don't you agree that a third party should be brought in – even if it is just to clear your name?'

'If it is the only way I will be vindicated then so be it. I hope you can live with yourself, Martin. I assume that I will be suspended while these investigations take place and it's the residents that you will ultimately be harming – leaving this place rudderless.'

'Oh I'm sure Rob will do a very good job keeping your seat warm for you.'

'Hello, Mary?'

'Hello, sweetheart! What can I do for you?'

I loved calling my mother-in-law because she always sounded so thrilled to hear from me, even if I'd just spoken to her an hour before.

'Two things: one, can you help me interview for the new au pair next week, I made such a hash of it the first time I think I need another pair of eyes and ears?'

'Of course – I got the CVs. Just tell me when.'

'And, second, can you babysit tonight? Something really rather fabulous has happened and I want to go out and celebrate – till really, really late!'

'No problem.' She knew from experience that at this stage of my life 'really, really late' meant about ten-past eleven. 'I'll come over at six and help with tea. Can you let me know what's going on?'

'I'll tell you tonight.'

'Alright, my love. See you then.'

Once it had become clear that Martin Sharp was going to take our accusations seriously, Rob had insisted that we go out and celebrate. Wary that I was vulnerable in the Rob department and worried that I might make a drunken lunge for him as the night wore on, I suggested that we ring Lucy and get her along too.

So here we were, the three of us, sitting in a spit-and-sawdust pub in Camberwell near to Lucy's home, getting fabulously, deliciously pissed. When Lucy had suggested where to meet, I had assumed that food would be part of the deal but no, so as alcohol splashed liberally into my empty stomach, I was feeling remarkably good about life. I had devoured three packets of cheese and onion crisps and a lot of wine and wasn't driving home and Mary was holding the fort. At this rate I might even go clubbing. I was wearing a dress that I loved. As the all-body Spanx has yet to be invented, I had made do with the ones that stretch from your waist to your knees. Luke had said that I looked 'scary' but I thought I looked pretty good for once, and so did Mary.

Rob was talking Lucy through the morning's events in minute detail, from Stephen and his violin to the look on Denise's face when I took the phone from her to speak to head office.

I wasn't saying much but just sitting back and staring, as I had a legitimate excuse to appreciate Rob's handsome face for minutes at a time. Lucy said little but just kept gasping and squeaking and squawking with delight as the tale unfolded.

'What will happen to her?' she asked.

'Even if the police don't charge her with theft, Martin says there's no way she'll work for the borough again.'

'What about the house? What about Stephen? God, she won't get put in jail will she?'

Rob laughed. 'She'll have to live like the rest of us mortals and find somewhere of her own. She won't go to jail though, surely it'd be community service, wouldn't it? Now that would be a sight I'd pay to see, Denise in an orange boiler suit, scrubbing at graffiti.'

Our laughter was a little forced as we all avoided thinking about Stephen and where he would lay his head and his violin case. Denise had absolutely got what she deserved but beneath his bravado I knew Rob wished it hadn't ended so badly.

After another glass of wine, it was becoming imperative that I eat something, otherwise I could see myself being removed from the pub by Rob in a fireman's lift as I vomited cheese and onion crisps down his back. Rob was telling Lucy about how he had agreed to stay on at Clifton Avenue as Acting Head, and then to my relief said, 'God, I'm famished. Do either of you want to get something to eat?'

'No,' said Lucy. 'I've got to get back. My sister's babysitting – she doesn't ask for money but she turns very stroppy after ten-thirty. Thinks she's being taken advantage of – which she probably is. No, you two go off and get hammered.' She was too drunk not to smirk.

We waved goodbye to Lucy and set off hazily to hail a cab to get us back from south-east London to the green pastures of Queen's Park. Sod the expense.

Once in the cab, I sobered up in an instant. I felt tired and on the brink of a headache. Being alone in such a confined space with Rob made all the leisurely joy of the evening disappear and I felt clumsy and self-conscious. And my breath smelt of cheese and onion.

Rob had not sobered up in quite the same way. He sat back in the cab and grabbed my hand. 'In case I forget to ever say it to you, you were bloody magnificent today. You were amazing. I think you might be my saviour.'

I sat forward awkwardly, with my hand outstretched as if it belonged to someone else. Then I tried to snatch it back and said weedily: 'Don't.'

Rob let my hand go. 'What's wrong?' he said.

I sighed. 'I haven't done this sort of thing for a very long time and think it would just about kill me if I were to find out that you have a beautiful blonde waiting for you at home.'

'But I don't. God, I wish I did . . . no offence.'

'But I saw you the other night getting into your car. There was a blonde driving and she kissed you when you got in. And there's a woman on your answerphone message and you never, ever talk about your private life so I think it's fair to assume that although you can flirt for Scotland, you are probably not single.'

I'd hoped he was going to laugh and say, 'Oh that beautiful blonde. You fool. That's my old friend, Brenda the Bull Dyke,' but he didn't. Instead, he knitted his hands together between his knees and let his head droop. 'That is Megan. You have correctly deduced that she is the blonde waiting for me at home, but alas she is my ex. Do you want the full story?'

I nodded.

Once the cab had let us out, we found a wall outside a pub to sit on and stared at the road.

Rob took a deep breath. 'We were briefly married about six years ago now. We have a son, Will, and things stayed amicable, with us sharing him fifty-fifty, after she decided that I was not her Mr Right. Last year she announced that she wanted to return home to Australia to be with her family. She took Will with her – I couldn't stop her, she was so determined to go and so miserable here – and I've been a bloody wreck ever since. A month or so ago, she said she was coming back to see friends and that she was bringing Will, but then at the last minute she left him with her mother saying it was 'too complicated' to travel with a child. It turns out her purpose for coming back was to see if there was anything left between us. For Will's sake I wish there was but . . . I worry she's just a malcontent. She's never settled, never happy. It just doesn't ring true that suddenly she's in love with me again. After all this time! It's weird to have loved someone so much and then to discover they might actually be an idiot.'

A bus trundled past and I watched it disappear. 'I try hard not to hate my husband,' I said. 'Because if I do then it makes a mockery of the most important years of my life. And anyway, I don't want to hate my children's father.'

Rob nodded. 'Sometimes I think that love actually is blind and when you stop loving someone the scales fall away and you see them for who they really are . . . and it's not what you thought at all.'

'Or perhaps people just change . . .'

'All this time I thought I wanted nothing more than for Megan to come home and now she has, I realize it's just about the worst thing that could ever happen for me and for Will.'

'But you've got to try for Will's sake, haven't you? When did you last see him?'

'Oh I went over in the summer and we're on Skype and we talk every day, but I still feel I've lost him.'

'If it's any comfort, Alec lives less than three miles away with his father and I know exactly how you feel.'

'You never said.'

'*You* never said.' He was laughing and shaking his head. 'It's you that's thrown everything! God, Rachel, it's you!'

And with that he leant forward and kissed me, properly on the mouth. His hand went up to my face and then through my hair and down my back. My heart started to hammer in my chest and I felt like the abandoned house again, coming to life with the lights being switched on one at a time. My worry was that if Rob's hand strayed anywhere near my Spanx, all my bulbs were going to blow simultaneously.

'Can I come home with you?' he asked simply.

'No,' I said sadly. The kiss had been nice, but a mistake. 'I think that would be a very bad idea.' I hadn't been through everything with Dom only to bulldoze another family – no matter how big a mess it was in.

The next morning and Mary and I were sitting in my kitchen opposite Hope, our possible new au pair, and things were going well.

'Yes,' Hope was saying, 'I looked after Ayron who was five, Catja who was three and the baby was Sam, he was nine months when I left.'

'And how long were you with the Rogers family in total?' I said formally.

'Just under two years.'

'And where do they live?'

'Oh not too far. Muswell Hill, so I know this area pretty well. I've got lots of friends here and I really want to stay around North London.'

'Why did you leave?'

'Well, I just felt it was time to move on.'

'And can I go to them for a reference?'

'Oh yes, no problem. Absolutely no problem.'

Hope was Kiwi, fresh-faced and sweet. Her sandy-coloured hair was swept haphazardly back in a huge clip and her youthfully angular face shone with enthusiasm and commitment. She wore sneakers, jeans and a vintage T-shirt and her wrist was the mass of beads, threads, bands and tattered friendship bracelets that denote the seasoned traveller. Her skin was gingery, honey-brown and the nooks between her fingers were marble-white by comparison. She appeared to have arrived like a very cool snail, with her house on her back in the form of a giant rucksack. She said she could start as soon as I wanted as she wasn't working, having just stepped off a plane from Marrakesh.

'This would be a very different job,' said Mary gravely. 'Luke and Jess are older and at school all day and so you would be expected to help Rachel with the running of the house while they're out and you'll need to be familiar with all the school runs, kit, clubs, et cetera, plus you'll need to make sure they have a good tea on the evenings Rachel is working. What sort of food would you make?'

'Oh I love cooking. It's a bit fiddly but I always think you can trust your own cooking better than any supermarket stuff. So, I would do homemade chicken nuggets –' I didn't know you *could* make chicken nuggets in your own home '– shepherd's pie, with carrots and other veg hiding inside so the kids don't even notice they're eating healthily. Nothing fancy just good, wholesome stuff. I'm veggie so I use a lot of fruit, chickpeas, nuts and pulses and I managed to get the Rogers kids eating them too. I sometimes struggled a bit with Ayron's five a day but I definitely managed four and a half.'

'Great!' I said, resisting the urge to kiss her. We went upstairs and she managed not to gag at the sight of Luke's room. I was pretty sure I had found my girl. Mary and I had seen six girls in total, all of whom had been deeply disappointing until the lovely Hope.

When she popped to the loo, Mary and I exchanged grateful glances and I mouthed, 'She seems great, doesn't she?'

'A dream,' said Mary.

We'd asked everything we needed to ask and as we steered her to the door, I said, 'Did you have a good trip?'

'Oh, amazing,' she said. 'I didn't sleep for about a month!'

I was madly dredging through my memories of Inter-Railing with Dom, many centuries ago. 'I loved Marrakesh,' I said. 'So busy and such an amazing light.'

'God yes!' said Hope. 'I think if I'd stayed another week I would have been dead. *So* busy. Have you been there a lot?'

'No, just a short tourist trip when I was a lot younger . . . and cooler!'

She laughed. 'Oh, I think you're pretty cool now.'

Dammit, a twenty-year-old had made me blush. 'Right, so I'll just take up your references with the Rogers family and get back to you. It's a real pleasure to have met you.' We shook hands and grinned at each other.

'Just one last thing?' she said airily.

'Yes?'

'When you speak to the Rogers, can I ask that you talk to Lloyd Rogers, the dad?'

'Yes, any particular reason?'

'No, everything's cool, it just might make more sense to talk to him.' And she winked at me!

I felt my smile dissolve. I looked at Mary and we exchanged uneasy glances. I was worried I'd overdone it on the just-off-the-hippy-trail mum bit and rather misled her over what sort of a person I was.

'Oh, OK. I'll talk to Lloyd.'

I went back into the house and rang the Rogers' family home. A man, presumably Lloyd, picked up and so I asked to speak to Mrs Rogers. I told her that I had just interviewed Hope and was ringing for a reference.

There was a terrible silence and then Lloyd came back on the phone. 'Hello? This is Mr Rogers here. Look, I'm very sorry but I really don't think we're in a position to give Hope a reference. She left us under something of a cloud.'

Someone in the background went '*Ha*!'

'Oh, only she said that you would be happy to recommend her.'

'Well . . . no . . . actually.'

There was another 'HA!' and the sound of something smashing. Then a voice said, 'Tell her she's good in the bedroom! Tell her she excels at sleeping with other people's husbands!' and with that the line went dead.

Mary and I trooped back to the kitchen. We had interviewed miserable Manoush and then Tanya-with-a-y who was a scantily dressed smoker and Tania-with-an-i who was a complete no-no because her only questions related to what days she would have off and whether the oven was self-cleaning. We had interviewed Theresa-Maria, who was lovely but who spoke English like a chihuahua and Lola, whose hair was so greasy I could smell it from across the table. Mel's Anna had come up with a few suggestions but after Marlene I was understandably cautious. I slumped down at the kitchen table and put my head in my hands. 'How hard can it be?' I said to Mary. 'I can't tell you how many CVs I trawled through and I can assure you, they were the absolute cream of the bloody crop.'

'Well perhaps you need to think outside the box a little more. Don't rely on the Internet and go for somebody closer to home.'

I looked irritable and uncomprehending. 'Like who for instance? Have you got anyone in mind because I'd truly love to meet them.'

'Well, actually, yes I have . . . me.'

There was a beat while I took this in.

'Are you serious?' I said, almost in a whisper.

'Completely. I've put a lot of thought into it and I think it's the obvious solution.'

'But what about the surgery?'

'Well, I've spoken to Dr Nigel, and he says that if I can make it work then I have his blessing. Jean is happy to swap to afternoons and Phyllis is happy to cover the early mornings once in a while. We're ladies nearing retirement age, we're incredibly flexible, the only thing we have to rush home for is *Countdown* and three of us don't even have husbands. So what do you say?'

'Oh Mary. I don't know what to say. Of course! Of

course! It just never crossed my mind. Will you be doing less hours? Will you be out of pocket?'

'Don't you worry about that, the girls at the surgery will see I don't lose any hours. And just to get it straight, I'm not moving into Luke's room! He can keep it. I'll stay in my little flat thank you very much.'

I walked over to her and put my arms around her. 'Oh Mary, you are the answer to all my prayers. I don't think I've ever been more grateful to anybody in all my life. The kids will be ecstatic. Why didn't you say anything before?'

'You didn't ask. And not everyone wants their mother-in-law poking about in their house. I thought I'd see if we could find somebody really super today and if not, see what you thought of my suggestion.'

'Well, you are most welcome to poke about wherever you please. Honestly, I feel as if a huge weight has been lifted from my shoulders. I feel as if when I look down at the floor my feet will be off the ground! Mary, this is just amazing.'

She'd gone a bit pink and was searching for the tissue up her sleeve.

'But just one thing?' I said. Thanks to Denise's downfall and now Mary, I could feel the mist clearing and everything beginning to look more straightforward.

'Anything.'

'Will you try and make it up with Dom? He misses you and you miss him and this has gone on for long enough. We've both got to move on.'

'I can't forgive and I can't forget – I never will,' she said bitterly.

'I didn't say you had to. Just move on.'

Lucy and I helped Margaret and Philip off the bus and we all waddled towards the leisure centre with our swimming bags bouncing against our hips.

I had looked forward all morning to telling Philip that I was going to remain as his key worker and had planned that ideally I would take him to the hot tub at the side of the pool and tell him, and if not, just take him to the café to spill the wonderful beans. Experience told me not to expect too much, but surely this would reach him, bring him back.

He hadn't reacted at all when I'd told him about the trip and now as we bought our tickets and went through to the hot, bright changing rooms, he remained utterly passive. Warm air and the smell of chlorine and damp clothes hit us. Someone somewhere was drying their hair with a noisy hairdryer. Lucy showed us through to a big changing room and there were two or three other carers like us and we all smiled at one another knowingly. Two old ladies were being got ready to swim, along with Margaret and a teenage girl in a high-tech wheelchair. I realized I would have to take Philip into another room. At these sessions communal changing was allowed but I thought I should spare Philip's blushes, and everyone else's.

I wriggled into my costume behind my towel and all

the while I talked as I got out Philip's smart new trunks and put them on him.

'Fabulous!' I said. 'Give us a twirl.'

But this was the same dead-eyed, disengaged Philip, the great wound on his forehead now yellow and purple.

'Now, we'll just take everything very very slowly,' I ploughed on. 'Perhaps today will just be a day to see the changing rooms and see how it all works. Perhaps today we'll just walk round the pool and you can see how you feel. If you want to go in you can, and if you don't that's fine. We'll stay in the shallow end. Maybe just have a little paddle and then go for a nice cup of tea.'

Lucy had had a limited choice of trunks in Philip's size and ended up getting a vibrant turquoise pair with an orange surfboard motif on the bottom of one leg. I was nervous and excited and it made me want to laugh out loud to see him standing slumped in front of me with his jaw hanging idly open and his eyes unfocused, all the while sporting a pair of trunks that subliminally said, Goin' to the beach, dude. Awesome!

When we were finally ready, I took his hand and he shuffled along beside me. Lucy and Margaret were waiting for us and Lucy and I smiled bravely at each other and she said, 'Let's do this!'

We walked gingerly on the damp, ridged tiles. I was worried Philip might slip so I clung to his arm and guided him as carefully as I could. Eventually, we were at the opening to the pool area. In order to make it there we had to step through one of those low baths of water that are supposed to clean your feet. Lucy and Margaret went ahead of us and waited on the other side. I made to follow, but Philip stopped dead. He brought his hands up to his chest and made two tight fists and then he buried his chin into the fists.

'Come on, Philip. Don't fall at the first hurdle!' said Lucy cheerfully. Margaret tutted and sniffed impatiently. This was the highlight of her week and Philip was holding her up.

'Go ahead, Luce,' I said. 'We'll take our time.'

She nodded and went to get into the pool with Margaret. I stood in front of Philip and walked into the two inches of chilly water that stood between us and swimming heaven. Turning to walk backwards I held onto his hands and pulled him towards me.

'Come on. It's only two steps and then at least you can see the pool even if you don't want to swim. And we can have a walk round.'

I was getting cold now. There was a wintry blast coming from somewhere and as I looked down at my cellulite, it was turning an unattractive shade of purple. Philip refused to move so I just took one hand and tried to coax him in.

'Come on, you can do this. This is easy.'

Still nothing, so I dropped his hands and went through myself. 'Follow me,' I said. 'You're out of it just as soon as you're in.'

I stood on the other side and looked back at him. Nothing. 'Oooh! Here's the hot tub!' I said optimistically.

It was right next to me. 'Let's treat ourselves and go and have a sit in there. There's something I have to tell you. A really good bit of news but I can't tell you unless you come out here.'

Now I was shivering so I folded my arms tightly across my chest. I pointed at the hot tub. 'Look! Shall we go in there? You don't have to go into the pool if you don't want to.'

My shoulders sank and I felt defeated. We were back to that very first day when I gave Philip his bath – only Rob wasn't here to help. The hot tub looked scummy and uninviting.

Keeping my eyes on Philip I walked over to it and put my hand in. 'It's lovely and warm. Please come in. I really want to talk to you.' As I whooshed my hand around in the lukewarm, flatulent water, I thought less of luxury spas and more of fungal infections and diseases multiplying in the heat. I thought of the bits of dead skin, toenails and hair clogged in the filter system and sat down on the edge to get a grip.

As I did so, Philip turned and began to walk back in the direction of the lockers.

'Fine,' I said to myself miserably. 'Let's just get changed and go home.' I looked over to Lucy and couldn't help but smile. Margaret was lying on her back, supported by Lucy, and both their bodies were swaying together in such a lovely, uncomplicated union. Margaret's eyes were closed and I could tell that just for a moment the mind of this poor fractured, frantic woman was calm and at peace.

Lucy caught my eye. I didn't want to disturb them, so I just shrugged my shoulders and mouthed, 'We'll see you in the café.'

She made a sad, 'I'm sorry' face and nodded.

Nobody was about so I took Philip into the big changing room again. I collected our clothes and as I carried them through I dropped my tights and skirt into a puddle on the tiled floor. 'Shit!' I said as I lifted them up dripping.

I got Philip changed and then struggled to pull on my damp tights over my damp feet. When we were both nearly ready I thought, well, now's as good a time as any and decided to tell Philip the good news. The café would be noisy and distracting, here it was just the two of us. I wasn't convinced but perhaps the day could be saved after all.

With Philip sat on a bench, I got down on my knees and very carefully started putting his socks on over his poor old feet. I looked up at him and said, 'You know I said I had some good news? It's the best news I've had all year.'

He stared blankly back at me.

'You remember that Denise told you that I couldn't be your key worker any more and that Scott would look after you?'

He gave no sign that he even registered what I was talking about.

'Come on,' I said. 'I know you remember that evening – it's certainly one I won't forget in a hurry.'

His head dropped and he looked at his knees.

I secured the Velcro straps on Philip's shoes and then sat next to him on the bench and took his hand. 'Well, the good news is that that whole plan has been cancelled. Denise is going away for a while and Rob is going to be in charge. He says that I can stay as your key worker. There's no need for Scott to be involved at all and you and I will carry on exactly the same as before . . . Are you pleased . . .? I am . . .'

'Here, puss,' said Philip distractedly, looking away.

I should have known better but I was hurt by his lack of response. Smarting, I pushed on: 'Scott isn't going to be your key worker. It's going to be me again, Rachel.'

We sat in silence for a moment, me wracking my brain trying to think of a way to get through to him. And then Philip said: 'You wanna watch her.' He spoke in a strange, spiteful voice I'd never heard him use before. 'You wanna watch that one. Trouble.'

And although I'd never met her, I knew that this was his mother talking. It was Muriel. Loving, devoted, bitter, mistrustful Muriel, who'd been suspicious of anyone who wanted to look after her son and who didn't believe he could achieve anything, so she kept him shut away.

'She wants locking up, she does,' he went on unkindly. This was Muriel's legacy. She was still there, a constant voice in his head.

I touched his arm. 'Oh, Philip . . . don't. Please don't.'

He clapped his hands loudly three times and shook his

head. He was agitated and wild. 'She wants locking up!' he said again loudly and jerked his chin upwards.

'Stop it,' I said gently. I couldn't bear it. 'Look at me. Look at Rachel.' I stood with my face close to his. 'It's not Scott any more, or Denise, it's me, it's *Rachel*. Look at me. Look at Rachel.'

It was useless. He never used my name anyway. He jutted his head upwards to look at the ceiling and clapped his hands again. I wasn't going to reach him.

I was cold and upset and I wanted to get out. 'Come on, let's go.' I stood up and tried to take his arm to leave, but he stared ahead at the wall and went rigid. Then he closed his eyes and started shaking his head, so I took his huge hands in mine. 'Get up, please!' I said, but I was holding his hands too tightly and as I went to heave him off the bench he panicked and started trying to get free with a frantic paddling motion. I wouldn't let go and kept trying to pull him up. We must have looked like two frenzied schoolgirls fighting in the playground. 'Get up!' I said again. 'Why won't you get up?'

Lucy came into the room. 'What's the matter? What are you doing?' she said, going to Philip's side, and I realized I was crying.

I let one big sob escape from my chest and I said, 'Sorry' and left.

I went into one of the lavatories and locked the door behind me. I pulled at the loo-roll dispenser but it was stuck and I pulled out a small ragged square of tissue. I couldn't even blow my nose. I rested my head back against the wall and took a deep, shaky breath.

Back at Clifton Avenue, Lucy was still quite cold towards me. I'd tried to explain what had happened with Philip, but she obviously felt I'd crossed a line. I heated up some soup for us all for lunch and we sat and ate it in the dining room in silence, except for the ringing of spoons against standard-issue china bowls.

Later I went to the office; it was the day to fill out the repeat prescription forms for the local GP. I was grateful to get lost in the task and it passed the time.

Unexpectedly, Rob arrived at 2 o'clock. I was so pleased to see him and felt a great whoosh of relief. I wanted to tell him what had happened with Philip and have him reassure me and put his arm around me. But that way was madness. After everything that had happened the other night, not surprisingly, we were uncomfortable with each other. So I found myself willing the shift to finish and for me to go and collect the kids as normal. Alec was coming home for the weekend and I was desperate to see him.

I was seeing what we were short of in the drug cupboard when the phone went. I picked it up and a woman's voice said, 'Oh hello, can I speak to Rob?'

'Yes,' I said. 'I'll see if I can find him for you. Who's calling?'

'It's Megan.'

'Oh right.' I tried to sound relaxed. 'I'll go and find him. I think he's upstairs so it might take a minute.'

'No problem, thanks. Is that Rachel?'

'Yes, yes it is.'

'Oh I'm looking forward to meeting you. I've heard a lot about you. Rob says you've been amazing.'

'Oh, I don't know about that. Yes . . . well. I'll see if I can find him.'

Then Rob walked in. I held the phone out to him and as casually as I could I said, 'It's Megan.'

'Oh right.' He took the phone. It seemed overly dramatic to leave the room but awkward to stay.

Rob was self-conscious and flustered. 'Hi,' he said. 'Why didn't you call my mobile?'

A conversation continued and I tried to concentrate on the drugs cupboard. It was obvious they were planning a weekend away and she was ringing to confirm the final arrangements. Thankfully the call didn't last long.

'Sorry,' Rob said as he put the phone down. 'For some reason she couldn't reach me on my mobile.'

'No problem,' I said.

'I've taken this weekend off, Vince's covering. We're going to get away. Only to Windsor but a mate recommended a hotel by the river and they've got a deal on, so . . . It seemed like a good idea after everything that's gone on. Get a bit of space, a bit of perspective.'

'Well you certainly deserve it,' I said as warmly as I could.

'I've only come in to make sure I've left everything in order. I'm going to try and get ahead of the traffic.'

'Good idea.' I buried my head in my notes but he wouldn't shut up. He felt he needed to give me an explanation.

'I think it's for the best. You were quite right. It's not the right time to . . .'

I thought I was going to cry again. Why wouldn't he just shut up? 'I know,' I said. 'It's fine. I hope you have a wonderful weekend. Don't give anything here a thought.'

'Thanks, Rachel. Thanks for being so . . . understanding.'

At that moment I was holding a large bottle of cough syrup in my shaking hand and it was all I could do not to throw it at his head.

When I got to school, Dom was there before me, saying goodbye to Alec and handing over his weekend bag. I nearly crushed Alec when I hugged him and as I ushered the children into the car felt relieved to be in their company and that it was Friday.

Dom was hovering. 'Look, I put Alec's bag together in a bit of a rush. I think I might have forgotten to put a few things in.'

The frustration and disappointment of the day had

compounded to make me tetchy and defensive and generally unpleasant. 'Dom, he's fine!' I snapped.

'I can always give him anything he needs tomorrow when we get the dog.'

Oh yes, I'd forgotten about the bloody dog. 'What on earth does he need that he doesn't already have at home?' I asked, exasperated.

'Well, just a towel and a few wash things.'

'For pity's sake, credit me with some sense. I've got a cupboard full of towels, as well you know.'

'Alright! I'm only trying to make sure he's got everything he needs.'

'Yes, but by doing so, you imply that I can't look after him adequately. I managed to do a pretty good job for eleven years.' I was about to tell Dom to just leave me to it and show me a bit of respect, when I saw Alec's worried face staring at us miserably. I sighed. God, could this day get any worse?

'Sorry, Dom,' I said. 'It's been a long day. I'll let you know if he needs anything. I'll call you in the morning about the dog. Thanks for bringing his bag.'

Dom gave me an incredibly irritating I-should-think-so-too nod and waved goodbye to the kids.

It was dark and pouring with rain again as I pulled away from school, having to edge the car nervously around a massive wheelie bin that was on the corner as we turned left. I was forced to veer over to the other side of the road and the driver coming towards me looked incensed, as if my driving was not that of a sane person.

My weekend with Alec had begun, so despite the rain and the traffic and such a terrible day, I tried to get my spirits to lift. I distributed Jaffa Cakes – a Friday treat – and they were chewed noisily by Luke and licked avidly by Jess, while Alec nibbled the edges in order to eat the orangey bits separately.

'Anybody got any news for me?' I asked, trying to sound cheery.

'I got sixty-five per cent in general knowledge!' exclaimed Luke.

'That's brilliant, darling. Well done you. Was Mrs John pleased with you?'

'Not really.'

'Why not?'

'The average mark was eighty.'

'Oh . . . well. As long as you did your best,' I said lamely and Alec sniggered.

'How about you? How has your week gone?'

'Not bad,' Alec sighed and I wondered if I detected a slight air of deflation. 'Oh I know what I did have to tell you,' he said, perking up.

'What?'

'Mrs Graves might be leaving.'

'Oh I love Mrs Graves! Why?'

'Well, she hasn't said anything but we're pretty sure she's pregnant because she hasn't had a school dinner since the beginning of term and at registration she just sits with her head on the desk and eats ginger biscuits.'

'Well yes, that does sound like you may be right. Either pregnancy or clinical depression at having to teach you lot.'

'Or maybe she just loves ginger nuts!' interjected Jess. 'Why when you're having a baby do you feel sick? Why does a little, tiny baby make you sick?'

'Oh I don't know.' I searched around for a brief explanation that would satisfy Jess for the journey home. 'I think your body just needs to adapt to all the changes that are going on.'

'Like what?'

'Well the mummy's womb is growing and the lining of it fills up with blood to make the baby comfortable and safe as it grows and –'

'Blood! How does blood make it comfy? Blood?!'

'Well the tissue that lines the womb –'

'Tissues?!' Luke joined in.

Alec gave me a conspiratorial 'forgive them for they are young and know not what they do' look. 'Plus the mother's breasts are getting ready to make milk,' he said.

Luke and Jess guffawed both at the concept and at Alec trying to be so matter-of-fact on the subject of breasts.

'They always have milk in them, don't they, Mum?' asked Luke.

'No! Of course not. I haven't got milk in them now, have I?'

'Haven't you?'

'No!'

'What are they filled up with then?'

It was Alec's turn to guffaw. 'You only have milk in them when you have a baby to feed. The rest of the time they're just filled with blood vessels and muscle and fat.'

'Fat boobies!' Jess whispered to Luke, thinking Alec and I couldn't hear and the two of them began to shake with the delicious mirth that only the forbidden induces.

Alec and I smiled at each other and I was about to start all over again with an explanation of morning sickness when my phone rang. It was in my pocket so I wriggled around and got Alec to take it out and answer it.

'Hello, Rachel's phone,' he said so efficiently that I was rather taken aback. God, that boy is growing up, I thought sadly as he carried on. 'Oh hello, this is Alec her son. I'm afraid she's driving at the moment. Can I get her to ring you back?'

'Who is it?' I was saying. 'Tell them we'll be home in ten minutes.'

'Oh right.' Alec waved his hand at me to say sssh. 'Well, just a moment, and I'll tell her to pull over.' He looked at me. 'It's Lucy from work. She says she needs to speak to you urgently.'

I lurched into a bus stop and took the phone.

'Lucy, hi. What is it?'

'Oh, Rachel, I'm so sorry. It's Philip.'

'What? What's happened?' I felt sick.

'He's been arrested.'

'What! Why?'

'It's a long story. We're all in the park and the police are threatening to take him to the station but he won't move. I said I'd get you. You need to come now.'

'Where in the park?'

'We're just in the car park by the south gate. After everything that happened today, I thought I'd take him for a walk and we got separated. I'm so sorry, Rachel. I'm so sorry.'

I turned the car around and we got back onto the main road. The traffic was appalling. A journey that should have taken fifteen minutes took half an hour and all the time my mind was racing and Lucy was ringing and talking to Alec and saying 'Where are you now? Where are you now?'

When we got to the car park it was freezing and dark and the first thought I had was of the night Alec went missing. There were three police cars, a van and someone was cordoning off the area with plastic tape. The police cars all had their headlights on so there was a great pool of artificial light reflected in the wet gravel and muddy puddles. In the middle of it all stood Philip, his head and neck stretching towards the black, evening sky and his hands clutching the front of the waistband of his trousers, kneading the loose fabric as if it were a rosary. He was swaying ominously back and forth like a drunk about to drop.

Lucy raced to meet us and began talking urgently as I

parked and opened my door. 'Oh thank God you're here. I just didn't know what to do. I've called Rob but I think he's away. The police don't understand. They won't listen to me.'

'What's happened? What on earth's happened?' I got out of the car and began to stride over to where Philip was. The children instinctively knew to stay behind and Lucy chattered hysterically next to me.

'I thought a walk would do him good, get him out of himself, but he got lost, I just don't know how it happened. One minute he was with me and the next ... anyway he frightened these two young girls –'

'Frightened them? What do you mean frightened them?'

Lucy grabbed my arm to stop me. She took a deep breath. 'They're saying Philip exposed himself to them.'

I looked at her incredulously, hoping for more of an explanation, trying to process exactly what she'd said when a stout, officious-looking police officer came prancing towards us. I remember thinking, You're a policeman, you really shouldn't be enjoying this.

'Mrs Bidewell? You're the gentleman's key worker, I understand. We're hoping you may be able to help us. We need Mr Johnston to come down to the police station. A very serious accusation has been made against him and we need to get it all sorted as soon as possible but I'm afraid he is very frightened and needs someone to calm him down and explain the situation to him.'

I took in the scene as quickly as I could. I looked over at two young girls, they were no more than twelve or thirteen, and leaning against the bonnet of one of the police cars. They had police blankets draped across their shoulders and their little faces looked tear-stained and shocked. They were flanked by grave and upset-looking men who I assumed were their fathers.

'Right,' I said to the police officer. 'I don't for one minute think that Philip has done anything that can't be explained rationally. I'm sure we can get it all sorted very quickly and with a minimum of fuss.' As I spoke, my voice shook and I frantically wondered what the best way to approach him was. All I could picture in my mind was that night and how he had hit his head again and again in his bedroom at Clifton Avenue. How he was unreachable. How removed he had been from anything but his fear and pain ever since.

'Well, we need to get him to the station and get a statement from him. At the moment he is refusing to come and if this continues to be the case then –'

'I'll do what I can,' I said quietly.

As I walked over to the area where Philip was standing, I saw an elderly woman talking to a police officer. At her feet was a horrid Jack Russell and it yapped and yapped as I went past, pulling on its lead and baring its teeth at me. In order to avoid it I veered off the path and stuck my foot into a wet, black puddle. The freezing water went over the top of my shoe and into my sock and had the effect of making me feel nauseous as I stepped closer and closer to Philip.

'Philip?' I said. 'It's me.' I went to put my hand on his shoulder. 'It's Rachel.' And I have to admit that just a small part of me was scared. Scared that this might be the angry Philip from the swimming pool or the one who beat his own head against the door frame. Scared that he would lash out. Not to hurt me. Just a reaction to his confusion and panic. So I stood very still, with my hand on his shoulder, hoping that my presence alone would calm him.

I looked back at the tableau behind me. Another police car had arrived and a WPC was talking to the stout officer. I could hear him saying 'potentially violent and very disturbed' and phrases like 'utmost care' and 'proceed with caution' like something from a bad soap opera. And all the while the nasty Jack Russell yapped and yapped.

I took a deep breath. 'Philip . . .? Whatever's happened we will fix it,' I said, 'but you have to come with us now. We'll have a cup of tea and make everything right.'

To my relief, he turned his great head towards me, he looked me in the eye and I felt something in him relax. It was as if he was finally seeing me after what seemed like such a long time. I took his hand.

'What would Muriel say if she was here? She'd say, "Come on Phil, let's get you home," wouldn't she? She'd know what to do, she wouldn't let them hurt you. Well neither will I, I promise.'

And slowly, he turned to walk towards the police. Despite the anguished look in his eyes, he nodded his head at me and tried to smile. His eyes were watery and red and he whispered, 'Here's trouble, here's trouble, my Rachel.' And he put his hand on top of my head. Then we shuffled a few steps forward and the newly arrived WPC stepped towards us with her arms outstretched.

'Hello, Mr Johnston, I'm PC Craig . . . Val,' she said kindly and I felt relief surge through me. 'And you're Rachel, his key worker?'

'Yes,' I said gratefully.

'Pleased to meet you both,' she said and gave my elbow a reassuring pat. 'Now, let's see if we can get this whole thing sorted out.'

'Look, Val,' I said, 'I haven't had time to hear exactly what happened, but whatever it is, Philip has severe learning disabilities, it's very easy to misread his behaviour and his size can be quite intimidating. I think once we've all calmed down there will be a very simple explanation to what has gone on.'

'Yes. I'm quite sure there is. There's nothing to be frightened of Mr Johnston. We'll just get it all sorted for you. What a night to be out in the cold! We all need to go and get warm. I don't know about you but I need a hot drink.'

'You see, Philip?' I said. 'It's going to be fine.'

And as Val put her hand on his other shoulder we guided him towards the cars and she chatted reassuringly. 'That's it. Come on now, let's get you into the warm . . . What a night . . . I'm quite sure you meant no harm . . . I bet you like the ladies, don't you, Philip. Big fella like you?

Nothing wrong with having a bit of a look at a couple of pretty girls, is there? You wouldn't be human if you didn't, would you?'

Philip stopped dead and turned his head away from me. The strength drained out of us both. The little dog yapped, yapped, yapped and I couldn't get Philip to move an inch.

'I need to talk to you,' I said shrilly to the WPC. 'You must listen to me. Philip would never have . . .' I shot Val a pleading look but she turned her back on us, saying she needed to contact her superiors about the best way forward.

She walked back to her car leaving Philip and me, hopeless and helpless and stranded in the middle of the dark, freezing car park. Then I saw Rob's old Audi, one headlight down, slew into the car park. He got out and looked around him. Bypassing the police, he ran towards us, and as he did I saw the doors of my car open and the kids all slither out.

When he was near enough to hear me, I yelled, 'Get the kids back in the car. Please! Tell them to wait there.'

The dog was making so much din that Rob shook his head and came closer. 'What? What's going on?' he called anxiously. 'What can I do?'

'Get the kids back in the car! I can't help him, Rob. I can't get him to move. I don't know what to do.' And hearing the panic rising in my voice, the dog seemed to redouble its efforts and Philip began to thrash his head around. One of the girls had started crying noisily and nearby there was the shriek of another police siren. Perhaps to block out all this clatter, Philip started to make a high-pitched cry himself.

Rob sprang forward and put his hands on Philip's shoulders. 'Mate!' he barked and cupped Philip's jaw in his hand. 'What's going on, Big Guy? Come and tell me about it?'

Philip fell silent and his eyes moved slowly to look into Rob's, and to everyone's relief, the dog stopped barking. We turned to see what had shut it up and saw Luke sitting on his bottom in the mud with the dog scuttling around in his lap, licking his face as he tickled his tummy and said: 'You're a lovely boy. A lovely boy. What's your name? Eh?'

'Look, Philip. It's Luke,' I said. 'Luke, my son. The one you haven't met.'

Luke looked up and waved cheerfully. The dog's owner looked on horrified as Luke fed it a Jaffa Cake to keep it quiet but she had the good sense to say nothing. Philip still didn't move and we all waited, breathless, hoping for something to happen in the now silent car park.

'Mummy? Come back to the car now. Please?' It was Jess, clinging onto Alec's side and looking very frightened. I opened my mouth to speak, to tell her to go back to the car and wait for me but Alec said calmly, 'Hello, Philip. This is Jess – the little one. Jess?' Alec got down on his haunches and looked into Jess's face. 'It's Philip. The one I told you about. Tell him we've got Match Attax cards in the car. He loves them, don't you, Philip? Fancy pants?'

He stood up. 'I've got the full Man U set in the car. Will you come and have a look?'

Alec held his hand out towards Philip. 'Come on,' he said. 'We're all here. Mum and Rob . . . and Luke and Jess. We'll sort this out, I promise you, Philip. It's a promise.'

Philip looked at me, his face unsure and afraid; it was definitely the old Philip, willing to please but now so confused and frightened that he was paralysed, rooted to the spot and shivering. I felt such a rush of sympathy and love for him and almost laughed at all of us crowded around him, begging him to budge. This great bear of a man and me, Jiminy Cricket at his side, urging him to move like I had done that first day at Clifton Avenue to get him in the bath, and then to go for his first walk and then to brush his bloody teeth.

'Come on, Philip,' I said again. 'I will sort this for you. I will make it alright. You've got to trust me . . . Who else is there?' And as I reached out my hand again, desperation and hysteria really did kick in and I started – in a very small, quivering voice – to murmer: "'*Daisy, Daisy . . . give me your answer do . . . I'm half crazy . . .*'"

Rob did a double-take and the kids looked at me appalled, as if I had taken leave of my senses. But I went on staring at Philip. "'*. . . all for the love of you.*'" His eyebrows stretched up his forehead with surprise and then recognition and gratitude. Finally, his huge shoulders seemed to melt down his back and hesitantly he took a little step towards Alec, Rob and me and he took my hand.

\*

'Thank you for this,' I said nervously. 'I'm so grateful. I honestly do think it's the best option.'

I was standing in the harsh, bright light of the office in Clifton Avenue. The stout police officer, Inspector Gregory, had agreed to move proceedings here at least to start with, recognizing that dragging Philip to a police station wasn't going to get anybody anywhere. However, it seemed inevitable that Philip would be charged.

Rob was in the kitchen and I could hear him crashing and banging as he made tea and tried to disperse some of his anxiety before he had to face the police again as the now head of Clifton Avenue. The kids were hungry and tired and I'd made them go to the TV room to watch television with a wretched Lucy.

Philip was clutching a set of Manchester United Match Attax cards but he looked far from peaceful. As the inspector listened to me, his eyes kept darting over to Philip anxiously.

'He simply isn't able to make a statement,' I said. 'He doesn't have the ability to articulate what happened – whatever it was. Can I talk to the girls with you?' Other police officers were with the girls and their fathers in the meeting room. 'I know it isn't doing things by the book,' I went on, 'but I don't see how you can in these circumstances.'

'No . . .' Inspector Gregory was shaking his head. 'But we do have procedures for when a suspect with poor verbal skills is unable to give us a full statement, and they do involve the suspect coming to the police station.'

'But can't you use your judgement? Surely it's better not to waste everyone's time if this really is just a misunderstanding – as I'm sure this is.'

'Yes, but the thing is . . . I have talked to the girls and I have talked to their fathers. I'm afraid there seems to be no doubt that Mr Johnston wilfully exposed himself to them.'

'Why?' I said. 'Why do you say that?'

He began to look at his notebook. 'Well, piecing together the afternoon, it appears that your colleague, Lucy Cook, took Philip Johnston for a walk. They encountered Mrs Betty Wright who was taking her Jack Russell, Ricky, for a run and Mr Johnston took fright and began shouting.' He flipped to the next page. 'Mrs Wright was offended by his behaviour – she was unaware of his special needs – and so Lucy stayed to pacify her. When she had finished, Philip Johnston was nowhere to be seen. Lucy looked for him for a period of fifteen to twenty minutes – from about 4.10 p.m. to 4.30 p.m. – but only found him when she heard the girls' cries. Mrs Wright had helped in the search and advised the girls to call 999 and their parents.' Another page flip. 'The girls say they had been chatting, leaning against the wall by the south gate. They maintain that they were dismayed when they saw the large figure of Philip Johnston running towards them and that he stopped directly in front of them and dropped his trousers.'

'Just his trousers?' I asked.

'Yes, just his trousers.'

'So he didn't actually expose his genitals, as has been implied.'

'Apparently not.'

'Well, that's very different isn't it? Completely different surely?'

'I don't think those two young girls through there or their fathers make a huge distinction between the two acts and I don't blame them. Would you, Mrs Bidewell?'

'Philip!' I said. 'Come here. Stand up and come here.'

Philip looked nervous and unsure but nevertheless did what he was told. He stood up and shuffled over to stand next to me, all the time clutching the top of his trousers.

'Let go of your trousers,' I commanded. 'Go on!'

He looked confused but let go of the pointed tuft of material he had been clutching. The minute he did so, his trousers slid gently down to his ankles, revealing his skinny, mottled legs, beige socks and clean, white under-pants.

Immediately, without taking his eyes off the police officer, Philip bent down and pulled his trousers back up.

Rob had come into the doorway and was standing with a tray full of mugs. 'Oh, Philip,' he said gently. Then everyone turned to look at me.

'Philip hasn't been with us very long,' I said. 'He came to Clifton Avenue ... Actually, can I say this to the girls and their dads as well?' The inspector nodded sharply, relieved I think to leave the room and gather his thoughts, and went to find them.

When we were all assembled I smiled nervously in the hope of easing the tension in the room. The girls looked exhausted and the fathers anxious. I made a start: 'Philip came to Clifton Avenue after his mother died just a few months ago and he's made a huge amount of progress just in that short time. Haven't you?'

I looked at Philip, who shook his head, smiled painfully and made a noise like a Clanger.

'One of our first priorities has been to get Philip to lose some weight. As you can see he's a big lad but when he came to us he was even bigger. Well, he's lost a couple of stone since he arrived but he's not that happy about wearing new clothes. I think the clothes he has remind him of his mum and, well, we all feel comfortable in old clothes, don't we?'

Everyone nodded.

'I bought him a belt not long ago. Where is it, Philip? That new blue belt I bought you. If you'd had that on none of this would have happened.'

Philip looked at his waist and then back at me.

'He never meant to frighten you,' I said, looking at the girls directly for the first time. 'He would never have knowingly upset you. He just wouldn't.'

The dads looked awkwardly at each other and for a terrible moment I thought they were not convinced. But thankfully they were decent, reasonable people and seemed to understand what had happened.

Inspector Gregory looked relieved, and happy to be bustling about again, spouting all sorts of police jargon regarding paperwork and sensitivity and compassion in the field and judging each case 'as each set of unique circumstances dictate'. I could have hugged him.

As everyone was putting on their hats and coats to leave, Alec stuck his head round the door to get an update. Luke and Jess followed him in.

'It's all sorted,' said the inspector. 'A misunderstanding. You did a great job, Alec. I honestly think if it hadn't been for you, we'd still be out there now.' I felt very proud but also as if we had drifted into the epilogue of *Dixon of Dock Green*.

Alec's ears went pink with pride and Rob said, 'He's right you know. You were fantastic. Alec Bidewell Saves the Day. You should be in the papers.' Then he scooped up Jess and said, 'Come on you lot. Let's get you in the car.' I held Luke's coat up for him to put his arms into. 'And you! Luke the Dog Whisperer,' said Rob. 'That Jaffa Cake was a stroke of pure genius.'

'If ever you want a place on the force . . .' said the inspector, looking at all the children. Luke looked shyly up at him and was obviously delighted. Alec looked embarrassed. Jess looked horrified. 'What a family,' he went on, shaking his head, and as he left, patted Rob on the shoulder in a congratulatory manner.

Rob and I shot each other uncomfortable looks.

When we were walking out to the car I said sharply, 'Sorry about that. I think he thought you were "Dad".'

Before he could respond, Rob's phone went. He pulled it out of his pocket and I read the name 'Megan'. He slumped a little. His face clouded and he looked exhausted. He rejected the call and then said wearily: 'To be honest, Rachel, right now there is nothing I'd like more.'

I didn't know what to say. I couldn't quite believe I'd heard him correctly. He went on: 'Can you get the kids looked after? I need to talk to you.'

'Yes – I think so, I''ll call my mother-in-law. It'll take me an hour to get them settled and into bed –'

'OK – I'll meet you back here at nine thirty. I'm going to go home now. I'm not going back to Windsor. I'm –'

Alec came careering in and Rob and I jumped. 'Can I ring Dad when we get home? I want to tell him about all this.'

'Of course.' I put my arm around him as I looked back at Rob. 'I'll see you later,' I said. 'Now! Let's go and see if Philip has managed to get some supper without traumatizing half of North London.'

At 9.20 I got in the car and pointed it towards Clifton Avenue once again. I hadn't bothered to get changed or even showered – there hadn't been time. Understandably, the children had taken a while to settle and I didn't want to leave Mary with them all up and about. It was raining again as I pulled away from home and the windscreen wipers made their rhythmic squeak and thud as I half-listened to a radio programme about bats. My eyes felt sore and gritty in the glare of other headlights and my palms prickled with heat and anticipation as I tried hard not to have any expectations of the meeting to come.

Such a big part of me was hoping that what Rob had to say would be good. And he wasn't in Windsor. But then I knew Rob too well, knew that he was decent and reliable and would feel that he owed it to me to keep me up to date, to inform me face to face that he was going to Australia the following day with Megan and was there any chance I could find a home for his cat?

Just before Clifton Avenue, I stopped at a red light and took a quick look at myself in the mirror. I looked tired and piggy-eyed but my face was blank. It managed to belie the nervous, hot twitching of my scalp and the churning of my stomach. My clothes were still slightly damp from the car park earlier and I felt uncomfortable and clammy in my skin.

I drew into the car park and Rob was already there. He dashed over to me in the wet and I wound my window down.

'Shall we just go round to The George?' he asked, hunching his shoulders and screwing up his face against the rain.

'Fine,' I said and we set off again in tandem for the two-minute drive to the pub. Once there it was raining so hard that I had to skip balletically to the entrance to avoid all the puddles in the deeply rutted car park. My prancing disguised the leaden feeling that dragged at my knees.

We burst into the pub and the doors thudded heavily behind us. I'd never been there before and it was crowded and noisy and the lighting was harsh. A row of machines competed to make the tinniest racket and in the corner an enormous screen was showing Chelsea versus Queens Park Rangers. A huge mass of sweaty punters was roaring and moaning in unison as I padded across a sticky carpet to the bar. The boy behind it ignored us and was yelling, 'Come on my son! Get in there!'

I looked at Rob hopelessly and he jerked his head back towards the door and to my relief said we should get out.

I got back into my car and Rob got into the passenger seat.

'Sorry,' he said. 'Not one of my best ideas.'

'It's fine, honestly,' I said but my voice sounded harassed and frustrated.

'We could try The Ram or do you want to get something to eat?' he asked, so amiably that I felt a great stab of irritation.

'Look, I've left my mother-in-law with the kids and she came round at such short notice, I don't want to be long. Can you just say what it was you wanted to say here?'

Rob looked surprised but shrugged and mumbled, 'Sure. Of course.'

And then a cold silence descended upon us and I

thought defiantly, I'm not going to make this easy for you. I swept my hand across some dust on the dashboard in front of me and rubbed my palms tackily together. We were surrounded by tickets for the multi-storey, sweet wrappers, 3D glasses for the cinema and biscuit crumbs. Dom had been really good at keeping the car clean inside and out, but since he'd left it had become a skip. I suddenly felt self-conscious and ashamed of the state of it. I let my gaze shoot nervously to Rob and he met it gravely, took a long, deep breath and reached for my hand. I stared awkwardly at his knuckles, blood beating loudly in my ears and my spine hot and prickly.

'Megan has got money worries,' he said eventually. 'Megan has always got money worries but this time it appears to be quite serious. God only knows what she does with the money I send her. Hence her trip back here minus Will – she wanted to sort some things out.'

'And has she?' I asked in a strangled whisper.

He shrugged. 'Who knows. I think she thought that if she could do a bolt and came back here to live, brought Will home and moved in with me, that would get her out of paying any rent or any bills or overheads. Plus, I'd cough up for childminder fees while she got a job and saved a bit. I really don't know if she was kidding herself that we had a future together or whether she just thought I was the mug that would get her over a temporary financial hump.'

He started to pick distractedly at a shred of faux leather curling off the glove compartment.

'Megan's a fun girl to be around,' he went on. 'She's a great girl and she's funny, really funny. Always first at the bar and first to get a party started. She has so much energy!' He was smiling warmly at the thought of her. I pulled my hand away uncomfortably. 'However, she's always lived beyond her means. Always been able to rely on her charm or a friend or her parents or some new situation to make everything right again. She moved in with me approximately one week after we first met and looking back I think it was the free board and lodging that attracted her just as much as I did. But now she's got Will and she's just not such a free spirit any more. I think it's come as a bit of a shock.'

'Is she a good mum?' I asked.

'Yes. She's a very good mum. Thank goodness. I can't fault her there. She's just a bit flaky.'

Rob had been looking at the rain-dashed windscreen but now he shifted a little and looked directly at me. 'The funny thing is that if she'd come up with this proposal just a couple of months ago, although I'd have known it was a path to almost certain misery, I probably would have agreed. I'd have done anything to get Will back, even condemn him to living in an unhappy household until Megan decided to flit off again in six months.'

'And now?' I looked away. I thought that by the time Rob answered I was going to have had a heart attack.

'Now, I want to be with you. Isn't it obvious?' He was laughing and had an incredulous grin on his lovely face.

I shook my head stupidly. 'No, not to me.'

'Rachel, I feel like a different person. As if Megan was the very last residue of a foolish and selfish existence. God, around you I feel like a grown-up. I feel like such a better person. I'm in my forties, I have big responsibilities now – it's about time I grew up.'

'It doesn't sound very romantic,' I said, confused.

'Doesn't it? Really? It does to me. I've been waiting for ages for someone like you to make it all make sense. To stop me feeling so directionless. I feel as if everything's slotting into place; Will's happy, I'm over Megan and work is going to be great. It feels great. And I think that's incredibly romantic.'

'I've got three kids and you've got a son?'

'You've got three great kids – so what? And look, Will's settled in Melbourne now. His grandparents are there and they love the bones of him. They've offered to give him and Megan a home with them – I think that's what she's running from. But she has to grow up too. Of course I want him home here with me. I wanted it more than anything but I've realized not at any cost. Especially because I know he's happy where he is.'

'I don't think you should give up on Will for what might or might not happen between us.' I couldn't believe what I was saying. I wanted to bang my thick head against the dashboard.

'I'm not! And I'm quite prepared for it all to fizzle out – not least because I'll never have any money because it will all go to Will and flights to Australia. Not least because you have three children and a complicated life. No least because we'll be working together and that is a well-known recipe for certain disaster. But can't we just give it a go?'

'But what if Will –'

'Shut up about Will! God! Can you not just listen to what I'm telling you and for Christ's sake let me know if I've just made an unholy fool of myself!'

I let my breath out slowly and shakily and smiled. 'Possibly,' I said, turning to look at him. 'Probably.' I leant forward and cupped his face in my hands and leant my forehead against his. 'Who knows. When things appear too good to be true, in my experience, they usually are.' And then I kissed him and he kissed me back for what seemed like an age.

'*Now* can I come back to yours?'

'Yes,' I said. 'Absolutely.'

To give her her due, Mary managed not to look shocked as I came through the door later that night with a sheepish-looking Rob in tow. She said hello to him politely and introduced herself as 'the children's grandmother', which seemed unnecessarily complicated. I saw her to the door and as she kissed me goodbye I knew that she was upset but nevertheless she whispered, 'He seems very nice.'

'He is,' I said and watched her get into her little car and drive away.

Once back in the house, I offered to make scrambled eggs for us both and Rob agreed to eat it as long as he could wash it down with a glass of wine. Fortunately there was a bottle in the fridge – I was tempted to down it in one in order to hold my nerve.

In the harsh light of my little kitchen, the intimacy from the car had evaporated and as Rob poked about, looking at the pinboard with all the kids' school paraphernalia on it, a self-conscious silence descended upon us. '"Year 4 Trip to Shakin' Shakespeare Consent Form"', he read. '"PTA Curry & Quiz Night – RULES for Participating Teams" … "Good Book Certificate Awarded to Jess Bidewell for her Excellent Listening in Class and for Being Kind" … "Ishmaelite Costume Requirements" … It's another world.' Was he laughing at me?

'Well, it's my world,' I said, trying to sound light.

I poured us both a glass of wine and as I handed Rob's to him, I saw his eyes flick down to my shaking hand – lust was being overwhelmed by cold fear. I had been with Dom since I was nineteen. I had forgotten how to react or how to behave and was terrified that Rob would find me gauche or needy or inept when I wanted to be tender and passionate and raunchy. He reached out and held my hand to steady it. Then, taking the glasses from me, he slowly put them down on the counter and kissed me.

I'd like to say that what followed was a beautiful experience, the like of which I had never known before and would never know again. However, although it was good – very good – gone are the days of my underwear being strewn across the stairs as my lover carries me to bed. My Spanx were puddled unattractively in a corner and still connected to my tights. We were confined to the sitting room as I was worried we would wake the children, so while I should have been in the throws of passion I constantly had one eye on the door, anticipating Luke or Jess's arrival and the inevitable question, 'Who is that man and why isn't he wearing any trousers?' At one point I broke away from Rob in order to spring to the door and wedge my handbag in front of it to stop any small person from coming in. The main light was on and I felt horribly self-conscious, so as I ran to the door I grabbed a cushion from the sofa to hide my bottom and as I ran back I used it to obscure my front.

Rob laughed out loud as I hopped back again. I appeared to be performing some coy, 1930s fan dance but done with an old and slightly baggy Ikea cushion.

'Come here, woman!' Rob shouted eventually and when I finally made it back to him he stood up, still laughing. He pulled his white T-shirt up over his head in one motion and then looked at me, his hair ruffled, his eyes wide – and it was the single most unbelievably sexy gesture I think I'd ever seen anyone make in my entire life.

'You're as posh as a dog,' I said laughing. 'As handsome as a fox.'

'I'm as randy as a rattlesnake,' he growled. 'I'm as horny as a hyena.'

He left very early the next morning, leaving my sitting room looking as if I had pleasured an entire rugby team. We said goodbye grinning – self-conscious but really rather pleased with ourselves.

And then it was back to real life and the kids' breakfast.

## Chapter Ten

# Revenge is a Dish Best Served Never Because It Has Become Irrelevant

'Right! "Empty contents of sachet into warm water and soak feet for a minimum of twenty luxurious minutes. Allow the rich, relaxing aromas of ylang ylang and jasmine to evoke the blah blah of the blah blah blah until the skin is soft."'

I was on my knees reading the back of a foot-massaging kit I had bought from Boots for Philip. He was sitting in an armchair with his feet in a washing-up bowl of cooling, boiled water. His trousers were rolled up and he looked as if he'd just come off the beach at Clacton. Six other residents were in the room with us watching *The One Show* and Rob was sprawled in an armchair finishing a cup of coffee.

'Right! Twenty minutes for normal folk, that's three days for you, mate. Just keep them in there and wiggle them about for a bit and in half an hour we'll exfoliate, massage in this cream and then see if we can make any progress with the clippers.'

Battle-scarred chiropodist Leslie-Ann had been kind enough to take a phone call from me and recommend a course of action for Philip's feet which we could try at home. Our hope was that he would get used to someone touching them and in time we could return to the hospital for some expert help or get someone to come to Clifton Avenue. Leslie-Ann was even prepared to take the appointment herself. I told her that single-handedly she had restored my faith in human nature.

'Are you the main point of contact there,' she had asked when I rang, 'in case I think of anything else?'

'Yes,' I said. 'I'm Philip's key worker, so anything concerning his well-being goes via me.'

Philip's feet remained resolutely still in the increasingly scummy, lukewarm water. Eventually I removed the right one and laid it in my lap on a towel. I wiped it dry and looked up at him.

'Now, if you kick me in the face, I'll kick you back. Is that understood?' But he just looked at the television screen and randomly jerked his head back a couple of times. I sighed and gave his knee a pat looking up at his face and then turned to Rob and shook my head sadly. Rob stood up, crossed the room and gave my shoulder a squeeze as he passed.

'Give it time,' he said. 'Just give it some time.'

After what seemed like years of feeling permanently tired, I felt as if I had enough energy to drive a tank. I started to get the house straight, all the little things that had been driving me mad like leaky taps, a messy garden, broken photo frames, the wonky loo seat that nearly slid off and shot you across the bathroom every time you had a wee, unhung pictures, the grill pan's missing handle, the socket hanging alarmingly off the wall in the sitting room. I didn't feel the need to introduce Rob to the children yet as 'The Boyfriend'. What was going on with him, while lovely, felt separate and special and mine. The only people who knew about it were Mary and Lucy, and for now that was the way I wanted it.

'You know,' he said one day when we were in bed at ten-past one in the afternoon, when the kids were at Dom's and everything felt calm and wonderful, 'the more this goes on the more I worry that at some point I'm going to have to choose between you and Will.'

I felt my heart sink. I didn't want this. What attracted me most about him was that he was practical and independent and no-nonsense and fun. Dom had always been a bit touchy and neurotic and I felt as if I'd ditched Woody Allen and taken up with Huckleberry Finn. Consequently I spent my days swimming in warm honey.

'Well you don't have to choose,' I said. 'Not yet. It's too early. But if you do decide you have to be with your son, I will be the one person in the world who will most understand.'

'What if Dom suddenly decided to move to Mexico?'

'He wouldn't and anyway I'd prevent him from leaving the country.' I so didn't want to talk about all this.

'Yes, but just imagine Alec was taken to the other side of the world. Would you follow him?'

'I'd follow him to Jupiter,' I said irritably, 'and so would Luke and Jess.' There was an awkward silence while Rob took this in.

He ploughed on: 'I think the thing with Dom and Megan is that they are the sort of people who are used to having their own way. Maybe it was instilled in them as children or maybe they were just born with a predisposition to go right on marching through until things just go their way.'

I sat up and started searching for my top. I tried to sound matter-of-fact: 'I think that Dom believes he's absolutely doing the right thing for Alec – that's why he's so unstoppable.' I knew I was being obtuse but I had just wanted to lie dozing.

'Yes, but you of all people understand that Megan –'

I was suddenly angry. 'No, I don't understand! Your situation is completely different. Alec is eleven, Will is five. I was with Dom for twenty years, you weren't with Megan five minutes! I don't want us to be victims together. I don't want the only thing that we have in common to be that we've got shitty ex-partners who have custody of our sons. I don't want to be bonded by misery and nothing else!'

Rob was taken aback and so was I. 'Neither do I. I just –'

'Then just leave it alone!' I was up now and pulling on my clothes. 'Let things play out in their own time. I'm trying to accept that Alec has chosen to live with his dad and Deborah and their bloody dog, but you talk as if I'm calm about it, as if I've got it all sussed. Well I haven't! I miss Alec every day he isn't here and I feel like a failure and an idiot for having let him go. Don't presume to know what I feel about Alec – or Dom for that matter – and I won't presume to know what you feel about Will.'

'Fine. OK. I'm sorry.'

I got up and went down into the kitchen and busied myself emptying the dishwasher. Bloody Dom. I thought. Still pervading everything, along with perfect Deborah and my perfect, sweet Alec who only sleeps in his own bed for two nights out of every fourteen.

Eventually, Rob put his head round the door. He was fully dressed. 'Do you want me to go?'

'Yes,' I said. 'I'm sorry.'

'Suit yourself.'

As I heard the front door click shut, I sat at the kitchen table and felt stupid and terrified that in the space of five minutes I'd blown everything.

Luke and Jess got back that Sunday evening having spent a long day at a football tournament in Orpington. Alec had been playing in the school's B team. It had been cold and wet, they'd lost heavily and I think everyone regretted agreeing to go and hadn't realized it would take up the entire day. Dom didn't even see the kids to the door, just let them out of the car, hooted the horn and drove off.

I hadn't rung Rob. It wasn't that I didn't want to, I just couldn't fathom why I'd hit the self-destruct button.

The kids were tired and subdued, so I gave them a quick bath and put them to bed early. I was watching a dull but nasty thriller on ITV and doing some ironing at about 9.30 when the doorbell went. My heart leapt, knowing that it would be Rob. I would say I was sorry and whatever he needed to hear to get things back on an even keel. Why had I thought I couldn't speak to him?

As I went to the door, I looked at my haggard reflection in the mirror and ran my hands through my hair. God bless him for coming round. I was so grateful.

But when I opened the door, it wasn't Rob. It was Deborah. Her hair was dishevelled and she had obviously been crying. She was leaning against the wall as if she had no energy to support herself any more. She even looked a bit drunk.

'What do you want?' I said flatly.

'Can I talk to you?' she said, her voice wobbling. 'I really need to talk to you.'

I stepped back and opened the door for her.

She followed me into the sitting room and I said nothing, but just stood and waited for her to speak. She began wringing her hands and looking at the floor as if she didn't know where to start.

'I'm sorry about this, Rachel. I really am. But Dom and I have had such a massive row. We've had a terrible day and we've got to resolve things, we've got to get things sorted but we can't talk about anything because Alec is in the house. Alec is *always* in the house so we can't talk anything through.' Tears had started to slide down her face again and she seemed hopeless.

'What's happened?' I said.

She pulled herself together and took a deep breath. 'I'm twenty-nine, Rachel. I like children, I really do. But I'm not ready to have them yet. I've still got a few years and at the moment I am loving my job, and the people I work with and the travel and . . . everything.'

She took another deep breath and wiped her hands anxiously across her face. This part of the speech was rehearsed.

'When I agreed to have Alec come and live with us, I really did think that we could make it work. I will admit to having had some reservations but I knew how much it meant to Dom, and I wanted to do it for him and Alec is such a great kid. So, so lovely . . .' Her voice was cracking again. 'None of this is his fault.'

She looked at me imploringly, as if she wanted me to finish the speech for her.

'That night he came to see you on your birthday, I knew I should have driven him to you but I had something on at work. Dom wouldn't leave his office to get Alec and I thought, Why the hell should I? We're supposed to alternate picking him up, but the longer things go on the more it seems to be me doing all the work because Dom's work is bloody sacred and mine doesn't seem to matter to him any more. My boss agreed a few weeks ago to let me work on a more flexible basis to accommodate Alec and school, but what's the point of working at home, when you've missed anything worthwhile that happened because you were stuck outside a primary school in Queen's Park?'

She was obviously straying off her script now and not giving a shit what she said next. In for a penny . . .

'I wouldn't mind but one of the things Dom said that attracted him to me in the first place was that I was driven and ambitious, and yet now he wants me to compromise all of that. I wanted to get some help – my mum offered to pay! – but Dom wouldn't hear of it. He says we've made a commitment to look after Alec and that we've got to stick with it. That if we get a stranger to pick him up we may as well send him home to you again!'

There was a pause. Her nose was running and she was forced to wipe it on the back of her hand, so I went to the downstairs lavatory and returned with a loo roll which I passed to her. She looked grateful, blew her nose and carried on immediately. She'd nothing to lose; the dam had burst.

'I love your children, Rachel, I really do, but they're not mine! I don't marvel at their ability to draw or kick a ball.

I don't find every other thing they say amusing or extra-ordinary. And you know the really mad thing is that all the things that Dom was most blown away by when we first got together are all the things that he seems happy to sac-rifice, just like that!' She clicked her fingers viciously. 'We've lost our freedom. We can't go out, we can't have sex unless it's in the bedroom and we know Alec is asleep. Even the weekends we have to ourselves Dom's fretting about Alec, and if he's not fretting about Alec, he's fret-ting about you!'

I looked incredulous.

'Oh yes, *you*!' She looked at me hatefully with her mouth quivering. 'Perfect Rachel; the paragon of all motherly virtue. "Rachel always reads to Jess before she goes to sleep. Rachel always lets Luke into her bed when he's had a bad dream. Rachel doesn't allow fizzy drinks, Rachel doesn't allow more than thirty minutes at the computer. Rachel looks after the *handicapped*." Sometimes, I want to say "Well if she's so bloody perfect why did you leave her? She can't be that bloody great!"'

'I'm not, I can assure you,' I interrupted but she was on a roll.

'When we were first together,' she went on, 'he thought all my friends were so young and inspiring but now they bore him and so we don't entertain. A dining room and we never use it! And, of course, now he's got an excuse: "We can't have anyone round because of Alec. Alec's got his homework. Alec's got to revise for his exams."'

Her indignation was growing and her voice had become high-pitched and whiny.

'And now . . . now! . . . we have a bloody dog. Pissing and shitting all over my new house. He's chewed everything – EVERYTHING! – and Dom and Alec just think it's funny! Now we'll never be able to go away – even on our weekends. I tell you, that's what's sent me over the edge. I love Dom, I really do and I thought I could do anything for him just as long as we were together. But now? Now I'm scouring the Internet for dog-friendly hotels. My parents won't have it. Why do you think I never had a dog when I was growing up? Because my father hates dogs. He thinks they're vermin! We're tied down enough with Alec and now on top of everything we've got a bloody dog! And what's more he has the nerve to pretend that he did it all for me!

'I'm out of step with my work colleagues, I'm out of step with my friends. I'm twenty-nine years old and I have an eleven-year-old stepson waiting for me at home who still needs to be looked after, cooked for, who leaves his clothes all over the floor. Who doesn't *ever* flush the toilet! I love him, I really do. But if he carries on living with us I'm going to stop loving him and maybe even Dom and Dom and I have caused too much pain to too many people to let it all just slip away. You think Dom's determined? Well, I'm a very determined person too and I will not give up on the life that we had planned together.'

She plonked herself down on the sofa. 'And my head is crawling with nits.' She had run out of steam.

I was breathing evenly. I wasn't an agony aunt, I didn't care what strain her new relationship was under, I just knew that Alec needed to come back, and this was my chance. 'Well, why don't you let Alec come home?' I said simply.

She had started to cry again. 'That's what I want, Rachel. I'm so sorry but I think it's the only way forward.'

'What does Dom say?'

'I told him I was coming over here but I think he thought I was bluffing.'

I went over to the phone.

'Dom, it's me,' I said before he could speak. 'Deborah's here and I think we all need to talk.'

Dom came over with Alec. It was late now so I told Alec to go to bed. He looked confused and worried – he wasn't stupid, he knew exactly what was going on. I stroked his head and said, 'Don't worry. I'll come up and see you before you go to sleep.' He looked grateful and hovered in the doorway for a minute before disappearing up the stairs.

Dom looked exhausted and defeated. Deborah couldn't stop snivelling. Scrubbed of any make-up, she looked vulnerable and deeply unhappy. The growing up you do when you have children is immense; in the last decade I'd learned so much about myself and my limitations and my strengths – a process that had been accelerated after Dom's departure. I looked at Deborah and thought that I wouldn't be twenty-nine again for the world.

At what point do tears stop making you look younger? As she tried to pull herself together, Deborah looked about sixteen. These days when I cried I looked a hundred.

'Does anyone want a drink?' I asked.

'I think I've had enough,' said Deborah apologetically and Dom looked at her with such affection I felt I should leave the room. I went into the kitchen and found a bottle of wine in the fridge and three odd glasses. I rested my head against the fridge door, telling myself, 'Don't fuck this up.'

When I came back into the room, Dom and Deborah were entwined and Deborah was bawling her eyes out. They stepped apart as I came in and we all sat down, Dom and Deborah on the sofa and me on a hard, upright chair. They both looked so miserable the only reasonable thing was to take control.

'It sounds as if,' I said evenly, 'it's time for Alec to come home.'


An hour later we had come up with a plan. We would continue to have the children alternate weekends. Alec would come home and spend the majority of the time with me, but would stay with Dom and Deborah every Wednesday night.

I'd dreamed of this moment, but now it was here relief and euphoria fought with the worry that Alec would feel rejected. Eventually, all three of us went upstairs to his bedroom.

He was still wide awake, playing on his Nintendo, which he put down when we came in. He looked at me nervously and I smiled and sat down next to him on the bed. He'd got ready for bed and was wearing an over-sized T-shirt commemorating a half-marathon that Dom had run for heart disease a couple of years ago. It had been a beautiful day, the sun had shone, Mel and Grace's husbands had taken part as well, and Grace had made a picnic. It struck me for the first time that Dom must have already been sleeping with Deborah, even back then. They hovered guiltily and I turned to Alec and smiled.

'We've all had a chat,' I said, 'and it's obvious that much as Dad and Deborah love having you live with them, it probably makes more practical sense for you to come home. Now obviously I'm very happy about that, but what do you think? Weekends will still be the same, but you'll spend every Wednesday night at Dad's house.'

'What do you think?' he said to Dom.

'I think it's for the best. Mum misses you very much and I know you miss her –'

'And Deborah and Dad,' I interjected, 'don't work part-time like me or have anyone like Grandma to help after school.'

'Grandma?' said Alec.

'Yes, she's the new Marlene, only she puts cheese and butter on baked potatoes and she's learned the art of smiling.'

'Really?' said Dom. 'Mum's going to help you out?'

'Yes,' I said.

'Awesome,' said Alec. Then we all fell silent until Alec said, 'I think it probably is the best thing to do, Dad. I think I do want to come home.' His cheeks had gone scarlet and I was worried he was going to cry. 'I'm so sorry,' he said.

'Sorry!' said Dom. 'Sorry? What have you got to be sorry for, Alec? None of this is your fault. I just wanted you with me so much that I didn't think it all through properly. When I moved out I don't think I ever really realized just how much I would miss you all. I didn't think it would be easy but I didn't realize how hard it was going to be on us all. Please, please don't think you've done *anything* to be sorry for.' He sat the other side of Alec and clasped his head to his chest and kissed it. 'You've *nothing* to be sorry for, darling.'

As I watched them I thought that maybe that was Dom's biggest crime; not falling in love with a girl from the office, not calling time on me and our marriage, but on underestimating the consequences of leaving. We'd bent Alec out of shape, there was no getting away from it. Was it irreparable? I didn't think so. Would it make him a bad person? No, but he wasn't the same Alec as a year and a half ago. He was too anxious now, too nervous, too

365

eager to please and scared of confrontation. As for Luke and Jess, we'd just have to wait and see.

Alec disengaged his head from Dom's tight grasp and looked at Deborah. 'What about Rufus?'

'We're going to have him,' I said. 'We'll sort of do fifty-fifty.'

Alec's eyes widened.

'Grandma will think she's died and gone to heaven, you know how she loves Labradors. But he's not allowed on the beds and he's not allowed on the sofa – that's going to be an absolute rule.'

It was now ten past eleven, but the doorbell rang and the others all looked at me with a 'Who the hell could that be?' expression. But I knew who it was. Here we go, I thought, and prepared to introduce Rob to the wider world.

That night at about 3 o'clock I went downstairs, sat at the kitchen table and wrote a letter:

*Dear Deborah,*

*I've come to the conclusion that there are three types of marriage: Fabulous Ones, Mediocre Ones and Rubbish Ones. If you are stuck in a Rubbish One, then get out: you can be happier with someone else or on your own – you only have one life, children or no children, so make the break. If you have a Fabulous One, then lucky you – enjoy it and never, ever take it for granted. But if you are in a Mediocre One, then if children are involved, at the end of the day, it's probably best to stick with it and hope for the* best. Perhaps you only have the capacity to be mediocre at marriage and if you swap a Mediocre One for another, you will break people's hearts in the process and then it will be really difficult to be happy ever again. Plus, if you stick with it, maybe just the very act of sailing through all the shit life throws at you and knowing that you've survived it together will see your Mediocre Marriage transform into a Fabulous One. My suspicion is, Deborah, that Dom belongs well and truly in the mediocre category.

I've also realized that I can't really hate you because I don't really know anything about you. It would be so much easier if I could as then I wouldn't have to hate the man who, until very recently, I loved dearly and whom I thought loved me back in the same way. If I blame you for everything then I don't feel foolish for having thought that Dom was one thing when in fact all the time he was something completely different. Much as I have dreamed of the day when I would open the door to find you weeping on your hands and knees, covered in snot, begging for my help, the reality was quite a let-down. Knowing that Dom had misjudged everything so badly just made me respect him even less. There was a time when I wanted you to beg for my forgiveness, but part of me knows that it will only be in years to come that you will realize the enormity of what you two have done. At the moment you are just too young and inexperienced to see it.

You think that Dom is a special, wonderful, unique human being who needs very careful handling and understanding and that only you can do this. You think that I got it all wrong, that I didn't understand him. Therefore, although you are sorry for all the upset you have caused, you believe you are still a decent person and that you have done the right thing, that you have set free the poor, tortured soul that was Dom. When your friends have the nerve to look disapproving or to ask after me, I should imagine that you justify your actions by saying, 'Well, he would never, ever have left his wife and family and I'm no home-wrecker but you see he'd been unhappy for a very long time.' It's what Dom said to all of my friends. He believes that now because it eases his guilt and of course you believe him, but it's bullshit; he was bored and tired and fearing middle-age, but he was loved and comfortable and contented for the majority of our married life. I really do believe that and I think he knows it deep down. And then you came along. I know that you think that you're the love of his life but I'm coming round to the idea that rather than it being your fault for tempting him away, in reality it was just a matter of time. If he was going to go, he was going to go and you or somebody else down the line would have facilitated it. It just needed someone to make his pulse race and make him the centre of attention after years of playing second fiddle to three children. And it was you.

Presumably you tell your friends – because once again this is what Dom told his – 'We fell in love. It was so powerful that we just couldn't resist it. It was too big for both of us to handle alone. We couldn't turn our backs on such a mighty force.' Yadda yadda yadda. Does it never occur to you that Dom and I were in love like that once? He may have told you that he was young and that it was all too long ago to count but it isn't. We loved each other with all the intensity that you are feeling now, except it grew into something much greater because we had children together and we grew up together.

Because of all that shared experience I foolishly thought that we were strong enough to have moved onto the next stage, the one I watched my parents enjoy until my mother died. I thought we were allowed to fancy other people in the office because, God knows, we're only flesh and blood, but that we saw these mild flirtations for what they were and would always come home to each other. I'm sure I took Dom for granted, that I put the children first and didn't tend to our marriage as much as I should have and I do regret that more than anything – I'm certainly not blameless in all of this. But for me the love hadn't died; the spark was still there. I still had faith in our relationship. We might go for months in the same old cosy, if dull, routine, but then we'd go on holiday and get a bit drunk one night and suddenly I'd remember just what it was that I fell for in the first place. Although in the morning around the pool I might find myself looking a little too long and a little too critically at his expanding waistline, I thought, Well, it's expanding at the same rate as mine and I love every inch of it. What's more, I can still see the boy of nineteen lurking within and I always will. That was enough for me.

I always thought that deep down we both knew that we were in it for the long haul, that we were going to be one of those couples who are interviewed by the local newspaper when they hit their hundredth birthdays. When asked what the secret to a happy marriage is, in a quivery little voice Dom would say something like, 'Well, the secret is to pipe up when you're wrong and pipe down when you're right.' And I'd say, 'And take the

369

*rubbish out!' and we'd laugh and clasp our yellow, papery hands together and feel so fortunate for having found one another and shared our lives.*

*I used to hope that your relationship would crash and burn spectacularly for all to see with me standing on the sidelines cheering. But what good would that do anybody now? Much to my surprise I realize that I really do want you and Dom to work because otherwise what has this whole bloody mess been for? And besides, I don't want the children to think their father is a complete prat.*

*I used to think you were superior and smug and I couldn't stand it. But now I think of your trusting little face and how much you love Dom. What you haven't yet realized is that your relationship will always be born out of poison; the hurt and misery of infidelity, betrayal and abandonment and who's to say Dom won't go out and do the whole thing over again? I might be the dumped first wife, but I will have the upper hand because I never hurt anybody, I never lied and I never took what wasn't mine. Now I feel smug.*

*I don't resent you for not being able to cope with Alec and now that he's home with me, I know you're hoping that Dom will be feeling free and alive and rejuvenated again. If on a Saturday lunchtime he wants to have sex on the kitchen table then sex on the kitchen table he shall have. If he wants to whisk you away for an extreme water-sports weekend at the drop of a hat, then so be it. He can be impetuous, unpredictable and romantic, all the things he hasn't been able to be for years within the confines and demands of family life. But what if you have babies? The kitchen*

*table will be covered with nappies and baby sick and you won't be
able to just take off because your boobs are too sore and besides,
where would you plug the sterilizer in? This is the moment you
will realize what you did to me. And this is the moment you will
both realize that Dom swapped what he had with me for the
identical situation: same dance, different partners; same circus,
different clowns. Only now he is older and fatter and balder and
has two mortgages to pay. Will you be nervous that he looks at
you and thinks, Why on earth did I go through all that just to
find myself right back where I started? Only he isn't where he
started; he's a lesser man because of all the hurt he caused. He's
lost old friends who couldn't forgive him and, as I say, no matter
how good his relationship is with his children, they will always be
slightly wary of him. He has damaged his connection with them
in ways that are permanent. They will always love him, adore
him, but they will never quite forgive him or trust him again. Or
take their dad for granted in the way that kids should. Believe me,
I'm not crowing, none of these thoughts bring me any pleasure.*

*You think that my children are resilient and that we could all
just get along fine if only I would move on. We could all holiday
in Devon together, sit together at the school play and jointly
organize their birthday parties. You and Dom think I'm selfish
and stubborn and vindictive for not doing this. And maybe you're
right. But until now I couldn't. I couldn't give you my blessing; I
couldn't sit at your table and say everything was alright because it
wasn't. I couldn't implicitly say to Alec that what has happened is
OK by me. For a start it would be dishonest, but above all I don't
want him ever to inflict the sort of hurt that you and Dom have*

371

*inflicted on all of us and think that it is OK. The books all say*
*that I should work on a positive relationship with you for the sake*
*of the children and until now I thought, Why should I? Why*
*should I give you and Dom that satisfaction? I wanted to punish*
*you both and be a constant reminder of the hurt you'd caused. But*
*now I've come to see that it really isn't about me, is it? It's about*
*the kids and doing what's fair isn't always doing what's right. I*
*think it's unlikely that we'll ever swap recipes and borrow each*
*other's clothes, but I think I can be civilized given time.*

*I feel good about myself now. And so I say, 'Good Luck to*
*You!' I'm pretty sick of playing the wronged wife and I've had*
*enough.*

*So, I'll move on, but don't forget that when Alec passes his*
*driving test or has a child of his own, or on Luke's first day at*
*university or the first time Jess has her heart broken, I'll still be*
*thinking, Damn you, Deborah, because nobody will know how it*
*feels other than Dom and me, and I won't be able to share the*
*moments with him.*

*Yours,*
*Rachel*


End of rant.

I printed the letter off and then shoved it straight in the bin.


Today is a beautiful day. I am standing in the kitchen trying to wash the barbecue tongs that were obviously put away without being washed the last time we had a barbecue –

about two years ago. They were shoved in the garage and are now encrusted with charcoal, grease, dust and possibly mouse droppings. But I'm actually finding the task quite satisfying. I'm back in my Marigolds.

Rob isn't here. He's gone haring round to the One Stop Shop because he faithfully promised to get Luke some Heinz Salad Cream. It is one of Rob's great loves in life – Dom wouldn't even have it in the house – and he has got Luke to share his passion, only to run out on the one day I might actually get the children to eat a bit of salad.

I am watching the children from my vantage point at the sink. In my small garden there is a whacking great trampoline. When Alec came home I just thought, Sod it! and bought one – an early birthday present for Jess. I will be paying it off for another year.

Bouncing on the sagging trampoline are Alec, Luke, Alec's friend Thomas and Jess. They are all laughing wildly but not as wildly as the man in the centre of the circle who refuses to stand up or even move from his rigid sitting position. That man is Philip. He is sitting with his legs stretched out in front of him and the children are doing great leaps in unison that send him flying about five feet into the air. He whoops with total elation and looks over at me, waving and shouting delightedly: 'Here comes trouble! Here comes trouble!'

'Not too high!' I warn the children through the open window, with visions of him sailing off and breaking six ribs.

'Oh come on, Mum,' says Luke. 'He's loving it!' And indeed he is. He's come to us for Sunday lunch as he does most weeks when we are home. Sometimes he even stays on a Saturday night. But he's not as reliant on me as he used to be. He has excellent relationships with all the new staff at Clifton Avenue and most of the residents too. He's come such a long way and is now on an intensive programme, which Rob, Ruth and I put together, to prepare him for independent living. I'm so proud of him.

It is warm and Rufus is conked out on the sofa next door. When Philip visits the dog has to be banished into another room, which he hates, but we're working on a bit of aversion therapy and I think, one of these days, Philip will be able to tolerate him in the same postal district. Give it ten to fifteen years.

As I stand, looking out of the window, I realize it's one of those moments when just for a second your mind isn't racing, everything stops and you are flooded with such a sense of well-being that you can almost taste it. Any minute now the dog will kick off or a child will boing off the trampoline into a hedge. I'll stab myself with these tongs and the sun will go in. But for now it's a beautiful day and I'm going to take a very long, deep breath, stop what I'm doing, and enjoy it.

# Acknowledgements

Firstly thanks to Georgia Garrett and Lissa Evans for giving me the confidence to sit down and write a book.

Thanks to Louise Moore, Mari Evans and Celine Kelly at Penguin for their encouragement and patience.

Thanks to the Jubilee Library, Brighton, for warmth, light and quiet.

Thanks to my sister, Sarah Elton, for finding the time to read every draft and for her practical, incisive notes.

Thanks to Clair and to those friends who read early drafts and understood that when I asked for an honest opinion I was lying. And to those who let me steal shamelessly from their own lives.

Thanks most of all to Andy, the boys and the twins, whose excitement and enthusiasm have been the best part of this whole experience.

And finally, thanks to Jac Palmer and the Windsor girls – you can now say, 'I told you so.'

# An interview with Kate Anthony on the themes in *Beautiful Day*

You explore various themes in your novel *Beautiful Day*, such as the many repercussions of divorce, the challenges of being a parent and the bureaucracy of social services. What was the most difficult to write about?

*It was hard writing about Rachel's short fuse around her children. Describing Rachel at her lowest ebb and taking her misery out on her children was a challenge; as soon as there is a child in a scene it is very difficult to keep sympathy with a character who is yelling, no matter what the extenuating circumstances are.*

The theme of divorce – the impact it has on the children from the marriage, how it can change the financial situation of one or both partners and how a person can lose their sense of self and purpose through a marriage breakdown – is explored in detail in your novel. Did you find this theme interesting to write about and was it difficult to tackle any aspect of it?

*Again, the hardest parts to write were the scenes when Rachel's bitterness and exhaustion got the better of her. I wanted to add a footnote saying 'Bear with Rachel. Honestly, this isn't like her.'*

*I suppose the aspect of the break-up that I found the most interesting to write was that of Rachel's recovery; of her realization that just by keeping her head down, waiting it out and trying to do the right thing no matter what, her strength would return. Plus her acceptance that one black day where she lets herself down and it all goes pear-shaped is OK, it doesn't mean she's irrevocably lost the plot and that she can't make amends. I was also interested in looking at how the means to healing can come from the most unlikely of places.*

As a working mother yourself, did your own experiences help you when writing about the challenges Rachel faces?

*Yes, although my biggest fear is being beaten up by my friends who are PTA reps. None of whom, I hasten to add, bear any resemblance to RebeccaClassRep.*

You spent some time working in social services. How much of your own experience did you draw on when exploring this theme in *Beautiful Day*? Did you meet anyone like Philip? And did you ever work with anyone like Denise?

*Of course, I drew heavily on my time as a residential social worker, especially the period when I was with an agency because you would get a phone call in the morning and be sent off to do a couple of shifts here, a week there, so you got to see all sorts of different set-ups and meet a real mix of people. Philip is probably an amalgam of some of the residents that I got closest to and Denise is a highly-fictionalized version of the colleagues that I didn't! In the main, the group homes that I found myself in were warm, friendly places to be but some weren't, and those are the ones that have stayed with me and that I wanted to write about.*

Rachel, to her surprise, finds love again with Rob – a man very different from her first husband, Dom. Do you think she would have fallen for a man like Rob had she met him before Dom? Do you think people look for something different in a partner later in life?

*Although at first glance Rob is a very different character from Dom, he probably embodies the qualities Rachel thought Dom possessed for all those years – only to find he didn't. If my husband ran off with a Deborah tomorrow, initially I might crave a very public fling with a ski instructor half my age, but ultimately I think I would end up looking for the same qualities that drew me to my husband before it all went wrong. But then again I didn't marry till I was in my thirties – things might be very different if you marry when you are young and you may not still have the same perspective and priorities as you get older.*

*I think we tend to believe that if you lose a partner in later life you are more likely to settle for companionship and comfort, but in reality marriage or a partnership is a massive commitment and takes up so much of your emotional energy that embarking on it just to have someone to help with the washing-up is probably pretty rare.*